"Looks like the rumor was t... Destiny was one of *The Trib*'s long-time business writers and an African American, one of only three people of color on our staff. The others were photographer Erica Martinez, who was Hispanic, and Connie Lee, an Asian American. Critics who pointed to *The Trib* as a pillar of structural racism were right.

"You mean the rumor we were for sale?" I said.

"What else could it be?" Destiny said.

We were standing in the lobby with our good friend, reporter Bud Fuller. A film crew was loading tripods and cameras into the elevator to the fourth-floor auditorium.

"But Gordon vowed we weren't for sale," I said.

Just last week, in fact, publisher Randolph E. Gordon IV had issued a written statement denying persistent rumors of a takeover.

"And two years ago he insisted we weren't downsizing," said Bud. "His word means shit."

Bud was right.

Three days after his written statement, Gordon slashed the staff by twenty-five percent, albeit through buyouts that left many of the remaining three-fourths jealous. For the record, that was the last of the buyouts. What came next was good old-fashioned firings: a call to visit HR, where you were told you were terminated, your email and card key would be deactivated in a half hour, and you had until then to clear your stuff out and be off premises or security would be called.

"So, who's the new owner?" I said.

"Must be SuperGoodMedia," said Destiny. "It's the only chain based in Florida."

My stomach churned.

"They're worse than McClatchy," I said.

"There's something worse than McClatchy? Destiny said.

"Hard to believe, but yes, and they're it," I said.

UNFIT TO PRINT
A MODERN MEDIA SATIRE

BY G. WAYNE MILLER

DISCLAIMER

This is entirely a work of fiction. Real-life people do appear, but in imagined situations with imagined dialogue and depiction. All other characters are fictional, and any resemblance to actual persons, living or dead, is coincidental.

DEDICATION

To my journalist friends and colleagues, some still working in the field and others retired, moved on to other professions, or involuntarily forced out in this click-bait era, when locally controlled and reported news dies in many parts of the country.

Arguably more than any other historical figure, Benjamin Franklin, were he to magically appear, as he does in *Unfit to Print*, would understand the threat to American democracy.

INTRODUCTION

I have written many books, but none as long in gestation as *Unfit to Print* if you count the real-life experiences behind it.

You could legitimately assert that this book began during my freshman year at St. John's Preparatory School in Danvers, Mass., when my first stories were published in the school newspaper. In junior year, I became co-editor of that newspaper, *The Paper*, with Richard Howell, a classmate who went on to become a noted comics artist and writer. Richard and I also wrote and published what I believe was St. John's first-ever underground newspaper, *The Mole*, which we used to disseminate controversial opinions we knew would never clear *The Paper's* faculty censors. You will see an echo of that dynamic in the pages of this book.

After graduating from Harvard College and free-lancing stories to papers including my hometown *Wakefield (Mass.) Daily Item* and *The Boston Globe*, I became a full-time professional reporter in August 1978, four years after *The Washington Post* was awarded the 1973 Pulitzer Prize for Public Service for its coverage of the Watergate scandal. Bob Woodward and Carl Bernstein were the lead reporters in that investigation and they inspired many journalists and journalists-to-be during a period when their profession was held to be a noble, if not sacred, calling.

I was among those who answered that call, by way of legendary New England journalist Rod Doherty, who in August 1978 was city editor of *The Transcript* in North Adams, Massachusetts. Rod hired me—me, a 24-year-old baggage handler for Delta Airlines at Boston's Logan International Airport who had taken the job after graduating from Harvard. That weekly paycheck supported my passion for writing, which began in grammar school, but until Rod brought me on staff, it didn't seem like a career in journalism was in the cards.

Rod took a big chance on me—me, someone who had never taken a journalism course, let alone majored in it—and for that, I remain eternally grateful. In return, I have tried over my long career to mentor and support young and new writers. Read more about this at *http://gwaynemiller.*

blogspot.com/2018/08/chances-and-lesson-on-coffee.html

In April 1979, I left *The Transcript* (a family-owned newspaper that no longer exists) to join the staff at *The Cape Cod Times* (now owned by Gannett and a shadow of its former self), where another editor, the late Bill Breisky, took a chance on me, too. In October 1981, I became a staff writer at *The Providence Journal*, where yet another editor, the late Chuck Hauser, also took a chance on me. I remained a staff writer at *The Providence Journal* (now also owned by Gannett) until November 2022.

During my long career, I have witnessed firsthand many changes in newspapering—I was in the room where an historic transformation of the press happened, you could say. It was not the only profound transformation since the first newspapers in America—those were one-page broadsides published in 1689, followed by the first paper with more than a single page (*Publick Occurrences Both Forreign and Domestick*, published in Boston, on September 25, 1690)—but *Unfit to Print* is my argument that changes in the last decades are the most threatening to our democracy.

In my early days in journalism, I saw all-time highs in display and classified-advertising pages, which brought record revenues to many papers and an annual profit margin in the range of twenty percent, which any corporation would envy. I witnessed the growth of the internet, which initially seemed a wonderful adjunct to traditional newspapering.

It wasn't.

Beginning in the mid-1990s with the dawn of free online advertising, those record revenues began to decline—and a business, which American journalism has been from the start, experienced unprecedented pressures. A landmark year was 1995, when Craigslist was founded.

The next year, I witnessed the sale of the family-owned *Providence Journal*, the oldest continuously published daily newspaper in America (1829), to Dallas-based A.H. Belo Corporation, which for a while nurtured its investment, then bled it for profit as staff members were laid off and bureaus closed.

In 2014, I witnessed another sale of *The Journal*, from A.H. Belo to GateHouse Media, which was owned by Fortress Investment Group, a hedge fund manager. GateHouse continued cutting *The Journal* staff, just as it did other papers it owned.

Five years later, GateHouse merged with Gannett, whose flagship paper is USA TODAY. Its first editor was the late John C. Quinn, a Rhode Islander who began his career at *The Providence Journal* and worked his way up to assistant managing editor before leaving for Gannett. (Quinn's son, John C. "Chips" Quinn Jr., who also worked at *The Journal*, died tragically in a car accident in 1990. I wrote his obituary. Yes, a sad irony.)

In the year 2021, Gannett cut its overall head count by 24%, according to Nieman Lab (https://bit.ly/3QsDP2I). The cuts continued during 2022, with layoffs in August at many Gannett papers, including two *Providence Journal* workers. Approximately 400 employees chain-wide lost their jobs. Another 400 or so open positions also were cut.

In October 2022, the cuts continued. Buyouts were offered, remaining employees were required to take unpaid leave in December, hiring was frozen, and Gannett temporarily suspended 401(k) contribution matches, according to *The New York Times* and other media outlets that reported on the actions.

In December 2022, Gannett cut some 200 additional news staffers at its papers, including the executive editor of *The Providence Journal* and one of the paper's long-time and highly respected photographers. Gannett was not alone as 2022 ended and the new year began. In January 2023, *The Washington Post* laid off 20 staff members and announced another 30 vacancies would go unfilled.

During the long decline, I witnessed first-hand how journalists became expendable, their careers and livelihoods discarded when their bosses said it was time.

Many were the best of the best—and then one day, they got the call to visit HR.

Some returned to our *Providence Journal* newsroom in tears, gathered their belongings, hugged friends, said goodbyes and disappeared, never to set foot inside their newspaper again. The diminishing number who were left arrived at work every day wondering if it was our turn.

Some who had dodged the ax began job-hunting and found employment at places that value accomplishment—universities and newspapers not owned by hedge funds or chains, for example. Those of us who were left at *The Journal* still believed local journalism mattered, even as the pillaging continued and some Americans, led by former President Donald Trump, reviled journalists as enemies of the people, not people whose profession had been endorsed as a bedrock of democracy by the Founding Fathers in the First Amendment.

During what could be called the glory days, *The Journal* owned and occupied the entirety of a four-story building in downtown Providence. It operated more than a dozen bureaus, including two in Massachusetts and one in Washington, D.C., and employed approximately 200 editors, reporters, photographers, columnists, critics, librarians, editorial writers, copy clerks and assistants in features, business, news, sports, photography, and editorial departments.

The Journal staff now numbers about a dozen news reporters, one columnist, one sportswriter, one staff photographer, and a handful of editors and online producers. They are dedicated professionals, working... in part of one floor of the four-story building that once was all *The Journal* and is now owned by a developer who rents the rest to Tufts Health Plan, Virgin Pulse, Infosys, Saladworks and Charles Schwab. Insurers, tech firms, food chains, and financial service companies thrive while local journalism withers.

This was the newspaper where I had worked for forty-one years and nine days when, on November 4, 2022, I left voluntarily to become head of *OceanStateStories.org,* a non-profit, non-partisan news publication where I have been able to continue my writing about issues that matter to residents of Rhode Island.

Nationally, the picture is grim. According to the Hussman School of Journalism and Media at the University of North Carolina at Chapel Hill, which has studied newspapers for years, the situation continues to worsen.

"News Deserts and Ghost Newspapers: Will Local News Survive?", the school's latest report (fourth in a series), published in 2020, states that "in the 15 years leading up to 2020, more than one-fourth of the country's newspapers disappeared, leaving residents in thousands of communities— inner-city neighborhoods, suburban towns and rural villages—living in vast news deserts. Simultaneously, half of all local journalists disappeared, as round after round of layoffs have left many surviving papers—the gutsy dailies and weeklies that had won accolades and Pulitzer Prizes for their reporting—mere "ghosts," or shells of their former selves. Compounding the problem, there has been a lack of capital and funding available to support a variety of for-profit, nonprofit, and publicly funded news organizations attempting to thwart the rise of news deserts...

"In the years immediately following the 2008 recession, the decline has been relentless, and it appears to have been accelerating in the years leading up to 2020. Since our last report, *The Expanding News Desert*, was published in the fall of 2018, 300 newspapers closed, another 6,000 journalists employed by newspapers vanished, and print newspaper circulation declined by 5 million. Consolidation also increased, with the largest chains, backed by private equity firms and hedge funds, racing to merge with the last surviving publicly traded companies and form mega-chains with hundreds of newspapers, and management focused on shareholder return over journalism's civic duty."

In this era of so-called "fake news" and "alternative facts" and QAnon— when some media outlets, left- and right-leaning and in between, will do just about anything for clicks—when Russia uses social media and other platforms to undermine our democracy with disinformation—when extremists and politicians inspired by Trump erode it further with lies and conspiracy theories—when social media platforms purport to be ethical but care mostly about profit—truth still matters.

But why did I write a novel and not a memoir or exposé?

In part, because fiction allowed me to wring dark humor from a sickening reality. As the old saw has it: If you don't laugh, you cry.

But mostly because as Ralph Waldo Emerson is purported to have said, "fiction reveals truth that reality obscures."

So, yes, truth still matters—and so do morality, social justice, quality local journalism, and doing the right thing.

Those are among the lessons that Nick Nolan, the protagonist of *Unfit To Print*, embraces as he eventually rejects the click mentality and hollow sensationalism driving much of what's left of newspapering today.

Nolan comes to believe we are better than that.

I hope he is right.

G. Wayne Miller
October 2023
Newport, Rhode Island

CAST OF CHARACTERS

In order of appearance.

The Boston Daily Tribune

The Trib, a Pulitzer Prize-winning newspaper published every day since 1823. After years of layoffs and downsizings, SuperGoodMedia, an out-of-town chain, has just bought it.

Nick Nolan

The narrator, a once relevant and prize-winning journalist at *The Boston Daily Tribune* whose column in recent years has become pathetic. Needs something big or it could be curtains.

Destiny Carter

Trib business reporter. Only African American on the paper's staff. Nolan's best friend.

Randolph Gordon IV

Longtime *Tribune* publisher and member of family that owned the paper for generations. Until an out-of-town chain made a lucrative offer, that is.

David Chamberlain

CEO of SuperGoodMedia, aka SGM, a Florida-based national newspaper chain whose motto is "Good News Rules!"

Paul Peters

SuperGoodMedia's Chief Fun Officer, or CFO.

Ron Hawkins

SuperGoodMedia's Chief Motivational Officer, or CMO.

Bradley Winthrop III
SuperGoodMedia's Chief Diversity Officer, or CDO.

Roger Rogers
SuperGoodMedia's Social Media Pal, or SMP.

Danny D'Ermo
SuperGoodMedia's SuperOptimizerSupervisor, or SOS.

Bruce Hill
New *Trib* publisher. His background includes an MBA from Harvard and years in marketing at Frito-Lay. Wears Superman t-shirts.

Bob Jones
Trib executive editor.

Terry Winters
Trib investigative reporter. Won the paper's most recent Pulitzer Prize, which is likely to be its last, now that SuperGoodMedia owns it.

Jennifer Abbott
A former actor who claims the Virgin Mary speaks to her comatose daughter, Amber. Old flame of Nolan's.

Amber Abbott
Eight-year-old girl in a persistent vegetative state.

Bud Fuller
Trib suburban reporter. President of the Newspaper Guild local. Good friend of Nolan.

H. Henry Harlow III
Arrogant member of old Yankee family whose bank is one of *The Trib's* last major advertisers. An entitled and despicable man.

Luke Turner
Wealthy Massachusetts developer. Also despicable. And corrupt.

Ted Matthews
Trib freelance reporter.

Courtney Lawford
Columnist for CoolBostonWeekly, an "alternative" weekly and web site. Nolan's soon-to-be-ex-wife.

A.J. Johnson
Last lifestyle columnist left at *The Trib*. Lawford's source inside the paper. Lives with chronic fatigue syndrome, or is that only what she claims?

Benjamin Franklin
Yes, him.

Greta Ricci
A true believer.

Office Gerry Maloney
A Boston cop.

Robert J. Dixon
A creepy sportscaster and drunk.

Erica Martinez
Photographer and *The Trib*'s only Hispanic staff member.

Aaron Schiffman, MD
An oncologist at Dana-Farber Cancer Institute.

Mark Zuckerberg
Chairman and CEO of Facebook, now Meta.

David M. Wehner
Facebook CFO.

Rose Redwing Brown
Central character in "Nipmuc Nation: Here first, Native Americans work to bring the real story of Mass. to the masses," an award-winning series Nolan wrote before turning columnist.

Henry Spinelli
Another true believer.

Carol H. Thomas, MD
A neurologist at Brigham and Women's Hospital.

Tony Callahan
Another true believer.

Gina Pulaski
Mother of an only child who is at risk of dying of cancer.

Jimmy Pulaski
Young boy with kidney cancer.

Chris Hackett
The Trib's new marketing chief.

Marjorie Rudd
New Lifestyle editor, whose last job was at *Vogue* magazine.

Donald Sabella
Former Chief Judge for the U.S. District Court of Massachusetts. Bribed by Mexican drug lord Joaquín Archivaldo Guzmán Loera, El Chapo.

Margery Eagan and Jim Braude
Hosts of Boston Public Radio.

Michelle Wu
Mayor of Boston.

Natalia Perez
Chamberlain's executive assistant.

Garth Vader
Manager of The Alkil Global Capital Fund.

Donald J. Trump
45th president of the United States.

Rudy Giuliani
Former mayor of New York City.

Mike Lindell
Founder and CEO of My Pillow.

Jose Cardinal Cruz
Archbishop of Boston.

Elizabeth Turner
Devout Catholic and wife of developer Luke Turner.

Cindy Leroux
A photo editor and friend of Nolan.

Joseph T. Cicilline
U.S. Attorney for the District of Massachusetts.

Pope Francis
First Jesuit Pontiff.

Dave Roderick
Weekend editor.

Michael Adams
Trib press foreman.

Ted Sorenson
Retired restaurant owner.

CHAPTER ONE: MARKET VALUE

Once upon a time, I, Nick Nolan, wrote exclusively about marginalized people who had little or no voice in the mainstream media. Socioeconomic and health disparities, mental health, and intellectual and developmental disabilities were among my topics. My stories prompted change. Some won awards and three were Pulitzer finalists—but, more importantly, I helped advance the social-justice agenda as only a crusading journalist can do.

When I left hard news to become a columnist, a move I believed would afford me greater power to prompt change—think Anna Quindlen and Nicholas Kristof—I was merciless when I took aim at corrupt politicians and judges, self-serving civic leaders, misogynists, unethical corporations, climate deniers, opponents of LGBTQ+ rights, and racists and demagogues wherever they were found.

My column was always on the front page, I was nationally syndicated, and I hosted a popular TV show. My website, Facebook, Twitter, Instagram, and YouTube accounts had hundreds of thousands of followings. Simon & Schuster published a collection of my columns and in its review, *The New York Times* proclaimed me "brilliant." *The Los Angeles Times* went further, calling me "a writer who eloquently frames truths. The world needs more Nick Nolans." Promising millions, a Netflix producer had reached out to me, wanting a pitch for a series about the newspaper business.

How long ago this all seemed the morning we learned that our newspaper, the family-owned *Boston Daily Tribune*, had been sold.

It was August 23, 2021, the second year of the coronavirus pandemic.

By then, my social media activity was tepid.

By then, my column was buried deep inside metro/region.

By then, not even bottom-feeder agents contacted me.

By then, the January 6 insurrectionists had stuck another dagger into the heart of democracy—and out-of-town and hedge-fund newspaper chains that paid their executives obscene salaries and bonuses while laying off actual journalists as they ghosted and killed local papers were pushing it in deeper.

By then, my muse had forsaken me.

More correctly, the muse had been slain.

Using Google Analytics, a member of our marketing staff had "proved," as he phrased it, that social-justice columns did not generate the numbers of online views and engagements needed to justify my job.

Or anyone's job, this marketer said. *What do you think this is, socialism?*

The new reality? Newspaper executives wanted clicks.

Fuck public service, unless somehow there was a Pulitzer in it, which would be a marvelous come-on the shrinking sales staff could bring to certain advertisers. Well-endowed non-profits, for example. But not car dealers, real-estate firms, floor and rug installers, hearing-aid manufacturers, the Jitterbug cellphone company, and shyster companies promising cures for erectile dysfunction, which remained among our biggest advertisers.

And me?

Maybe a feel-good piece every now and then that hints of public service, for old times' sake, this marketing moron said, *but that's it. Maximize your clicks. You're no dope. You can read the tea leaves. You still like a paycheck, right, good buddy?*

Good buddy my ass.

But I held my tongue.

As real newspapering continued to die, I knew the inside game intimately. Not the time to shoot yourself in the foot. Definitely not the time to proclaim Dana Priest, Seymour Hirsch, Maggie Haberman, and Neil Sheehan as four of your heroes.

So what was getting the clicks on that August 23, 2021?

Consider a few of the so-called "recommended" headlines and accompanying stories—all from free-content providers—that were posted on our website that day,

Go Topless Day Draws Hundreds, Even a Few Men
Desperate Housewives Without Makeup, the Shocking Reality
Giant Rabbit Hops Across Wyoming, Arrives Hungry in Idaho
Texas Christian Has Proof She Walked on Water
She Hid Under the Bed to Spy on Her Husband But Instantly Regretted It
Sultry Country Star Steals Rival's Diamond Necklace, Hides It in Her Cleavage
Man Buries 42 School Buses Underground. Look When He Reveals the Inside
The Baddest Biker Girls in the World
We Can Determine Your Education Level in 25 Questions

Does Your Cat Throw Up Often? Try This One Trick
50 Photos That Show the Wrong Side of Cruise Ships
20 Hair Shapes That Make a Woman Over 60 Look 40
20 Southern Phrases Northerners Don't Understand
17 People Who Learned the Hard Way

And there was no escaping these abominations.

They populated the home page from top to bottom and owned its entire right side, and they popped up inside every second or third paragraph of every story. Adblocking software couldn't stop them. Rebooting and clearing the cache couldn't stop them. Clicking on the "X" next to the dread AdChoices button in the upper right-hand corner couldn't stop them.

You get the picture. A pathetic fucking picture. Not what I signed on for those many years ago, when journalists believed journalism really could change the world, not just line the pockets of newspaper executives and owners.

But ordered by management to get the clicks, I had "retooled my toolbox," as the idiot marketer phrased it.

The result? I was now writing nonsense, three times a week, except for July, when I vacationed on Block Island, where I fantasized I might live someday as I wrote novels and screenplays.

Nonsense about socks, for example—45 numbing inches about losing socks in the washer, finding socks under sofas, socks without mates, the amazing secret life of socks. I contemplated the greater meaning of winter sunsets (OK, not bad), spring robins (also not bad), and Jell-O (shoot me now), and I explored my separation from my wife, a columnist at CoolBostonWeekly, Boston's leading website. Cue violins now, please. Or barf, your choice.

I recommend the latter.

Alliteration, adjectives, and clichés had become my stock in trade, and I killed no darlings (see Faulkner, King, et. al.).

If anyone needed further proof of how pathetic I'd become, it could be found in how often I wrote about the difficulty of writing columns: 4.5 times a year, according to the smugly published calculation of my soon-to-be ex-wife. Her math, sadly, was correct.

I took comfort knowing I wasn't alone.

Our once-mighty newspaper—defender of truth, champion of the common man, Pulitzer Prize winner, published every day since 1823—through wars, pandemics, depressions, civil strife, patriotic and idiotic presidents, divided Congresses—was on the ropes, too.

Starting in the 1990s with the advent of the online era, *The Tribune's* daily circulation had tanked, from an Audit Bureau-certified 410,000 to less than 50,000 and still dropping. We couldn't even stabilize our flagship

Sunday edition, which once had a circulation north of a million, despite cutting the subscription price, lowering ad rates to peanuts, and sponsoring online crossword contests with $5,000 cash prizes. Not sure if we ever paid them, or just dangled that out there and followed up with excuses or movie passes, but whatever, I digress. I do that a lot.

There were even rumors of moving to five-day-a-week publication, or going entirely online—or even, in a worst-case scenario that increasingly seemed possible, ending publication altogether, the presses after two centuries silenced for good.

Had we been a two-rag town, by now we surely would have become another ghost paper, run by a skeleton crew working remotely from Texas or Indonesia.

But having bought and then folded The Boston Chronicle, the only other print competition in the metro region, The Trib owned a monopoly, which meant we had a new lease on life, for a spell anyway. It meant we could hold advertisers hostage, to a degree.

It meant we still had some market value, which is why I was not shocked by the events of that August morning, when I arrived at work to find a remote-broadcast trailer with Florida plates in front of our building. A satellite dish lifted toward the sky.

The Delta variant was ravaging the U.S. that summer, but we were in Massachusetts, which had one of the highest vaccination rates in the country. Nonetheless, fully vaccinated people—and that was all of our staff, to the best of my knowledge—were required to wear masks indoors, and we were working hybrid shifts, virtually from home on most days, with a rotating schedule of only small numbers of us at the paper on select days of the week.

This was the first time we had been summoned to be on site all together.

"Looks like the rumor was true," said Destiny Carter, my best friend. Destiny was one of *The Trib*'s long-time business writers and an African American, one of only three people of color on our staff. The others were photographer Erica Martinez, who was Hispanic, and Connie Lee, an Asian America. Critics who pointed to *The Trib* as a pillar of structural racism were right.

"You mean the rumor we were for sale?" I said.

"What else could it be?" Destiny said.

We were standing in the lobby with our good friend, reporter Bud Fuller. A film crew was loading tripods and cameras into the elevator to the fourth-floor auditorium.

"But Gordon vowed we weren't for sale," I said.

Just last week, in fact, publisher Randolph E. Gordon IV had issued a written statement denying persistent rumors of a takeover.

"And two years ago he insisted we weren't downsizing," said Bud. "His word means shit."

Bud was right.

Three days after his written statement, Gordon slashed the staff by twenty-five percent, albeit through buyouts that left many of the remaining three-fourths jealous. For the record, that was the last of the buyouts. What came next was good old-fashioned firings: a call to visit HR, where you were told you were terminated, your email and card key would be deactivated in a half hour, and you had until then to clear your stuff out and be off premises or security would be called.

"So, who's the new owner?" I said.

"Must be SuperGoodMedia," said Destiny. "It's the only chain based in Florida."

My stomach churned.

"They're worse than McClatchy," I said.

"There's something worse than McClatchy? Destiny said.

"Hard to believe, but yes, and they're it," I said.

"And you thought downsizing was bad," Bud said. "We need to see Gordon."

"Good luck," said Destiny.

Now the guys in uniforms were carrying sealed cardboard boxes up to the auditorium.

Destiny pointed to three guards who stood at the front desk. The friendly Albert "Al" Rosenthal, who'd manned that post for as long as I could remember and knew all of us by first name, had been replaced by a trio of unsmiling men with shaved heads, flak vests and visible sidearms. One had a tattoo on his neck which I thought was a Don't Tread on Me flag, but I couldn't be sure: I didn't dare stare for fear he'd draw a bead on me.

So now we knew why the entire staff was together at the paper for the first time since early March 2020.

After huddling in nervous clusters around the newsroom, one of the guards summoned us to the auditorium, where a monitor large enough to grace Fenway Park had been erected. Gordon stood on the stage, cameras trained on him. He was an overweight man who smoked, and today, when he took his mask off to speak, he wore a shit-eating grin.

"Welcome, dear friends and fellow employees!" Gordon said when we'd settled into our seats.

Many of the journalists I've known tend toward ADHD, like kids on sugar. But I'd never seen a room so quiet. No one even parodied Gordon's customary phony salutation.

"As you know," Gordon said, "for nearly 200 years *The Tribune* has stood for gold-plate standards of truth, excellence, and public service. But even a great tradition needs a vision to prosper today. And so, with all of our futures in mind, I recently entered into discussions with a man who is a visionary without equal."

This was bullshit.

The gold-plate truth was this: with the passing generations, the Gordon family had bred too prolifically for the center to hold. Gordons in Texas and Arizona and the Cayman Islands with their money in Swiss banking accounts had no emotional investment in stewardship of a Massachusetts newspaper. They wanted only a better return on their privately held stock so they could continue lounging by their horizon pools as staff brought them their Mojitos.

Gordon's first attempt at appeasing his pampered relatives had been buying, then closing, the Boston Chronicle, a move that had increased revenues, through the higher ad rates a monopoly afforded. But that bump was temporary. Next was the downsizing, which presumably increased dividends again, just not enough. I say presumably because Destiny tried to get a story in The Trib—and came away with "no comment" from every Gordon she contacted and an order from our publisher to kill her story.

The screen flickered alive, and, as patriotic music played, we saw a wide-angle shot of the Orlando, Florida, world headquarters of SuperGoodMedia: a sprawling, futuristic building designed by an architect the Disney company had retained for several of its projects. An American flag flapped in the breeze near a row of Mercedes and Range Rovers in the parking lot.

The image dissolved, leaving us inside the office of chairman and CEO David Chamberlain.

Chamberlain greeted "my fabulous new friends in New England!" and prattled on about "two great traditions that today are joined!" and blah-bah-blah.

My mind drifted to the scathing piece Columbia Journalism Review had run recently on Chamberlain, which began: "Is this what Benjamin Franklin and the Founding Fathers had in mind when they wrote the First Amendment? Hell, no. They wanted journalism, not a freak show."

The story went on to relate how Chamberlain had earned an MBA at Harvard Business School and after a lightning rise inside The New York Times Co.—the business, not news, side of the house—he became Chief Financial Officer of Rupert Murdoch's News Corp. Chamberlain was thirty-four when he left Murdoch to build his own company. He today led a national chain of daily and weekly newspapers, shoppers, and web sites.

Large in number, they were without exception journalistically undistinguished.

The chairman was still glad-handing us when Destiny whispered to me:

"Look—it's true."

"What?"

"His motto. Check out the sign on his desk."

And there they were, the three words and exclamation mark that CJR had criticized: GOOD NEWS RULES! They encapsulated Chamberlain's editorial policy: that so-called good news had gotten lost in the media's supposed infatuation with the "bad."

CJR had ridiculed this slogan and philosophy, writing "Did Chamberlain hire Don McLean as a consultant? Because it seems he has taken these American Pie lyrics literally: 'But February made me shiver. With every paper I'd deliver. Bad news on the doorstep. I couldn't take one more step.' Although Chamberlain actually did take one more step, into nonsense.

"Or perhaps Chamberlain took inspiration from Amy Sherman-Palladino. Herewith a transcript of 'Welcome to the Dollhouse,' episode 115 of *The Gilmore Girls*. Judge for yourself:

LANE: So, what's going on in the world?

LORELAI: Nothing.

LANE: Nothing.

LORELAI: - good. There's nothing good. There's absolutely nothing even remotely positive going on anywhere in the world. How can that be?

LANE: That's why I don't read the paper anymore.

LORELAI: You will mine. I'm starting my own. The Good News Daily. Nothing but good news, every day.

LANE: Sounds good.

LORELAI: "No civil war in Canada." Big article. "Cars drive down road without incident." Front-page news. "Puppies, how cute are they?" In-depth exposé and the subscription is free. How happy is that?

Chamberlain was committed to excluding so-called bad news from his papers—for example, they published nothing about how former president Donald Trump and his family were criminals who had used bad loans, a reality show, tax loopholes, and fake corporations to build their house of cards.

Nothing about Russian military intelligence, which by manipulating social media had helped hand Trump the keys to 1600 Pennsylvania Avenue.

Nor anything about how Trump had instigated the January 6 insurrection, which the House Select Committee was on the road to proving.

Did I mention that Chamberlain was a friend of Ted Cruz, Marco Rubio, and Mitch McConnell—and a big Republican donor? That he had dined with Trump at Mar-a-Lago? That he was a close friend of Florida Governor Ron DeSantis?

By shifting the balance between good and bad, Chamberlain had told CJR, his papers had experienced an increase in ad revenues. As proof, Chamberlain provided a statement from the CEO of Keep America America for Heaven's Sake, who said that "real Americans are fed up with the media's obsession with violence, negativity, wokeness, homosexuality and trans nonsense, and I applaud SGM for its bravery."

Chamberlain had defended his philosophy in a diatribe from which the publication had excerpted a quote: "I was deeply troubled by the crisis facing newspapers in the age of Google, Apple, Facebook, Twitter, Instagram, 1,000-channel TV, and the two-working-parent family. I feared that one of the foundations of modern democracy would go the way of the Edsel—with disastrous consequences for every citizen of our great land. I wasn't the only one concerned, of course. But where others tried Band-aid approaches, I knew something radical had to be done. So I did it. And if our audience size and stock price are any indication, I did it to overwhelming success."

Responding to critics who maintained that his Good News Rules policy amounted to censorship, Chamberlain had told CJR:

"Horsefeathers. We are simply deciding, as journalists have since Benjamin Franklin, what belongs in our newspapers—and what doesn't. This, I believe, is what is known as editing. The Founding Fathers envisioned a free and vibrant press, not one beholden to tired tradition or some woke ideal that Ivy League professors trot out every fall to indoctrinate their students. If consumers don't like our product, they have a multitude of other choices in today's wired world."

CJR closed its profile of SGM by declaring "If the stakes for local journalism weren't so high, Chamberlain could be dismissed as a jester, but the truth is he and the hedge-fund managers are killing it. Pay attention, America. Democracy is at stake."

To which Chamberlain had responded: "What's at stake is the credibility of the Columbia University Graduate School of Journalism in the new world they refuse to see."

Chamberlain's office lights dimmed and a soundtrack built in volume. It was Pharrell Williams' song "Happy."

"Come on, SuperGooders, clap along with me!" Chamberlain said.

A few *Trib* staffers did.

The rest of us sat in stunned silence.

The lights came back up as a parade of white men skipped in, clapping and singing.

"My new friends at *The Trib*, I'd like to introduce you to our super great—and I mean *super great!*—management team!" Chamberlain said. "First, meet our CFO, Paul Peters. Paul, take a bow."

Peters did.

"But if you folks in Boston think our CFO is our chief financial officer," Chamberlain continued, "you'd be wrong. We *do* have someone who fills that function, but Paul is our Chief Fun Officer—yes, today's cutting-edge CFO is the officer in charge of keeping things super-good and super-light! You'll be seeing and hearing a lot from Paul in the weeks to come as we work to instill a positive attitude up there in the Bay State. With Paul on your side, 'If it bleeds, it leads' will painlessly become 'If it's light, it's right!' "

Another man stepped forward.

"Meet Ron Hawkins, our Chief Motivational Officer, or CMO!" Chamberlain said.

Hawkins took a bow.

"I don't need to tell you *his* job!" the chairman said. "That's right, getting you super-charged as we awaken your super-tired paper! You'll be seeing and hearing a lot from him, too, as we push you to achieve your best—or shall I say *super*—success!"

A third man came forward.

"Meet Bradley Winthrop III, our Chief Diversity Officer, or CDO!"

The previous two were ridiculous, but this one blew my mind.

White, male, blueblood... surely this was when Chamberlain delivered the punch line.

There wasn't one.

"Next," said Chamberlain, "let's have a warm welcome for Roger Rogers, our Social Media Pal, or SMP, the man who will be sure all of your posts, personal and professional, on Facebook, Twitter, Instagram, TikTok, Pinterest, and wherever meet company standards—which is to say, are all super good! Roger that, Roger Rogers?"

"Roger that, Chairman Chairman!" said this fourth man.

"You will be emailed a copy of our Social Media Playbook, written by our Social Media Pal, which spells out what SuperGooders can and cannot post," Chamberlain said. "Cute pets, birthday parties, and setting suns are all permissible. But we will tolerate no politics, slurs, denunciations, supposedly clever witticisms, or personal opinions of any kind, not even what your favorite flavor ice cream is. And no emojis except for happy ones, right, Roger?"

"Roger that, our beloved chairman!"

"Finally," said Chamberlain, "meet Danny D'Ermo, our SuperOptimizerSupervisor, or SOS. He's the dude who'll be producing weekly spreadsheets of your numbers. Let's hope your clicks never drop to emergency lows, but if they do, send out an SOS to our Dashing Danny, and he will be your all hands-on-deck captain! Should that happen, who you gonna call?"

A man who resembled Don Knotts during his appearances on Hollywood Squares joined the CFO, CMO and CDO. He wore a Superman bow tie.

"Let me repeat," Chamberlain said. "Who you gonna call?"

"Your no-clicks buster!" D'Ermo said.

"And you will be happy to hear him roar as he refloats your boat!" Chamberlain said.

"My fellow SuperGooders, here I come to save the day!" D'Ermo screeched.

"Wasn't that Mighty Mouse?" I whispered to Destiny.

"I'm sorry," she whispered back. "I'm still counting the mixed metaphors."

"We're screwed," I said.

"Big-time," Destiny said.

Little did we know.

Chamberlain finished his dog-and-pony show, and then another scary life form materialized—next to Gordon, live and in person on the stage.

It was Bruce Hill, our new publisher.

He was dressed in a jacket, tie, and button-down-collar shirt and wearing a COVID mask with the SuperGoodMedia logo, SGM.

None of us had heard of him—but after removing his mask and saying he was fully vaccinated, he delivered an impassioned introduction that had the energy of a Tony Robbins TED Talk. A Harvard MBA, like his boss, Hill's entire career before Chamberlain hired him as SuperGoodMedia's national marketing director was in marketing at Frito-Lay. You would think a newspaper publisher would be ashamed to admit that, but not Hill.

Hill looked thirty but was actually thirty-nine. In well-rehearsed lines, he told us he was single, owned a golden retriever, drove a Lexus, and was an accomplished marathoner—"nine hundred and sixth the year before the pandemic right here in Boston," he said, "not bad for a ham 'n' egger!"

By this point, I was alarmed by something else.

I was remembering another of my columns—a light-hearted break from weightier topics that I wrote years ago when Olestra products were in the news for their tendency to, shall we say, soften and hasten the stool.

"Poop chips," I'd called them, a reference to their notorious side effects that the copy editor had used in a forty-two-point headline: 'Straight Poop on Poop Chips Makes Me Sick."

Back then, Frito-Lay had briefly resurrected Olestra with its line of

Light chips, but whether Hill had been involved was unclear. Chances were, he was.

"Now *I'm* fucked," I whispered to Destiny.

"That column was years ago," she said. "He never read it and never will. He's got bigger fish to fry. Like us."

"Want to bet? Ten bucks says he does within a week."

I had no shortage of detractors, inside and out of *The Trib*, who would be delighted to inform him.

Hill paused his remarks.

His face emotionless, he took off his jacket and undid his tie, tossed them to the floor, and did a 180, his back to us. Then he ripped off his dress shirt and swiveled back, revealing a tee-shirt with a Superman logo.

"There is a superhero in all of us, we just need the courage to put on the cape!" he shouted.

One lone person in the front row clapped.

Nerves, I had to believe.

"So many of our dreams seem impossible, indeed improbable—and then, when we summon the will, they become inevitable!" Hill continued. "Sometimes you have to take a leap of faith first, trusting that the trust comes later! Fellow journalists, place your trust in SuperGoodMedia and take that leap with us today!"

For a moment, I thought he was going to ask us to literally leap from our seats.

He rattled off a few more Superman clichés, Gordon put in his final two cents' worth, and then both men walked to the rear of the auditorium to fist-bump us as we filed out. Our last Human Resources worker was also there, distributing oversized manila envelopes from the sealed boxes we'd seen the guys in gray carrying in.

"Don't open until you are downstairs," he said.

Back in the newsroom, we did.

What ensued was a scene none of us will ever forget: some reporters finding a card key for the new security system that would restrict movement everywhere inside a previously internally unlocked building, and an employees' code of behavior that we were instructed to read and sign under penalty of dismissal. The envelopes also contained a t-shirt, a button, and a bumper sticker, each with GOOD NEWS RULES! printed in red. A note advised us that the tee shirt would be acceptable on the premises only on "dress-down Friday," a revolutionary concept in a profession that had never known what it meant to dress up, on any day.

I got one of those envelopes. So did Destiny, Bud, and several of our friends, together with others.

The rest opened theirs to find termination letters from Hill, who signed them "Super Sorry;" a $50 Walmart gift card "to celebrate the beginning of your new life;" and a note stating they had 30 minutes to leave the premises voluntarily or be escorted out by security.

Everyone cried save for one terminated reporter who threw his laptop on the floor and began stomping on it while shouting "Fuck you, you fucking fuckers. Your day will come."

He stopped when two of the three new guards, who now were wielding batons and wearing riot helmets with face shields, appeared.

"Twenty-four minutes and counting," one of them said.

A month later, on a Friday afternoon in September 2021, our executive editor called me into his office.

Bob Jones was the classic old-school newsman: a sharp-tongued, ruddy-faced man who wore rumpled shirts, drank to excess, didn't seem to own a comb, and loved a good cigar and sports, above all his beloved Red Sox and the New England Patriots until they let Tom Brady leave for Tampa Bay. You could picture him shouting "Get me rewrite!" into an old-fashioned phone or imagine him as Ed Asner on *Lou Grant*. If only we still lived in that era.

Jones had started as a high-school intern and moved up through the ranks until, at age fifty-eight, he'd been named top dog. It didn't hurt that he'd married Randolph Gordon's sister. He was sixty-four now, a year shy of retirement. If he could survive with SuperGoodMedia for one more year, I'd learned, his pension would double.

"Danish, Nick?" said Jones.

I noticed he was wearing a pin-striped suit—Brooks Brothers, if I had to guess. I'd seen him in a suit exactly once, at a funeral.

Jones pointed to a silver tray with an anemic-looking pastry. I assumed it was left over from some morning meeting of the publisher, who obviously knew how to dispose of them. Stale pastries, cold pizza, advance copies of books, samples of new air fresheners, the latest home-improvement software—just about anything, send it to the newsroom and it vanished quickly.

"No, thanks," I said.

Along with cheeseburgers and Coke, pastries and doughnuts had been my downfall. Lately, I was trying to shed a few pounds with an occasional visit to the gym—a losing battle that, sadly but predictably, had wound up in a column that began "With all due respect to soldiers who actually fought in it, My Personal Battle of the Bulge started when I...."

"The reason I asked you here," Jones said, "is I want to talk about your column."

"You're the only one who does," I said.

Jones laughed—a high-pitched, silly laugh that escaped him whenever he was anxious.

He was anxious a lot these days, and not only because his father-in-law was publisher no more and his pension was no longer guaranteed. After years of legal maneuvering, the biggest libel suit in the history of *The Trib* had just been scheduled for trial. The suit involved an essay Jones had written and then played on the front page when Gordon was publisher.

In it, he had expressed the hope that the once powerful judge he believed had ordered the killing of his son in retribution for a *Trib* investigation would "rot in hell."

"Actually," Jones continued, "a *lot* of people have been talking about your column. People the marketing department has brought on board."

That had been one of Hill's first acts: expanding what had been reduced to a one-person staff during Gordons' final days to a department with five employees.

"What kind of people?" I said.

"Readers selected at random."

"You mean focus groups."

"Yes."

"So a newspaper has become no different than McDonald's," I said.

"This is a new era," said Jones. "The subscriber is boss now."

"Subscribers want this shit?"

"SGM says they do. Even if I wanted to do differently, I'd have no choice. The publisher personally ordered this study. He's also read it cover-to-cover."

The spiral-bound book on Jones's desk was two inches thick.

"This is all on me?" I said.

In a gallows sort of way, I was flattered.

"No, they examined the entire news operation. But that's not why we're here: we're here to talk about you."

Jones opened to a page toward the middle.

"Let me share a few of the comments," he said.

"Must you?"

"I think it would be instructive."

Jones perched his glasses on his nose and began reading.

" 'The question is: if Nolan writes a column and no one reads it, does it make a sound?' "

"Was my about-to-be-ex in this focus group?" I said.

Jones didn't laugh.

"Here's what someone else had to say," he went on. " 'Nolan is about as funny as pancreatic cancer.' That was a doctor speaking. Someone who wasn't a doctor asked if euthanasia was legal in Massachusetts. Someone else wanted to know what size concrete shoes would be needed to send you to the bottom of Boston Harbor and keep you there permanently. I'd like to think he didn't mean literally."

"You've made your point," I said.

"And then there was this: 'Do the world a favor. Gag Nolan with one of his socks.' "

"Enough," I said. "We've already discussed what a terrible mistake socks was."

"If only it were that one column," Jones said. "But the fact is that across our key demographics—especially the critical eighteen-to-thirty-four segment, and the next most important, retired boomers, the ones with disposable incomes—your regular readership is... how best to put it... anemic."

Another of Hill's first acts had been hosting a weekend retreat for his senior managers, as top editors were now called. Danny D'Ermo had flown up from Florida to attend. The grapevine had it that they spent much of their time reviewing the findings from the latest focus groups—and digging deep into Google Analytics, which broke down audience engagement of every story, photo, video, audio clip, and chart we published online. Google also provided a wealth of demographic data that was useful in sales pitches to advertisers. Everyone at *The Trib* had access to D'Ermo's spreadsheets and the analytics, and many of us, myself included, had started obsessively checking the numbers, the way I imagined prisoners on Death Row checked the calendar as the days ticked down.

Jones turned the page, to a series of bar graphs charting frequency of my readership (never, occasionally, regularly, always) by age group. Only in OVER 80 was I even close to respectable. This was not a group advertisers coveted, given consumer spending for that demographic.

In case the message was unclear, the market research firm had charted the numbers for Dear Abby and Ask Amy next to mine. Abby and Amy trounced me in every category.

I was getting defensive.

"You could put Toni Morrison or Dickens in the paper and people would bitch," I said.

And it was true, as Jones knew. He'd often told me how he dreaded Monday mornings for the barrage of phone calls and emails about the weekend editions that always awaited him. Few concerned literary excellence. But a missing crossword puzzle or comic? That was a different story.

"Numbers don't lie," Jones said.

"Why don't you just cut to the chase," I said.

"The marketing department will be charting these numbers on a weekly basis and distributing them to the appropriate parties," he said.

"You mean Hill and Chamberlain. Are you also going to send them around by email to the whole staff so we can have a collective shaming?"

Jones dodged that one, saying only "I have every hope you'll turn things around."

"And if I don't?"

"I'm afraid we'll have to make some changes."

"Changes?"

"We'll have to realign your contributions to the company's needs," said Jones.

"Cut the corporate-speak," I said. "What are you saying?"

"I'm sorry," Jones said, "but we'll have to send you to the suburban staff."

For journalists like me at mid-career, the suburban staff, small as it now was with most of our bureaus closed, was death.

I mean death, as in demise of the soul. I knew reporters who'd passed twenty years in the boondocks without ever writing a front-page story again or finding a moment of satisfaction with how their careers had unfolded. They were like actors who played characters on old TV shows that get recycled on UP TV or the Hallmark Channel: you never were sure if they were still alive, nor did you care.

"You wouldn't do that to me," I said.

"I'd have no choice," Jones said. "As you know, the publisher has taken a keen interest in all aspects of the news department. He's involved in everything here now."

"How long do I have?"

"A month."

"That's twelve columns."

"I really am sorry, Nick. Off the record, I'm not happy about this. I'm not happy about any of this."

"But you're doing it, aren't you," I said. "That's Okay, Bob. I understand it's a whole new world. I understand your pension is on the line. So they've reduced you to a mercenary."

Jones seemed wounded. For the first time since the sale, I caught a glimpse of my long-time mentor and friend, not a newly minted SuperGoodMedia team player.

I met Destiny Carter at Ernie's, a working-class bar a few blocks from *The Trib*. Bud Fuller often joined us, but not tonight.

"So how'd it go?" she said as the bartender lined us up with Sam Adams draft beers.

"Awful."

I filled Destiny in.

"I have more bad news," Destiny said when I was done. "Poop Man's hiring consultants."

"Poop Man?"

"Hill. That's the nickname for him that's started going around."

Destiny told me that someone had started a group text that included a reference to my column—and a printout of my column with "Poop Man" written in red had appeared on the newsroom bulletin board. In the column, I had castigated Frito-Lay for reviving its WOW brand of chips under the new name of "Light."

You may recall WOW, introduced in 1998 as fat-free Ruffle's, Doritos, Tostitos and Lay's snacks. Fat-free was achieved with use of the ingredient olestra, which apparently had not been market-tested on actual people before the launch. The snacks were hugely popular—until actual consumers began reporting unseemly after-effects.

What I could not have predicted but had recently learned was that Hill during his career at Frito-Lay had handled the marketing for Light, the rebranded name for Wow. Light had remained on the shelves until 2016, when Frito-Lay discontinued Light products.

"So now it's official," I said. "I am truly fucked."

"I doubt he'll find out about that column," Destiny said. "I shredded that printout and what are the chances he'll find out about the group text?"

"I'd say 100 percent. So, about those consultants. What's their mandate?"

"Reorganize the news organization. 'News efficiency experts,' they're called."

"Suits. The kids from middle school we hated all grown up now."

"They start next week."

"Time for the grape Kool-Aid," I said.

"Wrong. Time to kick ass."

I looked to see if Destiny was indulging her quirky sense of humor, but she wasn't. She was animated, the way she got when inspiration struck.

This was not always a good thing.

"I've been thinking about this a lot," she said. "I've decided we can beat them at their own game."

"You've totally lost me."

"Their bottom line is the bottom line, right? Profit. Ramp up the ads and the clicks and keep the stock price high and shareholders happy."

"Are you looking for a new career as hedge-fund manager?"

"Can I finish my thought?"

"Okay, how—by delivering the damn paper, too?"

"That would be funny if we still had any print subscribers," Destiny said.

We did, of course, but the numbers kept dwindling as readers rebelled against the ever-rising prices of a subscription and elders who'd started reading in another era passed on.

"No, smart ass," Destiny continued, "by going back to what newspapering used to be. Remember those days—when principle and great stories were what mattered, not this crap we fill the paper with today?"

"You mean stories like 'giant rabbit hops across Wyoming, arrives hungry in Idaho'," I said.

"Yes, like those. Also, the stuff *we* write."

Destiny was on a roll. I ordered another beer and watched as she opened today's paper to the business section, where her story on the seasonally adjusted Massachusetts unemployment rate inching up two tenths of a percentage point had been cut to a brief buried deep inside.

"Look at this," she said. "Could you even get through the first sentence?"

I had to admit I had not read the story, nor planned to.

"Of course not," said Destiny. "It's a bloodless, boring piece of shit. Two-tenths of a percent—OK, who are they? I'll tell you who. Single mothers forced to decide between paying the rent or the utility bill. People of color, immigrants, and white folk who have lost their jobs during the pandemic. Small business owners ruined by COVID. Where are their voices? Not in my story, that's for sure. 'Just the numbers' were my explicit instructions."

"I'm surprised they wanted anything," I said. "Doesn't SGM consider rising unemployment quote-unquote bad news?"

"They do. I was told this is the last time we report on increasing unemployment. A drop, however—we'll be trumpeting that, if and when it happens."

"So your story was both buried and boring. Point is?"

"Point is that is just one example of our useless journalism. It's not just the business section. It's every section, every day. It's me, you, everyone on the staff writing play-it-safe crap or sensationalistic nonsense, all for clicks. With the exception of Terry Winters, that is."

Winters was the head of our I-team—head and only investigative reporter left after his three colleagues had been laid off. Terry had won our last Pulitzer Prize. Given SGM, it was likely to be the final one.

"Look at today's front page," Destiny continued. "Our six-millionth story on the Minuteman Mall being almost completed; yet another insipid feature on *American Idol's* next season, which hasn't started filming yet; and a story about gasoline prices dropping again after the latest rise, like that's news we haven't been reading for a thousand years. And the centerpiece? A name-the-baby-flamingo born at the zoo contest. Not a word about the pandemic or the humanitarian disaster in Afghanistan. We've become more superficial than Justin Bieber. And that was before the assholes in Florida bought us."

"You're tough," I said.

"Also, right. We need to get back to the basics."

As I started into a third beer and Destiny elaborated, kindly not singling me out as Exhibit Number One, I reflected on my own career.

Back when I was a beginning reporter (cub, they quaintly used to say), I believed we could change the world—or at least where we lived in it. It was near the end of the last century, when journalists still were inspired by—or at least remembered—Seymour Hersh, Neil Sheehan, and Woodward and Bernstein. I may be over-romanticizing, but back then, the First Amendment was a sacred charge, pursuing justice a noble calling.

We sought to inform and to right wrongs—to afflict the comfortable and comfort the afflicted, as the saying goes. We gave voice to those whose voices were not heard in corridors of power, if anywhere. And we managed to entertain and amuse as well. Story reigned supreme, as Destiny noted—tales of ordinary people doing extraordinary things and everyday things, as the writing coaches taught us. Remember writing coaches, my old journalism friends? There really was a time when newsroom budgets had line items to hire them—and we once hired the best, the late Pulitzer Prize-winning Don Murray, who encapsulated his craft this way: "I write to say I am, discover who I am, create life, understand my life, slay my dragons, exercise my craft, lose myself in my work, for revenge, to share, to testify, to avoid boredom, and to celebrate."

I wrote my share of those give-voice-to-voiceless stories, including a series titled "Forgotten Children: Our National Disgrace," about the socio-economic and health disparities faced by a Black mother, Brenda Davis, and her three school-age children. They lived in an apartment contaminated by lead, and my series led to meaningful changes in state law and criminal charges and prison for the landlord, who owned many such properties.

"Forgotten Children" was my first Pulitzer finalist—and while I appreciated the honor, it was beside the point. My career accelerated and within four years, I was *The Trib*'s flagship columnist. Thomas Friedman in an NPR interview called me the best emerging columnist in America. I got the TV show: a weekly news program "with your host, the amazing Nick Nolan!" I married CoolBostonWeekly's star columnist, and *Boston Magazine* put us on the cover as their Power Couple of the Year.

And then, Google Analytics became *The Trib*'s overlord and marketing told me: *Maybe a feel-good piece every now and then that hints of public service, for old times' sake, but keep it occasional.*

Thus began the death spiral. Athletes, actors, and socialites found a ready forum for their points of view in my column. I wrote columns about skating a shift with the Boston Bruins, serving as honorary bat boy for the Red Sox, and playing a bit part in a revival of *Jesus Christ Superstar*. I parasailed from Hyannis to Martha's Vineyard, parachuted from a restored B-17 bomber, flew with the Blue Angels, waited tables one Saturday night at Top of the Hub restaurant, and emerged from the clown car at a circus to the roar of the crowd.

Fame proved fickle. Eventually, my TV show was cancelled, my Amazon book rankings plummeted to the millions (and available only from third-party sellers), and my column was moved off the front page to inside metro/region.

Before long, the stunts ended and I was writing about socks and the difficulty of writing columns.

"Don't say we should embrace Chamberlain's asinine motto," I said to Destiny.

"No," she said, "I'm saying we need to write more stories about real news. No wonder approval ratings for reporters are lower than for Congress. We've abandoned the very people we should be clamoring to cover. Instead of another piece about Netflix trends, we need to write about working families struggling to get their kids off to school or manage remote learning. We need to get out of the newsroom and into the neighborhoods—into the mom-and-pop stores and the veterans' homes, into communities of color and the homes of immigrants. Along with stories about Black businesses, I need to write about Black Lives Matter. About Ferguson and the militarization of the police and George Floyd. About health, social and economic inequities for BIPOC communities. About the #MeToo movement. I'm talking the kinds of stories local TV rarely does and no papers are committed to anymore, certainly not *The Trib*, this sad remnant of a paper that traces its heritage to Benjamin Franklin."

Funny she would say that—I'd had Franklin on my mind lately, wondering what he would think about journalism today, were he to come back to life.

"And don't give me the argument about staff size because that's only part of it, albeit a big part," Destiny continued. "This is more than head counts—it's about inertia and elitism and comfort. When we're not worshipping influencers or chasing fads, we're rewriting press releases. One by one, we've bled most of the real issues and people out of the paper. And I'm ashamed to admit that I, an African American, have gone along."

Destiny was right on principle, but I had to wonder about practicality. Forget her glorification of the past, which was justified; we lived in the era of TMZ and TikTok and attention spans that have shrunk to a millisecond. Did anyone really want what Destiny proposed? Or had the culture killed great local newspapering? Rare was the issue of Editor & Publisher, Nieman Journalism lab, or Dan Kennedy's Media Nation that did not contain a story about the latest paper closing or gutted.

"You've got one big problem," I said. "Hill's not kidding about good news rules. I don't believe that racial profiling fits that description."

"When circulation goes up, that will be the best news ever," Destiny said. "I'm going back to the *real* basics. And you?"

"I'm trying to keep my ass off the suburban staff."

"Well, now you know how to do it."

CHAPTER TWO: A DEAR LITTLE GIRL

The next Wednesday, as I scrounged through folders and emails for an idea for tomorrow's column, the phone rang.

"Hello, Nick," the caller said.

My heart raced. I hadn't heard that voice in years.

I didn't respond immediately.

"Are you there?" the caller said.

"I'm here."

"Do you know who this is?"

"Of course," I said. "Jennifer. Jennifer Abbott."

Jennifer was an old girlfriend, the only woman I had ever truly loved.

"How are you, Nick?" she said.

"Fat and boring and basically without purpose, if you must know," I said, intending humor but only shooting myself in the foot, something I'd gotten good at lately. "At least I don't have COVID. And I do still have my hair."

She laughed—and I remembered how much I had enjoyed that laugh.

"How are *you*?" I said.

"Also happy I don't have COVID," she said. "I'm fully vaccinated, as I assume you are."

"Yes," I said. "Which one did you get?"

"Pfizer."

"That makes two of us. I'll be getting the booster as soon as I'm eligible."

"As will I," she said.

"So where are you living these days?" I said.

Her number had come up with a California area code.

"I'm your neighbor now, can you believe it?" Jennifer said. "I just moved to Middleton."

Middleton was a suburb north of Boston.

"Last I knew, you were in California," I said.

"I was, for a long time. But La-la Land finally got to me. Everything's fuzzy out there, like there's something in the air, if you know what I mean."

"I do," I said.

In truth, I didn't.

That, too, was the Jennifer I remembered—sometimes eerily mysterious, a quality she herself acknowledged. She traced it to continuing trauma from a chaotic upbringing: Only child of an addict mother and a man who'd walked out when she was a toddler, the young Jennifer and her mother had been victimized by a succession of other bad men, dealers mostly.

But as a teen, Jennifer had found sanctuary in a Catholic parish in the last city where she and her mother had lived. During the time we dated, she still talked fondly of the pastor, Fr. Mateo Silva, a priest who had immigrated to America from his native Chile. According to Jennifer, he often spoke of Chile's first saint, Teresa of Jesus of Los Andes, a Carmelite nun who had succumbed to typhus in 1920 at the age of nineteen. Teresa was canonized by Pope John Paul II in 1993 after so-called confirmation of a modern miracle attributed to her: the healing of a critically ill child.

"Cool dude," I recalled Jennifer describing Silva. "Loves sitcoms. Big fan of *Friends*."

That was Jennifer's story, anyway. I was not into fact-checking at that point in my career.

"Are you married?" I said.

Shouldn't have been my next question, but it just slipped out. Actually, it was something about which I had wondered for years, increasingly as my own marriage crumbled.

Jennifer laughed again.

"God, no," she said. "What about you?"

"I'm separated and soon to be divorced," I said, "the sordid details of which you can periodically read in CoolBostonWeekly."

Jennifer was too new in town to get it.

"Courtney Lawford, my soon-to-be ex-wife, is one of their columnists," I said. "Her favorite punching bag is me."

"Well, I didn't call to make you feel bad," Jennifer said. "I called to say how much I love your columns. Especially the one about socks."

"You're kind, but you don't lie well."

"Honest to God, I *loved* that column! It could have been me you were writing about. The washing machine part especially—where *do* those socks go?"

"I guess some things are universal," I said, and let it go at that.

We chatted a while longer, and I learned a few details of Jennifer's life, including the fact that she had a daughter, Amber, eight years old.

"I have another reason for calling," Jennifer said, "besides catching up. I have an idea for a column."

"Socks II?" I said. "The world's dying for a sequel."

Jennifer laughed.

"Something better," she said.

"Don't say lint. I don't do lint."

I laughed.

"My idea isn't funny," said Jennifer.

Her voice had shifted back to mysterious.

"What is it then?" I said.

"Why don't you come see for yourself?" she said. "I'll put on some coffee."

As I drove to Middleton, highlights of our relationship ran through my mind.

I met Jennifer when she was 23 and I was 26, a relatively new reporter at *The Trib*, having been hired, thanks to nepotism—a sort of it, anyway. My father worked at the paper then—not in news, but as the longtime head of maintenance, a man who'd been hired straight out of Dorchester High School as an apprentice and worked his way up.

Growing up in Boston, I felt the pull of its history—the colonial, Revolutionary War, and early-republic periods especially. Many times I walked the Freedom Trail with my father, who raised me after my mother died while giving birth to my sister, who also died during delivery. I was eight years old, a student at Saint Brendan School, soon to be an altar boy at St. Brendan's Church, our family parish.

My favorite stops on the Freedom Tail were Faneuil Hall, Old Corner Bookstore, and the original site of Boston Latin School, with its statue of Benjamin Franklin, who was a student there. I was lucky to be accepted into the modern-day Boston Latin, where teachers supported my interest in writing and I developed an obsession with Franklin.

Unlike Dad, who pursued no further education after graduating from Dorchester High, I went to college: the University of Massachusetts, where I majored in Creative Writing and minored in history. My senior English thesis was a fantasy novel, "What If He Came Back?" about Franklin time-travelling to the present day. I received an A for it, and thus encouraged, I mailed it to dozens of publishers.

None bought it and only one, a small university press, even responded. In her rejection letter, that editor wrote words I have never forgotten: "Decent imagination, mediocre writing, although your use of 18th-century English was a nice touch. You may have a career somewhere, but it won't be in books."

That stung. And while I didn't want to believe it, I needed to get a job, not chase a dream. So I worked in a Borders bookstore and began writing short stories. They didn't sell, either.

After a few years of this, my father suggested I apply for a reporting job at *The Trib*.

"It would be writing," he said.

My initial reaction, which I kept to myself, could be summarized in "The Tender Bar," a movie that came years later: "When you suck at writing, that's when you become a journalist."

But when I pondered Dad's advice, I concluded otherwise. Woodward and Bernstein didn't suck at writing, and weren't they journalists?

You might say meeting Jennifer was serendipity. Fresh from Georgetown University, where she'd majored in theater, she was tending bar at a nightclub that I, the new *Trib* hire, was profiling for a summer entertainment guide. I painted a flattering picture of her in my story—it was deserved—and then I asked her out. New to journalism, I had yet to learn that ethically that was wrong.

After a summer of dating, we moved in together. Jennifer auditioned for plays and bit parts in movies that were filming in the Boston area but landed nothing. All she found was a car commercial voiceover, which she hated.

I said Jennifer was sometimes mysterious—but the truth was, she could be beyond mysterious. I didn't get this at first, of course—I was in love. So when her mood would shift into what she called her "hyper speed," her thoughts and words racing, I was enchanted... at first. And when her mood swung back from euphoria to brooding, I was intrigued, if not exactly enchanted. Jennifer's other quirks—such as her belief that guardian angels really did exist, and she'd met hers—those were charming, too... at first.

After we broke up—after two more summers had passed and *The Trib* made me their top columnist and Jennifer had gotten no further in her career than ad voiceovers—she left for Los Angeles, where she took acting lessons and hired an agent. For a while, she seemed to be headed toward stardom: she landed a cameo role in a Spielberg film and she was, for one year, a regular on a Fox sitcom.

Then her buzz fizzled. Jennifer was reduced to bit parts in indie movies and the occasional guest appearance on such forgettable TV shows as *Do Not Disturb*. I knew this for a fact, because one night when I was channel-surfing I came across her in an episode.

Last I'd heard, and it was third hand, she'd become pregnant by an actor who'd left when their child was a baby.

Jennifer's directions were good and confirmed by Google Maps I had no trouble finding her house, located on a dead-end street near Middleton Pond and St. Agnes Parish. Her house abutted an empty field that had been part of an old farm.

Jennifer must have been watching, because no sooner had I parked my car than she opened the door and waved.

Age had taken its inevitable toll, but the degree was small, and from a distance she looked amazingly similar to the last time I'd seen her—in tears at Boston's Logan International Airport.

"You look great," I said.

"So do you."

"Once again, you're kind—and a terrible liar."

"But it's the truth. And you're not fat, as you claimed, unlike many men your age."

"I stay in shape hunting socks," I said, and Jennifer laughed.

"Welcome to my humble abode," she said.

"It's not humble," I said. "You want humble? I'm renting a room these days."

"You poor thing," said Jennifer. "Come inside. Coffee's on."

She brought me through her living room into a kitchen made cheerful with bright-colored curtains and potted plants. The smell of fresh-ground coffee filled the room.

"Cream, no sugar, right?" she said.

"You remembered."

"I remember a lot, Nick."

"I do, too," I said.

Through three cups of coffee, Jennifer did most of the talking.

She told me of her career sputtering, and how, as I'd heard, her daughter's father had walked out years ago. She told me of her decision to finally leave California—of returning east to be near her mother, who had been in recovery for years and then, in a cosmic fuck-you, had been diagnosed with terminal cancer. Last spring, she had died in hospice.

Hopeful of a return to acting, Jennifer was auditioning, but so far she'd only been hired to narrate an audio book and voice-over a few ads.

I don't know at what point I became convinced I heard labored breathing from somewhere in the house.

Did Jennifer have a boarder?

She surely would have mentioned that. My imagination had brought me to Edgar Allan Poe's "The Tell-Tale Heart" when I finally said:

"What is that?"

"What?" said Jennifer.

"That breathing sound."

"That's Amber. My dear little girl. Would you like to meet her?"

"Oh, I don't want to disturb her," I said.

It was a school day, so I figured her daughter was home sick.

"You won't disturb her," Jennifer said. "You can't."

"Can't?"

"Come with me," Jennifer said.

I followed her down a hall into a bedroom.

"Meet Amber Abbott," Jennifer said.

My breath caught in my throat.

The girl lay on a hospital bed, her eyes and mouth closed, her face frozen into a lifeless mask. A bag of chocolate-colored liquid hung from an IV pole and a tube disappeared under the sheets. I smelled antiseptic. Medicine bottles crowded the bureau, where a little girl's stuffed animal collection might have been. A box of Attends lay on the floor. A suction machine and catheter sat atop a cart with wheels.

"Oh my God," I said. "I'm so sorry."

"Don't be," said Jennifer. "This is my beautiful daughter."

"Does she have COVID?"

I knew that a rising number of kids were seriously sick with the disease in that fall of 2021 as the Delta variant brought another pandemic surge.

"No, she doesn't," Jennifer said.

"Is she in a coma?"

"Yes—and no. I mean, she doesn't wake up, not like you or me. But the doctors say she can still hear. And dream—they say she's constantly dreaming. Happy dreams, I know for a fact, because she visits me in my dreams, and I visit her in hers."

I couldn't tell if Jennifer was fantasizing—if this was how she coped, by convincing herself that Amber was sentient and at peace, the mother and daughter meeting in each other's dreams.

"What happened?" I said.

"We were in a car accident."

"I'm so sorry."

Jennifer told a story of a rainy night on the Pacific Coast Highway when she, Amber, and a Catholic priest had been driving to a weekend retreat— this following Jennifer's recent rediscovery of the religion of her youth. The priest died in the crash, Jennifer said, and this was how Amber had wound up. Jennifer herself had escaped unharmed—"miraculously," she said.

I remember the word exactly.

Miraculously.

"It's an extraordinary story," I said.

"Do you think so?"

"God, yes."

"I've learned a lot about the important things in life though all this," said Jennifer. "Lessons that might help others. Lessons I thought might make a good column, one only you could write. I wouldn't trust anyone else. We live in such crazy times. So many sleazy reporters spreading lies and disinformation. And not just on Fox, either."

Back to the basics, Destiny Carter had said.

If this wasn't basic, what was?

A single mom. A child living with a disability. A middle-class family surely crushed by medical debt headed by an actress during a pandemic that had devastated the entertainment industry. All while sustained by the power of will and faith.

"You'd let me write this?" I said.

"She's beautiful, Nick," said Jennifer. "I know how that sounds, but there is dignity and courage in her quiet simplicity."

"And in you," I said, "there is an extraordinary example of a mother's unshakeable love."

"That is so kind of you," Jennifer said. "Now let's get going. I only have a half hour before I have to suction my dear little girl. Not so pleasant to watch. Let me tell you the rest of our story."

I got out my pen, notebook, and cell phone and hit voice-record.

"One more thing," I said when she had finished. "May I take a photo?"

"Not of Amber," Jennifer said. "Not at this time."

"A photo of you?"

"Of course," Jennifer said. "Just let me freshen my makeup."

On my way back to the city, I stopped by *The Tribune's* Lynn bureau.

Years ago, *The Trib* operated 15 bureaus, but all that survived were one in the old industrial city of Lynn and a second in the State House—less a bureau than a corner of a cramped space shared with other media outlets. The others had closed over the years, the leases terminated, the reporters, photographers, and assistants let go, leaving communities with only a toll-free number that was rarely answered and the email address of the suburban editor, who only opened corporate communications. Death by a thousand cuts to local journalism.

Bud Fuller worked in the Lynn bureau, which was two rooms (counting the bathroom) on the third floor of a cinder-block office building located near a Domino's Pizza and an old cemetery, the Western Burial Ground (read into that what you will).

Bud was a good man—and a sixty-two-year-old dinosaur. A native of Deer Isle, Maine, who'd moved with his family to Massachusetts after he'd graduated high school, Bud had started as a copy clerk when he was nineteen, then been hired as a reporter. Bud never went to college, nor did he need to: he was smart, he wrote fairly and accurately, he met deadlines, and he'd handled a succession of beats with distinction.

He also, for the last twenty years, was president of our Newspaper Guild local. The brass would never admit it, of course, but it was Bud's unionism that had caused Bob Jones, acting on Gordon's direct orders, to demote him to the suburban staff. The only reason he wasn't fired was

Gordon's fear of a lawsuit.

Bud was in a rotten mood. Since the sale to SGM, that was his default mood.

"Don't even ask," he said, looking up from his screen.

"I'm asking," I said.

"I get sick to my stomach writing this shit."

"Another zoning board story?"

"Worse," said Bud.

"The zucchini contest?"

The Lynn Lions' Club Zucchini Contest was a late-summer staple for Bud's edition. Fifty inches and four photos minimum, every year. With SuperGoodMedia now, it would probably lead the home page and be played above the fold in tomorrow's print edition.

"Even worse," said Bud. "A man-on-the-street. I just pushed the button on it."

Meaning he'd sent it to the copy desk, essentially the point of no-return.

"Now if you'll pardon me," Bud said, "I think I'll slash my wrists."

Also called a walk-and-talk, a man-on-the-street piece was arguably the silliest creation in the history of journalism. A reporter approached strangers with dumb-ass questions to produce an unscientific poll that revealed nothing except lack of editorial vision—if said strangers didn't pull out pepper spray or a .38, that is, this being the age of Enemies of the People. Not to mention that the potential for fraud was enormous—we could hardly ask for IDs, which meant that respondents could give aliases and fabricate opinions.

But editors loved man-on-the-street stories: they filled space and imparted a phony sense of accomplishment. Especially the man-on-the-street Bud had just completed. It was about the soon-to-open Minuteman Mall, a *Tribune* sacred cow since before SuperGoodMedia bought us.

More on that in a moment. But first, a bit more about Bud's hatred of man-on-the-street. His last prior to the mall had sent him over the edge. He'd been assigned to count the traffic cones along a stretch of highway that was being rebuilt.

Let me put Bud's experience in screenplay format. It will capture the Buñuel-esque quality of what happened.

EXT. A HIGHWAY UNDER CONSTRUCTION—MORNING

We OPEN ON a scene with equipment, laborers, mounds of material, Jersey barriers, and orange traffic cones. BUD FULLER, a journalist in his sixties, leaves his car, which he has parked near a police vehicle. A COP steps out.

COP
Hey, Bud, you can't park here.

BUD
Do I know you?

COP
Huh?

BUD
You called me 'Bud.'

COP
I call every loser that.

Bud extends his hand, but the cop doesn't take it.

BUD
Bud Fuller, with the *Daily Trib.*

COP
They still publish that rag?

BUD
Ow. That hurt.

COP
Sorry. I get my news on Facebook.
Anyway, Bud, how can I help you?
First, can I see an ID?

Bud hands over a timeworn photo ID. The photo and printing are barely legible.

BUD
They haven't given us new ones in
years. Not in the budget.

COP
Seriously?

BUD
Seriously.

COP
Maybe you guys should have a car wash
or a bake sale. Like high school football teams.

BUD
Not funny.

COP
I wasn't being funny. How can
I help you, Bud?

BUD
I'm here to count the traffic cones.

The cop leans in and takes a sniff of Bud's breath.

COP
You haven't been drinking. Are you high?

BUD
If only.

COP
May I ask why you want to count the cones?

BUD
I'm on assignment.

COP
To count cones.

BUD
(sarcastically and pained)
Specifically, these cones.

COP
I take it this wasn't your idea.

BUD
Most of the shit I write isn't my idea.
My editor is a brainless prick.

COP
Also, off his rocker. Should I arrange
for a mental health intervention?

BUD
How about pray for a stroke. I don't mean
that literally, of course, officer.

COP
Maybe you should. You wouldn't have to
count cones again.

BUD
I wouldn't bet on it. Depending on the clicks,
the clowns down in Florida might love it.

COP
You mean Disney World?

BUD
I guess I do.

COP
Go ahead, then, knock yourself out.
Just be careful of the 'dozers. Wouldn't
want one of the last *Trib* reporters left

COP (CONT'D)
getting crushed or anything.

Bud begins counting cones, tallying them one-by-one in a reporter's notebook.

CLOSE ON:

Bud's reporter's notebook. He is tallying with hash marks.

CUT TO:

INT. TRIB NEWSROOM—THE NEXT MORNING

Bud has been summoned in from the Lynn bureau to meet with EDITOR BOB JONES. He walks sullenly past colleagues into Jones' office.

INT. JONES OFFICE—DAY

JONES
Have a seat, Bud.

Bud sits. There's no love lost between these two.

JONES
I got an email this morning from a
regular reader. A subscriber, no less.

BOB
Let me guess: H. Henry Harlow III.

JONES
That would be him.

Harlow is an arrogant member of an old Yankee family who delights in taunting *The Tribune*, Bud Fuller in particular, following a story Bud wrote years ago about Harlow's son being arrested for cocaine possession. He writes letters to the editor incessantly and calls Jones whenever he has a hair across his ass, which is always. He also happens to be an officer of a bank that is one of the paper's last remaining major advertisers.

                    BUD
          So what is it now? Did I use a comma
          where a semicolon was preferred?

                   JONES
           Your cone count is wrong.

                    BUD
          Why do I know you're not kidding.
                By how much?

                   JONES
                    Four.

                    BUD
                    Four.

                   JONES
          Four. You had two-thousand-sixty-one
          and the correct number is two-thousand-
          sixty-five. He sent one of his people
                out there to check.

                    BUD
             The cop allowed it?

                   JONES
          Once he said who his boss is, yes.

                    BUD
          Was the cop looking for a loan?

                   JONES

This is no laughing matter, Bud.

BUD
I wasn't laughing.

JONES
Anyway, Harlow had him count three
times to be sure he was correct, all while
video-taping so that, as Harlow put it, 'I
have the evidence.' He attached the video
to his email. I watched it and he is
right. Can I play it for you?

BUD
How long is it?

JONES
Forty-five minutes.

BUD
Jesus Christ, Jones. Forty-five minutes.
Don't you have a paper to run?

JONES
It was actually quite fascinating,
watching all the cones in their many
different locations. And the ones that
had been knocked over provided a dose
of drama. Wish I'd sent a photographer
with you. Would have made a great video.
I can see it going viral. Anyway, I've already
written and posted the correction.

BUD
Remind me to send you a thank-you note.
Now if you'll excuse me, I have to barf.

Bud stands over Jones' desk and vomits. Jones runs screaming from his office.

OK, so the barfing didn't really happen. But it would be a wonderful touch in a movie.

Bud's disgust was deepening as he prepared to vent about today's man-on-the-street assignment.

"Our suburban editor, the moron," he said, "decided we needed to tap the public pulse on the Minuteman Mall again. This time, the developer issued a press release with some bullshit about time running out. So there I was, asking strangers what they thought about a possible delay. Most didn't give a crap. Of course, I couldn't put that in the story and still have a job, and I need a job, much as I hate this one. So, I quoted the handful of clowns who claimed they need—and that was their word, 'need'—the mall. And we wonder why America is heading the way of the Roman Empire."

Bud had nailed it. Refugees could drown crossing the Mediterranean and we'd play it on A-17—but Minuteman Mall developer Luke Turner opened his mouth and it was a lock for page one. Particularly in 2021, with so many malls across America having closed and few new ones on the drawing boards.

Under construction in Danvers, on choice property along Routes 1 and Interstate 95 near the Middleton border, the Minuteman Mall promised acres of shopping—and conceivably a fortune in ad revenue, a fact conspicuously absent from our shameless coverage and editorials. To my certain knowledge, *The Tribune* had run exactly one negative story on the mall: about a "disgruntled" and "recently fired" steelworker who'd testified before the rubber-stamp State Mall Commission that inferior iron had been used on the job, a contention that Turner, the iron supplier, and state inspectors had all vehemently denied.

The story—four inches long and off the AP wire—had run at the bottom of page B-23.

No surprise there. Gordon had made the mall a cause célèbre that Hill had embraced by appearing before a legislature that had already granted generous tax breaks—but now balked at the additional $75 million in interest-free loans Turner demanded before he would approve the last few weeks of work left before Minuteman could open.

Some considered this blackmail. But in an op-ed piece Hill had personally solicited, Turner called it "good business practice."

"The suburban editor is an asshole," I said.

"Bigger than ever since he's started management training," said Bud.

"They let him in?"

"They're doing it for all the editors—except copy editors, that is. You wouldn't believe the shit that goes on. Like locking them all in a room and pretending they're trapped in an earthquake with nothing but a can of Coke. Team building, they call it. I wish they really were trapped in an earthquake with a can—of gasoline held by a sicko team member with matches."

"Tell me what you really think," I said.

"I really think I need a cigarette."

"But you quit years ago."

"Then Chamberlain bought us. Let's go outside."

Leaving, we passed the bureau's only other reporter, a twenty-five-year-old named Ted Matthews. He was actually a freelancer willing to accept a pittance per story, a desk and a phony Staff Writer byline in hopes of advancing his career. He was not on staff, he drew no paycheck, and he had no health insurance or other benefits, but for him, a growing body of clips was enough. That Gordon had allowed such an arrangement for him and others in the final years of being publisher spoke to hypocrisy and servitude.

In which we, members of the Guild, had participated. Fearful that Gordon would try to bust the union, in our last contract we had voted to approve the system in return for one percent raises and a one year cap on our health insurance co-pay. It was a devil's deal that did none of us proud.

Matthews and the "Staff Writers" who'd come before him were pleasant, hard-working, and thrilled to be at *The Trib*. They filed cop logs with enthusiasm, never whined about night meetings, and thrived on writing cheery profiles of *Trib* advertisers in stories that lacked the "advertisement" tag. They had prodigious energy: one had actually interviewed more than a hundred people when she was assigned a man-on-the-street titled "My Favorite Color," surely a world record, although it did lack the special panache of counting cones.

And that's why they annoyed old schoolers like me and Bud: they loved their work, were still imbued with youthful optimism, and probably did have meaningful careers ahead of them, albeit not at *The Trib* and probably not in newspapers, since the numbers of dailies and weeklies continued to dwindle in 2021 with no end in sight.

"Hi, Nick," Matthews said. "Loved your column today."

"Thank you," I said.

I couldn't tell if he was being sarcastic, but I gave him the benefit of the doubt.

"Where *do* you get your ideas?"

Utica, Stephen King once replied in answer to that question.

"I guess they just come," I said.

"I wish it were that easy for me. Bud here tells me that will all happen in time."

"I'm sure it will," I said.

What torture the suburban staff was for Bud.

What torture it would be for me, too, especially since I'd heard my soon-to-be ex-wife was dating Matthews.

Bud bitched some more, finished his smoke, and went back into the bureau. As luck would have it, Courtney was getting out of her car as I headed toward mine.

"Until yesterday's masterpiece," she said, "I wouldn't have believed there was a more regal topic than socks."

My column: Top Ten Reasons to Live in a Rented Room. I'd listed "the hotplate is all yours" as reason number ten and "no complaints about underwear on the floor" as reason number nine. Eight through one were no better.

"In case you missed it," I said, "that was self-parody."

"So that's what we're calling it these days."

"At least my readers are familiar with the concept."

"What few you have anymore. Speaking of readers, I hear Jones put the wood to you."

"Word gets around, doesn't it."

"I have my sources."

"You mean source, singular."

Like all of our recent conversations, this one had quickly reached its end.

"I've hired a lawyer, Nick," Courtney said.

"Why?" I said. "You know I don't have shit."

And I didn't. I drove a twelve-year-old BMW and I had no other significant assets or savings. Suze Orman I'd never been.

"It's what you do when you divorce," Courtney said.

"So now I have to get one, too."

"That's how it works, Nick."

"Well, you do what you have to do," I said, walking away.

Once upon a time, night reporters checked in with the city desk, then headed over to Ernie's, where they sat by a police scanner drinking as they waited for some dirt bag to murder somebody. From what I'd been told, they could run from Ernie's back to the newsroom, crank out a hell of a story, and get back in time for a nightcap. But those days are gone, along with most of the night reporters.

With copy editors working remotely this evening, the newsroom was deserted when I arrived after leaving the Lynn bureau. Before going to my desk, I stopped at the newsroom bulletin board. Since becoming publisher, Hill had issued a torrent of printed memos, distributed also by email, to "My Dear Super Colleagues." When they didn't chill us, these pronouncements were good for a laugh.

But there were no new memos from Hill. The only new item was a printout of a confidential note he'd sent Jones before Jones called me into his office last Friday:

"Nolan seems innocuous enough, and that's the problem: see marketing report, pp. 223 - 229. I don't know how much longer we can afford him a column. As we discussed, see if there's room for him on the suburban staff or the copy desk. If not, well… Remember—GOOD NEWS RULES!"

I had a pretty good idea who had posted the memo. I tore it off the board and walked across the newsroom to The Scene, The Lifestyle division of the features department, to see if A.J. Johnson was still there.

Ob Scene, as some insiders called the Scene, was victim of another of Gordon's ax-wielding legacies.

Lifestyle had lost three reporters, a copy editor, and a page designer to the downsizing, and none had been replaced—even though management in the ensuing two years had added a weekly tab for women called Gals, a name so pathetic we couldn't further ridicule it with one of our infantile nicknames. The tiny and overworked staff of Ob Scene made do with wire copy, clip art, and freelanced features that cost $25 and looked it.

Whether Lifestyle could still afford their last surviving staff columnist was increasingly in doubt under Hill. A woman in her late thirties, A.J. Johnson wrote mostly about dating and her lack of success finding anyone suitable on eHarmony and Match, columns that barely registered in the analytics. Like me, she was pretty much down to navel-gazing and nonsense.

Once the award-winning anchor columnist of metro/region, A.J.'s columns now ran in The Scene, below Ask Amy and Dear Abby. This had hardly endeared me to her, but I was not alone: A.J. disliked most of her colleagues, and based on her recent columns, she seemed to hold scorn for most of humanity, too. Betting was that her days with SGM were numbered. In print and in person, A.J. personified bad news.

But Lifestyle was deserted this evening. A.J. had left for the day.

Back at my desk, I called her at home.

"A.J.," I said, "It's Nick Nolan."

"What do you want?" she said.

She sounded exhausted and weak, as if the chronic fatigue syndrome she claimed to suffer from was flaring up again. I sensed another medical leave on the horizon. That, at least, would be genuine good news. Sounds heartless, but I knew from someone who'd since been let go from HR that no doctor had ever diagnosed her with CFS, which when real is nightmarish.

"You're an idiot," I said.

"And you're an asshole," A.J. said. "Is there a reason for this call?"

"You posted Hill's memo."

"The hell I did. Why would I need to? The whole world knows about you and Jones. Or soon will. If I'm not mistaken, tomorrow's Thursday."

CoolBostonWeekly was published on Thursdays. Courtney's column would be there, likely bannered across the front and the online lead.

"You leaked the memo to her, didn't you," I said.

"Ever hear of the First Amendment?" A.J. said. "Live by the sword, die by it."

Then she hung up on me.

I tossed down a cup of coffee, threw a few words up on the screen, then stopped.

I couldn't get Hill's memo off my mind.

Not A.J. posting it, but Hill's other threat, which Jones hadn't mentioned: the copy desk.

Copy editors are the foot soldiers of a newspaper, the journalists who daily save reporters and columnists from themselves. Those who are along in years have paid dearly with deteriorating vision from decades of staring into monitors—and often with wrist braces or surgical scars from carpal tunnel syndrome in their pursuit of excellence.

Also, in keeping us out of court. I couldn't count the number of times they had saved me and my colleagues from libel suits. No one needs one of those, trust me.

So God bless.

I refer here to the remaining handful of old-timers, not the copy editors brought on since the downsizing who worked part-time at low wages and without benefits. No wonder our corrections box had grown into a serial novella.

Long way of saying: a seat on the desk would not be the preferred capstone to my career.

For half an hour, I stared at a blank screen.

Then, deadline looming, the proverbial muse, a stranger for so long, visited. In an hour of frantic typing, I portrayed Jennifer as a saint, her daughter a martyr, their fight for dignity and survival a noble cause.

This wasn't a sob story, nor your basic disease-of-the-week piece. This was solid storytelling—my hallmark, back in the day.

CHAPTER THREE: VISIONS

I could hardly believe it the next day when I logged onto *Trib.com* and scanned the e-edition, which offered PDF files of the printed paper. My column was the online lead and the front-page print centerpiece. As I later learned, the night editor, uncharacteristically wowed by what I'd written, had called Jones at home and gotten permission to move me off metro/region. More than three years had passed since I'd escaped its confines.

And this was the headline the night editor had written:
Mother tends, keeps faith in young comatose daughter
An extraordinary lesson in 'the important things in life'

More amazing still was the reaction to the story of Amber and Jennifer.

"Way to go!" said Destiny Carter, when I arrived in the newsroom. "Awesome story."

"Am I back to the basics or what? Sure beats socks."

"Forget socks—that's ancient history now. We're turning the corner here, my friend. You and me both."

My phone's message-waiting light was blinking when I got to my desk. I had dozens of voice mails—it was only ten o'clock—and more than a hundred emails. *The Trib* Facebook post had more than 2,000 engagements, and our Tweet had been liked and retweeted hundreds of times. Many readers wanted to help Amber and Jennifer with donations.

Jennifer had already opened a GoFundMe page and in an online update, I included the link. Jennifer set a goal of $10,000, but before the day had ended, more than $35,000 had been pledged. It was a dramatic start to what soon would be the biggest GoFundMe campaign in Massachusetts history.

The good news for me was I had enough material for another column.

"Heart-warming" and "outpouring" were among the clichés I had in mind.

What most mattered to my continued employment, of course, were the analytics. With Jennifer and Amber, I finally had a winner.

Since midnight, when it posted on *Trib.com*, my column had received more than 133,000 page views, with 66,078 unique visitors and nearly 100,000 total engaged minutes. Digging deeper, I learned that people around the world had read it, with especially high readerships in Italy, The Philippines, Spain, The Democratic Republic of The Congo, Brazil, Mexico, and other countries with large populations of Catholics.

Had these been numbers for nine days, they would have been impressive—but nine *hours*? "Go Topless Day Draws Hundreds, Even a Few Men" couldn't hold a candle to "Mother tends, keeps faith in young comatose daughter, An extraordinary lesson in 'the important things in life.' "

If anything soured the moment, albeit briefly, it was two journalists.

One, A.J., made a show of snubbing me. The second, Courtney, offered online reaction when this week's CoolBostonWeekly was posted.

Courtney had written a hodgepodge—one of those bulleted "for what it's worth" jobs that proved the muse hadn't paid her a call again this week. I was the third bullet, a fat graf about my meeting with Jones and a quote from Hill's memo.

"*Daily Tribulation* insiders say they're warming a seat for Nolan right now on the copy desk," Courtney wrote. "The late-night copy desk, no less. What a loss to literature that would be."

I was tempted to call Courtney, but I resisted. My cell phone was ringing.

It was Jennifer, with an invitation to dinner.

As marinara sauce simmered on the stove, Jennifer and I drank red wine— Merlot, my favorite. After our third glass, I managed to forget that a comatose girl lay just around the corner.

Jennifer had already thanked me for my column, so I was puzzled when she picked up today's *Trib* and drew my attention to a passage half-way in.

"That was really something, this part here about me praying," she said.

In our interview, Jennifer had in fact discussed her faith—but only touched on her belief in the power of prayer. I had embellished, describing a woman who was on her knees by her daughter every night, "sometimes for hours."

"I got carried away," I said. "I shouldn't have. I'm sorry."

I feared Jennifer would want a correction, something I could ill afford. Bad writing was one thing, but corrections were like stab wounds: the bleeding was impossible to hide and too many would kill you, especially now with consultants combing the archives to calculate a corrections count on each of us since we started at *The Trib*. Protection against lawsuits from terminated staff members, past and future, I figured—and in the meantime, a tool for shaming.

"I don't think you went too far at all," Jennifer said. "On the contrary, I think you showed amazing insight and understanding. I *do* believe in prayer, you know. The image of me kneeling by Amber is perfect. Even if I don't kneel, I do sit with her every evening for hours. And I pray and pray and pray."

"It's part of your devotion."

"And more than that. Much more."

Jennifer was drifting out there again.

"In what way?" I said.

"I hesitate to tell you this," she said. "It will sound unbelievable."

"Tell me."

"Sometimes late at night, Amber talks to me. Softly, often unintelligibly—but she is talking, definitely talking."

"But she's in a coma," I said.

"I knew you wouldn't believe me."

"I didn't say that."

"The tone in your voice said otherwise," Jennifer said. "So let me explain. There are different kinds of comas. I know because I've asked her doctors. Amber's state is like a form of autism. When inspired, she speaks."

"What inspires her?"

"Mary."

"Mary who?"

"The Virgin Mary," Jennifer said. "Amber wants me to know that she's happy and safe with Mary's help now—that Mary will take care of her and me, that I should stop worrying. 'Mary talks to me, Mommy,' Amber says. I couldn't tell you yesterday, Nick—I figured you'd think I was crazy. But your column suggests I can trust you. Can I, Nick? You don't seem like other reporters, but are you? I don't want to look like a nutcase."

Jennifer was six inches away from me and I was on my third glass of wine. I couldn't help but notice she wasn't wearing a bra.

"Of course you can trust me," I said. "How long has this been going on?"

"Since last winter, when we moved into this house. I thought I was crazy at first—this has been so traumatic, as you wrote so eloquently. Then, two months ago, Amber told me a number. I'll never forget it: Six-four-one-one-seven-nine. She said Mary had whispered it to her."

"What did it mean?"

"I didn't know, at first. All I knew was we were about to be evicted."

Faced with medical debt and expenses related to her mother's death, Jennifer explained, she'd fallen behind on the rent.

"I said extra prayers that night," Jennifer continued, "including to Saint Teresa of Jesus of Los Andes. By any chance, do you remember me talking about her when we went out?"

"I do," I said. "She was a favorite of that priest when you were a kid."

"That would be Fr. Mateo Silva," Jennifer said. "A good man. How strange we would both wind up in California."

I didn't immediately make the connection.

"So the next night," Jennifer continued, "Amber repeated the number—and added two words: 'Mega Millions.' "

"You're kidding," I said.

"I'm not. 'This is Mary's gift to us, Mommy,' Amber said. So I bought a ticket and played it—and won five thousand dollars, enough to get caught up on the rent. I just wish she would give me another winning number so I can pay off the rest of my debt!"

"GoFundMe will help," I said.

"Yes, it will," Jennifer said. "Thank you for including it in your update."

Jennifer went to a desk and returned with the stub of a ticket and a receipt from the Lottery Commission.

"I knew no one would believe me so I saved these," she said.

I examined the stub and receipt, which had been stamped by the commission and signed by Jennifer. Both appeared genuine.

Whether the Mother of God was responsible was another matter.

"Has Amber said anything else?" I asked.

"Many things—she says Mary's been very talkative lately. I've been writing everything down. Amber speaks very slowly, so I am able to get every word."

Jennifer went to the desk again and returned with a hardbound diary.

"Some things I don't understand—I just repeat what Amber says. But some things are clear. Here in the early years of the new millennium, Mary is proclaiming her love for all God's children. Just as she has taken care of me and Amber, she promises to take care of everyone—provided they renounce Satan and draw closer to her son, Jesus.

"And that is all good news, I think you would agree. But there is also something else that Mary is telling us through my dear little girl. 'Something terrible is coming,' Mary said. 'Something you will know with horror when the water rises and the fierce winds blow and Delta death is catastrophic. And then, as my Precious Son always preached, only faith and love will be our salvation.' "

"Wow," I said. "What do you think that means?"

"I thought at first another horrible hurricane, maybe one hitting the Mississippi Delta," Jennifer said. "And then I thought about the Delta variant, but the death toll already is catastrophic. Maybe it will get worse? A terrible new variant will arise? Honestly, I have no clue. Maybe Amber is relating it wrong. There's always that possibility.

"But forget Delta and wind for now. Let me read another of Mary's missives: 'Dear Children! I am your mother and I invite you to come closer to God through prayer, because only He is your peace, your Savior. Therefore, little children, do not seek comfort in material things, rather, seek God. I am praying for you and I intercede before God for you. I am looking for your prayers, that you accept my messages. Only then, when you open your hearts and pray, will miracles happen, large and small, and one will be large indeed. Thank you for having responded to my call.' "

The words struck me as wooden, as if a bad translation of a foreign language. Then again, didn't much of scripture have this same tonality?

Maybe Jennifer's in the early stages of a breakdown, I thought.

Then a new thought pushed that one away:

Maybe there's something here. Isn't the history of Christianity filled with tales of mystics? Augustine. Saint Thomas Aquinas. Francis of Assisi. Joan of Arc.

I remembered the names from my Catholic childhood.

I remembered a headline from earlier in the year, and the blockbuster reaction to the story: Texas Christian Has Proof She Walked on Water

That story, of course, had provided no such proof, only a Photoshopped image and a "sworn affidavit" from some alleged notary public in Hillsboro, Texas. And yet, the online story had generated an all-time *Trib* record 1.8-million page views, which had attracted new advertisers and put a smile on then-publisher's Gordon's face.

"I don't know what to say," I said to Jennifer.

"Tell me about it," she said. "If it hadn't happened so many times, I'd be sure I've been imagining it."

"Have you recorded your daughter?"

"I wanted to—but Mary, through Amber, refused to allow it. She said: 'Your mother's faith must guide her, not the false comfort of a machine.' "

In light of Jennifer's past, warning bells were sounding, an echo from that time in my career when I cast a skeptical eye on everything.

But what a story!

What timing for me!

Throw in caveats—an "alleged" here, an "apparent" there—and I would be golden. The numbers would be stratospheric.

I was just about to ask if Amber might talk to me when Jennifer kissed me on the cheek.

"You coming back into my life is another answer to a prayer, Nick," she said. "I've been so lonely. Now toodles. I need to tuck my baby in."

Back in the newsroom, I wrote my second Jennifer/Amber column, then began wading through the latest emails from SuperGoodMedia about the many "Incredible!" changes that were coming under the new ownership. I'd listened to the grumblings of colleagues who'd already dug into them, but until now, I hadn't comprehended how bizarre they really were. The bureaucrats were super-busy. If SGM had devoted even a quarter of those resources to actual journalism, we might have had a glimmer of hope.

Herewith a sampling:

• HappyWare

The name of our new publishing platform.

The buffoonery only began with the name. HappyWare was big on key words; advertising, content, and system tags; SEOs, for search engine optimization; structured data, which no one at corporate could explain in real words; and a bunch of other bullshit aimed at… you guessed it, clicks.

We had to fill all this out when creating a story package, then enter the package asset number into the daily budget spreadsheet, along with the print folder name, estimated length, estimated deadline, and digital assets if any (podcast, video, etc.). Images had to be separately uploaded, with their own keywords, SEOs, etc. Ditto for videos and fact boxes. Each story was required to have links to at least three other stories.

There also was the so-called planning card, which no one ever created because it was indecipherable and annoying beyond measure.

As Destiny and Bud remarked, you could easily invest more time in completing the package than in writing your asset. And there was this: the parent company had announced that in a few weeks, HappyWare would be replaced by a superior platform "that is now the subject of an exciting international search!" Meaning, it would be riddled with bugs that the SuperGoodMedia IT team—if you could reach anyone, that is—would be unable to fix.

Meanwhile, to become "fluent" in HappyWare, we were invited to participate in live webinars and watch pre-recorded videos from "trainers" who looked and acted like survivors of a psychiatric experiment gone badly awry.

• Passwords

True, we were hardly the only ones in 2021 bedeviled by the process of selecting and resetting passwords. Or cursed by forgetfulness.

But with SuperGoodMedia came requirements for separate passwords for email, timesheet, story packaging, expense reimbursement, mileage reimbursement, the digital library, health benefits, the daily budget… and that's the short list. The parent company demanded that passwords be changed monthly, and that each meet these specifications: Must be between 50 and 125 characters (these are not typos); must have upper and lower case letters, at least ten numbers, five special symbols (though NEVER %); must NOT be your first, last or middle name, nor any component of any previous password; and must have three new security questions, from the following selections: Who was you second-best friend in sixth grade? How many cats have you owned in your life? What is the longest you've ever been able to hold your breath (in seconds, please)? What is the name of the first haiku you were able to recite from memory? Where were you at 12:27 p.m. on December 5, 2013? What was your great-grandmother's favorite dessert?

This was all for setting a password.

Re-setting after forgetting or losing it was worse. These were the steps, annotated by me:

1. Send email to passwordhelp@sgm.com requesting assistance.

2. Wait days for response.

3. When response comes, open a ticket. Choose "urgent" priority, "high" priority, "routine" priority or "low" priority, knowing it makes no difference, since IT considered all tickets "no" priority.

4. Receive a phone call from an outsourced firm in an unknown country.

5. Ask for a link to reset password.

6. Get placed on hold.

7. Call back and ask to speak with supervisor.

8. Get placed on hold.

9. Repeat step 7, this time threatening to file a report with the office of David Chamberlain.

10. Open link in email that was instantly sent and follow prompts to reset password.

• Training

Aka "potty training," as we dubbed these condescending, never-ending, mandatory sessions.

In what areas did the bureaucrats contend we needed training? Inclusion and diversity was one. And it was the only one with merit, albeit accompanied by twisted irony, given that Chief Diversity Officer Bradley Winthrop III, spokesperson for privileged whites, was in charge.

But the rest were time-consuming insults to the intelligence. Consider: Training in "spotting news," as if reporters were birdwatchers and not journalists. Training in "identifying the perfect photo opportunity." Training in "creative use of bullet points."

And training in internet security. Here's one of the 68 quiz questions we were required to answer in pursuit of our required certificate. Failure would result in disciplinary actions, up to and including termination.

Q. Which of the following is a phishing attempt in an email you receive:

1. Your PayPal account has been suspended, click here to restore. Sent from   fortunegckdick9asjsv1-160tm9dickp05xrctheresdickagain0p2z@ zeaggcvn-93901179.world

2. Your bank's central headquarters burned to the ground and now the heroic bank employees who did not die a fiery death are working tirelessly

to restore online services, after which a new building will be erected. Click here to get access to your account(s) back.

3. Your best friend named Abrahanne Lincolnn was visiting Antarctica when he was robbed and left stranded in a Winnebago on the river Sticks edge. Click here to wire him American dollarz to save their livers.

4. Amazing news! This week's Russian Powerball winner has been personally chosen by Vladimir Putin and you are the lucky person! Click here to find out how much you won, and how to claim your prizes in rubles or U.S. dollars.

5. All of the above.

6. None of the above.

• My Care!

SGM's so-called health and well-being site, which Destiny christened "Daycare" for its childish approach.

"Proper Popcorning!", as one of the My Care! tutorials was titled, will illustrate the absurdity.

"Did you know that popcorn kernels can get stuck between your teeth?" the model in the video stated. "Well, they can!!! And it's not good for gum health or keeping those Pearly Whites white. We recommend flossing after eating popcorn, and don't stop until every kernel is gone, baby, gone! Then follow with a thorough cleaning and mouth washing. Not at home when you are popcorning? Carry a proxy brush! Maybe two, as they bend easily and popcorn kernels are a mighty adversary! Proxy brushes can be used discreetly. Swallow what they dislodge and wash that down with a nice cool drink. And make that drink WATER, not soda, right, SuperGooders?! Don't want kernels caught in the esophagus! That would open a whole 'nother can of worms!!! And always remember: Good Gums = SuperGood Yums! Be the Boss of Your Floss!"

• 'Develop and grow'

SGM's euphemism for what I would describe as "waste yet more time to satisfy bureaucrats who justify their jobs with emails, town halls, all-hands-on-deck Zooms, 'pop-up pump-you-ups! Super Morale Boosters,' training programs and Team sessions.

We learned about this program in an email from Chief Fun Officer Paul Peters and Chief Motivational Officer Ron Hawkins. The CFO and CMO wrote:

"With our 2022 goals now created and filed, we must create our plans to nourish ourselves, flourish with and bask in the glow of our fellow SuperGooders, give feedback, and raise a toast to our accomplishments in the year 2021."

Our year had sucked on every level, but I suppose that didn't count as accomplishment.

"What's on the horizon, My Dear SuperFriends and Colleagues?" the email continued. "Starting on Monday, we commence the Grow Our Seeds Exercise, in which we review what we have planted and the Wonderful Flowers we expect to bloom. More details from People Communications (supergoodpeople@sgm.com) will follow, but for now, here is a summary of the stages. All stages will be conducted online on Teams Meetings."

The first stage was the "SuperGooder Moment," in which we were required to "complete your Seeds Planted list and send to your Manager. The list will derive from the 115 questions that we, CFO Peters and CMO Hawkins, have created and which, after careful scrutiny, have received the personal blessing of our beloved Chairman Chamberlain. If it will help you in compiling your lists, try remembering this slogan: Plant Seeds, NOT Weeds. From Seeds Come SuperGood Deeds!!!"

The second stage was "Your SUPERMANager Moment," during which "SUPERMANagers review their team member's Seeds Planted list and complete a SUPERMANager Moment for each Planter."

The third stage: "Department SUPERvisor Moment. In this exciting exercise, Department Heads will holistically do their thing."

Stage four was the "Flowers Blooming Performance Conversations."

The name brought to mind Mao Zedong's Hundred Flowers Movement. That didn't end so well for the Chinese, did it?

For the Flowers Blooming Performance Conversations, our chairman advised us to "check off that check list every week, adjust the water and fertilizer as needed, and keep growing the future you SuperGooder!"

The email ended:

"Let's thrive together! Your SUPERGOOD buddies, Paul and Ron!"

I left the newsroom late. Too tired for a stop at Ernie's, I went straight home. Sleep came quickly.

And so did Benjamin Franklin, in a dream.

It began with me impulsively deciding to travel to Philadelphia, a city I had only ever passed through on my way to Washington. I went online, ordered an Acela ticket, packed a bag, and took an Uber to Boston's South Station.

Remember, this was a dream, though when I awoke, it seemed disturbingly real—and it made me wonder if there really was an afterlife and whether the dead could return. I thought of getting in touch with Amy Bruni, host of Ghost Hunters and now Kindred Spirits, someone I knew by casual acquaintance. I pondered writing a column about the dream, but only fleetingly. Why muddy a game-changer story about extraordinary lessons in "the important things in life" with a relapse into the ridiculous?

Acela got me into Philadelphia at dinner time and Yelp led me to Red Owl Tavern, a restaurant a block from Independence Hall, where the

Constitution was signed. I ordered a veggie burger and salad and imagined Ben Franklin walking in.

He did.

At first, I did not recognize him, this older man who took a table near mine and began looking curiously at me, as if he had made an appointment with someone he had never met and he was trying to ascertain if I met the description. The Benjamin Franklin I envisioned from that famous portrait had long hair and bifocal eyeglasses, which he had invented, perched on the end of his nose. This man had short hair and no glasses.

But on closer scrutiny, he did look like Franklin, even under his COVID mask.

"Mind if I take it off?" he said. "I'm fully vaccinated."

"Go ahead," I said.

"So what's up with the veggie burger and salad?" the man said. "That's really not what you want. Let loose, my friend. Indulge. Order a real burger and fries, sweet-potato fries if you want a touch of healthy. Go ahead. You need a break."

Within the dream, I thought I must be dreaming.

"Nice to meet you, Nick," the man went on. "I know what you're thinking: where are the bifocals? I wear contacts now—wish I'd invented *them* instead of glasses, to be honest. So much lighter, if not quite as easy to put in. And that hair was *so* 1700s. While it worked again for the Hippies and still does for Arlo Guthrie, it's *totally* yesterday's news, if you'll pardon the pun. The kind of shopworn pun one might find in one of your silly columns."

I struggled for words, but none came.

"Let's get down to business, shall we?" the man continued. "I'm here because I couldn't keep quiet any longer. I've been following you for quite a while—almost since the start of your career. What a dramatic rise and fall. Seems like you're in the member mug now."

"Excuse me?"

"Chamber pot. The shitter, to use a contemporary term. You've hit a low point. Your writing sucks, to be blunt. Your soon-to-be-ex is right about that, not that I'm on her side. I'm on yours, Nick. *You* are a journalist, or were. She's a hanktelo, a mere codshead."

"Definition?"

"A hack, a loser, to translate how we would have put it back in my day. She ought to get into some other line of work. Used cars, say."

"I can't say I disagree. But can we get to something more pertinent?"

"You want me to confirm who I seem to be," the man said.

"Yes, for starters."

"OK, then, I will. I am an American polymath, one of the Founding

Fathers of the United States, and leading writer, printer, political philosopher, politician, Freemason, postmaster, scientist, inventor, humorist, civic
activist, statesman, and diplomat. That's what Wikipedia says and not to
be immodest, they pretty much have it right. What Wiki doesn't say—and
how could it, since I never admitted to this—is that after that first electric
experiment, I developed a terrible phobia of kites. But that's a story for
another time."

"Haven't you left a few things out?" I said.

"Would you wish me to recite the entire Wikipedia entry? My good
man, it's over a hundred pages long, not counting the references. And all
the books that have been written about me! I never lacked self-esteem, but
goodness, I did not expect that. A certain college student even wrote his
senior thesis on me. Quite flattering. Authors hope to make money but
students generally follow their passions."

"You know what I mean," I said.

"I suppose I do," the man said. "I am, after all, a polymath. You mean
the fact that we didn't give women the right to vote."

I detected shame in his voice.

"You could begin there," I said. "Then get into why you gave no rights
at all to African American slaves. And the fact that you yourself owned
two slaves," I said.

The man sighed.

"It's true—although that certainly pales in comparison to Jefferson.
What a total piece of shit *he* was."

"You don't have a slang word for shit?" I said.

"There are too many to count," the man said. "Most have left the
language, likely in inverse relationship to the advent of indoor plumb-
ing. But as I was saying. In my defense, I did toward the end become an
abolitionist."

"Too little, too late?" I said. "Surely you know that saying. And there's
more. For instance, your stand on Native Americans."

"As in the people whose land we stole, who we killed with firearms
and smallpox, and who we referred to as 'the merciless Indian Savages.'
I cannot deny these facts, or those very words, which are written into
the Constitution. Let me recite from memory: 'He has excited domes-
tic Insurrections amongst us and has endeavoured to bring on the
Inhabitants of our Frontiers, the merciless Indian Savages, whose known
Rule of Warfare, is an undistinguished Destruction, of all Ages, Sexes, and
Conditions.' Good lord, how horrible we were."

The man seemed close to tears.

"Not proud of any of that," he said.

" 'Ashamed,' 'racked by guilt,' 'wish we could do it over' might be better responses," I said.

"Would it help to know that behind the scenes, I fought for the rights of women, Native Americans, and Blacks—and lost?"

"Prove it," I said.

"I can't," he said, "and while you paint me as a moral troglodyte, I was anything but. If there had been a Black Lives Matters movement, I would have marched in the front ranks."

"Well, we'll never know, will we?" I said.

"I suppose not. And not for nothing, but at least I did not elect that orange-haired buffoon to the presidency."

"Nor did a majority of Americans. And of course he wasn't alive or running back then."

"Had he been, I can assure you we would not have elected him," the man said. "Maybe the Federalists would have, but certainly not me and my kind. I was the original Independent, if you will permit me a strut."

Another pause. Whoever this guy was, he was entertaining.

"There's something else," I said.

The man brightened.

"The fact that I attended the original Boston Latin School, whose contemporary form is your alma mater?" he said. "Or the fact that I became publisher of *The Pennsylvania Gazette* at the tender age of 23? One of, if not *the*, most influential newspapers in the colonies, if you will permit me anther swagger."

"No, not more of the past," I said. "The present. If you really are Ben Franklin, how did you get here?"

The man laughed.

"Perhaps I also invented a time-travel machine," he said.

"Seriously."

The man rolled his eyes.

"For the moment," he said, "let's dispense with the how, save for the disclosure that The Founders did not publicly reveal all their powers. I, at least, did not. As for 'why,' another question surely on your mind? That one I can answer: I want to help you, Nick."

"How?"

"I have in mind four things. First is help with your journalism."

I was about to say that I was hardly the only journalist—at hardly the only newspaper in 2021—who needed help when Franklin said:

"Don't be flattered. It's not only you. I have a *very* long list. Journalists and the press today have become purveyors of fiddle-faddle."

"I suppose you don't mean the popcorn snack."

"Good lad, you're starting to catch on," he said. "No, poppycock was a word from my era that Conagra co-opted. Not that there could be a copyright claim. And yes, I learned about Conagra on Wikipedia. I mean fiddle-faddle as in nonsense. Though when the ad popped up I must confess I watched it and then I *did* take the next bait, which was 'Giant Rabbit Hops Across Wyoming, Arrives Hungry in Idaho.' Remind me, what is Idaho?"

"A state out West."

"Oh, right. I've been reading about it recently. Home to white supremacists and anti-vaxxers. Weird, how they gravitate to places like that. Maybe you have a theory you could share some day. But that rabbit story was a good one. So was 'Go Topless Day Draws Hundreds, Even a Few Men.' I clicked on that hoping to find risqué pictures, but all I saw were images with blurred faces and bars mid-chest. False advertising, I say. But it surely helped with your ad revenues."

A smile spread across the Franklin character's face.

"Scrolling down through 'Topless Days' I happened upon 'Famous Bosoms: Then and Now.' I couldn't believe it. Or, to be honest, my luck. In my time, you never saw the female breast—or the male, for that matter—outside the shadowy confines of a brothel or bedroom, and then, only rarely. At least that was the case for me.

"But today, seems every other image on your site is of the female bosom. Young bosom, middle age bosom, old bosom, the same bosom 50 years after the young bosom of some aging star's early TV days. From a salacious point of view, I suppose there is merit. From the journalism perspective, what rubbish. This Chamberlain fool ought to be flogged."

"I won't disagree with that," I said.

"Allow me another observation on headlines," the man said. "Whatever happened to the great ones? 'Headless Body in Topless Bar,' for example. Classic! Told the whole story in just five words! Or 'Man Bites Dog,' 'Nixon Resigns,' 'Diana Dead,' 'War on America,' even 'Mush From the Wimp,' though as we know it wasn't intended for actual publication. At least it had spirit! So many of the headlines I see today lack imagination."

The Franklin character furrowed his brow.

"Speaking of headlines reminds me of an episode of *The Big Bang Theory* that I just watched. Season 10, Episode 10, I believe it was. Sheldon says 'He's expecting a newspaper in the morning. Apparently, they still make them.' He referred, of course, to a print edition. Did you see that one?"

"I did," I said. Another sobering reminder of the state of my profession.

"And then there was 'The Solo Oscillation,' episode 13 of the 11th season," the dream man continued. "A newspaper has reviewed Raj's planetarium show. Penny takes the paper and folds it into a boat and then wears it as a hat. It would have been funny if it didn't speak volumes about newspapering. So that's where you are today, Nick. Click bait and the culture sneering at you. I suppose you don't know what 'click' meant back in my day."

"I don't."

"A blow or knock in the face, as in 'a click in the muns.' Which is what click bait has done to journalism in the year 2021, wouldn't you agree?"

I nodded my assent.

"And who is pushing the click bait? Pretty much every publication I've read. Some are worse than others, and of those, I put SGM at the top of the list. Your chain—"

"Not 'my chain,' " I said. "They bought us. I had no say in the matter."

"Then let's call it 'the chain.' From Chamberlain on down to Hill, that oaf in Boston, the chain is an assemblage of grifters and fools. They'll get theirs and it shan't be pretty. And you will play a role in the royal comeuppance, though you will first become their best boy and momentarily line their coffers—a role you will eventually renounce, much to your credit."

"And you know this how?"

"Intuition."

I was done with the dance.

"Well, sir, you are a clever fellow," the dream me said. "Also, delusional, though seemingly harmless. I don't know what your game is, but you are certainly not Benjamin Franklin, time-travelled to 2021."

The Franklin character turned indignant.

"As I have already stated, I am here to help you and hopefully others in a profession that was so dear to me," he said. "Beyond clicks, what have these monsters done? We could start with all the time and effort spent on nonsense like tagging. And keywording. And SEO-ing. And Assets. Really now? Oh, yes, I've mucked around inside HappyWare. Even watched one of the training videos. 'Make it part of your DNA,' is how the instructor referred to tagging. What a cock lane, he be. Count me as an Autem Cackler, or Prickear, if you prefer."

"You've totally lost me," my dreaming self said.

"Forgive me," said the Franklin stand-in. "I do drift off into the old vernacular sometimes—like you and your grinagog nonsense. Where *do* those socks go? Perhaps witches or gremlins swoop in after dark and whisk them away!"

He laughed mightily.

"So that is my first task: tossing you a lifeline for your journalism. Are you not curious about the other three tasks that comprise my mission?" the man said.

"Not really," I said.

"Suffer me. Second is I propose to support you in writing a book. Not a collection of your useless columns, but a book about the state of the media today."

"I think Bob Woodward or David Brooks would be far better qualified than me."

"They don't do novels, which is the only format that can do justice to a treatise of this magnitude" the man said. "Nor would they ascribe to an essential element here, namely, the willing suspension of disbelief."

"That you actually appeared to me."

"Exactly. More critically, as Emerson supposedly said, only in fiction can the deepest truths be revealed. I'm thinking satire would be the preferred format, or perhaps a sort of modern media morality play, but let me get back to you on that."

"The other two?" I said.

"Third is guidance on your romantic life. You've put yourself in a terrible pickle and I might be of some help."

"The fourth?"

"I want to give you the Tip of the Century."

"Thanks but no thanks," I said.

"You'll want this scoop, trust me."

"Goodbye."

I stood and signaled to the waiter to bring my check.

"How about I offer some proof," the Franklin wanna-be said.

"Of what?"

"My identity."

"And how do you propose to do that?"

"By taking you on a little walk."

"I don't have time."

"Sure you do. Come on. Christ Church Burial Ground is only two blocks away."

I followed the man out of the restaurant, and we were walking toward the graveyard where the real Benjamin Franklin is buried when my dream ended.

When I awoke, it was so clear in my head—so *cinéma vérité*—that I did something I never had before.

I began keeping a dream diary.

For what purpose, I did not yet know.

The reaction to my second story on Amber and Jennifer was what I had hoped for, and then some. Our social media accounts blew up. Google Analytics were beyond stratospheric.

I owed a measure of thanks again to the night editor, who wrote this headline:

Mother claims comatose daughter speaks
'Miracle' from Virgin Mary said to result

For the record, I did balance Jennifer's claims with real-world references.

I acknowledged that many believed that Mary had appeared at such places as Lourdes, Fatima, Medjugorje, and more recently Trevignano Romano, Italy, where a woman named Gisella Cardia claimed to experience supernatural visions. According to Cardia, Mary in September 2019 had prophesized COVID, stating "Pray for China, because new diseases will come from there, all ready to infect the air by unknown bacteria."

And I noted that the Catholic Church officially recognizes such claims only after long investigations "that have proved effective in weeding out frauds. I tossed in caveats—many "claims" and "believes" and "says" and "asserts" and "apparently"'s and "supposed"'s.

And only once did I use the word "miracle": when quoting what Jennifer "insists" was one of the messages from Mary.

None of that mattered.

With COVID still raging, people in the fall of 2021 were desperate for good news.

I was barely settled into my desk when the new publisher's secretary summoned me to his office.

"Sit down, Nick," Hill said when I got there. "Make yourself at home."

Nervously, I sat—in one of his chairs that we'd heard cost a grand apiece. Hill was a bear with the newsroom's budget, but he'd spent lavishly redecorating his office with fine furniture and carpeting, and two of the original Norman Rockwell paintings he collected.

The only tacky touches were the GOOD NEWS RULES! brass plate he had on his desk and a freshly opened bag of Frito-Lay potato chips.

"Chip?" Hill said. "Don't worry, they haven't contained Olestra in years."

"I'd love one," I said.

You know the phrase *breaking out in a cold sweat*? Until that moment, I'd never believed it was an actual physiological reaction.

"Help yourself," Hill said. "I've got plenty."

Hill whistled and a purebred golden retriever appeared at the door of the publisher's conference room. It was a beautiful animal. Hill undoubtedly treated it better than his employees.

"Chip, Tom?" said Hall.

The dog took it gently from his hand, then lay down at his feet.

"Good boy," said Hill.

"He's a great dog," I said.

"The best. If only all my employees were so loyal."

I wished I had the ability to faint on command.

"He's even a hell of a runner," Hill continued. "Comes with me on all my jogs. I named him after my father, who died when I was eight. Dad loved dogs, goldens especially."

A saddened look came over Hill's face—and was quickly gone.

"What did he die of?" I said.

"Cancer," said Hill. "Leukemia, to be precise. He left my mother to raise me alone. She waitressed nights and weekends to support us."

"I'm sorry, Mr. Hill."

"Shit happens," the publisher said. "OK, down to business. Are we off the record?"

"Of course," I said.

"No cute little publisher anecdote ever winds up in your column?"

"Never."

"Because that would be a very bad move."

Hill waved a printout. It was my poop chips column.

"When I read this," Hill said, "my first impulse was to fire you. My second was to keep you on, as my dog groomer. Pay you minimum wage and give the Mary story to A. J. Johnson."

I nearly choked on my chip.

"How well I remembered when word first began to spread about 'fecal urgency' and 'loose stools.' I was still in B-School, contemplating what company I wanted to work for after graduation. The tree-huggers with their phony righteous indignation started to piss and moan, and jerks like you began to put their every word in the paper. I wanted to take a bag of Wow! chips and ram them down the throat of every fucking sanctimonious reporter until they came out their worthless fucking asses."

"I'm sorry, Mr. Hill," I said. "Sometimes a columnist up against a deadline—"

"I understand about the difficulty of original ideas on a consistent basis and all that happy horseshit," Hill said. "My point is that after I calmed down, after I took my first job at Frito-Lay—believe me, the signing bonus was an enticement!—after I was assigned to the team that was attempting to make lemonade from the lemons of Olestra—I took bad PR as a challenge. As opportunity!"

He was standing now, his arms raised, as if giving a T.E.D. talk. He had once, as I had discovered when Googling him. Damn thing had more than ten million views, too. Another measure of the sad state of our culture.

"I realized consumers didn't want the bad news about the one or two percent who couldn't enjoy Olestra," Hill went on, "and I'll grant you there's a certain tiny percentage of people whose intestines are different than mine or yours. Undoubtedly inferior genes, but that's neither here nor there. No, consumers wanted the good news about the ninety-eight or ninety-nine percent who *could* enjoy the product! They wanted to know that almost anyone *could* eat an entire bag of chips without an ounce of fat! In a nation of couch potatoes—pun intended—what could be better than that? And that's how we retooled our marketing, to such great, if fleeting, success with Lay's Light line. So, forgive me if my instinct on reading this was to fire you. Consider it a hiccup. Guys like you actually taught me a valuable lesson. Thank you, Nick. Thank you from the bottom of my heart."

"You're welcome, Mr. Hill," I said.

"Please call me Bruce."

"You're welcome, Bruce."

"Now to the matter at hand—this coma kid. Do you have any idea of the response?"

"I've had a lot of calls and emails."

"And so have I—hundreds, actually. The social media and analytics are unprecedented. What's more, this morning we ran out of newsstand copies—every single one, from Portland to Providence, gone by six-thirty. We ran off another five thousand—when was the last time *that* happened at a newspaper?—9/11?—and they went, too. It wasn't the Dunkin' Donuts coupons that blew out the doors—it was you, Nick. You!"

"I don't know what to say."

"As long as you keep writing like this," he said, "you can say you have a job for life. And not on the suburban staff or the copy desk, either. You know, sometimes I'm slow to see what's under my own nose. Mea culpa. You, Nick, are a genius."

"Wanna know what kind of sickening brownnose I've become?" I said when I called Destiny.

I briefed her on my visit with Hill.

"At least he likes you," she said. "I had my first performance review today."

That had been one of the consultants' first recommendations: twice-yearly assessments, resulting in a six-page "blueprint for action." Both documents had to be signed by manager and employee and filed with Human Resources. So far, I'd not been scheduled.

"Was it bad?" I said.

"Overall, I got a three on a scale of one to ten. I have three months to, quote, 'achieve performance expectations.' And there's more. According to my assessment, I do not keep 'readily documentable' hours, my telephone skills are 'deficient,' I keep a 'disorderly desk,' my page views are 'laughable' and my byline count since I've started my series is 'grossly inadequate.' "

"They're counting bylines now, too, along with corrections?" I said.

"And plugging them into a program that generates an 'inches-to-hours-worked ratio.' A productivity measure."

But Destiny said she could care less about performance reviews and action blueprints. She was exhilarated, like that night at Ernie's.

"My first story's done," she said. "A hundred and twenty inches, ready to run Sunday."

True to her word, Destiny had ignored the press releases that crossed her desk and successfully fought off the business editor, who'd assigned her the first story in ENTERPRISING, a weekly feature Hill had cooked up after being invited onto the board of the Greater Boston Chamber of Commerce. According to Hill's memo on the new feature, each ENTERPRISING was to be "a lively, colorful, upbeat look at an innovative local business."

A vehicle for ads, in other words.

No, Destiny had concentrated on the first installment of her "The New Disparities" series. Whether it would actually become a series remained to be seen, but she was determined to fight. Her first story was a profile of a Black man who'd lost both legs in Vietnam and whose life today was a daily struggle, economically and emotionally.

For Destiny, it would be a return to her past. Born and raised in Newark, she was the daughter of public-school teachers who had been active in the civil-rights movement of the 1960s. Her parents had demonstrated during the 1967 Newark Rebellion, before Destiny was born, and they had inspired their only child to a similar commitment to social justice. After graduating from Rutgers with a dual degree in economics and journalism and media studies, she'd been hired at *The Star-Ledger*, her hometown paper. She won awards there before joining *The Tribune*, which under the leadership of a new executive editor, Bob Jones, was aggressively recruiting women and people of color.

A bygone era, that was.

"Can I read it?" I said.

"Absolutely."

"Is it in the system?"

"Yes"

Destiny gave me the asset number, and I began reading.

I was blown away. A long while had passed since a story of this caliber had run in *The Trib*. It flowed seamlessly, it captivated and informed, and it exposed an injustice without being heavy-handed. I figured even Hill would have to be impressed, even if he would discover why ENTERPRISING hadn't premiered yet.

Just before lunchtime, Jones called me into his office. Hill was there. He was in the editor's office a lot these days, often with one or more SGM executives joining in via Zoom.

"Have you talked to Jennifer Abbott today?" Jones said.

"I haven't had a chance," I said. "You should see all my messages."

"So you don't know what's developing out there."

"No."

"Then look at this."

The noon news was on. A reporter was doing a live remote from Middleton, where a crowd had gathered in an old field that abutted a raised ranch on a dead-end street. Crime-scene tape ringed the house, and police patrolled the lawn. I thought it was a mass shooting scene—until I recognized Jennifer's residence on close-up.

Jones turned the volume up.

"According to police," said the reporter, "the crowd began to grow early this morning, after Nick Nolan's story in *The Daily Tribune*. As you can see from the crucifixes and statues they carry, these are the faithful. Like pilgrims to Lourdes, they come seeking miracles."

"Holy shit," I said.

"Shit it ain't," Hill said.

"Greta Ricci drove all the way from Cape Cod," the reporter said. "Greta, would you like to tell us why?"

The camera cut to an older woman in a shawl. She was clutching rosary beads.

Impressed by the numbers for my first story about Jennifer and Amber, Hill had put my second story behind a pay wall. Only subscribers could read it.

"I read Mr. Nolan's first story, which was free," Greta said, "and when this one required a subscription, I didn't think twice about signing up, even if a month costs $50 and every penny counts when you're on Social Security. The moment I read this one, I knew I had to come. I have liver cancer and the doctor's given me a month to live. But I know Mary will save me."

"I can't believe this," I said.

"Believe it," said Hill, "and thank the guy upstairs for it. Stories like this don't come along every day. Or year, for that matter."

Jones turned the TV off.

"Bruce is right," he said. "We've got ourselves a monster. And as great a job as you've done, Nick, it's time to hand it over to hard news. You can do the occasional column, of course, but there are a lot of angles here that we need to get going on immediately."

"It's not that easy," I said.

Jones looked at me blankly.

"I don't think Jennifer will talk to anyone else," I said.

"She told you that?"

"In so many words, yes. It's an issue of trust. Frankly, I'll be surprised if she even talks to me again. She was worried what the reaction would be. And now look at this. A feeding frenzy."

Jones launched into a discourse about how reporters, not subjects, must decide coverage.

Hill was rolling his eyes when a voice behind us said: "Did he tell you he used to live with this woman?"

A.J. was standing in Jones's doorway. That was another of her annoying habits—barging in.

"They were shacked up for more than two years," A.J. declared.

"Is that true, Nick?" Jones said.

"We dated for a while," I said, lying, "that's all. Until now, I hadn't seen her in two decades."

"But you'd like to start something again, wouldn't you?" said A.J. "What with your marriage ending and women not exactly clamoring to hook up with an overweight loser journalist."

I said nothing.

"Well? *Wouldn't* you like to get into her pants again?" A.J. said.

"That's ridiculous," I said.

"Oh, really?" A.J. said. "I hear she used to be in Hollywood."

"And your point would be?" Hill said.

I couldn't tell if he was being deliberately cantankerous—or if he really didn't get it.

"The point is objectivity," said A.J.

"Conflict of interest," Jones agreed.

"No," said Hill, "the point is that for the first time in years people are tripping over themselves to subscribe to *The Trib*. More than 3,000 new subscribers so far today and it's only noon. The point is, we have the beginnings of a story with legs and that isn't super-good news—it's super-*great* news, single mom overcoming impossible odds, the Virgin Mary speaking, manna from heaven, etcetera etcetera. Who cares who writes the story so long as we stay on top of it. This woman wants Nick. I want Nick. He's got the touch."

"I'm not comfortable with that," said Jones.

"Would you be comfortable if I ordered you? Let me, then. Nick covers the coma kid, and everyone else—the disgruntled and unlikeable Miss Johnson here especially—butts out."

"Bruce, there might be a middle ground here," Jones said, weakly.

"Middle ground, baloney," Hill said. "As for you, Miss Johnson—"

"—That would be Ms. to you," A.J. said.

"As for you, Ms. Johnson," Hill said, "let me show you something."

He opened the manilla folder that was on his desk.

"Believe it or not, I much prefer to read from paper, not a screen," the publisher said. "And when a colleague of yours who shall remain nameless—no, it wasn't Nick—suggested your drivel might amuse me, I had my secretary print out a sample. And guess what? I *was* amused, in a depraved sort of way. You, Ms. Johnson, may be the worst writer in newspaper history—a history, I would note, that goes back to Benjamin Franklin."

A.J. stormed out of Jones's office, saying as she left, "I am going directly to H.R.!"

"Knock yourself out," Hill said. "I've already let them know you might be coming."

Hill was wearing a smirk.

"I used to think tree-huggers were crybabies," he said. "Then I met reporters. My God, what a bunch of miserable self-centered whiners. Not *all* of you, of course—not *you*, Nick—but for every one of you, there's ten of her. Never happy with anything. 'The copy desk fucked up my story,' 'why wasn't I on page one?' 'why do I have to cover this,' 'why can't I cover that,' 'photo-taking is not in my job description,' 'I couldn't reach my source,' 'seriously you didn't get my email?' 'I can't do this in fifteen inches,' 'I hate man-on-the-streets,' 'I need another hour or maybe a week,' 'are you authorizing OT?' and blah-blah-blah-blah-blah-blah-blah-blah."

For the first time today, Jones smiled.

"Welcome to my world," he said.

Then he left for lunch.

"Is it true?" Hill said when he'd gone.

"Is what true?" I said.

"That you have romantic interest in Jennifer Abbott?"

"I did, many years ago."

"And do again, I can see it in your eyes," Hill said. "I say go for it. I remember her from *Do Not Disturb*. Yeah, I've got a weakness for bad TV. She's one good-looking woman, Nick. Just don't screw up. This one really does have legs. Legs enough if we play things right to carry SMG to our most profitable year ever. Not that I want to pressure you or anything."

"Sorry, buddy," said a cop, one of several on duty, "we can't let you in."

It was five o'clock, and I was standing at the edge of Jennifer's lawn. The crowd had grown past 1,000 and I counted 13 TV vans, including ones from *Inside Edition* and TMZ.

"I'm Nick Nolan," I said to the cop. "I wrote the column."

He instantly warmed.

"Great story, my friend," he said. "Sorry about stopping you like that— I didn't recognize you."

"Happens all the time," I said. "I haven't updated my mugshot in a while. I'd like to hang on to the illusion of a single chin a little longer."

The cop laughed and extended his hand.

"Officer Gerry Maloney. I'm happy to meet you. Is Mrs. Abbott expecting you?"

"Yes."

"Then right this way, please. And can I give you a tip?"

"Sure."

"Are we off the record?"

"As off as off is."

"Don't stop writing about this. I'm not real religious or anything, turned my back on the church years ago when the news about priests diddling little boys broke, but something's happening here. I feel it. I swear I do. It's got me thinking maybe I should go back to Mass. Just a thought at the moment, but even a thought is a minor miracle in itself!"

Maloney escorted me past the crime-scene tape and down the walk to Jennifer's house. I couldn't help but notice that all of the curtains and shades were drawn—and that an army of TV and still cameras were suddenly trained on me.

Jennifer opened the door, double bolting it once I stepped inside.

"Thank God you're here," she said. "This has been a terrible day. Crowds terrify me, Nick. You know that."

I did. Jennifer never could attend a concert or game because of her fear of crowds.

"To see so many people out there," Jennifer said, "and then all the TV. One guy was even in the backyard, trying to shoot into Amber's room, before the cops, God bless them, chased him away. Thank goodness I'd already pulled the shades."

"There's nothing to worry about," I said. "Everything's under control now."

"Hug me Nick? I'm scared."

I hugged Jennifer, and she led me into her kitchen, where she made coffee. We talked some, and I told her I was obligated to write another column about the crowds and all. She was cool with that—and adamant she wouldn't talk to any other reporter.

"How do they put it in your profession?" she said. "This is an exclusive?"

"That's how they put it," I said.

"I've already got a new cell phone number," Jennifer continued. "You can have it—but no one else. Swear on the bible?"

"I swear."

"I just can't deal with a media circus. I know that sounds crazy given my career, but there's a huge difference between a set and a live audience. I never could do theater, you know."

"I remember."

"If only I'd found beta-blockers then. I think I would have liked Broadway. Or off-Broadway. Or even community theater."

We finished our coffee and there wasn't much more to say. Jennifer was right: it was impossible to ignore what was happening outside.

"I'll call you tomorrow," I said as I was leaving.

"First thing?"

"First thing, I promise."

"Thanks, Nick. I don't know what I'd do without you."

"Probably still lead a nice quiet existence," I said, and we laughed.

"We'll get through this, right?" Jennifer said.

"Piece of cake."

"I hope so," Jennifer said, "because I have a feeling it's just beginning."

Officer Maloney escorted me past people in wheelchairs, on crutches, and on stretchers inside ambulances. They were all races, seemingly all socio-economic classes. I even saw a woman with an infant—and a boy with a Tom Brady cap covering a bald head whose gaze caught my eye.

I was about to get into my car when microphones and cameras were thrust in my face.

What timing. It was exactly six o'clock—top of the evening news.

The questions came in a barrage:

"Did you see the kid?"

"Did she say anything today?"

"Is there any new message from Mary?"

"Mega Million's one thing, but has the kid actually ever healed anyone?"

"Does it strike Jennifer as strange that she played the mother of a handicapped kid on that Fox show?"

"How's it feel, Nick, to be caught up in all this?"

"What's your column going to say tomorrow?"

I probably should have brushed by. Let them get their own damn stories.

But I'd done a lot of TV myself, once upon a time. Lights and cameras still cast a spell.

"Amber has nothing further to say at this moment," I said. "That doesn't mean she won't at some other time."

"Like holding a press conference?" said a reporter.

"Not happening," I said.

"So this is only you."

"Sure looks that way," I said.

"How do we know you're not making it up?" said another reporter.

"You'll have to take my word for it," I said. "And if you think it's fake news, well, nothing says you have to cover it. My guess is you will. Nielsens, you know."

"How's the mother holding up?" the reporter from *Inside Edition* asked.

"Jennifer is overwhelmed—as any of us would be. She asks that everyone please respect her privacy. I'm sure at the right moment she'll have a statement of some kind."

"Are you paying her for this story?" said the TMZ reporter.

"Of course not," I said. "Do I work for you?"

"Maybe you should," the reporter shot back. "You've got what it takes. And my bet is we pay better than some dying rag."

"Do you honestly believe it's Mary speaking?" another TV person said.

"I believe something is happening here," I said.

"What about all these sick people who've come to be cured?"

I was about to answer when an old woman in a shawl elbowed her way to my side.

"If you have faith," Greta Ricci said into the cameras, "all things are possible."

My second Ben Franklin dream picked up where the first had ended, walking toward Christ Church Burial Ground in Philadelphia. For a man of 75 or so, old Ben walked briskly. He was in good shape.

Dream characters can read minds and this one read mine.

"My secret?" he said. "Treadmill 30 minutes daily, minimum. Weights every other day. No more than two glasses of wine at dinner ever. And that would be red wine, with its resveratrol. Love the research on that, BTW, even the Cleveland Clinic gives it a thumbs-up, along with dark chocolate, another of my indulgences. Plenty of fiber daily, keep sugar to a minimum, which means no more Twinkies, and organic fruits and veggies whenever possible. Also, keep the salt low. And check the Fitbit hourly."

He smiled.

"And no poop chips, I can assure you of that!" he said, laughing. "Despite what Hill said, there was no good news in Olestra."

"Can we please get serious?" I said.

"You think your publisher isn't serious?" the man said. "Be careful of that one. When a ship is taking on water, you don't want a captain who orders full speed ahead."

"Regarding Hill," I said, "I expect he eventually will lay me off, along with most everyone else."

"Not a chance in the world," the man said. "He has big plans for you, none of which I approve. But that can wait. Olestra brings something most curious to mind."

I knew where this was heading. I'd seen the click-bait story on our site myself.

7 Things That Cause Green Poop, the headline read.

"Until I saw that ad on *Trib.com*, I hadn't the faintest that blueberries could turn your crap green," Franklin said. "Seems paradoxical, doesn't it?

Broccoli and kale, I get. But who eats broccoli and kale? Granola-crunchers mostly. And may I ask if you can offer any insight into this other headline? 'If your dog is dragging his bottom on the ground here's what it means.' "

"Don't we have a more serious purpose today?" I said.

"You think green shit isn't serious? Seeing it in the outhouse might be fright enough to cause you to fall in. I had that experience as a young lad, and trust me, it's not pleasant. Cause enough for PTSD. And had I ever seen a dog dragging its buttocks on the ground I would have been deeply disturbed. But you're right. We do have serious purpose today. Before we get to that, however, I want to emphasize that I am on your side and the side of every journalist left at *The Trib*. This Stupid Good Media chain—"

"Super Good," I said.

"Like I don't know that? Have you lost your sense of humor?"

"It's hard to maintain it working there these days."

"Well, fuck them and the horse they rode in on," the man said. " Okay, I have that off my chest. While we walk, may I ask you two questions?"

I was expecting more nonsense, but Franklin surprised me.

"In your opinion, what do you suppose the proper diagnosis for Trump is? I've been brushing up on the DSM-5 and I think it must be a personality disorder. Histrionic personality disorder or narcissistic personality disorder or maybe both. Your take?"

"Both," I said.

"I suppose you are right. What was behind all the tweets, before he got banned? Some days, there were dozens. He barely had time for a Fox News appearance."

We were nearing the cemetery.

"Before we arrive, we have time for my second question," Franklin said. "And it is: Wassup with yo obits, bro?"

"Excuse me?"

"You don't like my 2021 lingo?" Franklin said.

"I think the last time anyone said 'lingo' was in 1970," I said.

"Practice makes perfect, I suppose. I mean obits. Obituaries. What's up with them?"

"You mean *The Trib*'s?" I said.

"Pick your paper," Franklin said. "Since when did your final farewell cost money?"

"Since the suits discovered a new revenue source."

"That's what I suspected. It's the old saying: 'In this world, nothing is certain except death and taxes.' "

"One of Will Rogers' quotes," I said.

"Not actually. That one was mine, though Will did capitalize on it. My point is obits used to be free. A staff member wrote it, not a funeral director who then billed the deceased's relatives for tortured and ungrammatical pablum. To add insult to injury, I see that with obits of certain newsworthy individuals you apply the pay wall, looking to grab even more money off the souls of the dead. 'You've reached your limit of free articles, subscribe to read more' is what I see on those.

"How ghoulish, and all to learn that the dearly departed left us 'peace-fully' and 'surrounded by their loving family'! Who defines 'peacefully'? Not the dead person. And no doubt there are such loving families, but in my experience, they are few and far between. 'Surrounded by family members who haven't spoken in years and will now be hiring lawyers in a battle over the estate, if the bastard left anything,' would be more truthful."

"It would," I agreed.

"And why must newspapers today use such euphemistic phrases as 'passed' when the reality is better phrased as 'croaked,' or just plain 'died?' Although in my time, we weren't honest, either, with use of such nebulous terms as 'turn over the perch,' 'yield the crow a pudding,' or 'put to bed with a shovel.' And please, if truth be served, the manner of death should be included, not hinted at or unmentioned. A heart attack is a heart attack, not 'suddenly.' Same with stroke, brain aneurysm, and aortic dissection."

"Is this how you wanted *your* final mention?" I asked.

"Final mentions, plural, that would be," Franklin said. "And they *were* rich with details of the physical conditions that led to my demise. Consider what my personal physician, Dr. John Jones, told my own Pennsylvania Gazette four days after I died: that sixteen days before croaking, I was seized with fever and five days before the end, an abscess in my lungs burst and amidst vomiting and struggling for breath, I expired. And it is reputed, reliably I can confirm, that my final words were 'a dying man can do nothing easily.'

"The truth is that my health had been the subject of numerous sto-ries throughout my life—my attacks of pleurisy and gout, for example. But against the odds, mine was a long stay the first time around, allowing me ample opportunity to write my own epitaph. Have you read it?"

"No."

"I can recite it from memory: 'The Body of B. Franklin, Printer; like the Cover of an old Book, Its Contents torn out, And stript of its Lettering and Gilding, Lies here, Food for Worms. But the Work shall not be wholly lost; For it will, as he believ'd, appear once more, In a new & more perfect Edition, Corrected and amended By the Author.' Not bad, right?"

"Damn good, actually," I said.

" 'Food for Worms' was a special touch."

"I'd say."

"And did not my prediction of appearing again in a new and more perfect edition—this glorious man you now know—come perfectly true?"

"It did," I said. "And I do like the new look."

"And you probably have not read the obituary published by another newspaper of the time, *The Federal Gazette*. It wrote '"Died on Saturday night, in the 85th year of his age, the illustrious BENJAMIN FRANKLIN. The world has been so long in possession of such extraordinary proofs of the singular abilities and virtues of this FRIEND OF MANKIND that it is impossible for a newspaper to increase his fame, or to convey his name to a part of the civilized globe where it is not already known and admired.' A blush doth redden my cheeks recalling that. And also, recalling how many attended my funeral—some 20,000 people, in a city whose population was about 28,000."

"So this is the route newspaper obituaries today should go?" I said. "Description of lung abscesses and worms?"

"Of course not! Would I want to deprive you of a revenue stream? You poor folks need every penny you can get. Speaking of pennies, do you not find it ironic that a man of arguably greater stature than I, Abraham Lincoln, is on that lowliest of coins, while I grace the $100 bill?"

"Like anyone carries cash anymore," I said.

"Right, not even I do," the man said. "It's Chase Sapphire for me. Best rewards out there and only a $95 annual fee. Cheaper than Amazon Prime. But we were speaking of obituaries. If truth mattered today, they would be more factual and less flowery. Let me dictate what I would describe as a model obit that serves both masters, truth and revenue. You of course remember the late Robert J. Dixon, the longtime sportscaster for radio station ABCD-AM."

"Who could forget him? Everyone in the media had the misfortune of knowing him or about him. A drunk who was totally lacking in social skills and notorious for hitting on women. When one filed a sexual harassment lawsuit, he was fired. He should have been years before."

"Probably had something on someone," the man said.

"Our guess was the station owner, a toad who was cut from the same cloth," I said.

"Good guess."

"Somehow he wound up with a job at a pathetic little web site that never caught on, *isntsportsthebestwellyoubet.com*," I said. "That's where he was when he died—there and in and out of court on the class-action suit. Apparently, he was too poor to afford a lawyer so he was representing himself. I heard he'd croaked but I never saw an obit."

"Because there wasn't one" the man said. "When you have no survivors, no friends and no estate, you disappear without a ripple. It will need polishing, but off the top of my head this is the obituary I would have written:

BOSTON—Robert J. Dixon, a sportswriter at rinky-dink web site isntsport-sthebestwellyoubet.com *whose earlier undistinguished career at radio station ABCD-AM was characterized by sexual harassment of women, drunkenness, food-stained shirts, body odor, and dandruff died yesterday at the age of 59. The apparent cause of death was cirrhosis of the liver, though it could have been alcohol poisoning. We will never know, since the state Medical Examiner said she would not waste resources on autopsying his bloated corpse.*

Dixon leaves no survivors, only individuals who knew him and are relieved that he has left the earth. There will be no funeral or memorial service as no one has come forward to claim the body, which is now on ice at the Medical Examiner's office. For how long remains uncertain.

"We can't keep people like this forever," a medical examiner's spokesman said. "Electricity costs enough as it is."

Asked for comment about Dixon's passing, no one contacted at radio station ABCD-AM would say anything. However, another member of the media who asked to remain anonymous, did have a remark.

"If only he'd died 30 years earlier," this person said.

It is anticipated that in the afterlife, Dixon will be doomed to spend eternity in a place where boorishness and peevishness comprise existence. The Ninth Circle of Hell in Dante's Inferno, that would be."

I let this settle in and said: "Sounds right to me. Off the record, can you say who the source was?"

"You know who," the dream man said. "It was you."

We reached the burial ground and the man sat by the iron gate to Franklin's tomb.

"That's me under there," he said. "My mortal remains, that is."

"And that's your proof?" I said.

"Nick, may I suggest you take a chill pill? We came here to discuss task number one: transforming your pathetic pitter-patter into Pulitzer-caliber journalism."

"Can you get me a ghost writer?" I said.

"Good one, my lad! But no, that shan't be needed. Just a few simple rules and we'll turn you around in no time. Rule Number One: No more socks."

"I though you already established that."

"It bears repeating," the man said. "Rule Number Two: Do not trust

Hill for a second. The man is a snake."

"I think I've gotten that, too," I said.

"Have you? I wouldn't be so sure. You've been disturbingly buddy-buddy with him lately. One could almost imagine you've sold your soul."

"That's mean," I said.

"Sorry to hurt your feelings. In the end, you will redeem yourself. Rule Number Three: Question everything Jennifer says. She may be telling the truth but you *do* realize she also could be making this up?"

"I do," I said. "And I've been careful with my qualifications."

"Not careful enough. Rule Number Four: Read and re-read Stephen King's book *On Writing: A Memoir of the Craft*. It's as applicable to journalists as to fiction writers. And when it comes time to write *your* book—more on that in our next session—you will thank me mightily."

"We'll see," I said.

"Now that I think of it," the man said, "I'd like to add one more writer to Rule Four: Dan Barry."

"Of *The New York Times*?"

"Of *The New York Times*. One of the finest writers of his generation."

"I know Dan Barry," I said.

"Apparently not well enough," the man said.

"For a supposed mentor, you lack finesse."

"The truth hurts. But you're a grown man and can take it. There is an interview with Dan in *The New York Times* that you should read. 'A Reporter Striking Universal Chords,' it's titled. Here's the nut graf. I urge you to take it to heart:

"My aim is to make the reader see and feel everything the protagonist sees and feels. I try to do this through intimate interviews and well-chosen details that include all the senses. Then I try to craft a few first paragraphs that all but dare the reader to stop reading. Now, of course, I have to honor the promise of those first paragraphs by maintaining a narrative topspin through to the end. This means that I am always alert to where a reader's interest might wane—where ponderous explication or unnecessary description disrupts the rhythm. So I rewrite and rewrite, trim and tighten, work with an editor to make the story the best it can be—begging the editor to flag any purple prose—and then pray that the reader stays with the story through to the end."

"That's it?" I said.

"That's it," the man said. "Follow these rules and the world of writing shall be thy oyster."

"Well, thanks," I said.

"My pleasure. And may I now seek *your* insight?"

"Me, the hack?"

"Give yourself more credit," the man said. "You once were *The Trib*'s shining star, before you turned featherweight."

He was right about that.

"What insight do you think I can give you?" I said.

"What is this brouhaha about the Oxford Comma, also known as the serial comma?"

"I wasn't aware of any such brouhaha."

"It's raging in certain circles," the man said. "Circles in which you clearly do not travel. Literary circles, they would be. But I find it fascinating."

"I suppose you would."

"If I may quote The Oxford Companion to the English Language, 'usage varies as to the inclusion of a comma before and in the last item. ... This practice is controversial and is known as the serial comma or Oxford Comma, because it is part of the house style of Oxford University Press.' But the Oxford Comma is also known as the Harvard Comma.'

"So, the insight I seek is which of these two esteemed universities do modern writers choose for the proper name? It may surprise you to learn that I favor Oxford. Harvard, in my estimation, is *so* overrated, so full of itself."

"Look, Mr. Ben Franklin or whoever you are," I said, "I really don't have time for this. Nor, I was led to believe, do you. Don't we have more pressing business to attend to?"

"We do," the man said, and the dream ended.

CHAPTER FOUR: LIVE AT SIX

The days passed and Amber—Mary—had nothing further to offer. I wrote one more story—a bulleted recap of past developments, just to keep my numbers up—and then I, too, had nothing further to offer. TV drifted away and the crowds thinned. Only a hundred or so fanatics remained, including Greta Ricci, who'd pitched a tent on the empty lot next to Jennifer's, vowing to stay until she was granted an audience with Amber.

Back in the newsroom, new discord was brewing. It involved a Sunday supplement that every SGM paper carried: "The (Super) Goods!" it was called.

The (Super) Goods! was something of a successor to Parade Magazine, that once-proud weekly publication that now existed mainly as a venue for pizza coupons and Nutrisystem ads. Oh where have you gone, Walter Anderson?

Herewith a sampling of The (Super) Goods categories, with descriptions:
Good one!
A funny anecdote!
Good luck!
With anything!
Good point!
That you made to someone else who was forever grateful!
Good riddance!
To anything annoying!
Good Golly!
Only for those named Molly, lol!
Good Fido!
Times when pooch didn't chew on a shoe!
Good Tabby!
Times when tigger didn't turn up her nose at Meow Mix!
Goodness Gracious!
A most embarrassing moment, but no sex or bathroom stories. Farting is OK, however, if delicately phrased.
The (Super) Goods! national stories originated every week from

corporate headquarters, and every reporter at every SGM property on a rotating basis was required to localize it. If it was your week, regardless of your beat you were required to drop everything and "Get Down and Goody!" as Chamberlain phrased it in an email blast.

There were murmurs among the staff of a picket or walkout to protest The (Super) Goods!—just as there had been before publication of this year's "Super Readers' Choice Awards," in which readers supposedly voted for their favorite businesses, the votes were tallied, and the winners and runners-up revealed in another supplement.

There were 175 categories in the "Super Readers' Choice Awards," including clam shack, spa, hearing aid center, sushi, bowling, laundromat, pest control, mattress store, credit union, oil change, brewery, bankruptcy, and places to be buried and/or cremated. It's possible that readers actually *did* vote and the results *did* play some role in declaring winners and finalists, but we in the newsroom found a suspicious correlation between winners and finalists and businesses that bought ads in the supplement.

In the end, no one protested the awards or the "The (Super) Goods!" supplement, which also was thick with ads. We sucked it up and wrote them. The specter of "fries with that?" was a strong disincentive to disobedience.

So The (Super) Goods! was not the topic of conversation as Destiny, Bud and I drank at Ernie's that day after work. An email from Chamberlain was. He'd written:

"During our last Town Hall, I emphasized that we all belong to a village that will prosper with a common set of values and a common purpose."

The purpose is not journalism, I thought.

"When we properly nourish our culture, we all feel inter-connected, intertwined, interlocked, and integral to the core mission. We can be ourselves and grow. Together, sharing our kinship, memories, expectations, hopes, dreams, skills, opinions—and, I daresay, our very hearts!—we will flourish in unimaginable ways. Super good ways as yet unimaginable!"

He remembered we were journalists, didn't he?

"So I ask you to join me in the Widen My Circle Challenge," Chamberlain continued. "During the next two months, connect to 30 people for a 30-minute 'hello, I'm Me, and who are You?' conversation—in-person with COVID protocols in place, or by Zoom."

Thirty people, a half hour apiece… that was 15 hours lost, at a minimum, although surely we could find plenty of actual friends who would check that box with a ten-second chat, bringing the actual time invested down to minutes.

Under "Circle Ideas," Chamberlain proposed the following:

"A You who would adore Me. A You who could teach Me. A You who is the yang to My yin. The You from another department who only ever sees Me microwaving lunch in the kitchen."

Chamberlain offered "Circle Set Up" tips.

For "meeting title," he suggested: "Help me cultivate community at SuperGoodMedia." The "meeting message" he proposed was "I'm looking to broaden my Super Circle, so come on in! Let's You and Me relate!"

And once we had met, we were advised to use one of his "Convo Starters," which included: "What's your favorite color? Do you have a lucky number? What's the Super Big Thing on your plate now? What's the best thing about your job at [name of your property]? What's your superpower? What makes you unique? What questions do You have for Me? Fire away, because in the Widen My Circle Challenge, anything goes [except criticism of SGM, not that we'd expect any of that]! And for those who are wondering: Yes, there will be prizes!!!"

"Lost his fucking mind," Destiny said over our first round.

"That presumes he had one to begin with," Bud said.

"I think we need to see the results of his mandatory drug test," I said, "although I don't believe they test for LSD."

"Wonder how we start a conversation with an IT person, given that I've never actually been able to speak to one," Destiny said.

By our third round, we'd come up with some conversation starters of our own.

"Besides suicidal ideation, how do you spend most of your time after you've lost another shift to company emails when you could have been engaged in journalism?" I proposed.

"What's your superpower? Oh, that's right, you don't have one. Only the bureaucrats at SGM are comic-book characters," Destiny said.

"Anyone besides a good shrink I can connect you to?" Bud said.

"Do you believe you were Atilla the Hun in a previous life and working here now is proof of karma?" Bud said.

"If you had the chance to waterboard Danny D'Ermo, how quickly would you?" I said.

Thus it went for another few fun minutes, until Bud, who like me was fascinated by Benjamin Franklin, said: "I wonder what Benjamin Franklin would think of it all."

"Funny you should ask," I said. "I've been wondering the same thing lately."

"Well, we could make a pretty good guess, couldn't we," said Destiny.

"Yes, we could," Bud said.

"No need to guess," I said. "I have it on good authority."

"What does that mean?" said Destiny.

"Like Mary and Amber, he's been visiting me in my dreams," I said. I laughed, weakly.

"You need a sleep aid," Bud said.

"Or another beer," Destiny said.

"Another round," I said to the bartender. "This one's on me."

I'd stopped calling Jennifer daily when one afternoon she telephoned me saying we had to meet. I asked if I could bring Erica Martinez to photograph her and Amber. I expected her to decline, but she said yes, on the condition she have final say on the images.

I agreed, despite this being a violation of a basic tenet of journalism. Journalism as it once was, that is.

"I'm not comfortable with this, as I know you're not, either, but I see no way around it," I said to Erica as we drove over.

"Nor I, with Hill flipping out over Mary News," Erica said. "Need I remind you that I have two kids and rent to pay?"

"This sucks," I said.

"So does shooting class photos when the unemployment runs out," Erica said. "But just this one time, Nick. If you need more photos, try someone else. I don't ever want to make a devil's deal like this again."

Arriving in Middleton, we passed Greta, who was sitting outside her tent with her rosary beads, and went into the house.

"It tears me up, looking at that poor woman every night and every day," Jennifer said. "I've heard liver cancer is the worst. Eventually it spreads everywhere."

"She left me a message begging me to intervene," I said. "I haven't responded. I don't know what to tell her."

"This is in my hands now, Nick," Jennifer said. "Don't tell her anything yet."

Jennifer extended her hand to Erica.

"You must be Erica," she said.

"Pleased to meet you," Erica said.

"I'm sorry to insist on dictating how to photograph my daughter," Jennifer said, "but no one ever has since the accident. I must be certain she is not exploited. Not that you seem the sensationalistic sort—yes, I've gone through your online galleries. You have true talent, Erica, and are respectful of your subjects. You're like Annie Leibovitz "

"Thank you, that's high praise," Erica said.

It also was true. Erica was our best photographer.

"These are the rules," Jennifer said. "I will tell you what angle is allowed, watch your every shot, and then look over your shoulder as you delete all but the one I choose, OK?"

Jennifer beckoned us toward the kitchen table.

"Please sit," Jennifer said. "Would either of you like something to drink?"

Neither of us did.

"Well, I'm having an iced tea," Jennifer said.

She poured a glass and sat with us.

"As you know," she said, "Amber has been silent lately. The stress has gotten to her, too."

"Understandably," I said.

"But last night, she spoke."

"What did she say?"

"That Mary wants to see Greta Ricci."

"To heal her?"

"Mary didn't reveal her intentions," Jennifer said. "She only told me— through Amber as always—to bring Mrs. Ricci inside at midnight tonight. I'd ask you to be here, Nick, but I worry you might be an impediment. I hope you understand."

"Of course."

"But I'll tell you everything tomorrow, I promise."

We fell silent.

"That's really all I have to report," Jennifer said. "Are you ready, Erica?"

"I am," she said.

We followed Jennifer into her daughter's room. Erica gasped.

"I'm sorry," she said.

"I understand," Jennifer said. "It can be overwhelming at first. But let's watch quietly for a few moments so you can fully absorb what you are seeing. What's that saying photographers have? More than meets the eye?"

"Yes," Erica said, "that's the saying."

I don't know how much time had passed when Jennifer said: "Are you ready?"

"I am," Erica said.

The mother walked to her daughter, whose face remained the lifeless mask I'd first seen. Jennifer had placed a Teddy bear in her arms.

"You're surprised it's not religious, aren't you," Jennifer said. "But not everything is. A little girl deserves her Teddy, wouldn't you say?"

Jennifer stood at the head of Amber's hospital bed and signaled to Erica.

"I'd like you to shoot the back of her head, with her Teddy in the background," she said. "No face. No IV or medical equipment. Do note that I washed her hair this morning and put it in ribbons and curls for you."

"Thank you," Erica said.

"When you're ready, go ahead," Jennifer said. "I can assure you the sound of the shutter will not disturb her."

Erica clicked off several shots, adjusting the angle as she went.

"I think I have enough," she said. "Here, take a look."

Jennifer watched as Erica toggled through the shots and settled on the one she wanted.

"This is it," Jennifer said. "Now delete the rest."

Erica did.

"God bless you," Jennifer said. "Amber blesses you, too."

We headed back to the kitchen.

"We'll save this for the next story, whenever that is," I said.

"I suspect the next story will be when Greta Ricci is cured," Jennifer said. "As for the photo, no need to wait. You may run it tomorrow as a standalone, as you call it. I imagine it would work as a front-page center-piece. With an appropriately sensitive caption I will trust you both to write. Now be careful leaving. You never know where the media ghouls may be lurking. There's a special place in hell for them, wouldn't you agree?"

"Absolutely," I said. "Ghouls, all of them."

"Says Ghoul Number One," Jennifer said.

"Not funny," I said.

"Who said I was joking?"

I said nothing about Greta Ricci's midnight visit to Jones, Hill, or even Destiny or Bud, and Erica kept the visit secret, too. Later, when Jennifer texted me Ricci's phone number, I called her. Ricci confirmed that she'd been invited inside at midnight, then left to await her cure. She offered no more details. I said and wrote nothing.

But we did run Erica's shot of Amber.

And not as a print centerpiece, but most of the front page. Also the entire top of the *Trib.com* home page, both with a caption Erica and I had written: "In gentle repose, sweet Amber waits for word from above."

No image, video, story, podcast or anything we'd ever published sur-passed the numbers that photo brought. It broke all records not only at *The Tribune*, but also, as Erica and I learned in an email from Chamberlain, all records at SuperGoodMedia. The worldwide reach this time, the analytics confirmed, was even deeper.

It was time to rest on laurels, and I did, until several days later, when I called Ricci for an update and she said: "Praise Mary and Jesus! There's not a cancerous cell left in my body!"

The woman went on to relate how she'd felt better the instant she'd held Amber's hand—and that when she'd visited the hospital next, just this morning, they'd pronounced her cancer-free. I knew enough about cancer to doubt such a rapid reversal and when Greta consented to a story, I said

I would have to verify everything with her doctor.

"Oh ye of little faith," the woman said. "But talk to him with my blessing."

Oncologist Aaron Schiffman was no ordinary MD—he headed a department at the Dana Farber Cancer Institute. His input would lend credibility to my story.

" 'Cure' is too strong a word," Schiffman said in a Zoom call, "but the shrinkage in those tumors was so swift that I brought in a colleague for another opinion. We can reach no other conclusion but that she's in remission."

"Was it, for lack of a better word, a miracle?"

"I'll leave that to someone more spiritually qualified to judge," Schiffman said. "What I can tell you is that Mrs. Ricci had not responded to a highly aggressive protocol of chemotherapy and radiation. Spontaneous remission is not impossible—but it's extremely rare. I happen to specialize in this type of tumor, as you know. In reviewing the literature, I have found spontaneous remission in a case like this exactly twice. One of those was a dubious claim; the other, more credible, at least in the scientific aspects, was a visitor to Lourdes."

"Unbelievable," I said.

"I suppose the crowds out there will be ten times larger once your column hits," Schiffman said.

I figured I was in for a lecture on the irresponsibility of the dumbed-down press, but the oncologist surprised me.

"You know what?" he said. "If it brings another unexplained recovery—a miracle, if that's what you insist on calling it—that's all right with me. Many of us in medicine believe we have all the answers. The truth is, we don't."

"Thank you, doctor," I said.

"Reach out to me any time," Schiffman said.

The call ended and I received an urgent text message.

It was from SGM.

"Could your pet be the Super Good Media Mascot of the year?" it read. "Click on the link to submit your photo and learn about your chances for the Grand Prize, an all-expenses-paid trip to the pet-friendly amusement park of your choice! Dogs and cats only are eligible, no birds, snakes, hamsters, gerbils, tropical fish, goats, cows, or horses. Or humans, lol!!!"

Schiffman was right, of course: by nine o'clock the next morning, more than two thousand people had gathered at Jennifer's, according to police estimates. I suppose they would have come regardless of the headline, but the copy desk had put the magic word again into the headline:
Woman in Remission Claims Mary's 'Miracle'

Jennifer was buoyant when I made it into her house.

"Amber is delighted," Jennifer said. "Even though she plays a humble part in this, it makes her very happy. Would you like to see her? You can judge for yourself."

We went into Amber's room, illuminated by a candelabrum. The girl hadn't changed position since my last visit. Her face remained that silent mask.

"She seems at peace," I said.

I was lying. She still seemed like a comatose girl with only brainstem function.

"She *is* at peace," said Jennifer, "and she's eager to do more, in her own way. Amber tells me that the Virgin Mary has decided to embark on a mission of forgiveness and healing. We are to await details of her plan."

Some ancient reporting instinct surfaced, or maybe it was a memory of a Franklin dream, and I struggled with how to phrase my question.

"Don't take this the wrong way," I said, "but is there any chance, that, you know—"

"I'm hallucinating or on drugs?"

"Something like that."

"You can forget the drugs," Jennifer said, "because the strongest thing I've had since California is wine. As for hallucinating—I've obsessed over that, believing several times that I had to be. But then how to explain Mrs. Ricci?"

"Spontaneous remission," I said.

"The doctor told you how rare that would be," Jennifer said, "just two cases ever and one of them one obviously the work of Our Lady. As Mrs. Ricci herself declared, we must have faith. *Something* is happening here, Nick—don't tell me you don't feel it too."

This time, I didn't try to dodge the TV cameras. Jennifer had asked me to read a statement. It was six o'clock, top of the evening news.

"Jennifer wishes to convey the following," I began. " 'My daughter, Amber, has been in communication again with Mary the Mother of God, and the Blessed Virgin wishes everyone to hear the joyous news—that her love for all God's children is unlimited. Mrs. Ricci is proof of that love. Mary implores us to seek forgiveness for our sins, and to reject materialism. Now hear her exact words.' "

I read from Jennifer's Mary diary.

" 'Dear children! Today I call you to conversion. You are too concerned about material things and little about spiritual ones. Open your hearts and start again to work on your personal conversion. Decide every day to dedicate time to God and to prayer until prayer becomes a joyful meeting with God. Only in this way will your life have meaning and with joy will you contemplate eternal life. Thank you for responding to my call.' "

The questions erupted.

No, Amber had never spoken directly to me, I told the reporters. No, Jennifer did not intend to hold press conferences. Yes, I planned to be here every day from now on—if possible, at six p.m.—and I would share what I could.

"I'd like to say more," I finished, "but I'm afraid I can't; for the complete details, read my story tomorrow. *The Trib*: online, home-delivered, and in stores everywhere."

Hill had asked me to say that. I had no problem doing it: We'd taken a beating for so long from TV that it seemed justified.

Besides, the publisher had just given me use of a company car, a new Audi.

From then on, the phenomenon built, like a Category Five hurricane nearing land.

Cardinal Cruz announced that the Church was beginning an official investigation that could lead to confirmation of a miracle, and the Massachusetts Speaker of the House, Ronald Mariano, an Italian American, made a highly publicized visit to Middleton with former Congressman Joseph P. Kennedy II, scion of America's storied Catholic family. Mayor Michelle Wu visited. Matt Damon, Steve Carrell, Denis Leary, and Bob Kraft were among the celebrities with Massachusetts ties who made the journey. Stephen Colbert, a practicing Catholic, taped a segment of his show from in front of Jennifer's house. Luke Turner, developer of the Minuteman Mall, visited with his wife, Elizabeth, a devout Catholic who had made pilgrimages to Medjugorje, Fatima, and Lourdes.

Out-of-towners streamed in, too: Kim Kardashian, Tim Tebow, a Calvin Klein model who claimed to have found Jesus. Tom Brady and wife Giselle Bundchen, both Catholics and both still married, flew up from Tampa Bay. Reporters from mainstream publications, including *The New York Times*, *Washington Post*, *Wall Street Journal*, *The Atlantic* and *Huff Post*, came. L'Osservatore Romano flew in a correspondent from Rome, joining reporters from France, Spain, Portugal, Mexico, Poland, Brazil, and the Philippines. The Associated Press sent a reporter. The list went on.

And me—I had free reign with my stories, which wasn't as welcome as it sounded.

Some days, according to Jennifer's diary, Amber was loquacious, speaking of the depth of Mary's love, the need to reject materialism, the eternal reward awaiting the faithful in heaven. Those stories wrote themselves.

But other days, Amber was mute, and I was reduced to briefing the media at six and writing crowd pieces—glorified man-on-the-streets. I wrote stories about the media presence, Mayor Wu, Stephen Colbert, and a self-proclaimed "seer" who insisted on his Web site that he had detected a cirrostratus cloud formation in the shape of Jesus hovering high above Middleton. This man was obsessed with chemtrails and the fantasy that COVID vaccines contained nanoparticles that allowed the U.S. government to read an inoculated individual's thoughts. He and his garbage did not belong in any reputable newspaper, but when Hill found him online, he ordered me to write a story.

He sent me an email overloaded with exclamation marks when it passed 100,000 page views, which it did in fewer than three hours.

But no more miracles. If Mary had designs, as Amber had stated, she was taking her time.

The masses scarcely cared. The word "miracle" was out there now, swirling through the public consciousness—and like the proverbial genie from the bottle, there was no putting it back. The appetite for Mary News was unquenchable. The Nielsens confirmed a huge bump in ratings for every local station that broadcast Mary stories. *The Trib*'s print circulation continued to rocket, new subscriptions continued to climb, and the analytics set yet more records. Advertisers we'd lost swarmed back. And Chamberlain announced a paid day off for every employee who'd played a role in Mary News.

A giddy Danny D'Ermo, SuperGoodMedia's SuperOptimizerSupervisor, our SOS, took the trends as an opportunity to convene a "Super Special!" virtual meeting.

To state that D'Ermo was loathed would fail to properly capture the newsroom staff's feelings for him. He had no journalism experience, only employment at eBay followed by employment at PayPal followed by a stint at Uber and then Zillow before Chamberlain hired him. His LinkedIn account, which chronicled his career, boasted of him being "exemplary" and "multiply awarded" with a bundle of "skills," and it was rich with endorsements from prominent people... if any of it was real, that is.

D'Ermo himself didn't seem real.

Monotonous and humorless, he looked, moved, and spoke robotically, like a Matrix sentinel—minus the tentacles but equally nightmarish. We only ever saw his balloonish head, framed by one of those app-generated fake backgrounds that made you wonder what he was hiding (we soon found out).

His appearances, at least, had comic value for me, Destiny, Bud, Terry, and others in our circle. We spent most of his Teams Meetings sessions half-listening to him and group-texting our observations.

"I wish this guy would explode, leaving no trace behind," was one of Bud's texts. "I hate him."

"Hope he doesn't have kids," Destiny wrote. "Beyond hating him, they'd need psychiatric care for life, the poor things."

"He's definitely not real," Terry Winters texted. "Seth MacFarlane created him. We'll be seeing him soon on *Family Guy.*"

"Or on the news when they find the bones in his cellar," I responded.

"How many times do you think he's been called an asshole?" Destiny texted.

"To his face or behind his back?" I responded.

"Both," Destiny responded.

"At least 10,000," Bud wrote.

"And that's just since last month," Terry wrote.

Almost as annoying as his screen presence were his weekly spreadsheets, individualized and then sent in aggregate to everyone. These included data for views, engagements and how many subscriptions each story had generated. Subscriptions were labeled "subs," and the prize was "Super Sub wins," a story that had brought in fifty or more new subscriptions. Ten to forty-nine came under "wins," five to nine were "lackluster," and anything fewer than five was "pathetic, send out an SOS."

Like schoolchildren, our performance had been reduced to report cards.

Beyond what was on LinkedIn, we could find little about Danny. He wasn't on Facebook, Twitter, or Instagram, nor in any Florida voter, property, or motor vehicle registry. Terry Winters inquired of his sources, but they had nothing, either. Google and *Ancestry.com* searches of his surname turned up several D'Ermos in the U.S., but none in Florida. Destiny, however, did discover that the Russian word for shit, дерьмо, was phonetically translated as der'mo.

And here I must confess that with Mary News, I had become the only member of the Super Sub Wins club. My stories brought in so many new subscriptions that Danny created a new category, Super Stratospheric. I was the only journalist at all of SGM's properties to belong.

When that was trumpeted in an email blast, I texted Destiny: "I'm ashamed."

"Shame is insufficient," she replied. "You should be mortified."

As for Jennifer, she was holding up. The donations to her GoFundMe account continued to increase, allowing her to erase the remainder of her debt and then some. The local stations found old clips from *Do Not Disturb* and Jennifer's other shows, and she got a kick out of watching them. Her biggest complaint was being a prisoner in her own home.

One moonlit night, Jennifer hired a private nurse for Amber and snuck out of her house, taking a secluded path along Middleton Pond to where I was waiting on a back road in my new Audi.

"Sweet!" Jennifer said when she got it.

"I felt weird accepting it," I said.

"Tell me you'd rather drive that old shitbox," Jennifer said.

"That would be a lie," I said.

We drove north to Portsmouth, New Hampshire, to a small restaurant we figured would afford us privacy. It did—until dessert, when a middle-aged couple recognized us. After pointing and whispering, they finally approached us for autographs. We signed on a paper napkin.

"Isn't life strange," Jennifer said. "The whole time I was in Hollywood, no one ever asked."

As we waited for the tab, Jennifer was lost in thought.

"I'd like to see where you work," she finally said.

"*The Trib*?"

"Do you have another job?"

"Why?" I said.

"Because it's been so much a part of your identity," Jennifer said. "Your identity all these years we've been apart."

"The place is a shadow of its former self," I said.

"I'm OK with shadows," Jennifer said. "I live in them."

"It's almost eleven," I said, "you sure you don't want to go home?

"I'm sure. The nurse is on duty until seven in the morning."

Memory brought me back to *The Trib* when I arrived as a young man.

It was a four-story brick building on Tremont Street, about equidistant between the State House and City Hall and within short walking distance of Granary Burying Ground—where John Hancock, Robert Treat Paine, and Samuel Adams, all signatories to the Declaration of Independence, are interred—and Boston Common and the Public Garden. I had many happy memories of visiting all those places with my father when I was a kid.

You entered *The Trib* through an ornate lobby, where a kindly guard could direct you to the newsroom, features, sports, photography, the publisher's suite, marketing, circulation, classified and display advertising, the cafeteria, auditorium, and presses, which occupied all of a first-floor wing. I don't know exactly how many people *The Trib* employed, but it was well into the hundreds. The place buzzed with industry and purpose.

It was, looking back, a shrine.

Now, it was largely a haunted house, with entire floors vacant. One of Terry Winters' sources had told him that Chamberlain was secretly trying to sell it to any developer willing to pay the premium for the location—surely hundreds of millions of dollars. Terry had been unable to confirm his source's story, but it rang true to him. Once the sale was concluded, like many other dying papers we would be relocated to a rented office in a cheesy suburban mall. Maybe Lynn. At least Bud wouldn't have to move far.

We arrived at *The Trib* shortly after 1 a.m. The paper was empty. No nanny cams had been installed during our heyday, nor during the decline, so there would be no record of our visit except for that left by my cardkey. It was unlikely I would be monitored, but in the event I was, I could remind Hill about the virtually twenty-four-hour demands of Mary News.

"We used to have an army of reporters who kept city and town politicians in line," I said when we'd finished the tour. "Informing citizens and protecting democracy were what the Founding Fathers had in mind with the First Amendment. Except for my friends Bud and Destiny and a handful of others, all of those local reporters are gone."

"That's not right," Jennifer said.

"We used to have movie and TV writers, too, but no more. We had a book critic and a book editor and now we have freelanced reviews, $25 apiece, which run in the Sunday print edition—probably not for much longer—but not online per order of our SuperOptimizerSupervisor."

"Your what?"

"The creep who tracks clicks. Book reviews don't get any, he claims."

"Maybe people aren't reading books much anymore," Jennifer said.

"But they are. More than ever during the pandemic. Audio and e-book editions are hot and hardcovers have held their own."

"Does your super-whatever know that?"

"Doubtful. He doesn't know shit about anything. Back in the day, we also had a magazine with an editor and a staff, and we had a sports department with more than two dozen reporters and editors. All gone."

"There seriously is no sports department anymore?" Jennifer said.

"If you want to call it that, which I wouldn't," I said. "We have a sports editor and one writer who covers the Sox—home games only and no trips to spring training. The rest is AP and high school coaches sending scorecards."

"No one at *The Trib* covers the Pats now?"

"No one."

"The Bruins?"

"No one."

"Celtics?"

"No one."

"Wow, you weren't kidding about slow death," Jennifer said.

"Welcome to the funeral home," I said. "Come on, let's get out of here."

I headed toward the door, but Jennifer didn't follow.

"Speaking of death, don't you have a morgue?" she said. "The place where old articles and photos are kept? They're always in the basement, at least in the movies.Please take me there.What visit to a funeral home would be complete without a peek inside the morgue?"

INT. TRIB MORGUE—PAST MIDNIGHT

Nick leads Jennifer down a dimly lit staircase and then through an enormous maze of file cabinets and shelves. It's a god-awful dirty, dusty, dark mess. The bowels of the building, with leaking water dripping and rats scurrying.

                          JENNIFER
                          Creepy.

                          NICK
                       Hence the name.

                          JENNIFER
                    Who comes down here?

                          NICK
                          No one.

Jennifer opens a few drawers and looks at yellowed clippings and
                    black-and-white photos.

                          JENNIFER
                   How many photos do you think are
                          down here?

                          NICK
                  Hundreds of thousands. Millions if you
                       count the negatives.

                          JENNIFER
                  They must have incredible historical
                          value.

NICK
They do.

JENNIFER
They're rotting. I see mold. Can
they be saved?

NICK
Most of them, yes. We used to have librarians who
would know how. But they've all been let go.

JENNIFER
Why not donate them to a historical
society?

NICK
Our old publisher looked into that.
No organization had the money for such
a big job and the publisher refused to
underwrite the cost.

JENNIFER
So what happens now?

NICK
SGM will sell the building and the
new owner will hire a disposal
company to take everything to the landfill.

JENNIFER
You're kidding.

NICK
Do I sound like I'm kidding?

JENNIFER
That's fucked up.

NICK
History means nothing to these pricks.
Only clicks do. And it's not just
photographs that are lost. With every
layoff and firing, institutional memory
is gone, too. And that, unlike photographs,
can never be restored.

A long pause, as the weight of what will happen to this priceless archive
settles on them.

JENNIFER
So what happened?

NICK
To a newspaper that once was a shiny
beacon on a hill, if you'll allow me
a bad pun?

JENNIFER
No, not that. I know that story. What
happened to us?

NICK
What do you mean?

JENNIFER
You know what I mean. When you
dumped me.

NICK
We were young.

JENNIFER
So?

Nick is visibly uncomfortable.

JENNIFER
Young people can't stay in love?
We talked about marrying and
starting a family.

NICK
Is that what you really wanted?

JENNIFER
I really wanted you, Nick. Wanted
to wake up next to you every day for
the rest of my life. You said you
wanted that, too.

NICK
I was an asshole.

JENNIFER
No, but you weren't very nice.
Never returned a phone call or
email after I moved to L.A. Not one.

NICK
Like I said, I was an asshole.

Another long pause.

JENNIFER
Kiss me, Nick. Like before.

They kiss passionately.

Two months after being summoned to the auditorium to learn about the sale to SuperGoodMedia, Hill brought us back upstairs for what he called his first annual "State of the Paper Address."

We filed in—cheerlessly, again. No new reporters had joined the staff but Hill had hired new managers. Among them was the new Chief of Visuals: John Wright, who was in charge of photography, graphics, typography, and the overall look of the product, as managers now called newspapers.

Wright seemed a nice man—but he'd never worked for a publication of any kind, let alone a newspaper. A graduate of the Rhode Island School of Design, he came to *The Trib* from Honda, where his claim to fame was a bit role in the look of the new Accord. Wright believed that the traditional broadsheet was outmoded, and so he'd embarked on a study of a replacement. He wasn't thinking tabloid. He'd said that maybe a newspaper should be oval—or a different shape every day of the week, sedan-contoured on Thursdays, for example, when our auto section ran, or house-shaped on Sundays, when our real-estate section was published. Wright believed newsprint should be colored—maybe beige, with green for ad pages, wink-wink.

Then there was Katy Stein, the new head of circulation. She'd started at one of SuperGoodMedia's Web sites but soon jumped to the Interactive Division in Orlando, where she'd managed New Ventures. In Boston now, Stein put little stock in the traditional tools of circulation-building: radio and TV spots, billboards, and house ads. Twenty-nine years old, she believed in giveaways—free movie and concert tickets, free oil and filter changes, free pizzas with all the toppings to anyone subscribing to home delivery. She believed in hype and she'd had no trouble convincing Hill to sponsor a Midnight Madness shopping spree, a live broadcast of a local talk show, and a bungee-jumping contest from a construction crane in our parking lot—all of which the publisher played on Page One.

And then there was Paula Orton, the person Hill hired from Ernst & Young to be senior vice president of operations.

Thirty-two years old, Orton was athletic, a woman who, like Hill, ran marathons. Only her forced smile and cold eyes gave any clue into her true nature, which was sociopathic as best we could tell, given her delight in slashing budgets and absence of a sense of humor. Orton had issued new guidelines calling for pre-authorization of any expenditure over a dollar. She and her staff tracked phone and Internet use, sending emails requiring us to explain anything they deemed questionable.

During his State of The Paper address, Hill outlined his contest for a new slogan.

Open to all readers, it had been heavily promoted on social media, in house ads, and feature stories, and on drive-time radio—and had generated an enthusiastic response, undoubtedly because the top prize was an iPhone 13 with free AT&T service for life.

"Off the record," Hill said, "I like the one from the woman in Hyannis: 'All the GOOD News That's Fit to Print.' "

Of course he did. Hill hadn't been in town a week when, in the first editorial *The Trib* had ever published on the front page, he'd spelled out the new SGM policy. Henceforth, he'd informed our readers, "No disturbing stories or photos will ever again appear in our newspaper. Let those with prurient interest turn elsewhere because we believe in a strong sense of responsibility to our children and to society. Without compromising our long and proud tradition of journalistic excellence, we pledge to make *The Daily Tribune* a true family product. You are family and so are we!"

"So, he took off the cape and now he's Sister Sledge?" Destiny had cracked when she read that.

Internally, Hill had distributed a memo further defining his concept of news and encouraging us to aggressively pursue that which he deemed "good."

He wrote: "By no means do we intend to abdicate our role as our readers' primary, comprehensive, and most reliable source of information in a rapidly changing world. This is what our chairman means when he talks about our role as the bedrock of democracy. We will continue to cover politics, within reason. Next year's mid-terms remain important, but unless something truly earth-shattering happens, we'll be playing those stories inside. Ditto the wrangling over Biden's agenda. Ditto COVID, unless it's stories of miraculous recoveries or a date certain of when life returns to normal.

"Caught up as they are in the demands of daily living, our readers have a right to expect a degree of pleasure if not delight from their hometown newspaper each and every day. Think of us, if you will, as an oasis of joy in a desert of woe. And so I urge you to leave your old notions behind and bring to our pages hometown heroes, fiftieth-anniversary couples, brides and grooms, lottery winners, newborn triplets (or more, ha-ha!), First Communicants, flower show winners, giant pumpkin growers, Soap Box Derbyists, beauty pageant contestants, etc. etc. Always remember: Good News Rules!"

And Hill wanted all this delivered with a personal touch.

"In keeping with our exciting new direction," Hill said, "I'm thinking of replacing bylines with something more customer friendly."

We had no clue what he meant.

" 'By so-and-so' sounds so impersonal," Hill explained. "To use Nick as an example, imagine if we replaced the byline with 'Your friend Nick Nolan prepared this for you' or 'Your buddy Nick Nolan hopes this story makes your day' or 'SuperWriter Nick Nolan crafted this with loving care.'"

Hill prattled on some more and then his State of the Paper address wound down.

"Soon, the moment you've all been waiting for," he said. "Our first Employee of the Month award. But first, something super-special!"

The screen behind him lit up.

There was Chamberlain, in his Orlando office. CMO Ron Hawkins was with him.

"Surprise, surprise!" Chamberlain said. "But nothing like the *real* surprise. My dear Super Gooders, I present to you the one and only Mark Zuckerberg. Applause, please!"

No one clapped.

The big screen shifted from Chamberlain's office to what presumably was Zuckerberg's in Menlo Park, California. Zuckerberg and David M. Wehner, Facebook's CFO, appeared. This was just days before Zuckerberg announced Facebook had become Meta.

Chamberlain could still be seen on a smaller screen, bottom lower right.

He was trembling with excitement.

"Do I know you?" Zuckerberg said.

"Not personally, but what an honor it is to have you speak to us!" Chamberlain said.

Wehner looked perplexed.

"I'm sorry, mister… what did you say your name was?" he said.

"David. David Chamberlain! Thanks for agreeing to speak with us!"

"There's been a mistake," Wehner said. "Sorry, Mark. Wrong call. Thank you for your time, Mr. Whoever. We'll be in touch."

The Facebook screen went blank.

But in a tech glitch from the gods, the audio remained on.

"Who the fuck was that?" Zuckerberg said.

"CEO of some newspaper chain called SuperGoodMedia," Wehner said.

"Never heard of it."

"Neither had I until his people began bugging the shit out of us. Not happy with what we pay for their content."

"And that is?"

"A hundredth of a cent per article."

"I'm Googling them now," Zuckerberg said.

The auditorium was silent. I saw furtive smiles on some faces.

"Seems they're a bunch of weeklies and dailies no one reads," Zuckerberg continued. "One of them is *The Boston Daily Tribune*. Used to see it when I was at Harvard. Great newspaper then, but I wouldn't line the bottom of a bird cage with it now. No upside in insulting birds."

"Right," Wehner said. "Or fish."

"Don't get back to them," Zuckerberg said, "and stop using and paying for their content. We didn't get here by subsidizing losers."

"Got it."

"One more thing," Zuckerberg said. "Do we give them money through the Facebook Journalism Project?"

"Yes," said Wehner. "And they keep coming back for more."

"They all do," Zuckerberg said. "When they're not busy publishing stories about antitrust suits against us, they've got their grubby little hands out."

"You got that right."

"While we're on the subject, I want you to kill the whole damn Journalism Project," Zuckerberg said. "Talk about throwing good money after bad."

"Done."

"How did this happen, getting patched into some moron's meeting like I was the guest speaker or something?" Zuckerberg said.

"It was on the schedule," Wehner said. "Your personal assistant put it there."

"The new AI one?"

"Yes."

"Still too many bugs," Zuckerberg said. "Get engineering to work them out. And get back an actual person for me until they are. We can't have fuckups like this as we transition to Meta. Our stock price is too important and so is my time. I waste too much of it as it is in depositions and Congressional appearances."

Chamberlain squirmed in his seat, then regained composure.

"As you have just witnessed," he said, "even the best laid plans of mice and men sometimes go awry. But fret not, my SuperGooders. We have much to celebrate, starting with this year's Very Best of SGM winners—those stories, photos, and videos that showcase the super things we together can achieve! Ron, please roll the tape."

A cascade of images set to rousing music appeared—the winning stories, photos, and videos together with headshots of the journalists who'd produced them.

We recognized none of them.

"Shit," Hawkins said. "That was the 2019 winners. I screwed up."

"We'll be having a little talk when we're done here," Chamberlain said.

"I found the right one," Hawkins said.

"Play it."

Hawkins rolled another tape featuring winners for 2020, before SGM bought *The Trib*. Again, we recognized no one, but their lightweight stories foretold our future.

"Congratulations, everyone," Chamberlain said. "But before we go, let me announce that nominations are now open for our 2021 Very Best of SGM Awards. You will find all of the categories in an email you will soon receive but let me present a few highlights now. Ron, roll that tape. The right one this time."

We watched as the so-called "highlights" were described. They included:

• Reader Obsession Award
Open to employees who are "super-focused on providing an exceptional multi-media experience and always going the extra mile in hooking readers because new subscriptions and clicks are their only passion in life," Chamberlain said.

• Energizer Award
"No, SuperGooders, this is NOT a battery award! These nominees have found a dazzling new revenue stream (legal, please!) by Super-charging systems and Super-leveraging data to boost subscription retention."

• Heart Values Award
"These gifted nominees personify SGM's core values—clicks, analytics, and revenue, revenue, revenue—and tirelessly promote themselves internally and externally, empowering those around them. Those who aren't green with envy, that is!"

• And the highest award: S.U.P.E.R.G.O.O.D.M.E.D.I.A.S.T.A.R
Chamberlain spelled it out: "Some Unusually Perfect Employee Recognized Greatly [as the] One [and] Only Dominant Mesmerizing Excellent Dynamic Individualistic Agreeable Superb Terrific Adventurous Royal."
The screen went dark, but before Orlando signed off altogether, we heard Chamberlain threatening to fire Hawkins.

"So now, our first Employee of the Month winner," Hill said. "To confirm just how important this award is, I have decided to name it the Benjamin Franklin Good News of the Month Trophy. Yes, *that* Ben Franklin."
He reached into the podium and brought out a statuette of Franklin.
"Before I name our inaugural winner," Hill said, "let me show you something. Lights down, please."
The auditorium darkened and a chart appeared on the screen. It showed single copy sales and new print subscriptions compared to the year prior: all told, circulation had jumped by more than 75,000. If I had to guess, with the exceptions perhaps of *The New York Times* and *Washington Post*, no paper anywhere in America during the last decade had experienced such a dramatic rise in such a short period of time. Certainly, no paper of our size.

Hill projected another chart, this one with the Google Analytics. Here, too, the numbers were extraordinary. They trounced Go Topless Day Draws Hundreds, Giant Rabbit Hops Across Wyoming, Arrives Hungry in Idaho, and the rest of the previous leaders.

"Roll the video, please," said Hill.

The chart was replaced by a clip of Greta Ricci. The camera drew back, revealing the crowd in front of Jennifer's.

Hill said: "You may be asking yourselves: what do these have in common?"

The clip segued to video of me giving a six o'clock briefing.

"The answer, of course, is our very own Nick Nolan. My fellow Tribbers—let's have a hearty round of applause for *The Daily Tribune's* first employee of the month!"

The applause was less than deafening.

"Nick," Hill said, "would you please join me at the podium so that I may present you your trophy and your ten $100 bills, which of course have the image of Franklin."

He also had a custom Superman t-shirt for me.

My face was on the back.

The Ben Franklin character and I were still at Christ Church Burial Ground when my third dream began.

"I wish I could congratulate you," the Ben Franklin character said, "but the truth is I nearly vomited when I learned of my name on that award. Such an insult. The Edward Smith Trophy would have been much more appropriate."

I did not get the reference.

"Captain of the Titanic," Franklin said.

"That's harsh."

"Would you have preferred the Doctor Doom Award? Sorry, my lad, but as we have discussed, sometimes the truth hurts. But it is what it is. And it's not what it's not."

He smiled.

I stared at him blankly.

"Well?" he said. "Aren't you impressed?"

"By what?"

"By turning that expression on its head. 'It is what it is' becomes 'it isn't what it isn't.' We could also go future tense, as in 'it will be what it will be' and 'it won't be what it won't' Or past tense: 'it wasn't what it wasn't.' Or how about future perfect: 'it won't have been what it won't have.' Genius! I always did have a way with words. Speaking of which, we're here to discuss *your* words. But if you will suffer me, I'd like to return to Trump for a moment."

"You seem obsessed with him," I said.

"What good patriot isn't?" he said. "I refer not, needless to say, to the Proud Boys. If anything good can come from the January 6 insurrection, it will be life without parole for them, followed by eternal flames in the afterlife, where they join Benedict Arnold. Same for the Oath Keepers and the rest of their ilk. As we know, keeping ahead of right-wing extremists is a game of Whack-A-Mole. Don't know if we'll ever win."

"You were talking about Trump," I said.

"Oh, right. DeSantis and Pence make noise, but it looks like Trump still has a lock on the Republican nomination in 2024. Remember that term 'sheeple,' which people with tiny so-called brains thought was so clever? Well that's the Grand Old Party today. And old certainly fits. How old is McConnell? Ninety-five? One hundred?"

"Eighty," I said.

"Too old," the Franklin character said.

"You lived to 84 and were productive until the end," I said.

"Yes, but that was me. We're talking about Trump. In 2016, he lost the popular vote but won the electoral college. Another one of our really stupid ideas, the college. College of idiots it proved to be. Wish we'd not put it in the Constitution. My theory on how Trump pulled it off: Putin. Not a news flash, but it's the best theory I have. Sixty-three million voters couldn't really have believed someone whose most famous line was 'you're fired' was equipped to be president."

"You underestimate stupidity," I said. "Have you ever been to a NASCAR race?"

"As a matter of fact, I have," the Ben Franklin character said. "Talladega this year. I was rooting for Bubba Wallace."

"I mean the crowd," I said.

"I admit I did not see any brain surgeons in the infield," he said. "But I have studied the 2016 political polling. Along with the conservatives, many well-educated voters cast their ballots for Trump. Plus people who were just plain sick of the system—the system I helped create, mind you."

"Don't forget the Christian right," I said.

"Don't even get me going," the Ben Franklin character said. "Okay, let's get into the second mission. Support in writing your book. I do have a bit of experience there, as you know. First step?"

"Outline," I said.

"Wrong. First step: a topic. Which, as I mentioned, should be the sorry state of the newspaper business today. You have witnessed a lot. But don't make it a memoir or exposé. Remember what Ralph Waldo Emerson is believed to have said: 'Fiction reveals truth that reality obscures.' "

"Can't quibble with that," I said.

"So now that the topic is settled, you must brainstorm," the Franklin character said. "The characters, the plot points, the inanities, the whole nine yards. Take notes when ideas occur to you. When you get further along and a narrative begins to reveal itself, put ego aside, allow someone you trust to be honest to read what you have, and listen carefully. And it need not be a writer. In fact, I recommend that it be not. Read King's 'On Writing' again—and again. Also again, Dan Barry."

"Fair enough," I said.

"Second, write every day for at least an hour. I recommend early, before the daily slog begins and your brain is freshly caffeinated. Thirdly, do not bring me into it. The critics will crucify you if you mention our meetings."

"I don't care about critics," I said.

"You should," the man said. "I can hear them now: 'Cheap literary device.' 'Seriously, a series of *dreams*?' 'Should have stuck with socks.' Fourth step: use the diary you are keeping as the beginning of the outline. And make sure you back everything up. I can't tell you how many writers have lost material when their computers crashed."

"Maybe I should write it longhand," I said.

"Don't be ridiculous; Updike you're not. Fifth and final step, get yourself a thesaurus. I recommend Roget's. You are just killing me with your overuse of 'moron,' 'idiot,' 'clown,' and the like. How about 'imbecile'? Or 'nincompoop'? 'Chump'? 'Dolt'? 'Ninny'? The English language is loaded with such synonyms. Your book will be filled with blubberheads and putzes. Be creative in describing them."

"Are you done?" I said.

"For now. But trust I shall be available to you as you get deeper into your book."

"I can hardly wait."

"There is no need to be snide," the Ben Franklin character said.

"I wasn't being snide," I said.

And I wasn't. I needed all the help I could get.

"That's it for now on your masterpiece," the man said. "As you will recall, my third mission is guidance on your romantic life."

"Good luck with that," I said.

"Eventually, your divorce will be finalized," he said. "That chapter will close. In the meantime, steer clear of online flirtation."

"Tinder, you mean."

"Goodness, no. A tawdry site at best—and how shall I best put this, one that is not exactly for a man of your... ah, circumstances."

"What a relief," I said. "You *did* detect the sarcasm in my voice."

"I did. I refer to eHarmony, Match, and the rest of the above-board sites. Don't waste your money. Trust me, I took a trial run on a few of them and what they connected me to was mostly hussies and cracks."

"What?"

"Prostitutes. No rum morts."

"Which are?"

"Great ladies. Of course, I must say not many women of any ilk are clamoring for a penniless octogenarian."

"I thought you died a wealthy man."

"You can't take it with you when you go."

"You really believed a dating site was for you?"

"No, it was mere curiosity. But back to you. Sometimes what we are looking for is right under our nose."

"Jennifer."

"Yes! You two were meant for each other, Nick. You know it. You felt it on first meeting and you feel it now that she is back in your life. I rest my case with that morgue scene. Now *that* was a sort of Tinder moment. If only it had ended with…. Well, you know what. But more opportunity will present, I am certain."

I had no response.

The man said: "At the risk of digressing—"

"—again."

"Yes, again. Is there anything I should know about Bud and Destiny?"

"What do you mean?"

"They seem awfully interested in me," the man said.

"Like me, they respect what you did to establish a free press," I said.

"Please thank them."

"I will."

"What wonderful senses of humor you three have, particularly once the ale is flowing. I laughed myself silly over that 'connection' conversation at Ernie's. Have you ever thought of stand-up? A one-woman, two-man act? 'Destiny Calling,' you could label yourselves."

"And you claim I am the silly one."

"Touché. Did you know I became fluent in French when I was across the pond?"

"Don't we have a more important matter to consider?" I said. "You promised me a big scoop. 'Tip of the Century.' Those were your exact words."

"I did, didn't I?" the man said. "You're probably thinking I have Trump's tax returns. Or a copy of the pee tape. Sorry to disappoint you. It's neither of those."

"So what is it?"

"Follow me," the man said.

We left the burial ground and headed toward Independence Hall.

I'd like to say my newfound clout inspired me to revisit what Destiny called the basics in my next column. The truth was less laudable.

The truth was, Amber had entered another of her mute periods, and I'd maxed out on crowd pieces and celebrity pilgrims. I was back to old emails and dog-eared folders when one day at noon the guard called to announce a visitor. I went into the lobby to greet her.

"Well, if it isn't the media star himself!" said Rose Redwing Brown. "Can't turn the TV on any more without seeing your face. Happy to see it, I would add."

"Hello, Rose," I said. "It's been a long time."

"Way too long," Rose said. "Hug?"

"You're vaccinated, right?"

"Like I'd be one of those despicable antivaxxers? Of course I am. With Pfizer—three jabs, counting my booster."

"Kindred spirits," I said. "That's me, too. Want to see my card?"

"Don't be an idiot," Rose said. "Just give me a damn hug."

We embraced. I hadn't talked to Rose in a long while, but I never forgot her. More than anyone except perhaps Jones, my early mentor, she'd help launch my career.

"Have you eaten?" I said.

"No, and I'm starved."

"Shall we do Ernie's?"

"Where else?"

We headed toward the bar, which served a mean chicken salad sandwich and the best fries in town.

Rose was a powerful link to my past—the central character in "Nipmuc Nation: Here first, Native Americans work to bring the real story of Mass. to the masses." That series was the second of my three Pulitzer finalists, in the Local Reporting category. The third was "The Growing Season: Frank Beazley and the Meaning of Life," about a man who was paralyzed from the neck down. Living in a state institution, Beazley, now deceased, became an artist, poet, and extraordinary inspiration to people who lived with disabilities—and people who did not. His State House testimony had helped enact landmark legislation and raise social service budgets.

Rose was a member of the Nipmuc tribe, which had lived in parts of Massachusetts, Connecticut, and Rhode Island before European settlers had appropriated their land and decimated their people with violence and disease. After teaching at an inner-city high school, Rose had left the classroom to lead a campaign to educate students and the general public regarding the truth about the Pilgrims, Plymouth Rock, and the first Thanksgiving, and the untold history of New England Natives before and after whites arrived.

A Christopher Columbus fan she was not—and that, along with her lessons of genocide in New England and around the nation had angered nitwits who refused to accept the historical roots and contemporary existence of systemic racism against Natives and all people of color. Pilloried on social media by the keyboard cowards and on talk radio by right-wing hosts and racist callers, Rose was not deterred, even when the death threats began.

Her campaign caught fire and by the time I wrote about her she had been able to change the curricula in many elementary and high schools, and she had succeeded in lobbying for a legislative commission, "Indigenous in Our State," although its work had been slowed by opposition from Republican state representatives and senators. The commission eventually wrote bills making teaching of Native and Black history mandatory in state public schools, and while districts complied to varying degrees, it was a start. Rose established an educational foundation to broaden the work and that's when I'd lost track of her.

We took a window seat at Ernie's, ordered lunch, and told the waiter to prepare warm apple pie with vanilla ice cream for dessert.

"No guilt trip, Nick," Rose said, "but how come you stopped returning my calls?"

"I'm sorry. I honestly am. A lot of shit was going down."

"Like socks?"

Rose laughed.

"Where *do* they go?" she said.

Had I become the subject of a snarky Facebook group? I was getting awfully tired of that damn line.

"Joke," Rose said. "Sorry. I didn't mean to offend you."

"Knowing you," I said, "I'm guessing you have something more pressing than bad columns you want to bring attention to," I said. "I'm all ears, as Ross Perot used to say."

Rose laughed.

"Good to see you haven't lost your sophomoric sense of humor," she said. "Possessing one of my own, I always loved that about you. So let me get to the point. Three years ago, I turned fifty. I don't believe you've hit that milestone."

"Not yet, but I'm close."

"I didn't expect any mid-life crisis, and there wasn't one," Rose said. "But my kids had graduated college and left home to start their careers— Dawn in medicine and Nkéke in law—"

"—Congratulations!"

"Thank you. Very proud of them. As the months passed, I felt an intensifying urge to change course. The foundation was in capable hands and I stepped down as president and CEO, though I remain on the board. More months passed and then the Creator visited me in a dream. 'Mother earth suffers,' the Creator said. 'All must help.' I took that as the sign I'd been seeking. For the last year, I have been laying the groundwork for another foundation I will soon launch."

"And you'd like some press," I said. "You've got it."

"Don't you want details?" Rose said.

"Yes, but if your name is on it, I'm in."

"I'm leaving directly Indigenous work for something of urgent importance to every life form on the planet," she said.

"Climate change," I said.

"Exactly. The Creator has called me to use my skills to do my part. I have incorporated a new foundation and raised one hundred million dollars from a benefactor whose name you will recognize when it is announced."

"Bezos?" I said.

"Would I accept money from a union-crushing billionaire? Never. Think software."

"Gates."

"Yes, him. We'll have our first office in Boston, and eventually open a headquarters in Washington."

"It sounds incredible," I said.

"It is," Rose agreed. "Now that I have funding, I need publicity to begin recruiting staff and citizen supporters."

I got my notebook and cell phone out.

"You're on," I said.

I wasn't surprised that they ran my story on Rose Redwing Brown inside metro/region, especially in light of the play they'd given Destiny Carter's magnificent first installment of "The New Disparities."

They'd kept that in the business section, where Destiny had argued it didn't belong.

A few people complimented me on Rose's story, including Destiny and Bud.

But no one else said anything, save for Danny D'Ermo, who sent the staff an email with three words: "No more Indigenous." It was accompanied by a chart showing that the story logged less than five percent of overall page views that day.

The leader that day?

"Man Orders Pizza Every Day For 10 Years Until Employees Realize Something Is Very Wrong (But Was He Dead?!)"

CHAPTER FIVE: PERCEIVED MOTION

I was headed into Jennifer's house one afternoon in late October when I saw Henry Spinelli being interviewed by a mob of broadcast journalists.

I'd interviewed Spinelli for a recent Mary column, a bulleted roundup of sick and dying pilgrims. Living with advanced multiple sclerosis, Spinelli needed a motorized wheelchair for mobility; his doctor, he maintained, had declared he'd never walk again. Spinelli's brother had driven him up from his home in Manhattan in a handicapped-accessible van. The two men kept their vigil at a shrine they'd erected alongside the vehicle.

When TV had finished with him, I interviewed Spinelli. He recounted what he'd told TV: last night at a quarter to midnight, after the reporters had left for the day, Jennifer had opened her door and asked a cop to help him into her house. According to Spinelli, Jennifer said "Mary has chosen" as she brought him to Amber.

"The instant I touched that little girl's hand," Spinelli told me, "I felt an electric charge."

"And then what?" I asked.

"I heard the voice of Mary—faint, like she was at the end of a long tunnel. 'Child of God,' she whispered, 'walk.' 'I can't,' I said. 'You must have faith,' Mary said. 'You can walk.' And I did. I fell at first, then Mrs. Abbott gave me support, and I left that little girl's room on my own legs. Praise be Jesus."

Spinelli was overjoyed—and I was stunned.

I also was pissed: for the first time, TV had beaten me.

The local stations broke in for a live report that afternoon before we could even post a breaking-news flash on *Trib.com*—and Spinelli's story led the evening news. About the only original angle I could offer in my next column was an interview with Spinelli's doctor, Carol H. Thomas, a neurologist at Brigham and Women's Hospital, who'd given me her cell number when I'd interviewed her after first meeting her patient.

I'd reached Thomas at about seven o'clock that evening.

She was not pleased.

"As I stated in our last conversation, one I now regret," she said, "Mr. Spinelli was wrong when he claimed I said he would never walk again.

As I told him and you neglected to mention, MS is an unpredictable disease, rife with ups and downs, good days and bad, setbacks and triumphs, as Mr. Spinelli himself so pointedly attests. In case your recollection is unclear, let me repeat my exact words: 'The longer Mr. Spinelli is immobilized, the *less likely* it is he will ever walk again.' A shade of difference, perhaps—but a difference, and a critical one."

"He walked today," I said. "I saw it myself."

"Which only proves the wisdom of what I said," Thomas said.

The call ended. What Thomas hadn't revealed was that she had sent Jones an email critical of my reporting. The moment Jones read it, not five minutes after I pushed the button on my column, he called me into his office.

When I recounted my interaction with Thomas, he seemed satisfied.

"If I put any more disclaimers in these columns," I said, "I may as well go write ad copy for vaping."

"Just be careful," said Jones. "Even if the publisher doesn't think so, we're on a slippery slope here. Speaking of Hill, he's called a planning meeting for next week. You're invited."

"What's he planning?"

" 'How to take Mary News to the next level,' to quote him. I didn't ask what he meant. I didn't want to know."

I left Jones's office and called Jennifer. She'd anticipated my displeasure at getting beat.

"I called you at home the second I got up this morning," she said, "honest I did. I tried several times. Texted, too. No answer."

It was possible. Unless I was expecting a call, I usually had my ringer off. There were not many people I wanted to hear from that autumn.

"Spinelli went on his own to TV," Jennifer said. "You know I would never give anyone else a scoop."

"It's okay."

"Anyway, you're in luck."

"Amber's spoken?"

"Less than fifteen minutes ago. The Blessed Virgin has asked to see Tony Callahan."

Callahan was another of the pilgrims I'd profiled. Thirty-eight years old, he suffered from chronic myelogenous leukemia, a painful and often fatal disease. After a second failed bone-marrow transplant at Johns Hopkins University Hospital in Baltimore, he'd been sent home to die. On morphine and in the care of an elderly mother, he'd reached Middleton on a bus.

"Has Callahan told TV?" I asked Jennifer.

"He swore he wouldn't tell a soul until after talking to you," said Jennifer.

"I suppose there's no way I could join him when he sees Amber."

"Maybe someday, Nick," said Jennifer, "but not now. This is still so sensitive. I'd hate to do anything to ruin it for these poor people. I hope you understand."

I told her I did.

"So, when will Mary see Callahan?" I said.

"Tonight at midnight."

"If the mother of God can do anything," I said, "why can't she keep better hours?"

We laughed and we were cool again.

We were about to end the call when I said: "This is going to sound very weird, but has Benjamin Franklin appeared in one of Amber's dreams?"

"You mean *the* Benjamin Franklin?"

"Yes, him."

"That may be the craziest question I've ever been asked," Jennifer said. "Of course not. What would make you think he did?"

"It's a long story," I said. "Long and boring."

"Maybe you can make it into a column!"

"I have much better material now."

"And for that, you can thank me with another kiss when I see you next," Jennifer said. "The memory of the morgue lingers."

A week later, after returning to Baltimore, Tony Callahan emailed me.

"I'm bursting to tell the whole world but I promised Jennifer I'd let you know first," he wrote. "So here it is: My white blood cell count has risen two days in a row! It's got a ways to go before they start talking 'spontaneous remission' (you know what word I'll use!) but this is fabulous good news!!! I've already asked my doctor if he'll speak with you and he said okay. Here's his number."

I called Callahan's doctor, listened to a lecture on the irresponsible and ignorant press, then broke the story the next morning in my column. I used the word "miracle" three times—but only when quoting Callahan.

The reaction was predictable. I had to park a quarter of a mile from Jennifer's house when I arrived that afternoon.

By now, many in the crowd knew me by sight. I couldn't move far without someone touching me—and begging for an audience with Amber and Jennifer.

"Please, Nick," said a woman whose face and head were bandaged. "Third-degree burns from a stove fire and now I'm septic. The doctors have been unable to stop it."

"God bless you," said a legless man in a wheelchair. "Type one diabetes. They say I'll soon be blind. If you could just get me to the door. Or slip me her number."

I did neither, and felt like shit as I walked away.

I was almost to the police tape when a boy of about twelve tugged at my sleeve. He had big eyes and a wide smile, and he was wearing a Tom Brady cap over a bald head, presumably from radiation or chemotherapy. I'd seen him before in the company of a woman who apparently was his mother.

"Don't you get bored coming here all the time?" the boy said. "I do. All it is is people standing around waiting for basically like nothing to happen."

"Jimmy!" the woman said. "Please forgive him, Mr. Nolan. He's unusually cranky today."

"But he's right," I said. "A lot of this *is* boring."

We made our introductions: This was Gina Pulaski and her only child, Jimmy, who had Wilms' tumor, a type of cancer. He'd already lost one kidney and the other was failing, the mother said. But for the moment, at least, Jimmy did not need to be hospitalized.

"Your columns are beautiful, Mr. Nolan," the mother said.

"Thank you."

"I don't think they're so cool," said the boy.

"Jimmy!"

"What I mean is they don't answer the questions."

"What questions?" I said.

"Like whether miracles really happen," Jimmy said. "You're the expert, Mr. Nolan. *Do* they really happen?"

I wasn't prepared for that, so I turned the question back on him.

"Why don't you tell me what you think," I said.

"I doubt it," the boy said.

I wasn't prepared for that, either.

"Why?" I said.

"Because if there were really miracles, wouldn't everyone get one? God isn't supposed to be mean, but picking out only a few people and basically screwing the rest *is* mean, don't you think?"

"I've told you, Jimmy, the Lord doesn't work that way," said Mrs. Pulaski. "Isn't that correct, Mr. Nolan?"

Jimmy didn't give me a chance to answer.

"If it really *was* Mary, she'd definitely help Amber," he said, "not leave her lying there like that. And that's a fact."

"Well, you certainly raise valid issues," I said.

I was suddenly uncomfortable—and not only because of Jimmy's questions, which had occurred to me but which I'd never deeply pondered; Nietzsche I wasn't. Unlike many boys his age, Jimmy moved with grace and what surely had been strength before he got sick; he obviously was into football, and I could picture him throwing the winning touchdown as the clock ran out. He had spunk, and he was smart.

He was the kind of kid I'd once believed I would have.

"Has Mary chosen?" I asked Jennifer when I finally reached her house.

The question took a moment to penetrate. Jennifer seemed out there, beyond mysterious again.

"No, Mary has not," she finally said.

"Too bad," I said. "I was hoping she'd asked for Jimmy Pulaski."

"Who's that?"

"A kid out there who has kidney cancer. He shows up every day with his mom. Wears a Tom Brady cap. I figured maybe you'd seen him."

"I haven't," Jennifer said. "What you should know is that while Mary has not chosen, she has spoken. Through Amber, she has delivered a message regarding Halloween. 'Abandon false idols,' Mary admonishes her children."

"You mean costumes?"

"And black cats and skeletons and all of the other trappings of paganism."

"Are jack-o-lanterns okay?" I said, half-jokingly.

Frankly, I was surprised the mother of God cared about Halloween when war and famine and COVID and climate change cruelly punished her children around the globe.

"With their fiendish faces," said Jennifer, "they are the very image of evil."

"Is candy bad, too?"

"Candy rots teeth."

"Mary is worried about *teeth*?"

"She didn't address them specifically," said Jennifer, "but the Blessed Virgin holds every part of our corporal selves sacred. In this temple, God dwells."

Or doesn't, I thought. But now was not the time for that discussion.

"But nothing more about miracles," I said.

"No. As I said, today Mary is distressed by false idols—and the commercialism surrounding Halloween. 'In this time,' she said, 'due to the spirit of consumerism, one forgets what it means to love and cherish true values.' "

"Not to dismiss the Mother of God," I said, "but I always thought Halloween was harmless kids' stuff."

Jennifer sighed.

"Sometimes we must look carefully to see the hand of Satan," she said. "And sometimes many of us don't ever see it—which is precisely how evil has been able to prosper since the fall of Lucifer. I don't know where you come down on that, Nick, and frankly I don't care. Will you please deliver Mary's message on tonight's news?"

I did repeat Mary's admonition about false idols when I went before the cameras that evening at six, and then I returned to *The Trib* to write my story. I toyed with the possibility of profiling Jimmy—but what would I have said? That it took a twelve-year-old kid to frame the most troubling questions of all? That I, a seasoned journalist, hadn't dared, if I'd even seriously considered them?

So, I went with the slam-dunk: Mary's Halloween admonitions and a *Trib* exclusive on Tony Callahan.

His white blood cell count had risen for the third consecutive day, and John Wright, our new Chief of Visuals, had designed a new graphic to accompany my column. It looked something like a chart of the NASDAQ during boom times—a red line representing Callahan's blood cell count spiking upward. Wright's idea was to run the graphic every day, whether or not I wrote about Callahan.

"People will follow that sucker like box scores," he said, and he was right, as the analytics would confirm.

Wright also wanted a photo of Callahan, so he'd sent one of our photographers to Baltimore to get it. Hill insisted that Callahan wear a baseball cap, like Jimmy.

"Miracle or not," the publisher said, "I won't have anyone in my paper who looks like he survived Nagasaki."

I wondered if that's how Hill's own father had looked, before his leukemia claimed him.

Before Hill, bundles of CoolBostonWeekly were dropped off in *The Trib* lobby and the guard delivered copies to the newsroom. Hill put an end to that and he got rid of the CoolBostonWeekly honor box in front of our building, too. Few honor boxes for any publication survived in the new age—all but a handful of ours were gone, too—and I had mixed feelings when CoolBostonWeekly's disappeared. I remembered with sadness when the last Onion boxes had vanished, too.

The closest you could get the print CoolBostonWeekly was a few blocks away, inside Capitol Coffee House. I walked over and bought this week's edition and a coffee.

Opening CoolBostonWeekly brought back memories of the Power Couple and the beginning of my slide into journalistic irrelevance.

This was years ago, when declining ratings and new station management prompted cancellation of my TV show; soon thereafter, cartons of my Collected Columns were sold at discount in used bookstores. Courtney, meanwhile, was intensifying her efforts to leave CoolBostonWeekly for something bigger. She deserved it, too; unlike me at that point, she was still on top of her game. Slimy politicians and spin doctors still couldn't agree if hiding from her was better than consenting to an interview.

Her first choice of something bigger was a job at *The Daily Tribune*, but while Jones wanted to hire her, Gordon had overruled him.

"It would just be too cute," he said. "Besides, we already have three political columnists."

We did, although none was Courtney's equal.

Courtney blamed me for not being hired. I could have leaned on Gordon, she maintained; I could have threatened to leave. She didn't want to hear that having been banished to metro/region, I had no leverage. Nor that I would never leave Boston for the *Miami Herald*, where she'd been offered a position and where I probably could have been hired, too.

Eventually, we worked through this—or at least achieved a sort of truce. We began to talk about starting a family.

A year later, Courtney was diagnosed with ovarian cancer.

She'd long feared the disease—her mother and grandmother had both died of it before they were fifty. Courtney was saved, but only with a hysterectomy: the tumor had metastasized.

We drew closer than ever that year, the year I turned forty. We cried and passed sleepless nights—and we talked about second chances and stopping to smell roses and the importance of hugs, stuff that sounds corny until you've faced death by cancer. We vowed to adopt two children, a girl and a boy, the perfect family.

And so it seemed we were bound for a happy ending.

Another year passed, Courtney was declared in remission, and we engaged an adoption agency. It would take a year or longer before we had our family, but we were willing to be patient. As we waited, Courtney's writing began to change. You would think after beating cancer she would have shifted toward the philosophical or spiritual, but instead, being shadowed by death had left her seeking life's lighter elements. She increasingly forsook politics for puff pieces like those in my column. It was troubling to see a woman who had brought down a corrupt Speaker of the House write about cute pet videos.

Courtney's column this week began with a broadside at our redesigned front page.

John Wright hadn't made *The Trib* oval, or tinted ad pages green—yet— but he'd changed the headline type, to Rockwell Extra Bold, which projected a sort of cyber feel, which Wright said was "trendy." Our contest-winning new slogan, *All the GOOD News That's Fit to Print*, appeared under the flag, and Wright had expanded the index and put a burst of red around it. The lower left-hand corner of page one was now dedicated to a daily feature Hill had cooked up: Celeb-Rate!, a mini-bio with a two-column pic of the celebrity of the day.

The Celeb-Rate! editor—newly hired at a fraction of what we paid existing editors—rated each celebrity on a scale of one to ten and Hill insisted on personally approving her selections and ratings every day. I guess I didn't comprehend how repugnant Celeb-Rate! was until Hill featured Neil Parr, a local car dealer noted for his infantile radio jingles ("Everyone squeals for Neil's deals on wheels!" "Go far in a Parr car, ha-ha!"). Parr so happened to be one of our biggest advertisers.

"Remember how shocked real journalists were when *The Orlando Sunshine*, Chamberlain's flagship publication, that caricature of a real paper, debuted?" Courtney wrote.

"With its redesigned front page and its lamentable new feature, Celeb-Rate!, *The Daily Tribulation* has travelled further down that road than the most despicable hedge fund manager could ever have imagined. What's next, scratch 'n' sniff newsprint? If any chain will introduce that kind of newsprint, it will be SGM, as in SuchGodawfulMuck, the chain that buys and guts newspapers, turning them into farces that surely has Benjamin Franklin rolling over in his grave."

Or walking past it on his way to Independence Hall, I thought.

"SuchGodawfulMuck" was first in a line of SGM sarcasms from Courtney. In weeks to come, we would read "SuperGrossMush," "SuperGreedyMoney," and "SuperGarbageMaker." And she would satirize "Good News Rules!" as "Good Nonsense Rocks!", "Good Nothing Reads!", and "Good Ninnies Regurgitate!"

Sophomoric, all of them, but they still won big points from me and my friends at *The Trib*.

"Shall we look at some of SuchGodawfulMuck's legacy?" Courtney continued. "'Nuff said already about The Tribulation. Out west, we have *The Arizona Advertiser*: Once a Pulitzer powerhouse, staff now down to 14, half of them part-time, with a print edition only on Sunday. In the Midwest, the *Iowa Register*: online only, staff of six. Michigan: *The Detroit Courier*, another former Pulitzer powerhouse, staff now at 16, counting free-lancers. New Jersey: *Asbury News*, bought and closed. New York: *Poughkeepsie Chronicle*, bought and closed. Vermont: *Burlington Bulletin*, bought and closed. Texas: *El Paso News*, bought and closed.

"Those are just a few of the dailies and former dailies. The list of shoppers and weeklies is longer, but the story there no less depressing. And then we have these freak shows that have popped up everywhere: *Catch.*

com, 'Natch.com, Scratch.com, Batch.com, Latch.com and *Trash.com*. Okay, so I made that last one up, but when the SuchGodawfulMuck goons read this, you can bet we'll see it soon. Do we detect a pattern here? No, not the dumb rhyming names but the fact that the ludicrous content in every one of them is virtually identical, although they each purport to be 'your community's local news, locally sourced and locally published.' "

Done with mocking the design and SGM, Courtney started in on me.

I'd figured she would, perhaps ridiculing my Employee of the Month Award.

But Courtney didn't mention Employee of the Month. In a column that reminded me of the journalistic force she used to be, she examined the ethics of Nick Nolan profiling Jennifer Abbott, ex-lover.

Courtney knew bits and pieces of my old relationship, of course—details of one's romantic past inevitably emerge during a marriage. Courtney accurately described my meeting Jennifer, our dating, then our living together. She quoted from one of Jennifer's old love letters. I'd forgotten about that—how my soon-to-be-ex told me she'd come across it while cleaning our townhouse after I'd moved out and then, on the advice of her layer, had not returned it to me.

"I can't wait for tonight," Jennifer had written in that old letter, "I want you to do again what you did, my sweet, sweet lover, with champagne and strawberries like last night!"

Seeing that in print hurt.

"How can Nick Nolan, *The Daily Tribulation*'s suddenly hot columnist, expect us to believe anything he pens about these alleged miracles?" Courtney wrote. "Even with Poop Man's ethics, solidified while marketing Olestra, how can the Good News Fools rush everything Nolan writes into print without so much as a perfunctory fact-check?

"And there's more than the question of allowing him to cover someone with whom he once had an intimate relationship—and may wish to again, for all we know. As readers of his column will recall from his earlier reflections on his childhood, Nolan was raised a strict Catholic. He was an altar boy and attended parochial school. But Nolan fell by the wayside, becoming a lapsed Catholic, the kind you see in church only twice a year, Easter and Christmas."

In truth, I didn't go even then.

"At the very least," Courtney concluded, "in light of his religious background and previous relationship with his subject, his objectivity must be seriously questioned. This writer strongly believes that *The Trib* is obligated to take Nolan off the story. Let TV use him for their six o'clock standups, if they must—but not Boston's supposed 'paper of record.' And speaking of the record, several calls to publisher Hill went unreturned. Not that we're surprised. When it comes to its own affairs, *Trib* executives have always demonstrated that access and accountability are concepts they believe apply to everybody but them."

I prepared myself to face Jones, who, I was sure, would call me back into his office, but he never did.

A.J. smirked when I passed her in the hall and a few colleagues expressed support, but that was the extent of the internal response to Courtney's column—that and a note from the publisher.

"We know we're hot when the weekly pays such close attention," Hill wrote. "Keep up the great work. And never forget the old adage: 'The only bad publicity is no publicity!'"

On Friday, the day after Courtney's broadside, Hill invited our online producers, marketing staff and select sales and newsroom personnel to his office for a planning session on Mary News.

The publisher was in rare form—chewing an unlit cigar and shaking hands and slapping backs as we filed in. The coffee was fresh-ground and the Danish smelled like they were just out of the oven.

"I would like to open the meeting by Zooming in Roger Rogers, our Social Media Pal," Hill said. "Roger has been busy monitoring our social media posts and he has some interesting insights to share. Roger?"

The big screen came to life and there was our SMP from his office at SGM headquarters.

"Roger that!" this idiot said. "We have an amazing SuperGooder we are about to honor, but first, I must report that there is someone who no longer can wear the Super Shirt. You will recall what the chairman said when announcing our social media policy: 'We will tolerate no politics, slurs, denunciations, supposedly clever witticisms, or personal opinions of any kind, not even what your favorite flavor ice cream is.' Regrettably, a former—yes, former—reporter at another property violated that policy with a Facebook post about the events of January 6 in our nation's capital.

"This person posted, and I quote: 'As the Department of Justice pursues the insurrectionists, I hope they all get what they deserve: long prison terms for their attempt to destroy American democracy.' "

Rogers continued: "Big no-no. Whatever we may privately believe must be kept private. So, good riddance to this non-conformist, who I shall not name, since naming such people who lack proper SGM values would only embolden them. And don't go looking, because we've scrubbed it and every social media reference to this loser, who agreed under threat of a lawsuit.

"All righty then. It's time for honor and glory! Super kudos to Suzy Summers for her Super Instagram posts of her hamster Squiggles who performs daily at 9 a.m. inside her wheel! Suzy just joined the million-follower

Instagram club and I am betting her TikTok will soon be there, too! A round of applause please!"

No one applauded.

"And just when you thought it couldn't get any better," Roger continued, "the biggest news of the day is Squiggles has won the Super Good Media Mascot contest! Suzy, take a bow!"

"There is no one here named Suzy Summers," Hill said.

"Isn't this *The Houston Happy Herald*?" Rogers said.

"No," said Hill.

"Oh, my," Rogers said. "Over and out."

"Sorry, folks," Hill said. "Signals crossed. But I promise you they are not for our next guest. Super Gooders, a warm welcome for Danny D'Ermo, who is going to walk us through the latest numbers," Hill said. "Danny, come on in!"

For 15 minutes, D'Ermo bored us with data.

"But what I haven't shown you is the very good news," D'Ermo said when he'd finished, "and the reason is I am reliably informed that Chris Hackett has prepared a presentation that will knock your socks off and I wouldn't want to steal his thunder!"

Hackett was Hill's new marketing chief, a man he'd hired to oversee *The Trib*'s newly rejuvenated department. He'd come to *The Trib* from Omnicom, the New York-based agency that counted McDonald's, Apples, and Exxon Mobil among its clients. Just thirty years old and, he was rumored to make twice what the most senior reporter did, not counting his signing bonus.

"OK, SuperGooders, that's all from super-sunny Florida!" D'Ermo said. "Over and out!"

We waited for the screen to go dark, but it didn't.

D'Ermo hadn't signed off.

And he was touching himself.

We were too stunned to say anything.

Finally, Hill cleared his throat and said: "Danny? Hello, Danny?"

A look of horror crossed our SOS's face and the screen went dark.

"Fucking A," Hill said, "When Chamberlain finds out, there will be hell to pay. And he'll definitely find out, since we have a room full of people who loathe him, including me."

An honest confession had escaped Hill. For a fleeting moment, I respected him.

"Let me clarify," Hill said. "I don't loathe him. I'm just occasionally annoyed. His presentations can sometimes be, well, long and boring. OK. Chris is up now, with the latest results from our New England Area Continuing Market Study."

"Let's start with Nick," Hackett said, scrolling through a series of graphs. "As you can see, until this fall, his column for at least the past three years, as far back as I crunched the numbers, has ranked second to last—only a percentage point or two above Knitting Korner."

More ammunition for A.J. and Courtney, I thought.

"But look at this," Hackett said. "In the latest study, several weeks into Mary News, who leads the pack in page-one and online lead stories? Nick Nolan! With a readership of ninety-one percent across all demos, a stunning turnaround. I've analyzed candy, shoes, soft drinks, cars, pharmaceuticals, and deodorants in my career and I've never seen anything like it. You could almost call it a miracle!"

"Nick's the man!" Hill exclaimed.

"He is indeed," said Hackett. "When we put Mary News into focus groups, we confirmed this near-universal interest. Note I didn't say *approval*. A significant percentage of people—those describing themselves as atheist, agnostic, 'not religious,' and 'not that brand of religion'—doubted what they read. But they read anyway: black, white, Hispanic, Asian American and Pacific Islander, boomers, zoomers, Gen Xers, Millennials, singles, couples, straights, LGBTQ+, low-income, middle-income, high-income. Mary News has become like a modern-day Dickens novel—you know, how his books used to be serialized in the papers after they arrived by ship from England. People can't wait to see what happens next with Mary News, regardless of whether they think it's bullshit, the hand of God, or something else.

"Which brings me to the final area of the study: 'perceived motion,' a fancy way of saying: Do our readers think the newspaper as a whole is getting better or not. Here again we have a breathtaking about-face, with an incredible eighty-eight percent stating we are getting better, ten percent having no opinion and only a statistically insignificant two percent stating we are getting worse. Given the dismal year-priors, I couldn't believe these numbers when they came in—so I double-checked them. Ladies and gentlemen, they're real. Congratulations!"

Hill replaced Hackett at the laptop.

"You already know from the weekly numbers how this has propelled our strong online and print-circulation gains," Hill said. "What you may not know is the effect on advertising. In print, both display and classified show triple-digit increases over the past year. Digital ads are even better. Anecdotal evidence from our sales force suggests Mary News is responsible—but only partly. Just like our readers, our advertisers have enthusiastically embraced our motto of Good News Rules. As one said, 'it's about time you knuckleheads got it!' Said another: 'A new day has dawned and we welcome it!' "

Listening, I thought of the old days and I remembered Hill's response to those who had expressed concern that layoffs and downsizing had doomed institutional knowledge, the wisdom, memories, connections, and sources that staff writers carried inside their heads and kept in personal directories.

"Google is today's institutional knowledge," Hill had replied. "And it's free."

The meeting continued.

"The challenge now on Mary News," Hill said, "is getting to the next level. Here are the elements of the plan."

Hill described a social-media campaign that Roger Rogers would personally manage as "his Job Number One, seven days a week," Hill said. The "secret sauce," according to Hill, would be polarization—pitting the believers against the doubters, which would power the algorithms "to new heights of intense, can't miss-a-minute intensity."

Jones rolled his eyes.

"So, you want us to be Fox News," he said.

"No," said Hill, "I want us to be Fox News and CNN and the networks, all in one."

Destiny raised her hand.

"You do realize, don't you," she said, "that this will piss everyone on every side off."

Hill smiled.

"If politics in 2021 has taught us anything, it's a roadmap for audience engagement," he said. "So, yes, I am not only aware—I am in debt to the right and to the left and everyone in between. Now if I may continue."

Hill outlined the daily polls we would run—check "I am a believer," "I am a disbeliever," "Amber is speaking for Mary," "No proof, Amber isn't saying anything," and so on. He described the social-media advertisement blitz about to begin and the new radio, TV, and online campaign set to launch: all spots ended with the jingle, 'The *Daily Trib*: Where good news is no miracle, just what we do super-best!' *The Tribune* also would sponsor a contest whose grand prize was an all-expense-paid trip to Lourdes, and we were about to launch a Sunday print and online advertising section geared toward churches and religious bookstores—"long an under-developed market here in New England," Hill called it.

John Wright was designing a Mary News logo, and our lawyers would copyright it. Hill wanted audio and video clips on Trib.com. And even though our religion writer had taken a buyout during the downsizing and not been replaced, Hill wanted more stories about other miracle sites, notably Medjugorje and Lourdes.

"OK, those are some of the things already in the works," said Hill. "My next personal challenge will be partnering with the cardinal."

"For what?" Jones said.

"Licensed products," Hill said.

"You mean crucifixes and statues?"

"And limited-edition bibles, t-shirts, coffee mugs, tote bags, key rings, bumper stickers, trading cards, action figures, the works."

"But it's the Catholic Church," Jones said.

"Your point is?"

"The Catholic Church isn't a business."

"Really?" said Hill.

He got busy with his laptop.

"I'm on *www.vaticangift.com*, an official Vatican Web site offering an extensive menu of items for sale," he said. "Here's what they're featuring this week: Rosaries, saint medals, crucifixes, jewelry, icons, statues, and Pope Francis Precious Gifts. Free gift wraps, and fast shipping 'thanks to our partnership with FedEx.' Also, 'free shipping on orders over two hundred US dollars.' All major credit cards and PayPal accepted."

Jones said nothing.

Bud muttered under his breath: "Not listed on the site, but available at the right price: annulments and settlements in priest abuse cases."

"I'll be speaking with the archbishop," Hill said.

Good luck, I thought.

Fifty-two years old and a native of Argentina, where he'd been ordained by the then-archbishop of Buenos Aries, now the pope, Jose Cardinal Cruz was known for his anti-materialism and his crusade to find more clergy abusers and bring them to justice—not just Catholic justice, but legal justice. The Vatican had announced that he would accompany Francis on his next pilgrimage to America, a trip planned for late in the year that would include stops in Los Angeles, El Paso, Miami, Baltimore, and New York.

"Well, that's all I've got," Hill said, taking a Magic Marker and standing at a blank flipchart. "Now I'd like the News Department's input on reaching the next level. This is your chance to take ownership of the story of the century."

Grudgingly, we got to work.

We could run pieces about non-Catholic religious phenomena, one editor suggested—faith healing, rattlesnake handling, Hindu and Jewish miracles. Predictably, the suburban editor wanted man-on-the-street stories about spiritualism. Another editor suggested a series on Jennifer's Hollywood days. A city reporter suggested ongoing stories on crowd control. Marjorie Rudd, our new Lifestyle editor, hired by Hill from *Vogue* magazine to redo Ob Scene, wanted to publish fashion tips for the comatose and terminally ill.

I waited for her to say that was only a sick joke.

She didn't.

"They have to wear something, right?" Rudd said. "Why be defined by hospital johnnies? Just because you can't open your eyes, does that mean you don't need mascara?"

"Excellent!" Hill said. I could see the old Frito-Lay marketer in him planning a branded line of clothing and cosmetics for the comatose: Sleeping Beauties he could call it.

"John, I see your hand up," Hill said.

Wright complained, as he had previously, about the dearth of photos of Jennifer. She had consented to only one shot, to accompany my second column—the one that ignited everything.

"This is becoming very difficult to illustrate," Wright said. "Wire art from *Do Not Disturb* goes only so far."

"Well, she definitely is a reclusive celebrity," said Hill. "Have you thought of using an artist, like in court when a judge bans cameras? Better yet, why not cook up a digital composite?"

"Good ideas," said Wright.

"Don't put any disclaimers on it," said Hill. "Our readers won't know the difference."

"How about we put a webcam in there and stream her around the clock on *Trib.com*" Wright said.

"Brilliant," Hill said. "I wish I'd thought of it. Nick, what do you think? Work on her a little bit, maybe she'll soften?"

"I doubt it," I said. "If she won't do another photo, and I've asked, it's hard to imagine she'd allow a webcam."

"Put it in the kitchen," said Hill. "That's a pretty innocuous place."

"Why her kitchen?" I said.

"Because this is the age of cooking shows and Kardashians. People will watch anything. Try the reality-show star angle on her, Nick. I don't think you ever get Hollywood out of your blood. Okay, anybody else?"

Jones raised his hand.

"Where are we going to get the people to do all these stories?" he said.

"Not out of the overtime budget, that's for sure," said Paula Orton. "We've maxed out there and I won't authorize another penny. So freelancers it is. There will be a line around the block of scribes eager for their twenty-five-dollar shot at fame."

"This is too big to leave to freelancers," Jones said.

"What areas do our metro reporters cover now?" Hill said.

Jones listed them. They included Roxbury.

"Not true," Hill said. "Roxbury's in Connecticut. I know because I've vacationed near there. Stayed at the 1754 House. Great inn. Highly recommended."

"Roxbury is part of Boston," Jones said. Specifically, a largely non-white neighborhood."

"Whatever," Hill said. "What are our numbers there?"

"I haven't a clue," said Jones. "It's not how I run a newsroom."

"But it is how I run a newspaper," Hill said.

On his laptop, he called up the analytics.

"The numbers are dismal," he said. "No one reads us there."

"Maybe because we suck at covering Latino and BIPOC communities," said Destiny.

I hadn't seen her enter the room, nor had her name been on the email and calendar invite Hill had sent to convene the meeting. But I was happy she had come.

"Bi-what?" said Hill. "Is that some new sex thing?"

He chuckled.

No one else did.

"It stands for Black, Indigenous, People of Color," Destiny said.

"Yes, I know. Don't you reporters have a sense of humor?"

"Not with racism," Destiny said.

"I'm not a racist," Hill said.

And Nixon said, 'I'm not a crook,' I thought.

"Sorry, that came out wrong," Hill said. "As I was saying, not many people in Roxbury subscribe to our paper. Point is, this is a business, not a charity. Has been since the days of Franklin. You need revenue. Without it, you go the way of the horse-drawn buggy. I'm sorry, Destiny, this is how it is."

"Then make it not how it is," Destiny said. "Give communities of color news that's important to them. It's not rocket science."

"I'm open to any and all ideas," Hill said. "And I will be convening that meeting in the next few days. Let's get back to today's topic."

Destiny held her fire, for now.

"So, you take what's-her-name off the Roxbury beat," Hill said.

What's-her-name was Connie Lee, the paper's only Asian-American reporter, hired by Jones just before the downsizing to cover diversity issues. She wasn't at this meeting.

"Connie stays," said Jones.

"Then take someone off the copy desk," Hill said.

"Since you shipped most copy-editing and page design to Orlando, our copy desk is down to bare bones," Jones said.

"I'll let you figure it out," Hill said. "My only demand is Nick stays in the driver's seat. And speaking of our Employee of the Month, you've been silent, Nick. Any further thoughts?"

"Just keep doing what I'm doing, I guess," I said.

"Anyone else before we wrap this up?" Hill said.

"Aren't we guilty of exploitation?" Destiny said.

"Come again?" said Hill.

He seemed genuinely perplexed.

"The girl," said Destiny. "Amber Abbott."

"She's in a coma," said Hill.

"While we swarm around her like flies on shit."

"That's pretty strong," Hill said.

"How about 'buzzards on carrion,' " Destiny said.

"You do know you were not invited to this meeting, right?" Hill said.

"And you do know about discrimination lawsuits, right?" Destiny said.

"Look, there's no need to make threats," Hill said. "I told you we will soon have a diversity meeting."

"We'll see how that works out," Destiny said.

Hill said nothing.

"But you are right about one thing, Mr. Hill," Destiny continued. "This meeting was called to discuss so-called Mary News. No offense to you, Nick, but we've lost sight of dignity. Here's this tragically brain-damaged girl, unable to get out of her bed or feed herself. And what do we do? Obsess over logos and expanded coverage—and bitch about photos."

"Well, duh," said Hill. "Last I checked, weren't we a newspaper?"

"We've gone way overboard," Destiny said.

"Overboard?" Hill said. "Some would say that a hundred-and-twenty inches on a chronically unemployed basket case who lost his legs in Vietnam and sees Viet Cong in his backyard is the worst form of exploitation."

Destiny kept her cool.

"I'll let your description of 'a chronically unemployed basket case' pass for now, though I certainly will remember it, as will everyone in this room," she said. "So back to Amber and Jennifer. What if it was your kid lying there?"

"I'd be grateful for the publicity that brought the donations that allowed me to keep my house with plenty left over for a rainy day," said Hill.

"And you'd let it go on, week after week."

"No," Hill said, "I'd let Mary cure one dying person and then tell the rest to go fuck themselves."

"That's not what I mean."

"Then what do you mean? Nick's been careful not to go grotesque with the coma side of Mary News, and I applaud him for that: you won't find diapers or drool in any of his columns. We do this story because it's good— good for the Abbotts, good for us, good for everyone. It's a free country; if you're uncomfortable with what we do, Ms. Carter, you can go sell cars or something."

"If you think I'd make it that easy for you," Destiny said, "you've got another thing coming."

The meeting ended, people drifted away, and I was left alone with Jones.

I realize I've given the impression that Jones was an asshole, but that's because I was so pissed at him for threatening me with the suburban staff. That's because he'd done Gordon's dirty work during the downsizing, and now he was letting Hill and Orton finish the job—all, I believed, for the sake of a pension.

At the end of his career, Jones was no hero.

But once upon a time, he'd been a hell of a journalist. I could fill pages with examples of how his stewardship had honored our paper and our profession—the public service pieces, the corruption probes, the impeccable coverage of the economy, politics, sports, and the arts. Jones had put diversity and social-justice issues on the front page. He'd introduced the notion of story into *Trib* culture, enabling disciples like Destiny and me to carry its banner.

The basics, as we remembered it.

I could cite no better example of Jones's virtue than *The Trib* investigation, led by Terry Winters with the support and encouragement of Jones, that won us a Pulitzer.

The investigation brought down Donald Sabella, Chief Judge for the U.S. District Court of Massachusetts, who had presided over several cases involving dealers working for the Mexican drug lord Joaquín Archivaldo Guzmán Loera, El Chapo, as he is known. Sabella had thrown out every case on a technicality, during a time when the cocaine reaching Massachusetts and much of the country had been laced with deadly fentanyl. On its surface, the dismissals seemed plausible.

Acting on a tip, Terry learned that El Chapo had bribed Sabella by transferring hundreds of thousands of dollars to the judge's personal bank account. Edited by Jones and backed by a publisher who was still managing to keep grumbling family stockholders at bay, our story was picked up by newspapers and other media outlets around the world. The FBI investigated and Congress began impeachment proceedings, the only wa a federal judge can be removed.

Sabella hired a team of lawyers and mounted a defiant defense, but in the end, after two weeks of nationally televised proceedings in the House and then Senate, he was impeached. We ran a humiliating photo on the day the verdict was delivered and he was leaving the Capitol. It showed Sabella, pursued by a throng of reporters and photographers, stepping into a black sedan where a young woman, not his wife, was waiting. I remember the debate about running that photo: no one but Winters and Jones wanted to. The publisher left the decision to them.

"It's the picture worth a thousand words," Jones argued during a tense meeting. "It speaks to deception and disgrace and that's what this story is about. Run it and the story as our entire front page and make it the lead on our web site."

A week later, Jones's only child was murdered.

It was Robert Junior's twenty-first birthday, and he'd gone out with friends to a sports bar. His body was found the next morning.

I remember our horror when we heard the news. I myself had gotten a call from Jones at about 2 a.m. when his son was overdue—Robert Junior was no buddy of mine but worry-sick parents make those kinds of calls. And I was at *The Trib* that morning when the police scanner carried a report of a submerged car with a bullet-riddled corpse inside. The car was in Lower Mystic Lake in Arlington. Jones lived on Mystic Lake Drive, a 15-second walk away.

Robert's funeral was the largest I've ever attended—more than a thousand people filling a cathedral during a Mass celebrated by Cardinal Cruz. Jones eulogized his son, threw the last dirt on his coffin at graveside, then went home and wrote an essay *The Trib* would never have run if Robert Junior hadn't been the publisher's nephew and godson.

"May you rot in hell, Donald Sabella, for killing my boy," the essay began.

In it, Jones acknowledged that in all likelihood Sabella had not personally pulled the trigger—indeed, that he had no evidence the ex-judge was involved at all.

"I need no proof," Jones wrote, "for some things speak for themselves. My sweet boy is gone while a monster lives."

Perhaps surprisingly, given the public disgrace of his impeachment, Sabella sued *The Trib* for libel. A few people believed he hadn't been involved, but most everyone assumed that Sabella, bent on revenge, had asked El Chapo to send his best hit man to Massachusetts.

Having gotten the best, Sabella gambled he was safe forever, a gamble that paid off as the months passed and the FBI and Massachusetts State Police failed to identify a suspect in Robert Jr.'s murder. Sabella knew a libel suit would torment the grieving father. He knew that the threshold for proving libel against a newspaper is high and that pretrial maneuvering would be interminable, compounding Jones's torment.

The scenario held true: only this year, the case been scheduled for trial.

Jury selection was now underway.

"You look defeated," I said to Jones.

He'd just placed a call to our lawyers, who were in court.

"Not defeated," said Jones. "Discouraged."

He told me that *The Trib* had lost its last challenge to a prospective juror—yet another person admitting to "dislike of today's media" was now in the pool.

"Sabella's lawyers are the best," said Jones. "Ours are worse than ambulance chasers. I wanted Elizabeth Ritvo, you know. You can imagine Hill's reaction."

"Too expensive," I said.

"And too high-profile. He didn't want us to cover the trial in the first place."

"You're kidding."

"It's the only fight I've won with him. I told him we'd look like assholes if we didn't."

"He cared?"

"Not one iota. 'Libel suits don't sit well in Orlando,' he said."

"So what convinced him?"

"I showed him the medical examiner's photos of Bobby. Even then, he had conditions: no front page, no stories longer than ten inches, no photos. It may have been a Pyrrhic victory, but in this new era, I'll take what I can get."

I understood now why Jones had stayed on under Hill. It wasn't a pension—he only wanted to honor his son.

"I owe you an apology," I said.

"For what?"

"I'll tell you some time over a beer," I said.

"Only if you buy," Jones said.

"Deal."

"Now let's talk Mary News."

"Is there anything left to say?"

"A couple of things. Do you share Destiny's concerns?"

"Yes," I said, "but I see Hill's point, too. We're walking a very fine line here."

"In more ways than one," Jones said. "What about the miracles—do you believe they're real?" Jones said.

"That's tough. As you know, if anything I've gone overboard with my disclaimers."

"The labels on pretty much every medication go overboard with disclaimers. How many people do you suppose ever read them? I want to know what you *believe*, Nick."

I contemplated that for a moment.

"The honest answer is I don't know," I said. "It could be real—I mean, aren't Fatima and Lourdes?"

"Depends on who you ask. A southern Baptist might say they're baloney. An atheist might laugh in your face."

"I don't discount the possibility that Jennifer is mentally ill," I said, "and it's possible that these people could be experiencing some sort of mass hypnosis. But what I do know for a fact is this: *something* is happening there. I'm not saying the stuff on this flipchart is the right way to cover it, but we'd be crazy to let up. Good, bad, or inexplicable, it *is* news."

"What about Courtney's column," Jones said. "Did you have a relationship with Jennifer?"

"I told you before: we dated a few times."

I didn't like lying to Jones, but now wasn't the time for true confessions.

"Courtney makes a strong case for more than a few dates," Jones said. "That letter she quotes rings awfully true."

"I swear I don't remember that letter," I said.

And technically, that was true—I didn't remember it verbatim. But I remembered the notes and cards that shot between us like lightning that summer. I remembered champagne and strawberries.

I remembered a recent midnight encounter in a newspaper morgue.

The day was ending when I updated my social media, cleared my inbox, and went to Hill's office. It was time to trade on my new standing.

"Can I ask you a favor?" I said.

"Is the pope a Catholic?" Hill said, laughing.

I handed him a printout of the latest torrent of SGM courses, updates, revisions, plans, goals, projections, commitments, and certificate compliance concurrence affidavits to sign, whatever the fuck those were.

"Can I get out of some of this?" I said. "To complete it all, I'd need days off from Mary News."

Hill read the printout.

"Bureaucrats justifying their stupid positions with a touch of projected paranoia to keep the underlings in line thrown in—that's corporate America today," he said.

That pretty much nailed it, though it surprised me Hill was so frank.

"That's also China and North Korea today, not that you ever heard me say any of this," he continued. "You didn't hear me, right?"

"Right."

"Every once in a while, the boss has to vent. They don't pay me enough to deal with this crew up here. Not you, of course, Nick, but you know who I mean. Anyway, I won't get you out of some of this—I'll get you out of all of it. I'll copy Chamberlain, who's on the same page as us, and have corporate HR relieve you of this and everything like it going forward. We don't want nonsense, Nick, we want subscriptions! Now go get me more of those."

CHAPTER SIX: FOOTBALL

The following Thursday brought more trouble from Courtney: JAYSON BLAIR OR JANET COOKE ALL OVER AGAIN? the headline on her column read.

"In analyzing the so-called pronouncements of Mary that *The Trib* eagerly publishes," she wrote, "one finds an uncanny similarity to the statements of Our Lady of Medjugorje, available in pamphlet form in any Catholic bookstore and also on the Web."

To make her case, Courtney reprinted Mary's supposed message after Greta Ricci's improvement next to the Medjugorje revelation of April 25, 2000. They were almost identical.

"Okay, so give Ms. Abbott the benefit of doubt," Courtney wrote. "Assume Mary speaks in a universal tongue. But how do the roots of this increasingly bizarre tale check out? Not very credibly."

With the help of unnamed sources—probably friends she had made inside the U.S. Attorney's office during her award-winning days—Courtney had gotten access to a national law-enforcement database, where she'd found the police file on the accident that supposedly left Amber comatose and killed the driver, a priest by the name of Fr. Mateo Silva. Yes, him.

"There is nothing about the priest dying," Courtney wrote. "In fact, the report notes 'priest administered last rites to girl waiting for ambulance.' Ten minutes after I learn this, a cleric who the Boston-area public was led to believe is in heaven answers his phone in Los Angeles."

According to Courtney, Fr. Mateo told her he hadn't been hurt in the accident—and that he, Jennifer, and Amber were not headed for a weekend retreat, as Jennifer had claimed and I had published. Nor, the priest said, was he driving.

Jennifer was.

"I first met Jennifer when she was a teenager," Mateo told Courtney. "Watching her faith blossom was remarkable. Very satisfying to a pastor. And then, as happens, she moved on and so did I, me to California, she to parts unknown. Many years passed and one day, Jennifer knocked on my rectory door. Such a delight to see her again! Who would have imagined we would both wind up in L.A.? She was trying to make it in Hollywood and having a bit of a time with it. I encouraged her to keep going. 'Hard work,' I said, 'always pays off in the end.'

"You know what would really pay off, Father?' she said. 'A miracle!'

"We both laughed. 'Well, let's hope for that,' I said. 'Shall we bow our heads in prayer to Saint Teresa of Jesus of the Andes?'

"And we did.

" 'I have a daughter now,' Jennifer said after we'd prayed. 'A beautiful girl named Amber.' "

" 'I would love to meet her,' I said."

" 'Would you join us one day at the Santa Monica Pier?' Jennifer said. 'It's Amber's favorite place. The Ferris wheel is her favorite ride.' "

" 'That would be wonderful,' I said. And that was when the accident happened, driving on the Santa Monica Boulevard. She lost control where it turns left by Sunset Strip. I tried to find her after that terrible tragedy—to see how she was and if her daughter had survived—but I had no number and the hospitals would give me no information. I never saw her again, though I have many times prayed for her and her daughter. Are they OK?"

"Her daughter is in a persistent vegetative state," Courtney replied. "Jennifer is her caregiver."

"This is so terrible, my prayers will go immediately to them," the priest said. "But I must ask: What do you intend to do with what I have just told you?"

"Write the truth," Courtney said.

"She has not?" the priest said.

"Not exactly."

Courtney provided Fr. Mateo links to my stories. After he'd read them, he'd called her back and said: "Goodness, I don't know what to say except there *are* miracles and perhaps this is an example, the confusion about the details notwithstanding. But I cannot draw any conclusions reading these stories. They seem... perhaps the kind word is 'boosterish.' Do you have Jennifer's number? I'd like to call her."

"I'm sorry," Courtney said, "I do not."

Courtney concluded her article by writing: "Does Nolan take everything his old lover states as the gospel truth? Has he become another Janet Cooke or Jayson Blair, playing fast and loose with the facts? Apparently returning to the limelight from the shadows of inside metro/region is so important to him that he's willing to abandon the last shred of integrity separating him from TMZ. We know where Hill comes down on all this—profit before principle has been his corporate policy since SuchGodawfulMuck came to town—but where is the executive editor? Perhaps more importantly, where is Nick Nolan's conscience?"

This time, Jones did call me into his office. Hill was with him. I couldn't read the publisher's mood, but Jones was pissed.

"How do you explain this?" he said.

"Sloppiness," I said. "Carelessness. I really have no excuse."

Nonetheless, I offered one.

I said that I'd written that first column under extreme deadline pressure, which left no time to attempt to contact the priest or otherwise confirm details of Jennifer's story. I said I might have asked a librarian to dig into the accident—except all but one of our librarians had been pink-slipped during Gordon's downsizings and the last had been booted by SGM. I said that, unlike Courtney, I no longer had police sources. And I said that when no one challenged any detail of Jennifer's story after publication, the accident and priest left my mind. I was too caught up in Mary News.

"I'll call the priest myself and we'll correct it tomorrow," I said.

"No you won't," Hill said. "You know, you news types drive me crazy, always wanting to shoot yourselves in the foot like this. Live priest, dead priest, no priest—what does it matter? I don't care about the nuances of something that happened three thousand miles away and years ago—nor do our readers, as the analytics and research confirm. We're writing about what's happening now, things we can see with our own eyes. Did the priest cure that old woman? Does the priest make Tony Callahan's white blood cell count keep rising? Did the priest send two thousand people to Jennifer's yesterday?"

"Nick made an error," said Jones. "We correct errors."

"We do?" said Hill. "Now there's another cute J school notion! How about the errors no one ever calls a newspaper on—the misspellings and misquotes and wrong middle initials? Or the errors of omission—making exactly one phone call or sending exactly one email or maybe doing neither to get the other side's view, and then using those always-damning lines, 'unavailable for comment' or 'didn't respond to requests for comment?' Or the stories we run built entirely on memories—the old soldier looking back at the war, the retiring teacher's recollection of her first class, the all-American outfielder's version of his Little League days? How much of that is true? How much of *that* do we ever correct?"

Hill picked up today's *Trib* and opened to an inside business page—led by Destiny's story about Massachusetts unemployment, which had declined for the first time in months.

"A story chosen at random," he said. "Good news for the governor after months of bad—and what timing, in light of the polls showing him facing an uphill reelection battle in 2022. Did we collect these data? Did we run these numbers? The point isn't that we necessarily think the governor lies; the point is this is journalism, for crying out loud, not science."

Hill picked up Courtney's column.

"What about *her* credibility?" he said. "Who's to say she isn't making this priest stuff up? If I'm not mistaken, isn't she in divorce proceedings with Nick?"

"We should still respond," said Jones.

"How—by holding a press conference? Issuing a statement? Have you lost it, Jones? We're the elephant in this town and CoolBostonWeekly is the pimple on our ass. Let's remember that."

Jones was smoldering, but he put up no further resistance; it was 9:30 in the morning, and he was already late for court. Opening arguments in the libel suit were set for today.

When I looked at the news budget a few minutes later, I saw that the libel-suit story was down for ten inches of wire coverage, on page B-16. I knew it wouldn't make it online.

Jennifer was reading CoolBostonWeekly when I saw her next.

It was the day after Halloween, and I had not called her for a while, at her request; Halloween was the fifth anniversary of Amber's accident, and she said she needed to be alone and undisturbed with her daughter. I'd told her I understood.

"I had to laugh when I read Courtney's column," Jennifer said. "A woman like that will do anything—including trying to wreck your good name. She won't succeed, Nick. We all know the truth."

Considering what was on my mind, I found it an odd phrasing: *We all know the truth.*

Despite Hill's dismissal of Courtney's column, I did have questions for Jennifer.

"What about Father Silva?" I said. "Jealous or not, Courtney raises an issue. You said he died in the accident."

"Oh, no. I never said that. You must have heard wrong."

In fact, I was certain I'd heard right. I hadn't tape-recorded that initial interview but I'd rechecked my notes, and they confirmed Jennifer's claim that Silva had been killed. It was there, in my own hand, underlined and unambiguous.

"But I didn't hear wrong," I said. "You said it."

"So you think I'm a liar," Jennifer said.

"That's not what I'm saying. It's just that some of the details don't add up. And not only about the accident."

In the wake of Courtney's column, I'd also read all of the pronouncements of Our Lady of Medjugorje, which were published online every month and which ran to about two paragraphs each. Courtney was right:

Every message that Jennifer claimed Mary had delivered through Amber was almost word-for-word the same as one from Medjugorje.

"That seems like a weird coincidence," I said.

"The Mother of God speaks a universal language," replied Jennifer. "Some asshole with an ax to grind may doubt it, but it hardly surprises someone with faith."

Jennifer's flash of anger shocked me.

But it was only a flash.

She smiled and said: "Forgive me for such terrible language. But you know how her treatment of you bothers me. You deserve better. Speaking of which—don't move an inch!"

Jennifer ran out of the kitchen. She was carrying a wrapped package when she returned.

"For you," she said. "Go on, open it."

I tore the ribbon and gift wrap off—and found a signed first edition of *A Farewell to Arms.* Hemingway was one of my favorite authors.

"This must have cost a fortune," I said.

"The cost is none of your business."

"Where'd you find it?"

"On *abebooks.com.*"

"I don't know what to say."

"You sound disappointed," said Jennifer.

"I'm not," I said. "It's just that we're not supposed to accept gifts from people we cover."

"Why not?"

"It could affect our objectivity."

"As if anything in any newspaper is ever really objective," said Jennifer. "Anyway, no one needs to know. Where's your gratitude? It's not every day that a Hemingway fan gets a signed first edition of *A Farewell to Arms.* I know your favorite Hemingway is *The Sun Also Rises* but signed editions of those only a millionaire could afford."

The Sun Also Rises was her favorite Hemingway, too. I'd introduced it to her when we were dating and I remembered well an evening in a New Hampshire hotel: reading it together, my arm around her, she turning the pages, and making love after the end of Chapter 16.

"So you'll have to settle for this," Jennifer said.

"Settle?" I said. "I love it!"

"You could show it," said Jennifer. "Say, with that next kiss you promised."

"I don't recall any such promise."

"But you do recall that night in the morgue."

She pulled me toward her and we kissed.

The following day was the next-to-last time I would see Courtney in person—and the last time we would speak to each other, except by phone, and then only once.

The occasion was a No-fault 1A Divorce appearance before a judge in Probate and Family Court. If all went smoothly and both parties agreed to terms, a trial could be avoided. On this, Courtney and I agreed: get it done, as quickly as possible.

As we sat in a courthouse waiting room flanked by our lawyers, we said nothing. Until we were called into chambers, that is.

Courtney turned to me.

Look, I know how we crashed and burned but I want you to know that I did love you then, I imagined her saying. *People change. Things change. I wish they hadn't with us, but they did.*

I imagined her crying, and me as well.

I'm sorry, Nick, I imagined her saying.

What she really said:

"Does my hair look Okay?"

November 5 was Election Day in some cities and towns. For as long as I could remember, *The Trib* had published a Voter's Guide—but not this year.

Hill killed it.

"All the ads they used to attract from candidates go now to TV and Facebook," he told the political editor. "Run a list of polling places and voting hours—online only—and that's it."

Not that I had my eye on election coverage.

After three weeks of inching upward, Tony Callahan's white blood cell count on November 5 finally reached normal, prompting his doctor to proclaim: "We believe he is in remission." I broke the news in my column, which was the lead story online and played above the Election Day wrap-up on November 6.

That night, Elizabeth Turner, wife of developer Luke Turner, had a dream.

Fresh with its power, she awoke at dawn and drove to Jennifer's, where, she later claimed, she saw the Virgin Mary spread her arms in open embrace over the house.

From there, she went to morning Mass at the Cathedral of the Holy Cross, the archdiocesan seat. Later, she visited her husband in his office at the Prudential Center. Then she went home and called me.

"Talking with you gives me goosebumps," she said. "I'm such an admirer of your work."

"Thanks," I said, "but I'm really just a hack."

"No," said Elizabeth, "you are the herald of God."

Her words didn't surprise me: her pilgrimages to Medjugorje, her Sunday-evening prayer sessions at her home, and her friendship with the cardinal were all widely known.

But she was more than a zealot, I'd decided after reading a profile of her that we'd published a few years before. Daughter of a Massachusetts blueblood and a magna cum laude graduate of Radcliffe College, Elizabeth, a convert to Catholicism, was one of Boston's most generous arts patrons—donating as much to the Museum of Fine Arts annually as she did to the archdiocese. She was a trustee of the Boston Public Library, a member of the Board of Directors of the Massachusetts Audubon Society, and a trustee of the St. Mary's Center for Women and Children, which provides housing, economic and education help to those facing challenges.

We chatted a moment more, and then Elizabeth related her dream, which had two parts.

In the first, the Mother of God led Elizabeth through a city with buildings made of polished marble and streets paved in gold.

"Build this city," Mary instructed Elizabeth, "as a gesture of my love for all God's children."

"Is this city temporal, or of another world?" the dream Elizabeth asked.

But Mary didn't answer, according to Elizabeth.

" 'I leave that to you,' Mary said, and she was gone."

"That was quite a dream," I said.

"More than a dream," said Elizabeth, "it was a directive. I knew the second I awoke what Mary meant. My husband was to stop fooling around and put up the seventy-five million dollars himself to finish the Minuteman Mall."

Although you wouldn't have known it reading our one-sided coverage, Luke Turner, not the Legislature, was holding the project hostage. Only a month or so of work remained until it could open, but Turner refused to give the green light until lawmakers agreed to provide that final seventy-five million dollars—this after the House and Senate already had approved and the governor signed legislation for two hundred million dollars in site improvements, bonds, and a ten-year real estate tax-free status. The initial deal called for Turner to kick in the seventy-five million dollars, but he'd subsequently refused, citing a controversial clause in his contract with the state.

"Mary cares about the mall?" I said to Elizabeth.

"She cares about jobs for single mothers with mouths to feed, yes, she does," Elizabeth said. "She cares about a strong economy, which helps all. And I believe she cares about my chapel—rather, what will be *everyone's* chapel, a place where all will be welcome, regardless of faith."

No one knew how exactly, but Elizabeth had managed to convince her husband to build a Franciscan chapel inside the Minuteman Mall. I remembered it from one of our stories and the fun Courtney had with it—"Our Lady of the Shopper," as she labeled it in one of her early columns on the politics behind the making of the mall.

"So I told Luke what he must do," Elizabeth said. "There will be a press conference this afternoon at two during which he will announce he is personally providing the final seventy-five million dollars. Because I admire you so, I wanted to give you a heads up. I won't be calling anyone else or granting any other interviews. *The Trib* may post a news alert when we conclude this call."

"Thank you, Mrs. Turner," I said.

"Thank Mary, the mother of God," she replied.

In the aftermath of Luke Turner's press conference, mall madness overtook *The Trib* again. This episode was more fevered than ever—the web home page and front page of the print edition were an explosion of stories, photos, and charts.

As for me, I'd hesitated before recounting Elizabeth's dream in a story. I knew putting her words in print would leave the impression that she was not in her right mind, but Hill insisted I write it.

"If it sounds like *The National Enquirer*, so what?" he said. "There isn't a person out there who won't read to the end. And what an end! You're brilliant, Nick. No one writes like you. The wonder is you're still here and not scripting movies or signing million-dollar book deals."

So I had another exclusive.

The first part of Elizabeth's dream made for a grab-you-by-the-throat lead.

The second gave me an awesome kicker.

"Mrs. Turner hints of more to come," I wrote in my closing paragraph. "In the second part of her dream, she said that Mary promises 'a gesture of goodwill' to coincide with the birth of Jesus. 'I understood that to mean something on or near Christmas,' Mrs. Turner said. 'What exactly it is, I believe Mary in due time will reveal.'"

I'd nearly run the gauntlet into Jennifer's house that afternoon when I felt a tug on my sleeve. It was Jimmy Pulaski. He looked jaundiced and skinny and there were dark circles under his mother's eyes.

"Haven't seen you in a while, Jimmy," I said.

"I was in the stupid hospital again."

"He had a setback," said Gina Pulaski. "A problem with his pancreas."

"I'm sorry."

"You know what I hate about hospitals most?" Jimmy said.

"What?" I said.

"They won't let you throw a football. Children's took mine away and it sucks."

"Jimmy, how many times have I told you not to use that word," said Gina.

"Okay, so it stinks—big-time."

"It does stink," I said.

"Me and this kid Rick—he's got cancer, too—we were only throwing it around in the hall. It's not like we went into an operating room or anything. But they took it and wouldn't give it back. 'You can have it when you leave,' they said. And when it was time to go, they'd lost it."

"I told you we'll get another one," Gina said.

"Yeah, but not what I want, which is one signed by Tom Brady," Jimmy said. "You told me they cost too much."

"Maybe for Christmas," Gina said.

"Just like we're going to Disney World," said Jimmy.

"*Are* you going?" I said.

" 'Someday,' my mom keeps saying."

"It's hard," Gina said. "I haven't been able to work since Jimmy got sick. But you don't want to hear all that. Plenty of people are worse off than us."

"Yeah, like refugees and people in places where the pandemic is worst," Jimmy said. "That's what she always tells me."

"Well, it's true," Gina said.

"I know," Jimmy said. "That stinks way more than not going to Disney World."

"Excuse us a second," I said to Jimmy.

I beckoned Gina aside.

Out of earshot of her son, I asked if she knew what a trip to Disney World cost.

"Probably two or three thousand dollars," the woman said. "My ex-husband keeps saying he'll pay, but that's baloney. He doesn't even remember Jimmy's birthday."

I asked Gina if she'd contacted Make-A-Wish, which sponsors trips for sick kids.

"I've called," the woman said, "but this time of year they're overwhelmed with requests. We're on the waiting list."

"I know someone on the board," I said. "Let me give her a call."

"Would you really?"

"Sure. No guarantee it'll work, but it's worth a try."

"You're so nice," Gina said.

"But not a word to Jimmy," I said.

"I promise."

Jimmy was getting antsy.

"So what's the big secret?" he said.

"Oh, nothing," I said.

"Is it about Amber? 'Cause I have another question about her. I want to know what she looks like."

"She's pretty," I said.

"Not all gross with like drool and stuff?" Jimmy said.

"Jimmy!" Gina said.

"Well, they have to feed her, right? That's gotta be messy if she's in a coma."

"She doesn't eat like you or me," I said.

"That's right," the boy said, "she must get fed with a tube. There's kids like that at Children's. Let me ask you something else. Does she ever open her eyes?"

"I don't think so."

"Is she happy?"

"Very," I said.

"But how can she be happy? Wouldn't she rather be able to get up and play and stuff instead of lying there like some kind of zombie?"

Jimmy's mother cast him an eye.

"Jimmy—"

"Well, it's true, it's gotta be like *Dawn of the Dead* or something in there."

"Jimmy, no more," Gina said. "I'm sorry, Mister Nolan. It's disrespectful of him."

"It's Okay," I said. "Kids are curious. The best way I can explain it, Jimmy, is that Amber is at peace. She has a loving mother, which means she's in good hands."

Jimmy pondered that a moment and said: "I guess that much is true. Can she hear?"

"They say she can," I said.

"Will you tell her I hope she gets better? And tell her I didn't mean it about *Dawn of the Dead*. I never saw it, only ever heard about it. My mom doesn't let me watch horror movies."

I promised to tell Amber.

CHAPTER SEVEN: SACRED WATERS

"If I wasn't at the top of Hill's shit list before, I am now," Destiny Carter said.

It was Tuesday of Thanksgiving week, and today's *Trib* contained a full page of letters to the editor responding to Destiny's second installment in her "The New Disparities" series—about a single mother of four who had to quit her job so she could be home to oversee her children's' remote learning.

Many letter writers had hammered "The New Disparities," and the editorial page editor, last member of the department who had not been laid off, had not extended Destiny the courtesy of a chance to respond.

"Did you read these?" Destiny said.

I had, and also the social media posts, which were similarly scornful.

"Trumpsters," I said. "Besides, no one pays attention to letters to the editor."

"Hill does," said Destiny. "The consultants do. I'm sure Chamberlain does down in Orlando, too. If it were only letters, that might be Okay. But he'll see the social media."

To wit:

"Carter proves only how out of touch she is with reality," a woman wrote on Facebook. "This cancel-culture, bleeding-heart AOC-wannabee writes an insufferable sob story about the difficulty a welfare mother has finding day care. Did we, the taxpayers, bring these kids into the world?"

Wrote a man: "The answer to Destiny Carter's so-called 'daycare dilemma' is birth control. That's one thing I WOULD pay for for these welfare freeloaders."

Wrote someone else: "My husband died when I was thirty, leaving me with five children. We managed without daycare or a penny of government help. Sorry, Carter. Play your liberal violin elsewhere."

And that is just a sampling.

"You knew getting back to basics wouldn't be easy," I said.

"True," Destiny said.

That conversation was over. Destiny had something else on her mind.

"You're still angry at me, aren't you," she said.

"For what?"

"For speaking out like that at Hill's Mary News session."

Like Jones, after the meeting Destiny had talked to me about credibility and exploitation.

"We've been over that already," I said.

"And I'm more troubled than ever," Destiny said. "Things are spinning out of control. This Elizabeth Turner and her dream—I don't even know where to begin. And the fact that you've never heard Amber speak? It all comes down to Jennifer's word."

I turned defensive.

"You were raised a Catholic, too," I said. "Has it ever occurred to you that maybe it's possible—wildly improbable, yes, but at least possible—that what Jennifer claims is true? That Mary really *is* working miracles? Even if it isn't miracles, how do you explain Tony Callahan, Henry Spinelli, and Greta Ricci?"

"But you've built this whole thing on one woman," Destiny said.

"You know what I think?" I said. "I think you're jealous."

I not only ruled the front page—Hill had given me a raise, enough to afford a Back Bay apartment. The publisher had also hired a personal trainer and opened a line of credit for me at Brooks Brothers "Now that you're on TV," he said, "that shlumpy reporter look has to go."

"You're wrong," Destiny said. "Until recently, you've done some of your best writing ever this fall, Nick: the early Mary News, your story on Rose Redwing Brown. But things have gotten out of balance. We need more Rose Redwings and Frank Beazleys."

Hearing Frank's name brought me back. Inspired by the success of my "Nipmuc Nation" series, I had spent much of the next year at Sudbury State Hospital, an institution west of Boston for the long-term care of people with chronic and debilitating conditions. We were given that kind of time for in-depth journalism, back in the day.

Brain-damaged victims of strokes, accidents, and overdoses were hospitalized at Sudbury State, along with patients living with Alzheimer's disease and other neurological disorders.

Some were comatose, but Frank Beazley, the man I had profiled, was not.

Born in Nova Scotia, Frank had come to America after an abusive childhood with hope of building a new life. And he had. He found a good-paying job at a bakery, fell in love, and was ready to marry and start a family when, during a power outage, he fell down an elevator shaft at work and was left permanently paralyzed from the neck down.

Unable to independently get in or out of bed and confined to a motorized wheelchair, Frank had been moved to Sudbury State. His fiancé left him and friends eventually stopped visiting. These were circumstances that would have sent many into deep depression, understandably, but not Frank. Somehow, a rare spirit was born of his tragedy.

Holding a brush between his teeth, Frank began painting and was soon winning awards for his work. He wrote poems that were published in national literary magazines. In recognition of his championing of disability rights, he'd been invited by then-President Obama to visit the White House, where he'd been honored with a medal.

I spent many wonderful days with Frank over the course of a year's reporting, but my favorite hours were in autumn, when the vegetable garden he'd help plant was nearing harvest, and in spring, when the garden was being planted for the new season.

"It's a beautiful day," he said whenever we were in that garden. "Any day I'm still here is a beautiful day."

"I've been thinking a lot about Frank," Destiny said. "He gave us an appreciation for the moment. The proverbial stop and smell the roses."

"That series was a long time ago," I said.

"But the lessons are enduring. I remember you yourself saying that… way back when."

Hearing a commotion at the other end of the newsroom, I saw that a camera crew had arrived.

"If you'll excuse me," I said, *"60 Minutes* is here."

I did not expect Hill to convene the meeting on diversity coverage that he'd promised Destiny, but he did. Perhaps he wanted to have something to show if anyone—make that Courtney—came snooping.

If that was his intent, it backfired spectacularly.

The meeting began with the usual niceties, and then Hill said: "So what can we do to improve coverage of diversity and inequity issues?"

"A good start," Destiny said, "would be to cover them."

"But of course we do," Hill said.

He opened the paper to today's Celeb-Rate! feature: A story about an African American, Richard Prentice, who was marking his tenth year of delivering Meals on Wheels to elders.

"A most wonderful man," Hill said.

"He is," Destiny said. "But Celeb-Rate! features are not what I mean. You know that."

"Good news about good people is not good coverage?"

"It is, but we need more," Destiny said. "We need stories about health outcomes in communities of color. About educational inequities. Housing and food insecurity. Childhood trauma. The multiple stresses on women of color on low incomes living in violent neighborhoods. Disparities that COVID has magnified."

"Those are all important issues," Hill said. "But it's not what readers want today."

"You mean it's not what gets clicks," Bud said.

"Or pleases Chamberlain," said Erica Martinez.

"I wish it were otherwise," Hill said. "But I have my orders."

"But no moral compass," Destiny said.

Hill blew up then, unleashing a tirade of obscenities.

After which, he began to sob.

"I'm sorry," he said. "You can't believe the pressure I am under from Chamberlain."

If he expected sympathy, he got none.

As we returned to the newsroom, Destiny showed me her cell phone. An app was open.

"I recorded it," she said. "Someday I'll want proof."

The next day, Hill accepted an invitation to discuss Mary News on Boston Public radio, the top-rated talk show co-hosted by Margery Eagan and Jim Braude.

His appearance did not go as the marketing department, which had booked him but obviously never listened to the show, had promised him.

"I'm a third-generation Irish American who was raised Catholic, so I am well-versed in so-called miracles," Eagan said. "I also was a journalist for many years. Don't you think you've crossed some line with Mary News? Do you care about anything besides clicks?"

Before Hill could answer, Braude said: "Margery makes an excellent point. I've read the coverage, as much as I could stomach, that is, and all I see is shameless exploitation of a child and mother. Would you like to apologize now or would that clown in Florida you call boss fire you?"

And that was before things turned really ugly.

"Jim, look who's calling in," Eagan said. "Michelle Wu, newly elected mayor of Boston. Congratulations, Mayor! We have you scheduled for tomorrow to discuss your plans for the city, but we are always happy to have you on. What's on your mind?"

"The newspaper this lackey runs," Wu said. "Mr. Hill, do you really ascribe to the Good News Rules policy of your parent company?"

"Well, I—" Hill began, but Wu cut him off.

"That was a rhetorical question," she said. "The reason I called is to have you explain why you have only one African American, one Latina and one Asian American on your staff, and no Native Americans."

"We are in the process of recruiting more reporters of color," Hill said.

He lied.

"And who is handling the recruiting?" Wu said. "Bradley Winthrop III?"

"Yes, him," Hill said.

"SGM's diversity joker," Wu said. "Wealthy descendant of a man who made his fortune in the slave trade. Memberships in the Mar-a-Lago Club and the August National Club, which didn't admit a Black member until 1990 and no women until 2012. Shall I go on?"

Thus it went until Hill declared he was late for a meeting, and regrettably had to leave.

My next Mary column documented the outpouring of predictions sparked by the second part of Elizabeth Turner's dream: the foretelling of a "gesture of goodwill," which I described as "a so-called Christmas Event," a term that was soon ubiquitous, minus the "so-called."

Not surprisingly, many Catholics believed The Christmas Event would be Mary performing more miracles, and their wish lists on social media included "bringing back my son who lost his life to suicide," "ridding the world of war," "giving sight to my visually impaired husband," "stopping famines," "reversing global warming," and "ending the pandemic."

Others posted different takes. The Reverend Ezekiel Jackson, a Baptist minister, said the skies would open and a warm, christening rain would fall—in effect, a mass baptism. Wiccans predicted that the "Earth Mother," as they called Mary, would put people in touch with nature. Devotees of Nostradamus claimed Mary would herald establishment of a new world religion, with one declaring that "the great prophet foretold 'The Christmas Event.' " A New Ager believed "a cosmic portal" would open through which all could revisit previous lives.

Others saw portals of a different sort opening.

One person predicted punishment, not miracles, for sinners, and he cited the Book of Revelation, Chapter Eight, as proof: "The first angel sounded, and there followed hail and fire mingled with blood, and they were cast upon the earth; and the third part of the trees was burnt up." QAnon conspiracists predicted that Hillary Clinton and Huma Abedin would be arrested and charged with torturing and murdering a young girl and then drinking her blood, the ridiculous "frazzledrip" conspiracy theory embraced by kooks. A woman who wore a Stop the Steal t-shirt believed Biden would belatedly concede to Forty-five, who would return to the White House "since they will finally acknowledge reality, but that won't be a miracle, just the God-given truth."

"You've never seen such a bunch of nuts," I said in a newsroom conversation with Bud Fuller. "That dream's sent them crawling out of the woodwork."

"So why do you keep putting them in the paper?"

"Would you rather they saw it first on TV?"

"I'd rather they crawled back under their rocks."

"Well, that's not going to happen," I said. "As long as they're out there, we have an obligation to cover them."

"You can keep the obligation," Bud said. "I'm praying for the suburban editor to get canned. He gave me another man-on-the-street today—predictions for snowfall this winter."

"It's a weather story—at least you'll make Page One."

"If I don't get arrested."

"For a man-on-the-street?"

"For decking one of the men on the street who wasn't wearing a mask and started screaming shit at me about being an enemy of the people," Bud said.

"Why didn't you just back away?" I said.

"Because he was wearing a MAGA hat. I told him the Big Lie was total bullshit and Trump should get prison for life for the January 6 insurrection, and he ran at me cursing and spitting. So I punched him and he fell to the ground, his nose bleeding and whimpering like a baby. Then I kicked him in the balls. The people around us cheered. They also were taping it with their phones. Probably all over social media by now. Like I give a fuck."

"Good for you," I said. "But you know Hill or Roger Rogers will find out."

"And if I didn't head the Guild, I'd quit now. Sometimes I wonder why I even bother with that. SGM's going to win, sooner or later."

He meant the widespread belief that Chamberlain intended to bust the Guild, which was one of the only union shops left in his empire after he'd broken most other locals. Our contract—a leftover from the Gordon days—expired at year's end, and Hill, who did the dirty work, had refused to even schedule an exploratory meeting. Instead, he was girding for battle: rumor was he would soon threaten to eliminate employee parking, take back a personal day, increase our health insurance co-pay, end our life insurance, stop contributing to our 401(k)s, and end payroll deduction of union dues.

"Did you hear who Hill hired?" said Bud. "Levin and Howard."

I'd known about them: the principal partners in a law firm notorious for its anti-labor work.

"So, we hire someone big of our own," I said.

"We? No offense, Nick, but it's been a while since I've seen you've Zoomed into a Guild meeting."

"This fall's been pretty busy," I said. "At least I still pay my dues."

A small but increasing number of Guild members didn't. When Chamberlain finally won, they wanted a job.

That evening Bud, Destiny and I convened at Ernie's for supper and brews. The Guild didn't dominate our conversation.

What Bud described as a "brilliant" idea of his did.

"I've applied for the new position," he said.

"We're hiring?" Destiny said.

"Chamberlain apparently believes what he calls trend writers can save us. He's created open positions around SGM, including one here."

"I missed that one," I said.

"Me, too," said Destiny.

"Just went up today," Bud said. "This reporter, according to the posting, will obsessively cover trends in eating, vacationing, shopping, dating, exercising, entertaining, vacationing, binge watching, and more, all while building what is described as, and I quote, 'Super Huge followings on Facebook, Twitter, Instagram, and TikTok.' "

"Do you even have a Facebook account?" I said.

"Of course not," he said.

"Then what are you up to?" Destiny said.

"Wasting their time having to interview and deny me," Bud said. "And then watching them sweat when they learn I've hired a lawyer to file an age-discrimination suit."

"What if they *do* hire you?" Destiny said. "Hill might see it as a great way to stick it to you."

"Let him," Bud said. "I would make him regret it with my first story. But that seems extremely unlikely."

"You've gone off the deep end," I said.

"No," Destiny said, "he's become Einstein."

As Bud later related, he applied the next morning for the job. Within an hour, Roger Rogers scheduled an interview by Zoom.

"I am first required to read, for the record—and we *are* recording—the description of the position," Roger said.

"Please do," Bud replied.

"The Daily Tribune is looking to hire an exceptional reporter with an abiding interest in trends," Rogers recited. "Did we say trends? Yes, we did! Trends including shopping, dating, eating, exercising, entertaining, vacationing, binge watching, and dying. Ha! That last one was a joke. But not the rest. And there is no requirement that data and statistics are needed to confirm trends; what one or two people say is good enough for a story, and if you have the talent to start a trend yourself, you most certainly are the reporter we are looking for!"

"Roger that," Bud said.

"Are you mocking me?" Rogers said.

"Absolutely not," Bud said. "Only using the phrase we used in the military."

"You were in the military?" Rogers said.

"National Guard," Bud said.

Bud had served in the Maine National Guard's 121st Public Affairs Detachment after graduating from high school. It was the job that headed him into civilian journalism.

"Well thank you for your service, sir," Rogers said. "So next, I must you read the qualifications."

"Please do."

"The perfect candidate can immediately attract tens of thousands of followers on social media platforms including Facebook, Instagram, YouTube, TikTok, Pinterest, Post, and Twitter. Writing, spelling, and grammar skills would be nice, but absolutely are NOT required! We don't want to scare away the next Kardashian! And if you're worried about covering ISSUES, don't. We are looking for clicks, plain and simple."

"Got it," Bud said.

"So let's look at how your social media accounts are doing," Rogers said.

He scrolled through his computer and frowned.

"Not what I would call top of the funnel," he said. "Seems you do not have a Facebook account and you only have thirty-two Twitter followers."

"But I do have a very active Myspace account," Bud said.

He was spoofing Rogers.

"Myspace?" Rogers said. "That thing that went the way of Friendster and the BlackBerry?"

"Oh, no, you're wrong," Bud said. "Myspace rules the social-media roost."

"If you say so," Rogers said. "Now I must administer the screening test, which is required before we can decide if you will move to the next step."

"I'm ready," Bud said.

"Please rate in order, from most clicks to least, the following recent stories published on *Trib.com*," Roger said. "You can enter your answers in the chat box. Ready?"

"Ready."

"OK, here we go. 'Go Topless Day Draws Hundreds, Even a Few Men. Desperate Housewives Without Makeup, the Shocking Reality. Giant Rabbit Hops Across Wyoming, Arrives Hungry in Idaho. Texas Christian Has Proof She Walked on Water. She Hid Under the Bed to Spy on Her Husband But Instantly Regretted It. Sultry Country Star Steals Rival's Diamond Necklace, Hides It in Her Cleavage. Man Buries 42 School Buses Underground, Look When He Reveals the Inside. The Baddest Biker Girls in the World. We Can Determine Your Education Level in 25 Questions. Does Your Cat Throw Up Often? Try This One Trick. 50 Photos That Show the Wrong Side of Cruise Ships. 20 Hair Shapes That Make a Woman Over 60 Look 40. 20 Southern Phrases Northerners Don't Understand. 17 People Who Learned the Hard Way.' Take as much time as you need."

Thirty seconds later, Bud said: "I'm done"

"All of it?" Rogers said. He sounded incredulous.

"All of it," Bud said.

"No one else who's applied has finished it in less than ten minutes," Rogers said.

"So maybe I'm your man," Bud said.

"Let me tally your score," Rogers said.

He did, then said: "One hundred percent. That's not possible. No one has scored that high. You must have cheated. I don't know how, but you must have cheated."

"You do know this is being recorded," Bud said. "On my end, too."

"I didn't give you permission."

"You didn't have to. I have my cell phone capturing every word. Plus, I installed a screen recorder, which will give the video, too. Pretty good knowledge of today's trendy world for an old dog, wouldn't you say?"

"You do have access to the analytics, don't you?" Rogers said.

"Yes, but I never look at them," Bud said.

Silence for a moment.

"Well, Mr. Fuller, congratulations on your perfect performance," Rogers said. "This will have to be approved by corporate, of course, but this is all very promising! What trends shall I tell them you would be covering? With your acute sense of the zeitgeist, I would add."

"Cones," Bud said.

"As in ice cream?" Rogers said. "Marvelous!"

"Not ice cream," Bud said.

"But therein is a *super* trend!" Rogers said. "New flavors are being dreamed up and brought to market every day. Here in Florida, we now have DeSantis Delight, Cruz Caramel, Trump Turtle Toffee and Brady Brownie Batter. The boss loves them all. And who knows? Bud Fuller might start a trend of his own with Fabulous Fuller Fudge!"

"I mean cones as in traffic," Bud said.

Another pause.

"Those orange things you see on construction sites," Rogers said.

"Those orange things you see on construction sites. Very trendy. You may think they are found only on roads and around buildings going up and the like, but the truth is they are everywhere. College kids have them in their dorms. Sellers of vintage cones clean up on eBay. Pinterest is jammed with them. And did you know there are 17 cone museums around the U.S.?"

"I'm not sure I get it," Rogers said.

"But you would get an age-discrimination lawsuit if I don't get this job."

"What are you saying?"

"That you have no intention of recommending me for this job because I'm sixty-two years old."

"You could not be more wrong!" Rogers said.

He sounded pained.

"We'll see," Bud said.

Meanwhile, the *60 Minutes* broadcast opened the floodgates on me.

More publications and media outlets including Grupo Globo, *The Japan Times*, Agence France-Presse, the BBC, *Forbes*, and *Fortune* published Mary News. O, The *Oprah* magazine, sent a reporter to Middleton. A writer from *People* showed up at *The Trib* at the moment Hill walked into the lobby, and the publisher personally escorted her to my desk.

And you would think at least a few of my *Trib* colleagues would have been congratulatory, but mostly I overheard grumbling about camera crews in the newsroom and sniping like Bud's. A.J. whined again to Jones, this time insisting on a piece of Mary News for herself; her angle, Jones later told me, would be ongoing commentary about how non-religious types such as herself perceived miracles.

"She thought someone with chronic fatigue syndrome but little faith in God would bring special insight," Jones said. "And maybe she would have, but Hill would never have allowed it."

Only Ted Matthews was complimentary. "Awesome work," he wrote in an email. "I hope someday to be half the writer you are."

I couldn't tell if he was yanking my chain, but I didn't care. I had bigger issues. The *People* reporter had just left and the publisher was summoning me.

"The chairman wants to meet you," Hill said after closing his office door.

"Mr. Chamberlain?" I said.

"That would be him."

"I'd be honored," I lied.

"You'll be more than honored," Hill said. "You'll be pampered. He's sending the corporate jet to bring you to Orlando. Have you ever flown in a corporate jet, Nick?"

"Are you kidding? When I fly, I go Southwest."

"Worst airline ever. I'd rather hitchhike than fly with them. You'll love corporate travel, trust me. You'll love even more what the chairman has for you when you arrive."

"Which is?"

"My lips are sealed," Hill said. "This is the chairman's vision, which he insists on spelling out personally to you. Make sure you keep the next two weeks open. He'll be sending for you in early December."

I left Hill's office and drove to Middleton. The *60 Minutes* frenzy had swelled the crowd to the biggest size ever—more than three thousand people, according to the police estimate—and the sub-industry that had sprung up was going gangbusters. Like some medieval bazaar, vendors were selling bibles, crucifixes, scapulars, prayer cards, rosary beads, statues of Mary and Jesus, and more.

Other vendors were cashing in on Mary News in more creative ways. A travel agent had opened a booth and was offering discount tours of "Miracle America": several sites around the country including a statue in Miami that purportedly shed tears of blood, and Madonna of the Windows, an image of Mary supposedly visible on a bank building in Maryland. With the weather cold now, a woman was selling a line of custom sweaters, umbrellas, and wool caps with religious slogans ("Mary's Martyrs," "Amber's Angels," and "Jennifer's Jewels"). Another woman was selling Pastoral Pretzels and Fatherly Franks. Someone else was offering a line of Divine Drinks: radiant root beer, celestial soda, the messiah milk shake. A woman named Maggie McMurray was pushing her Maggie's Miracle Muffins. Some dude with a ponytail was selling Spirit Spritzers. Another man who had led protests outside Planned Parenthood was taking orders for Prolife Probiotics. An older woman sold Mary's Manna and Holy Hummus. A sales representative from Kraft Heinz handed out discount coupons for Miracle Whip. More hawkers were arriving, and the Middleton Assistant Town Clerk was busy at his booth, selling amusement licenses, ordinarily $35 but now $100, checks payable to Town of Middleton.

Seizing opportunity, the pastor of St. Agnes Parish had opened his church around-the-clock for the lighting of votive candles, suggested donation ten dollars. The candles were so popular that the priest had arranged for two dozen new rows of holders and with those almost full, was considering a tent to hold more.

When I finally made it to her house, Jennifer was giddy with excitement.

"Come," she said, her hand trembling. "I have to show you something."

I followed her into Amber's room.

The girl looked no different than the last time I'd seen her: a child entombed in a coma. A sort of zombie, as Jimmy had said.

No, Amber had not changed—but her room had. Jennifer had bought new drapes, replaced all the furniture save for the hospital bed, and hung a gold-and-jewel encrusted crucifix on the wall. A large statue of Mary graced a bureau. Gregorian chant streamed from Pandora on her Bose. A candle flickered and incense burned.

"Very nice," I said.

It wasn't.

The room creeped me out: It reminded me of a funeral parlor, lacking only the lilies.

"Thank you," said Jennifer. "But what I really wanted to show you is this."

She drew my attention to a large painting that stood on an easel near the head of Amber's bed. It was an ornately framed, life-size reproduction of Fra Filippo Lippi's *Madonna and Child with Angels,* which hangs in the Uffizi. I'd been with her when she'd ordered it online. She'd paid five thousand dollars from her GoFundMe account, which continued to swell.

"Look at it," Jennifer said. "Go on. Get up close."

I saw that clear liquid had dripped from the Madonna's right eye, run down the painting, and pooled in a silver bowl underneath.

"What is it?" I said.

"Tears," Jennifer said.

"Come on."

"Not ordinary tears, of course. These are tears from the Mother of God."

I remembered enough from my upbringing to know that claims of weeping Madonnas had persisted for centuries, and some had been officially recognized by the Vatican. If memory served me, you could even purchase vials of such sacred oil from certain shrines in Europe.

"When did it start?" I said.

"Three days ago, just after the painting arrived. I placed in on the easelt immediately—and the next morning, tears."

I examined the painting. There didn't appear to be any hole in Madonna's eye—no seeming way the liquid could have been introduced from a source behind the canvas. I considered asking Jennifer if she owned an eyedropper but didn't.

"Have you seen it come out?" I said.

"No, but every morning there's more. I collect it in that bowl. I have two ounces already."

"But you've never actually watched—you know, sat there and seen what happens."

"Oh ye of little faith," she said. "You don't believe, do you?"

"I didn't say that."

"But you have doubts," said Jennifer.

"Who wouldn't?"

"No one, I suppose—no one who hasn't lived through the last many weeks. Mary's with us, Nick. Don't keep fighting her. Open your heart and let her in."

I'd tried that once, growing up Catholic. Whatever was going on here, it wasn't Mary wanting Nick Nolan to return to the fold.

"So what are you going to do with this stuff?" I said.

"This is not stuff," Jennifer declared, "this is sacred oil. Speaking through Amber, as always, Mary has instructed me to distribute it to the faithful."

"You mean sell it?"

Jennifer laughed.

"How absurd," she said, "that Mary should seek material profit from saving souls."

"Catholics sold relics during the Middle Ages," I said.

"These are not the Middle Ages. If the faithful choose to make a voluntary donation to a holy cause, that is their business. But we will not sell the Virgin Mary's tears. Never."

Jennifer dipped her finger into the bowl and made the sign of the cross, anointing herself.

"Shall you?" she said, offering me the bowl.

"No thanks," I said.

Jennifer lifted the bowl and poured its contents into a crystal cruet. She stoppered the cruet with a cork and handed it to me.

"Please take it to the cardinal," said Jennifer. "Have his people analyze it. That way, you can resolve your doubt."

"What if they say it's only water?"

Jennifer pondered that and said: "You don't have to keep doing this, you know."

"Do what?"

"Spreading the word. You could walk away today, and there would be no hard feelings. I would manage. The Blessed Virgin would see to that."

I fell silent. I looked at Amber, and Destiny's words came to mind—Jimmy Pulaski's questions, too.

"You know what troubles me most?" I said.

"That you've never heard Amber speak."

"That, too, but what troubles me most is this: If Mary's really here, why does she leave Amber like this? Why hasn't she performed the miracle of bringing her back to the life she deserves?"

"You think I haven't agonized over that?" said Jennifer. "You think this hasn't tested my faith? It has—and does. But as the saying goes, the Lord truly does work in strange and mysterious ways. It's not my role to question."

"It's heart-breaking," I said. "Cruel. It reminds me of when I was a kid and I asked a priest why wars happened if God was almighty and all-good."

"What was his answer?"

"Something about Adam and Eve and the apple, and mankind having free will."

"He was a wise man, that priest," said Jennifer. "Every turning point in our lives presents us with a decision. My own view is that, like Amber, you have been chosen. Much as St. John the Baptist cried out in the desert, the Lord has called you—*you*, Nick—to be a herald. It's your decision what to do with that.

"My guess is that were Amber to offer her opinion, she would beg you to be more resolute with your stories, stop the 'allegeds' and 'so-calleds' and speak truth. But perhaps I have misjudged you. Perhaps you are just another godless media whore."

"That's awfully harsh," I said.

Jennifer smiled.

"And I don't believe it," she said. "I was only hoping for a laugh."

"It wasn't funny."

"I'm sorry. My point is only that nothing's preventing you from speaking truth. Certainly your publisher would not get in your way. But *you* must decide, not me—and not Amber. Take this oil and do what you will. It's almost six o'clock."

Escorted by a policeman, I went to the trailer that Hill had rented from a movie-production services firm. The trailer had a reception area, dressing room, and small studio. I entered through the back door. Karen Swanson, my makeup artist, a woman in her twenties, awaited me.

"I was just about to panic!" she said, as she began applying pancake.

"I lost track of time," I said.

"That's okay. At least your hair doesn't need much work tonight. You used product, didn't you."

I confirmed that I had.

"Now if we could only get you to use teeth whitener, you'd be awesome."

It was five minutes to six; on the monitor, the WQZ-TV Channel 14 anchor was teasing tonight's broadcast.

Hill had recently signed an agreement with WQZ, which owned the highest ratings in Boston, to be the exclusive broadcast conduit of Mary News. The open briefings were history; from now on, my TV appearances originated from inside the trailer. If the competition wanted to watch from the screen mounted on the roof, they were welcome. Every other station and cable outlet in town had squawked at this new arrangement and one had threatened a lawsuit, but Hill wasn't budging. A torrid relationship had developed between WQZ and *The Trib* this fall as Mary News unfolded: over golf and dinners at The Commonwealth Club, according to one of Courtney's columns, Hill and the station's general manager had negotiated a broad strategic alliance. The two men were in final negotiations for what Hill trumpeted as "one-stop advertising": one call, one salesman, and one contract would buy carefully coordinated print and broadcast commercials (with discounts for extended plans).

Hill also was permitting WQZ to build a satellite newsroom in a corner of our own, and he'd authorized *Trib.com* to stream the station twenty-four hours a day; in return, WQZ agreed to tease tomorrow's paper in spots that aired daily during primetime. Inspired by my success, Hill was encouraging more of our reporters to go on air, with media training available on company time. Several reporters jumped at the chance. It could only boost their numbers.

"And as always," the Channel 14 anchor said, "*Trib* columnist Nick Nolan will have the latest from Miracle Middleton—live and on scene. All this plus Patriots and Eric Fisher with the weather, at six."

"Done," Karen Swanson announced with a final dose of hair spray. "You look marvelous."

"As Billy Crystal would say."

"When did he say that?"

"Before you were born," I said.

I opened the door to the studio.

"You're on after the first break—at six-oh-seven," my producer said.

"I think I should lead," I said.

"Too late."

"It's big."

"Can't do it, Nick. They need word downtown by five-thirty if you've got something breaking, otherwise it's six-oh-seven, you know that."

I took my seat, and the producer clipped a microphone to my shirt and ran a sound check. I watched the monitor as the news began, with a story about Luke Turner announcing the Minuteman Mall would officially open on December 11, "leaving plenty of time for all your Christmas shopping." I could see tomorrow's front page.

"How long do I have?" I asked my producer.

"Sixty seconds, same as always."

"Can't you give me ninety?"

"Sorry."

"Then how about a close shot of this when I open?" I took Jennifer's cruet out of my pocket.

"What is it?"

"Tears. Allegedly Mary's."

"Holy shit. Yeah, we can get close on it."

The commercial break ended, the anchor introduced me, and I was on.

"For those awaiting word from Mary," I said, "the news is unchanged: according to Jennifer, she has not spoken. But she may have done something more amazing. I have here a liquid that Jennifer claims originates from a painting of Madonna and child. If the claim is true, I have in my hand tears from the Mother of God."

"Incredible," the anchor said. "Does it have healing powers?"

"That remains unknown," I said, "but with Jennifer's permission, I will be bringing this to the archdiocese for testing. How long that will take—and what the outcome will be—I cannot predict. But let me repeat what Jennifer told me: 'The Lord works in strange and mysterious ways.' "

"Of course, you'll have more detail in your column tomorrow," the anchor said.

"A lot more—including a description of the painting and the story of the so-called tears in Jennifer's own words. *The Trib*: online, home-delivered, and in stores everywhere… and this week only, fifty percent off on subscriptions."

"Thanks Nick. And now Andy Rodmanwith the weather."

The red light went off and I was done. I removed my microphone, thanked my producer, and stepped outside.

The crowd had watched me on the big screen, and they knew what I carried.

I was immediately surrounded.

"Anoint us, Nick," one of them said.

"I have to take it to the cardinal," I said.

"The cardinal isn't dying. Anoint us."

"Jennifer will have more tomorrow," I said. "There will be plenty for everyone."

"I can't wait, Nick," a woman in a wheelchair said.

"Anoint us."

"Anoint us!"

Chanting "Anoint us! Anoint us!" the crowd closed in on me.

I was trapped.

"Anoint us! Anoint us!"

Now a woman with a gaunt face and hollow eyes was grabbing at me. I'd slipped the cruet into my coat pocket.

"Where is it?" she demanded. "Goddamn it, give me the oil! I'm out of time!"

She began hitting me.

A man grabbed me from behind.

He was about to bring me down when I heard the welcome shouts of the police.

"Break it up!" Officer Maloney said.

"Back off!" his partner said.

He was holding a Taser.

Reinforcements rushing over had them, too.

The crowd backed off.

"Follow me," Maloney said as the reinforcements opened passage through the crowd.

To them he said: "Ladies and gentlemen, don't ever try a stunt like this again. Mr. Nolan's got stories to write."

Courtney's column the first of December was another broadside at me.

"Could this be mass hysteria?" she wrote, citing the Salem witch trials as a possible precedent. "Or, like Orson Welles' War of the Worlds, is this blatant fraud—perpetrated by a one-time Hollywood actress in partnership with a newspaper that, until it found its golden goose, was on the ropes? Now we have the so-called sacred oil—flowing unwitnessed, of course. And speaking of the oil—isn't the Catholic Church the last agency that should be entrusted with analyzing it?"

I could have pointed out that the Church had allowed the very carbon-14 tests that had debunked the Shroud of Turin, but my days of sparring with Courtney were over.

No, it was the second half of her column that unsettled me. Courtney had obtained a copy of Hill's confidential memo to Chamberlain about *The Trib*'s plans for The Christmas Event.

By any standard, even his own, Hill was outrageous.

In the memo, Hill proposed to co-sponsor with Channel 14 a contest in which the winners of an essay on Mary, "to be judged by a panel of clerics," would receive vials of sacred oil—and, "if Nick can persuade her, and I have every hope he can, a private audience with Jennifer." He proposed having the Franklin Mint manufacture limited-edition statues and crucifixes, for sale only through our Web site, "something guaranteed to build traffic." He wanted me on the air at midnight Christmas, and three times Christmas Day. He wanted WQZ to charter a blimp and the cardinal to celebrate Mass outside Jennifer's. He wanted to pursue a strategic partnership with the makers of Miracle Whip, Miracle Ear, Miracle Gro, Miracle Cream, Miracle Spray, Nature's Golden Miracle, "and any other company or product with a similar name."

Hill's grand ambition was a ninety-six-page special supplement to be published seven shopping days before Christmas—not coincidentally, during the two-week-long "celebration" that would accompany the official opening of the Minuteman Mall.

The supplement, Hill wrote, would have a glossy keepsake cover with "a computer-enhanced rendition of Mary spreading her arms in a rainbow. Exclusive new Mary copy will be found inside. Online subscribers will get a QR code to read same. We can easily double our rates, and not just from religious advertisers. Luke's in for fifteen pages. With all of the negative publicity they get, cigarette companies will rush to be associated with a holy cause. Same should hold true with the wine and beer industries. Note to SGM Natl. Sales Force: Find the major supplier of altar wine and see if they want in. Think it's Christian Bros., though not sure."

Hill had handed Courtney dynamite.

"The question is," she wrote, "will anyone buy into this profanity? The sad truth is, in an era when spirituality has its price like everything else, many will. Thanks in no small measure to the resurrected Nick Nolan, pun intended, Middleton has more in common with the Super Bowl than God. Now Hill proposes to wring from Christmas the last vestige of holiness left by the marketers and retailers. I'm not much for religion, but this strikes me as sacrilege. Add the damage to what's left of *The Trib*'s credibility, and it almost makes you wish for McClatchy."

Half an hour later, Hill's secretary called me to his office. Her boss was in the bathroom when I arrived.

"Be right out, Nicky Boy," he said from behind the closed door.

A moment later, the toilet flushed and Hill emerged, smiling.

"It's funny how you do some of your best thinking on the throne," said Hill. "I was just thinking of you."

I believe he intended to flatter me.

"I was wondering if you golf," the publisher said.

"I don't."

"Too bad. I was going to tell you to pack your clubs. You're leaving for Orlando tomorrow."

"Nice," I said.

"Show some excitement, Nick—this is big. By the way, can I offer you a chip?"

Today's selection was ranch flavored.

"No thanks," I said.

"Tom?"

Hill's dog snapped one up, then settled back into his doggie bed.

"You seem out of sorts this morning," said Hill. "Is it Courtney's column?"

He had a copy on his desk.

"As a matter of fact," I said, "a few things in there do concern me."

"Such as?"

"Whether we aren't going overboard with our Christmas plans. Assuming what Courtney wrote is true."

"It's true," said Hill. "One thing I'll say for her otherwise unpleasant self: she got her facts straight this time."

"Even your accepting cigarette ads?"

"The First Amendment, Nick. The very same amendment that lets reporters ruin lives. Are we off the record, as always?"

I nodded.

"Courtney Lawford will soon be a moot issue. David is buying CoolBostonWeekly. He's been negotiating for two weeks and is ready to close the deal."

"Why would he want CoolBostonWeekly?"

"From a market perspective, it makes perfect sense: the advertising synergies will be breathtaking. And once we own it, Courtney's ass is grass, you have my word."

"I still think she raises legitimate issues today," I said.

Hill's face knit into a frown. I thought he might be having second thoughts about the sacred oil contest or maybe the pitch to cigarette makers, now that the world knew his plans.

"I *am* troubled by one thing," he said.

"What?"

"Do you guys really call me that?"

"Call you what?"

"You know. That vulgar phrase."

"You mean Poop Man?"

"Yes, that."

It seemed he couldn't bring himself to pronounce the words.

"I've never heard anyone around here use it," I said.

Could it have taken this long for him to learn about it? I thought.

"Because I believed in Olestra," Hill said. "I believe in it to this day. I estimate I have personally eaten a thousand bags of Wow chips and related products and I can honestly say I have never experienced a so-called complication, not even a fart. So, for Courtney or anyone to go on like that—I have to be honest, it hurts."

"I can see why it would."

"It hurts so much that I have just instructed Paula to fire A.J. She's the source of these leaks."

"How do you know?"

"An ingenious spyware program called Watch-It that Paula installed," the publisher said. "It screens every text, photo and email leaving and entering the building, as well as whatever's moving around inside. And not only does it monitor—it makes a copy of everything, providing us with an electronic trail that can be very useful in certain cases."

Union activity, for example, I thought. I made a mental note to tell Bud Fuller, who had not been reprimanded for decking the Trumpster. Hill had seen a video of the incident, and according to Bud, privately congratulated him "for doing what I would have done. And don't worry about Chamberlain. Our chairman may have friends at Mar-a-Lago, but he also finds humor in an old guy like Fuller decking some overweight dufus with a big mouth." But surely Hill would want to spy on his union activities.

"But the spyware program I especially like is called Furtive Forward," Hill continued. "Once we target someone—A.J., in this instance—it automatically sends copies of every communication to me or anyone I designate. I receive them just like regular email—they pop up into a special folder. Gives the old phrase 'you've got mail' special meaning."

"Do you monitor phone calls, too?" I said.

"We can, although it wasn't necessary in this instance: A.J.'s email provided ample proof. She's history now. Probably cleaning out her desk even as we speak."

"A.J.'s a profoundly unhappy person," I said. "I'll be surprised if she doesn't sue."

"Let her—the savings on her health plan will more than cover the legal expenses. That's another thing I've had enough of—her so-called chronic fatigue syndrome. You think I don't read the medical records? CFS is bullshit, we all know that. Nothing but a fancy name head cases put on their neuroses."

Actually, I thought, *a disorder recognized by the CDC and medical organizations everywhere. Whether she has it is another matter.*

"In any event," Hill said, "I didn't ask you here to gripe. I wanted to give you some friendly advice."

He waved my Rose Redwing Brown column.

"Don't mention this in Florida," Hill said.

"You didn't like it."

"Given your otherwise exemplary work," he said, "I could tolerate it. And with our successful emphasis on good news, I suppose it's permissible once in a blue moon to toss the do-gooders a bone—they buy papers and sit on contest panels, too. Just don't mention it to the chairman. David hates giving climate change attention. His father was an oil executive. Made a fortune from petroleum. Sits on Exxon Mobil's board. David himself is on the board of the American Enterprise Institute."

"Which receives funding from the Koch brothers."

"Correct."

"I won't talk climate change," I said.

"Good. I've been very careful in building your image, Nick. For example, I haven't published any of these."

Hill opened a manila envelope and dumped several dozen letters and email printouts on his desk.

"I'll spare you the agony of reading them. Most are from Catholic die-hards or whatever you'd call them who think we're dirtying their religion—as if priests raping altar boys didn't take the shine off long ago. Please. There's nothing worse than self-righteous zealots. Sure you wouldn't like a chip, Nick?"

"No, thanks."

"Well, there you go," Hill finished. "Off to Orlando for a one-on-one with the chairman. You really don't golf?"

"I really don't."

"Well at least bring your bathing suit. We'll have a driver at your door at six tomorrow morning."

Leaving Hill's office, I bumped into Terry Winters. We went back a long way—we'd started at *The Trib* the same week. Maybe it was that nostalgic touch that had kept us friends.

"I thought you were in court," I said. Because of his lead role in *The Trib* investigation that had won us a Pulitzer, Terry was a key witness in the Sabella libel case.

"I was," Terry said. "I've also been working on this."

He was holding a printout. Like the best of his kind, Terry was instinctively furtive: except for Jones, to whom he reported, no one knew what he was working on until it appeared in the paper, not even Hill. He worked on his own computers, never connecting to *Trib* servers and always protected by firewalls and encryptions. His sensitive phone calls and texts were exclusively on a Purism Librem 5 phone.

"It's a story about the mall," Terry said. "Remember that so-called disgruntled steelworker who testified before the Mall Commission last fall?"

I did. We'd run a four-inch story about his claim that defective beams had been used to build the Minuteman Mall. As far as I knew, no one had ever followed up on it.

"I decided to take a look," said Terry, "and it turns out he was right: they *did* use sub-grade iron. Not deliberately—it was a screw-up at the factory. Tons of it had already been erected when the contractor found out. By then, they would have had to tear half the place down to replace it, and Turner refused. He would have lost millions. Jones put the story on the budget for Sunday, Hill read it, and this morning he left a message on my machine ordering me to destroy it and all my files."

"You won't."

"Of course not," said Terry. "But I will have choice words when I go up to his office now. And if he still won't run it, I'll get it to someplace that will."

CHAPTER EIGHT: THE MIRACLE KID

As Hill's driver chauffeured me to Hanscom Field, I checked my voice mail. I had one message: Jennifer wishing me luck. Whatever time I got back, she wanted me to come by her house.

"I have a feeling a celebration will be in order!" she said.

At Hanscom, a sentry waved the limo onto the tarmac and we stopped next to a Gulfstream G700. I walked to the jet, where the pilot greeted me with a handshake.

"It's an honor to meet you, Mr. Nolan," he said. "I'm such a big fan. No one writes like you."

"You mean Mary News," I said.

"Of course," the pilot said. "You think I'd be complimenting you about socks?"

He laughed mightily.

I laughed, too, and said: "As a matter of fact, yes. I won a Pulitzer for that column."

"You're kidding," the pilot said.

"Of course," I said. "That was the worst drivel maybe ever in the history of journalism."

"Then you never read my hometown paper," the pilot said. "*The Houston Happy Herald.*"

I climbed in, the pilot got in behind me, introduced his co-pilot, and showed me to the cabin. I'd never been on an executive jet before, and it was larger than I'd expected. Grander, too—with leather-bound seats, wide-screen TVs, computer, stereo, telephones, chess set, bar, pantry, today's papers, and a selection of magazines.

"The seats fold down if you'd like to nap," the pilot said. "And here's fresh Starbucks coffee and croissants, in case you're hungry. Make yourself at home while we prepare for takeoff."

We ascended over Concord. I was reading the *People* magazine profile of me—again—when the cockpit door opened and the copilot joined me.

"Just wanted to alert you that we're expecting some mild turbulence," he said. "You might want to fasten your seatbelt, Mr. Nolan. Unless you'd rather use some of that sacred oil to buy us smooth flying."

"Seriously?" I said.

"My idea of a joke," the copilot said. "Sorry, I didn't mean to offend you."

"You didn't," I said. "I get this from my colleagues all the time."

"Probably jealous," the copilot said. "After all, how exciting can writing about politics or business be? You, on the other hand, get to have your fun."

"I try."

"And you succeed. It's a real gift, Mr. Nolan. I'd give my right arm for an imagination like yours."

It dawned on me what he was saying.

"You think I make things up," I said.

"You mean you don't?" he said.

"Of course not."

"Nothing?"

"Nothing."

"Not even a little something here and there?"

"Not even a little something here and there."

"Well I'll be darned. I thought this was good old-fashioned entertainment. Don't let the facts get in the way of a good story and all that."

I explained about my careful use of disclaimers.

"Take it from me," the copilot said. "No one reads the fine print. The only question is: *Do I want more?* And the answer with this miracle story is yes—I can't wait to see what tomorrow will bring. So, do I care if that painting really weeps—or Jennifer mixes her oil up in the kitchen sink? Don't be silly."

"What about Greta Ricci, and Spinelli, and Callahan?"

"Personally, I think the docs were right: those people were going to get better, anyway. But who cares? This thing keeps unfolding with more twists and turns than a John Grisham novel. I can't imagine what rabbit Jennifer is going to pull out of her hat for The Christmas Event, but I'll say this: I can't wait to see."

"What if nothing happens?"

"Something will," the copilot said with conviction. "That girl's on top of her game."

"You think she's scripting this," I said.

"Well, she *was* in Hollywood. But maybe she really does believe in all this hocus-pocus. And I suppose there's a chance, however remote, that it's really divine intervention. Whatever it is, Jennifer has sure milked it for all it's worth. I'm telling you, Mr. Nolan, you're on top of the world. You're the last person who should care if that miracle stuff is real or in her head."

Chamberlain's driver met me at the airport and took me to the world headquarters of SuperGoodMedia, which looked exactly as it had on screen the morning we learned *The Trib* had been sold: massive, impersonal, vaguely futuristic. Chamberlain's executive assistant, a woman named Natalia Perez, met me in the lobby.

A guard pinned a badge to my suit and told me it expired today at five o'clock sharp.

"Follow me," said Perez. "And keep your badge visible at all times."

We travelled a long hall whose walls were decorated with plaques and citations and entered a waiting room where a second guard checked our IDs. Perez escorted me to an inner door and punched in a code. The door opened into her office.

"You weren't kidding about security," I said.

She led me to another door and knocked.

"Mr. Chamberlain, Mr. Nolan is here," Perez said.

On-screen, Chamberlain's office had appeared massive—but in real life, it was small, about twenty-by-twenty feet, with one desk, one table, and a wall with TV monitors. There were no windows, no couch, and just one photograph: a shot of him golfing with Trump at Mar-A-Lago. His desk was surprisingly uncluttered—just a laptop, two neat piles of papers, two telephones, and his GOOD NEWS RULES sign. The windowlessness especially disturbed me. It reminded me of Dr. Strangelove.

"Nick Nolan," said Chamberlain, rising and offering his hand. "I can't tell you how delighted I am to finally meet you in person."

Once again, I was surprised—Chamberlain looked older in person than on screen. He looked hard, as if his success had brought little pleasure.

"The honor is mine," I said.

"Would you like an espresso?"

"I'd love one," I said.

I hated espresso.

"Natalia," Chamberlain said, "would you have Carlos bring two espressos? Sit down, Nick. We're going to watch some tape."

Chamberlain operated the remote control and a ten-year-old image of me hosting my old TV show appeared on one of the monitors. I was interviewing Miss Junior Massachusetts.

"That's sure an antique," I said.

"I show it to you to make a point."

"That I was a big loser," I joked.

"Bigger than any I've ever seen," Chamberlain said, "and believe me, I've seen a lot. You were wooden and embarrassingly trite. Am I correct in assuming you had no media training for this pathetic show?"

"You're correct."

"No fashion or makeup help."

"No."

Chamberlain worked the remote and another clip began. It was me displaying the sacred oil on the news two evenings ago.

"Now we flash ahead to today. Notice the difference?"

"I suppose."

"You *suppose*? This is a totally different person. You and the camera are not just friends now—you're lovers. I know from Bruce that you've had extensive media training this fall—he tells me you're quite a team player that way."

"I have a stylist now, too."

"Well, you certainly looked like shit ten years ago," Chamberlain said. "Wrote like shit, too. They should use that socks column in every journalism class as Exhibit Number One of the worst writing ever. But this you today—it's more than just new threads and a weekend with an overpaid media consultant. Something's happened down deep inside where no trainer or stylist can go, Nick. I've seen it before—rarely. You've been transformed. You've come alive on camera. I've watched all your tape and it's consistent—and quite remarkable."

"Thank you."

"It would be a terrible waste to confine you to the Boston market, Nick, big as it is. You have a national TV future—an international one, in all honesty. So, you will stay in Boston through The Christmas Event and then you'll move down here to a condo of your choice, for which I will pay. We'll continue to syndicate your column, but you'll be writing only once a week. Your main responsibility will be hosting a coast-to-coast, primetime and streamed TV show called *The Other Side.* You can continue with Mary News until it fizzles—everything fizzles, sooner or later—Zooming with Jennifer and flying up there as needed. But your main responsibility beginning in 2022 will be *The Other Side.* "

"Great title," I said.

"It's one of mine, naturally. The show, which we'll launch in the spring, will feature guests who embrace what, for lack of a better term, I call non-traditional beliefs. People who believe in Taoism, Buddhism, crystals, Tarot, feng shui, reincarnation, channeling, Area 51, ESP, astrology, mediums, Stonehenge, Carlos Castaneda, you get the picture. Our market research reveals a major untapped appetite for these topics, even among those raised with traditional beliefs. Boomers are especially interested as they creep toward the grave."

Chamberlain's phone rang.

"Scott's on line three," I heard Perez say.

Chamberlain looked pained.

"I'll take it," he said. "Nick, you can wait outside."

I left Chamberlain's office for Perez's. She wasn't exactly chipper now, either.

"Have a seat," she said. "Hopefully this won't be long."

I sat near the door to the boss's quarters—sufficiently close that I managed to catch a few phrases from Chamberlain's end of the conversation. Phrases including "Fuck the SEC... of course I know what a subpoena is... they get those over my dead body... no, Scott, I don't want another law firm... pay it out of cash reserves... the balance is *what*? ... Jesus Christ, how long do we have? ... you're shitting me, whistleblowers get full protection? ... I'll get IT to do a trace...."

At least, that's what I thought I heard. My head was reeling.

Chamberlain was still on the phone when Perez beckoned me to her desk. In a low voice she said: "Nick, can we speak confidentially for a moment?"

"Sure."

"We're off the record?"

"Yes."

"Way, way off?" she said.

"Absolutely."

"Cross your heart and hope to die?"

"Cross my heart and hope to die."

"You were raised Catholic," Perez said. "Know that you will burn in hell if you relate any of this to anyone, except at the right time to one person."

"Who?"

"You know who."

"Terry Winters."

"Right, him."

It occurred to me that I was being set up, but curiosity compelled me.

"You know what I think would be a *real* miracle?" Perez said.

"What?"

"If I finally had luck finding another job."

"What's wrong with this one?"

"You are seriously asking me that? You've met him. He's got the people skills of a piranha. Would *you* want to work for that prick?"

"I do work for him."

"Don't be cute with me, Nick. He expects me to be available 24/7 for calls, texts, whatever. And God forbid I don't get back to him immediately; I hear about it for the next week. And that's just for starters. You know what he pays? Let me spare you the guessing game. Sixteen bucks an hour. I could do better at Target. Plus, no health benefits, no 401(k), nada."

"Does the board know this?"

"You mean those asshole golfing buddies of his? Don't make me laugh. Wouldn't matter if they did know. To my knowledge, they haven't met except on the course for more than a year. The term 'rubber stamp' comes to mind. Also, white, male, and MAGA."

"Wow," I said.

"You're probably wondering how I got into this fucking mess. I blame my sister. Maybe not fair, but it's how I feel. Three years ago, she came over from Puerto Rico, where most of our family still is, seeking better opportunity. Greener pastures and all that. And for her it *has* been greener. She has a mid-level job at Publix that pays triple what I make. And they're sending her to business school, grooming her for an executive position. She always was the lucky one.

"Me? Not so lucky. I graduated college with a degree in economics and was considering grad school when I fell in love. With a big loser, as it turned out. And a criminal. Cleaned out my savings before he left, though I didn't have the evidence to go to the police. How many movies have this storyline? A lot, and there's a reason why: It happens. Happened to me. Fast-forward to when I was waiting tables in Bayamón and Hurricane Maria hit. The restaurant blew away and the apartment I was sharing with friends was flattened. Thank God none of us were hurt, but you know what shape the island was left in.

"My sister paid for me to come to the mainland. If only I'd listened to her when she said I should apply to Publix. Instead, I answered an ad on ZipRecruiter for a position at what was described as 'America's fast-growing media company,' interviewed, and was hired. Started the very next day. I later found out that Chamberlain had been through three executive assistants in the two months before."

"How long have you been on the job?" I said.

"Three weeks," Perez said. "Three weeks of hell. I've put in applications everywhere. It will kill me, but I may have to ask my sister to get me in at Publix."

I could hear Chamberlain's raised voice in his office, but could make out only 12 words: "A fucking *Washington Post* investigation? Do they know about 'complete treat,' too?"

Perez heard them, too.

"Why are you telling me all this?" I said to her.

"Because the Lord works in strange and mysterious ways. You know that Nick, perhaps better than most."

From Chamberlain's office came the sound of a phone slamming down and a torrent of obscenities.

Perez smiled.

"I do believe Mr. Chamberlain is off his call," she said. "Shall I buzz you back in? Before I do, you'll want to remember the words 'complete treat.' "

"So where were we?" Chamberlain said when I was back in his office.

His mood had lightened, but I couldn't help but notice what was on his screen: a chart of SuperGoodMedia's stock price for the last month on the Nasdaq Composite. It showed a tumble from a few dollars per share to pennies. The market had never been thrilled with the company, but this slide seemed evidence of something more than volatility at work.

"Don't pay any attention to that," Chamberlain said. "We'll be back in buy territory before you know it. So, what were we talking about? That's right *The Other Side*. I had the show in development before this Mary News thing hit. What's happened in Massachusetts only confirms the wisdom of the research. What you're probably wondering is what's in it for you."

"Actually I hadn't gotten that far," I said.

"I'm prepared to offer you half a million dollars a year, plus a $750,000 signing bonus, a percentage of the merchandise, and bonuses tied to the Nielsens to host *The Other Side*. If it hits the way I am confident it will, you could be looking at over two million dollars the first year alone. So what do you say?"

"I'm speechless," I said. "This is all so sudden."

"There's more," Chamberlain said. "I need you to write a book. The final draft is due May 1st."

"That's awfully fast."

"We're not talking Faulkner, Nick. If you need a ghostwriter, we'll get one. But whether you or Jesus Christ writes it, I need it by May 1. And the reason for that is we must be in full distribution by next Thanksgiving, in time for the Christmas release of the movie."

"A movie?" I said.

"A movie. The working title is *The Miracle Kid*—yes, I lifted it from *People* magazine. I've had screenwriters on it since October—they're into a fourth rewrite already, with only The Christmas Event left to script. We also have a commitment from Bradley Cooper to play you."

"Me?"

"You think you aren't a big part of the story—that synergies with TV and printed media aren't critical? Cooper is perfect. The only stumbling block so far is who plays Jennifer. I want Jennifer Lawrence or Dakota Fanning. Either would be perfect for the sex scenes."

"But this is a story about religion."

"So was Adam and Eve—you think they didn't screw? The way the screenwriters have it, we open with you and Jennifer twenty years ago with champagne and strawberries, just like in your soon-to-be ex's column. Fast forward to the eve of The Christmas Event, where we have you two today, naked by a crackling fire."

"But we don't have that kind of relationship," I said.

"This is a movie, for Chrissakes," Chamberlain said. "Lately, I've been pondering who plays you and Jennifer twenty-five years into the future."

"You have scenes that far ahead?"

"Yes, in one of the sequels. Christmas miracle saves the world, and the world twenty-five years from now is at peace. A happy ending."

"But the world twenty-five years from now may be melting," I said.

Oops. I'd forgotten Hill's warning.

"You mean climate change? Are you one of those nauseating liberals who believe every word out of every scientist's mouth?"

"Of course not, Mr. Chamberlain. "I just read about it now and then."

"Not in my newspapers you don't. And won't ever. Let's get back to the issue at hand. I could see Colin Firth or George Clooney playing the future you. Kurt Russell, even. Jennifer is trickier. My friends at Walt Disney Pictures make a persuasive case for Madonna."

'Wouldn't her name just confuse things?" I said.

"No, her name would be a huge selling point. And her daughter is named Lourdes, what could be more synergistic? Madonna would add a sort of mystical element to the project, which would help feed the buzz. So, what say you, Nick, are you in?"

I didn't answer immediately.

"Well? Are you?"

"I don't know, Mr. Chamberlain," I finally said. "This is an awful lot to digest all at once."

"Is that your way of saying no?"

"Can I think about it?"

The change in Chamberlain's face was frightening.

"Goddamn it," he said, "I'm ready to announce this today. I have *Entertainment Tonight, Inside Edition, Variety*, and Pax TV coming, not to mention the major networks, TMZ, and a bunch of others. I've flown analysts down from New York. The Donald will be making a brief appearance via Zoom."

"Donald Trump?" I said.

"Is there any other?" Chamberlain said. "You do see that photo on the wall, don't you?"

"Yes, but I wouldn't think he has any interest in me."

"He doesn't. But he sees opportunity in the golf course we plan to open."

"Golf course?"

" 'Major Miracles' we plan to call it. The president plans to invest. We'll probably build it in California."

"I'm speechless," I said.

"Also a pain in the ass with this 'can I think about it' bullshit. And Hill assured me you're a team player. I should have known when he told me you don't golf. What nobody who wants to be somebody doesn't golf?"

"I used to mini golf," I said.

"What a loser. So what is it, Nolan? In or out."

"I just need time to think, is all," I said.

"How about you think about this."

Chamberlain began reading a printout.

" 'The washing machine is the most mysterious of all, with a two-to-one ratio of socks-in to socks-out. So where *do* they go? Are socks congregating in sewer lines, like escaped alligators? Are aliens at work—beaming down in the middle of the night to steal them for their own mysterious purposes back aboard the mother ship? Do sock fairies line their little nests in hidden corners of our basements?' "

"Okay," I said. "I get it."

"I know a hundred people who would kill for this opportunity," said Chamberlain. "And you have hesitations. Is it the money?"

"No, the money's great."

"Because we can work on that. Give you a couple more points on the merchandise, a bigger advance on the book, a better cut on the video game, whatever. I'm easy."

"It's not the money."

"Then what is it?"

"My credibility," I said.

"Credibility," Chamberlain said.

"Yes."

"If credibility's the hang-up, I'll get you a Pulitzer Prize. No finalist this time, but a winner, complete with gold medal."

"I wish I had what it takes," I said.

"What it takes is connections. Do you know the members of the Pulitzer Prize Board?"

I shook my head no.

"I do," Chamberlain said. "Three worked for me before, and one still does: Dave Dupont, editor of the *Sun*. Then there's the crew from The Wall Street Journal, all of whom have been my house guests on Nantucket or down here. Surely you must have wondered why the same papers win the lion's share of Pulitzers, year in and year out."

"I thought because they were the best of the best."

"Nick, you are *so* naïve. Call in a few old favors, offer the right person on this year's Pulitzer Prize Board a lucrative position with SGM, and you could be uncorking champagne next April just as we're announcing your book. Talk about timing!"

I mumbled my agreement.

"You have a true talent, Nick, but it's not writing," said Chamberlain.

"It's the screen. Opportunity rarely knocks twice, and regret is a terrible thing to live with. So is unemployment."

We shook hands, and then Chamberlain brought in a man in a gray suit who had a stack of papers for me to sign.

When I finished, Chamberlain brought me into his private dining room. A table had been prepared for three, and a man of about fifty sat at the third setting.

"Garth, let me introduce you to the literal star of our movie, Nick Nolan," Chamberlain said.

The man extended his hand and we shook.

"Garth Vader," he said.

"Did you step out of a Star Wars movie?" I said.

I intended ice-breaking humor.

Bad call.

"And do you want to step back into socks?" Vader said.

"Nick sometimes has no inkling of what's funny and what's not," Chamberlain said. "I'm sure he meant no offense."

"Of course not and my apologies, Mr. Vader," I said.

"You may call me Garth," the man said.

"Sure, Garth it is," I said.

"Now, everyone have a seat," Chamberlain said. "The chef has prepared lobster tails and steak, his specialty. I am certain you will not be disappointed."

We ate, with Chamberlain and Vader providing most of the conversation. They seemed friends, albeit new friends, both with an interest in newspapers.

Vader's interest was chilling.

He managed The Alkil Global Capital Fund, notorious for its practices of buying newspapers, then gutting them, all in service to greed. I could only guess at Vader's annual income, but what I'd read about hedge funds suggested it was millions, while the journalists he'd laid off lost sleep worrying what they'd do when the unemployment ran out.

"Are you interested in SGM?" I said over dessert.

"If I were, do you think I'd tell you?" Vader said. "But the answer is no. I just happened to be in Orlando today, on my way to Mar-a-Lago. And when David told me who was here, I had to come by. It's not every day you get to meet a newspaper celebrity. Except maybe for Thomas Friedman, I don't think there are any anymore."

"I hardly consider myself a celebrity, Mr. Vader."

"Garth."

"Garth."

"Well, David does," Vader said. "I'd say you are SGM's shining star."

"You'll get no argument from me," Chamberlain said. "Now it's time to be off. My driver is here."

We headed to Disney World, where, Chamberlain informed me, a sound stage would soon be constructed for *The Other Side*.

"Trust me," said Chamberlain, "there could be no better place. If America has a national shrine, and I use that word intentionally, Disney World is it."

Chamberlain and his chief flack would handle most of the press conference, but I was to be introduced, make a short statement, and answer a few questions until I was signaled to stop.

"Your script," the chairman said as we rode in his limousine. "Don't deviate from it."

He handed me a two-page memo.

Written by his flack, it spelled out a list of DOs and DON'Ts. "DO mention Bradley Cooper," it stated, "but DON'T mention Lawrence, Dakota, or Madonna by name. However, DO tease with passing references to *Buffy the Vampire Slayer*, *Sabrina*, and *Evita*; we can count on TMZ and ET and social media to carry the ball. DON'T discuss money but DO say: 'Without getting into exact figures, let's just say I'm a happy man.' And DO make sure to give your autograph to every analyst. You can sign the posters we will be distributing in their bling bags along with bottles of Dom Perignon and personalized cans of Golden Russian Osetra Caviar. Finally, when President Trump Zooms in, don't interrupt. Don't say anything but 'I can never thank you enough, Mr. President.'"

Chamberlain had started a television production company, but he had not yet taken the plunge into films; for making and distributing movies, he still worked with Disney.

"On many issues, perhaps most," said Chamberlain, "Bob and I see eye-to-eye."

"Bob?"

"As in Robert Chapek, Disney CEO."

The limo stopped. We entered the side door of a small theater and entered an office. Awaiting us were Chamberlain's lieutenants: Peters, Hawkins, Winthrop III, and Danny D'Ermo, who really did look like Don Knotts.

Except, that is, for how he was dressed.

In a Cub Scout uniform.

Since his embarrassment, Chamberlain had assigned someone else the SOS responsibilities and given D'Ermo a new position: Chief Propriety Officer, or CPO.

"Wear what you are, that's my motto!" D'Ermo said. "And let me recite my new super motto: 'On my honor I will do my best to do my duty to God and my country and to obey the SuperGoodMedia Law; to help other people at all times; to keep myself physically strong, mentally awake, and morally straight.' Nick, I am honored to meet you in person."

The CFO, CMO, CDO and CPO were sycophantic with their praise for me.

I wanted to scream.

"Okay, gentlemen, there will be more time with Nick at the reception," Chamberlain said. "Now shoo."

Chamberlain escorted me to a dressing room, where a makeup artist did our faces, and then we walked backstage. Peeking out, I could see reporters and cameramen gorging from a large table that was piled high with cocktail shrimp, smoked salmon, scallops in bacon, crackers, cheeses, and a variety of fruit juices, soda, wine, and beer. Another few minutes, and they'd have the table picked clean.

Chamberlain's flack introduced his boss, who took the podium and welcomed all—joking to the analysts that if what they were about to see wasn't worth the trip from New York "I'll refund the price of your trip. Of course, since we flew you down, that would be nothing!"

The analysts chuckled.

The lights dimmed and the screen lit up with SuperGoodMedia's logo. A sizzle tape rolled.

"Just when you thought millennium fever was long over," began the narrator, "along comes the excitement of a century!"

SuperGoodMedia's corporate logo dissolved to a wide shot of the scene outside Jennifer's house, which in turn dissolved to a close-up of Tony Callahan rejoicing in his miraculous recovery from leukemia. "I never did believe in miracles, but I've a feeling it's time to try," some of the lyrics to Fleetwood Mac's "You Make Loving Fun," rocked the auditorium, and we were treated to quick cuts of my appearance on *60 Minutes*, and on the covers of magazines.

"As we enter the new age," the narrator declared, "an entire nation yearns for meaning. But only one man lights the way!"

Now we watched me working at my computer, me walking out of *The Trib*, me signing autographs outside Jennifer's, me leading the WQZ six o'clock news.

"Nick Nolan doesn't just tell the story," the narrator said, "Nick Nolan IS the story! And now SuperGoodMedia, in an unprecedented, multi-million-dollar, cross-media campaign, is bringing the man and the story to an international audience!"

Again, a series of fast cuts: mockups of a book cover and a video game logo, a virtual rendering of *The Other Side* set, the prototypical *supermiracle-kid.com* homepage, a shot of Bradley Cooper, models of the Nick Nolan action figures toy giant Hasbro had signed on to produce, mockups of the special-edition Nike shoes, photos of the McDonald's Super Good Burger, and the Apple Other Side phone, and more.

The sizzle tape ended.

"Ladies and gentlemen," said Chamberlain, "meet America's newest superstar, Mr. Nick Nolan!"

Bathed in spotlights, I crossed the stage. My hands shook as I took my statement out of my pocket and began to read:

"Ladies and gentlemen, words cannot express how excited I was when Chairman Chamberlain asked me to be the centerpiece of this incredible multimedia experience. Here is an unprecedented opportunity to combine entertainment with enlightenment—to marry faith to fun. This is not good news—this is *great* news, *super-great* news, for a world desperately seeking it."

I had five more paragraphs to go, but I didn't know if I could finish. I felt like an impostor—a stranger stuffed into a Nick Nolan suit.

But I did finish, and then I took questions, answering according to the script.

"So what's your package worth?" said one reporter.

"Without getting into exact figures," I said, "let's just say I'm a happy man."

"What's it like inside Jennifer and Amber's house?"

"Miraculous," I said.

"Any truth to the rumor that you're having an affair with that miracle lady?"

"I report the news, not make it," I said.

"Will you tell the truth in your book?"

"Yes, I will, just as I have in my stories and broadcasts from day one."

"If Bradley Cooper is signed on to play you, who's your choice to play Jennifer?"

"Not to rebuff you," I said, "but the question of girl is immaterial."

And so on and so forth, the most sickening ten minutes of my life.

Up until then, that is.

Because that's when Trump Zoomed in from Mar-a-Lago. He was sitting at a tiny desk in what looked like a ballroom. The stage behind him was crowded with boxes.

Our room fell silent.

"Where's his MAGA hat?" the former president said.

"Whose?" Chamberlain said.

"The dufus there at the podium."

"I don't wear hats," I managed.

"Just like you don't write fake news. You're a third-rate reporter, Little Nicky."

"Mr. President," Chamberlain said, "you agreed to join us to talk about your investment in Major Miracles and I was hoping—"

"—I would invest? Well I won't now because after seeing this nasty person you're not getting a penny."

Chamberlain found a MAGA hat, rushed with it to the stage, and handed it to me.

I threw it to the floor.

"Well, well, Little Nicky grew a pair," Trump said.

I was expecting Trump to cut out now, but I was wrong. He turned around to greet six people who had filed into his ballroom.

His wife, Melania. His daughter Ivanka. His son Donald Trump, Jr. Steve Bannon. Rudy Giuliani. Mike Lindell.

They stood behind him and Melania whispered, loud enough for us to hear: "Tee time, darling."

"Where are the clubs?"

"In the same room where you keep the rest of the classified documents," Melania said. "Come on, let's go."

"Not until I finish with him," Trump said.

"Who is he?" Melania said.

"Ed Asner," Giuliani said.

"Asner's dead," Trump Jr. said.

"Neil Armstrong?" Giuliani said.

"Armstrong's dead," Bannon said. "And there's no physical resemblance between Asner or Armstrong and this loser. Zero."

"Elizabeth Montgomery?" Giuliani said.

"He's an enemy of the people," Trump said. "Enemy! Enemy! Enemy!"

The group behind him took up the chant.

"Enemy! Enemy! Enemy!"

"Did they hit the Twin Towers again?" Giuliani said.

"Time for your nap, Rudy," Ivanka said.

"Come with me," Lindell said. "I have your pillow."

Lindell led Giuliani from the room.

"So Little Nicky and Chairman Meow thought they could pull a fast one on me," Trump said. "What a couple of losers. Wacky weirdos. Crooked, too. Go away."

The screen went blank.

"Well, that didn't go as planned," Chamberlain said. "Must have caught him on a bad day, but no worries, we'll work our magic on Donald and he'll be back. And now if you please, a round of applause for the man who is prophesizing a new era of profitability for SGM, Nick Nolan!"

The reporters lined up for their goodie bags, made a last pass at the food table, and the auditorium cleared. I was alone with Chamberlain, his flack, and the analysts.

"Autograph, Nick?" one of them said, offering the eight-by-ten glossy of me that came with the press kit.

"Me, too?" another said.

"He's the real thing, isn't he guys?" said Chamberlain.

The analysts nodded their assent.

"Don't worry about Trump," one said. "All the trouble he's in, you don't want to be associated with him."

"We have one more piece of business," the chairman said to me. "We have to visit the mouse."

"Mouse?" I said.

"Mickey. We need a photo of you with your arms around him."

I listened to my voice messages on the jet home. Jennifer had checked in again, reminding me to drop by tonight. And Gina Pulaski called to inform me that Jimmy was back at Children's Hospital.

"Probably only for a couple of days," she said. "The doctors have a new treatment they want to try. Jimmy says hi."

Damn. I'd forgotten about Make A Wish.

The driver was waiting for me when we touched down. He said Hill wanted me to join him for dinner at Luke and Elizabeth Turner's house. An hour later, we arrived in Concord, birthplace of the American Revolution—and toney home to contemporary millionaires.

Built after Luke had won a long court battle to raze a 1728 center-chimney colonial, the Turners' Mediterranean villa style house had twenty-two rooms, including a gym, theater, and indoor swimming pool. Turner had built a tennis court where a two-hundred-year-old barn once stood, and his four-bay garage was located on a former meadow where, legend had it, Henry David Theroux had contemplated nature. In a puff piece a free-lancer had written at Hill's direction, Turner had boasted that including legal expense, he'd spent twenty million dollars on his estate.

The driver left me at the front door, and Hill met me when I stepped inside. The house was noisy and crowded.

"Should I wear a mask?" I said.

"No need," Hill said. "We're socially distancing and the filtration and ventilation inside here is state-of-the-art. I wouldn't be here otherwise."

"Okay."

"The chairman tells me you were splendid," Hill said. "And the market agreed—our stock closed up three and seven-eighths! Obviously, no one gave a shit about Trump's rant. That's all he ever does is rant. And you didn't hear this from me, but bonus points for not wearing his hat. I met

Trump once and he gave me the creeps. So congratulations to America's newest star, Nick. You!"

"This is all for me?" I said.

"Don't be ridiculous," Hill said. "Do you read your own paper? The mall opened today."

The publisher had a copy of one section of today's *Trib* in his jacket pocket. It was The Minuteman Minutes, a seventy-two-page tab Hill had produced by pulling several of our best reporters off their regular beats for a week. I'd seen the final product after it rolled off the presses yesterday: rich with ads, it featured a 125-inch cover story ("All You Ever Needed Under One Roof"); numerous inside stories ("More Shoes Than Imelda," "Imax Theater World's Largest," etc.); a question-and-answer page ("Q. Is parking at the mall free? A. Until Christmas, Santa says 'you bet!' ") charts; graphs; interior, exterior and drone-shot aerial photographs; the address of the *Trib.com* Special Mall Bulletin Board ("Share your shopping experiences! Win a $100 gift certificate!"), and one of Bud Fuller's painful man-on-the-street pieces ("What Christmas Means to me!"). The online presentation with its videos and podcasts was equally ridiculous.

"So that's what this is about," said Hill.

He told me that the governor, mayor, Senate President, and House Speaker were here—along with the chairman of TD Bank, Red Sox owner John Henry, WQZ president Kevin Shaw and many entertainment celebrities, including David E. Kelley, back in his home state for a visit. Hill breathlessly informed me that Kelley had brought his wife, Michelle Pfeiffer.

"I'm sure it was an oversight, but you weren't on the invitation list," Hill said. "When Elizabeth found out, she hit the roof, so here you are. Come on, I'd like you to meet Mr. Turner."

We moved into the living room—an enormous space that brought to mind a Gilded Age ballroom. The room had been decorated with original artwork, Oriental carpeting, and Louis XVI furniture. The Breakers had nothing on this place.

"Champagne?" said a waiter in white uniform who carried a silver tray.

I took a glass and had managed only a sip when Hill introduced me to Luke Turner. He was talking to Paula Orton.

"The man of the hour," said the developer. "I can't tell you how much I love your columns."

"Isn't he the best?" Orton said. "So unlike your average reporter."

"This is quite the party," I said.

"Oh, this is nothing," Turner said, "just a few good friends celebrating good fortune. He may be too shy to say so himself, but Bruce has even more reason to celebrate tonight."

The developer made eye contact with my publisher.

"Can we tell him?" said Turner.

"So long as it's off the record," said Hill. "Okay, Nick?"

"Okay," I said.

"I've invited Bruce onto my board," said Turner. "No one has *ever* made it after such a short time in Boston. Then again, no one's *ever* had such a positive economic impact."

"Congratulations," I said.

I wasn't surprised: Hill had recently bought a condominium in Denton's Wharf, the upscale Boston Harbor front complex that Turner owned, and I'd heard that Turner had sponsored him for membership in the exclusive Down Town Club.

"Thank you," said Hill. "There'll be an announcement, of course—but not until all the excitement about the mall dies down."

"Timing is everything in life," said Orton. "Isn't that right, Bruce."

Hill put his arm around Orton.

Then Turner extended his hand to me. It was fat and sweaty and I didn't want to shake it, but I did. First opportunity, I'd stop at one of the hand-sanitizer stations I'd seen walking in.

"I hear some celebrating of your own is in order," Turner said. "You're going to be in the movies and on TV."

"Let's hope he remembers us when they're putting his star on Hollywood Boulevard!" Hill said.

"Speaking of which," Turner said. "I'd like you to meet Michelle Pfeiffer."

"Not so fast," said Elizabeth Turner. "I want to show Nick my spiritual home first."

I followed Elizabeth through the kitchen and down a hall. We passed the pool and entered a small chapel. I saw pews, an altar, statues of Mary and Jesus, and a row of votive candles.

"So, this is where you pray," I said.

"Morning and night. On Sunday evenings, I have Bible group here. The cardinal comes when he can."

"What about your husband?"

"He never steps foot in here. We fought terribly before he would build this. And you can just imagine the battle I had to get the chapel in the mall."

"Your husband doesn't believe."

"Only in money," Elizabeth said. "Money is his God. He never listens when I tell him that the Bible proclaims, in 1 Timothy 6:10, 'the love of money is a root of all kinds of evils.' "

Elizabeth genuflected, made the sign of the cross, and lit a candle.

"You're probably wondering how we wound up together," she said.

"The thought has occurred to me, yes."

"I was young when I married Luke—only twenty-two, and just out of Radcliffe. He was a decade older—handsome, charming, successful. We had a child a year later."

"I didn't know you have children."

"We don't, now. Kimberly died when she was eight. She was Amber's age."

"I'm sorry."

"She developed a brain tumor. The doctors tried everything—surgery, chemotherapy, radiation—but nothing worked, you could see her slipping away, day by terrible day. Then a friend suggested Lourdes. I was skeptical at first—when you're raised a Methodist, you don't put much faith in Catholic miracles. By the time I realized Lourdes was Kimberly's last chance, she'd already slipped into a coma. It was too late to bring her. She died in Children's Hospital a week later. Her birthday was Christmas. She would have been twenty-three if she had lived."

"It must make the day hard for you," I said.

"Terribly. Meanwhile, my husband and I began to grow apart, as often happens after the loss of a child. The very day we buried Kimberly, I had a dream in which a voice I later understood was the Virgin Mary's instructed me to convert to Catholicism. After much soul-searching and research about Lourdes and other miracles, I met with a priest that a Catholic friend recommended. I believe you know about him: Fr. Mateo Silva. This, of course, was before he left for California."

"An amazing coincidence," I said.

"No," Elizabeth said, "the hand of God. Fr. Silva baptized me and I was confirmed the next spring. Luke attended neither. He continued to worship money—and now it no longer was a big part of his life, it was his only life. And we were unable to have another child."

"So, why did you stay married?"

"Because I took solemn vows. Because I still kept hope of saving him. Because his company gives jobs to men and women with precious little ones to feed. Because his money is legally made and I demand he give twenty-five percent of his pre-tax profits to general charity and another twenty-five percent to the archdiocese exclusively.

"So you see, you have to weigh things in light of the greater good. It's like your columns, Nick: I could do without all the hoopla they've helped create, those obscene t-shirts and Papal Pretzels and what-not. But when we weigh that against the value of spreading the Lord's word, we see that the greater good is served."

"Doesn't Luke object to giving so much money to the archdiocese?" I said.

"Yes, but he does it."

"Why?"

"The tax benefits, obviously. Also the fact that should he ever divorce me, I would own his greedy ass. My family got him started in business. We have a controlling interest still and we know how to use lawyers."

The party was winding down when Elizabeth and I emerged from the chapel. I found myself in the entertainment room when the eleven o'clock news came on. Hill was with me, along with a few bankers and real estate agents, several of whom had already asked for my autograph. Hill was tipsy, and Paula Orton was drunk.

"They better have something on Nick's signing," said Hill, "or heads will roll."

But WQZ didn't have anything on the signing. The newscast led with the mall ribbon cutting. The off lead was Jones testifying at *The Trib*'s libel trial.

We watched as Jones, close to tears, recalled hearing sirens the morning they pulled his son's car out of Lower Mystic Pond. He told of the old newsman's instinct that sent him from his house to the scene—where he watched in horror as police opened the water-filled trunk.

"I couldn't look and I couldn't look away," Jones said, his voice choking. "It was my boy, his beautiful face already beginning to bloat."

Hill was furious.

"I don't believe it," he said.

"It was his son," I said.

"I don't care if it was Jesus. People don't want to see this. Who the hell put this on?"

"Not me, that's for sure," said WQZ president Shaw. "You know me better than that, Bruce."

Hill dialed Jones at home.

"I just saw you on TV," Hill said. "Did we have a reporter there, too?"

Jones said that *The Trib* had.

"Every other media outlet in town was there, too. I had no choice."

"Where are we playing the story?"

Jones told him.

"No fucking way," Hill said. "Not on my front page. Not on mall day. I'll deal with you later, Jones."

Hill hung up, then called the night editor and ordered him to remake the front page.

"I don't give a shit if you're a year past deadline," said Hill. "The pressmen can pound sand. Cut it to a brief and run it inside. No photo. And do not post it online."

It was midnight when Hill's driver dropped me off at my new apartment. I called Jennifer.

"I didn't wake you, did I?"

"No," said Jennifer, "I told you I'd wait up. I watched the press conference. You were great. And did you ever stick it to Trump by throwing his hat to the floor."

"I feel like I was bagged."

"By Trump?"

"No, by the deal I signed."

"You'll never have to worry about money again in your life," Jennifer said.

"If I go through with it."

"You sound hesitant."

"I am, the longer I think about it."

"But you signed a contract."

"I believe the legal term is 'under duress.' "

"Think of all the people a movie will reach," said Jennifer, "people who otherwise might never hear the word. I believe Christians and others of good faith will look past the hype and find the truths that lie within."

"But they want Jennifer Lawrence, Dakota Fanning, or Madonna to play you, for crying out loud," I said.

"That's Hollywood, Nick. Nothing's real there, as I've said. It's out of our hands now, anyway. God gives us the wisdom to recognize those things we cannot change—and the strength to let go of them."

Was I suddenly on Mars? Had Turner spiked the champagne? Or had Jennifer taken another of those crazy zigzags that had been her hallmark long before Mary News and miracles?

"Are you coming over?" Jennifer said.

"Do you want me to?"

"I don't want you to, Nick," she said. "I need you to."

I reached her house shortly after one in the morning. The moon hung low in the sky, and the lawn had a thin coating of frost. Many of the tents that had sprung up before the weather turned had disappeared, leaving mostly campers and mobile homes. I saw candles burning in a few windows, and a silhouette of a nun saying the rosary, but everything was quiet. The TV studio was dark and no one was afoot.

I parked, greeted the lone policeman on duty, and went to Jennifer's door.

Jennifer opened it. She was dressed only in a flannel shirt and her hair was down. A fire burned in the fireplace.

I stared, saying nothing.

"Is this wrong?" she said. "You liked it once upon a time. That night in the morgue, you seemed you might like it again."

"It's not wrong," I said, "just unexpected."

"Come in," said Jennifer. "The night is freezing."

Jennifer took my coat and led me to the fire. I thought, absurdly, of the proposed ending to Chamberlain's movie, *The Miracle Kid*.

"Poor baby," she said. "You've had such a long day. Are you hungry?"

"Not really."

"Not even for these?"

She pointed to a bowl of strawberries on an end table.

"Well, maybe one."

I reached—and Jennifer pushed my hand away. "How soon they forget!" she said. "Close your eyes."

I did, and Jennifer fed me.

"Keep them closed," she said.

I drank champagne and then I felt Jennifer's lips on mine. She kissed me and brought my hand to her shirt, which I began to unbutton.

"An important part of me has gotten lost in all this," said Jennifer. "Will you make love to me, Nick?"

She took my hand again and took me to her bedroom. Candles burned and I smelled incense. The covers were turned down on her new bed.

"I've waited so long for this," she said.

Coughing awakened me. I couldn't determine where it was coming from, and initially I thought I was dreaming.

Then I realized it was Amber.

"Jennifer?" I said.

I tapped her shoulder and she stirred. Outside, the day was dawning.

"I think I hear Amber," I said.

Jennifer sat up, rubbed her eyes, and kissed me lightly.

"We're lucky she was quiet through the night," Jennifer said. "The doctor thinks she might be getting pneumonia. Stay here while I check on her."

Jennifer ministered to her daughter as I got dressed. We met in the kitchen, where we drank coffee and I made scrambled eggs that neither of us ate. My head was full of new questions—questions piled on questions now—and I was struck anew by the realization that it's the answers where journalists often come up short.

But this wasn't the time for answers. The sex had been amazing but I didn't know how I felt emotionally about last night, and I didn't want to ask Jennifer how she was with it, either.

"Will you be back later today?" Jennifer said at the door.

Outside, a priest was already setting up for morning mass on the stage that Benedictine monks had built.

"Of course," I said. "I'll need something for my column."

"I love you, Nick," Jennifer whispered.

I started to speak, but no words came.

"Don't say anything," Jennifer said. "As you know, the Lord works in strange and mysterious ways. In due time, all of this will be clear."

CHAPTER NINE: A RELIABLE SOURCE

I went home, showered, and visited our website. Hill hadn't told me last night, but he had made me today's Celeb-Rate!, with a perfect 10 rating.

"Hey, we know he's our guy," the copy read, "but if we can't toot our own horn every once in a while, what fun would there be? At SuperGoodMedia headquarters in Orlando, Florida, yesterday, Nick Nolan inked a deal for a book, a video game, a movie, and a TV show that will soon be the talk of the planet. Here in Beantown we'll be able to say: 'We knew him when!' "

Things were no better in the print edition: the cover of The Scene had a photo of me with Mickey Mouse and a story from PRNewswire with details of my signing.

Except for Destiny's muttered congratulations, none of my colleagues mentioned any of this when I arrived at *The Trib* that afternoon. They were preoccupied with phones.

Rather, what had been phones.

Overnight, an IT person from Florida we'd seen nosing around the day before had removed them all from the newsroom. In the weeks prior, we had been bombarded with emails with links to training and instructions on how to convert to a computer-based telephone software system, Vonage, but the conversion steps were so convoluted and the training so long that most of us gave up, ignoring warnings about the deadline.

Eventually, we figured out how to log into Vonage and make and receive calls. When I checked voicemail, I found that several media outlets had left messages. But I returned no calls and read no email.

I left *The Trib* and drove to Jennifer's.

This time, I had a companion.

Concerned for my safety after I'd been mobbed when announcing the sacred oil, Hill had hired a bodyguard. He was a muscular man who packed a handgun.

"I have a Taser and pepper spray, too," he said as we drove up Jennifer's street. "Any of these wackos think they're going to mess with you, they've got another thing coming."

"Please don't talk like that," I said. "Most of the people here want only peace."

"Don't we all," the bodyguard said. "Take me. I did a tour in Iraq with the Marines and came home with my head all messed up. I get nightmares every night still. But I managed to find a job driving with Brink's."

"Thank you for your service," I said.

"Please don't, Mr. Nolan. You can't imagine how sick we get of hearing that line. Brinks laid me off when the pandemic started and no one was leaving their homes for anything. So when this gig came along, I jumped. My only intent now is to protect you. I'm sure we won't need force, but you never know. I thought Baghdad was safe and then I got here."

"Please wait outside," I said when we reached Jennifer's door.

"Those aren't my instructions," the bodyguard said. "I'm not supposed to leave your side."

"I'll be okay," I said.

"You got it, good buddy. Just don't tell Hill. One conversation with him and I saw right through him. He's a prick and a liar."

Jennifer offered no affection, not even a kiss on the cheek, when she opened the door. She was wringing her hands and I smelled alcohol on her breath. I assumed she was filled with regret over last night.

I followed her into the kitchen, where she made no attempt to hide an empty bottle of Merlot.

"I had to calm my nerves somehow," she said.

"It was a mistake, wasn't it," I said.

"What?"

"Last night."

"This has nothing to do with last night," she said. "The anxiety is about what awaits me. I'm going out there today."

"Into that crowd?"

"At three o'clock."

"What do you plan to do?" I said.

"Deliver a message from Mary."

"Has she chosen?"

"You'll have to wait to see."

"You really ought to think if this is what you want to do," I said.

"Oh, it's not, believe me," said Jennifer. "You know how crowds terrify me. But I have been ordered by the Mother of God."

We barely spoke during the next hour.

Jennifer started into another bottle of Merlot but gave no sign of inebriation; alcohol seemed unable to dim whatever was powering her. She'd shifted into hyper speed again. I could feel frenzied energy coming off her.

At three exactly, I heard a knock on the door. Jennifer had hired a private nurse to care for Amber in her absence. Amber's coughing had stopped, but I knew she remained worried.

Jennifer put on a white parka and white gloves, then disappeared into Amber's room. A moment later, she returned with the reproduction of Fra Filippo *Lippi's Madonna and Child with Angels.* Fresh liquid streamed down the Madonna's cheek.

"Let's go," said Jennifer.

We opened the door and found the crowd pressing against the police barriers. A loud murmur arose, and Officer Maloney tensed and spoke into his walkie-talkie. My bodyguard reached under his coat.

"You sure about this?" I said to Jennifer.

"I've never been more terrified in my life," she said. "Nor more certain."

Jennifer took a tentative step down her walk. I feared the crowd would break through the barriers, but they didn't; the murmur gave way to mesmerized silence as Jennifer approached.

When she reached the sawhorses and tape, some of the faithful knelt, others made the sign of the cross, and still others bowed in silent prayer.

Jennifer ascended the stage the Benedictines had built. After genuflecting, she went to the lectern.

"Behold the face of Mary," she said. "Behold Mary's tears, which she sheds for all God's children."

Jennifer lifted the painting toward the December sky, and liquid streaming from the Madonna's eyes glistened in the wintry sun. The tears were not there in Amber's room—I swear they weren't. They weren't flowing now, and I hadn't seen them materialize—but I hadn't watched Jennifer every second, either.

"Goddamn," the bodyguard whispered to me. "If I hadn't seen it myself, I never would have believed it. The painting is really crying."

"Praise Mary," Jennifer said.

"Praise Mary!" the crowd repeated.

"Praise the baby Jesus."

"Praise the baby Jesus!"

"Bless the children, the angels and the saints."

"Bless the children, the angels and the saints!"

"God bless us all."

"God bless us all!"

Jennifer settled the painting against the altar and leaned on the lectern for support; for an instant, I thought she would faint. Her face was drained of color, and she started to tremble.

"We all know about Mrs. Turner's dream," Jennifer began, "and, sadly, Mary is compelled to say that her vision was incorrect. The Mother of God will not mark her son's birth with what Mrs. Turner called a 'gesture of goodwill.' "

The crowd groaned.

"No," said Jennifer, "the Mother of God has something greater in mind than a mere gesture. What exactly it will be, Mary cannot at this time reveal to the world. But she has confided in me. And I can tell you that Mary's children will not be disappointed.

"But there *is* something Mary wishes at this time to publicly reveal. Speaking, as always, through my daughter, Amber, Mary wants her children to know that the terrible plague visited on us for nearly two years will be lifting—for The Father shall soon prevail against Lucifer, who with his variants continues to visit death and suffering upon us. This is the answer to our prayers and for that we shout Hallelujah and praise be God."

"Hallelujah!" the crowd chanted. "Praise be God!"

"But Mary also brings other tidings, and they are not of joy," Jennifer said. "She expresses her disapproval of the secularism destroying this sacred season. Starting before Halloween, we are overrun with advertisements to buy. Judges ban nativity scenes on village squares, and political correctness has ruined Christmas in our schools. Mary reminds her children that we celebrate the birth of Jesus, not worship the false idol of commercialism.

"Mary tells us, and now I quote directly: 'Dear Children! I invite you to decide again to love God above all else. In this time, due to the spirit of consumerism, one forgets what it means to love and to cherish true values. I invite you again, little children, to put God first in your life. Do not let Satan distract you with material things but, little children, decide for God, who is freedom and love. Choose life and not death of the soul, little children.'"

Her energy spent, Jennifer seemed about to collapse.

I ran to her and managed to keep her standing.

She handed me her notes.

"Finish this," she said, "before I pass out."

"You need a doctor," I said.

"Goddamn it, Nick, read it."

I began.

"Louder!" someone shouted.

I raised my voice.

"Beginning next Monday," I read, "the Monday before Christmas, Mary has asked the faithful to join her in prayer at Amber's side. Starting next week, every day at the conclusion of noon Mass, Jennifer shall admit groups of ten for an hour of prayer and meditation. The faithful shall be selected in a daily lottery to be conducted by the Sisters of the Sacred

Heart, who have accepted this role with humble determination. Thank you all, and may God bless."

For a moment, the crowd was silent.

Then someone shouted: "Only ten?"

"I've been here since September!" someone else yelled.

"Why a lottery?" another said. "The sickest should go first!"

The crowd closed in.

My bodyguard and Maloney jumped onto the stage.

Maloney took the microphone and said: "Everybody back. The woman needs medical attention."

No one moved.

"Ladies and gentlemen, please bear with us," I said. "Jennifer will be able to accommodate everyone eventually. It will just take time and your patience."

In the distance, I heard sirens.

"I called an ambulance," Maloney said.

Jennifer snapped to.

"No way," she said. "I'm going home."

"You need a doctor," Maloney said.

"There's a nurse in my house," said Jennifer. "I'm telling you no ambulance."

Maloney looked to me for direction.

"No ambulance," I said.

Supported by me and Maloney, Jennifer started toward her house. She smiled weakly and made a blessing with her right hand—and the faithful, almost as one, got on their knees. I had a mental image of Mary Magdalene, and then we were inside Jennifer's.

After settling Jennifer into her bed, the nurse told us she believed she was exhausted and likely would be refreshed after a good sleep. She'd given her a pill to ensure she got it.

Amber's condition, meanwhile, was deteriorating again. You could hear the girl's congested breathing throughout the house. It sounded like drowning.

"Pneumonia," the nurse said. "Her doctor is on her way."

At first opportunity, I met with Destiny and Bud in a quiet corner of a coffee shop not frequented by members of the media or politicians.

"I owe you an explanation, Destiny," I said. "I have no intention of doing a show or a movie or anything. I was forced into signing those contracts."

"That's bullshit," Destiny said.

"The whole day was like being on acid."

"Also weak. But go on."

"And get what I heard outside his office," I said.

I recounted the snippets of Chamberlain's conversation about the SEC, lawyers, and whistleblowers.

"You have to tell Terry Winters," Destiny said.

"Pronto," Bud said.

I texted Terry with an invitation to meet me later that day to discuss "something you'll want to know."

He texted back immediately.

An hour later, we met, outside and alone in a corner of Boston Common.

Christmas was just over a week away now. Events were accelerating and I'd been swept away again.

I realize that sounds clichéd, but the reality is certain events intoxicate the journalists covering them. Airplane crashes are that kind of story, as are presidential scandals. 9/11 was that kind of story. The death of Elvis or Diana, Princess of Wales. The election campaigns of Obama and Trump and Hillary Clinton and her husband before her. And on and on. In a truthful moment, a journalist covering such news would describe a rush like being high.

Which is how I felt when I got back to *The Tribune*, after taping my spot for the six o'clock news.

Writing madly, I captured Jennifer's passion, the drama of her performance, her finally defeating long-held fear—a timeless story of triumph against odds.

I pushed the button and went home. After taking an Ambien, I fell into a deep sleep.

My fourth and final Franklin dream found me with the Ben character inside Independence Hall. It was closed, but knowing the code to a back door, Ben had let us in. We stood for a moment in the Assembly Room, then started up a staircase.

"Follow me," he said.

We climbed to another door. Ben opened it and we ascended more stairs to the bell tower, a musty, dim space. The maintenance staff apparently had not been up here in a while.

"Have a seat," the man said.

We sat together on a small bench.

"That announcement scene was a horror show," the man said.

"You're being kind," I said.

"But there *was* an exquisite moment."

"Which was?"

"When you threw the MAGA hat to the floor."

"Like I was going to wear it?"

"A lesser man would have. And not for nothing, but Little Donny is the one who needs to grow a pair. A pair of fartleberries."

"Of what?"

"Never mind. What I mean is he needs to go away. For good. If I see one more CNN story about him, they'll hear my scream in Europe. Now to more personal matters. Your novel is coming along nicely. I'm proud of you."

"Thanks," I said.

"I do have one quibble, however," the man said.

"Which is?"

"You have an annoying tendency to jump around and expound on matters in the middle of a scene."

"That's how the journalist's mind works, so I am only being true to my subject," I said. "You were a journalist. Tell me you didn't act like that, too."

"Good point," the man said. "As for everything else, you are looking good. All the cheap plot devices are gone. Congratulations."

"I did my best."

"And that morgue scene with Jennifer—how hot was that! And the two of you in bed at her house… my oh my. You'll sell a ton of books just for the sex alone."

"That's not in my book," I said.

"Too bad, a little spice never hurts. Ask any best-selling author. While we're on the subject of your novel, I have a bone to pick. This epiphany that you are done sensationalizing—that your Mary News has exploited a poor little girl and that guilt-ridden you intend to make amends—seems to come from nowhere."

"Actually," I said, "it comes from self-examination, something at which admittedly I have rarely practiced and also from what Destiny Carter and others have impressed on me."

"Okay, good, just be clear about that," the Ben character said. "Otherwise we're back to square one with cheap plot devices. But 'Enemy of the Paper: When the Hedge Fund Comes to Town. What Franklin Would Say'—love your working title, by the way!—is not why we're here. That scoop I promised you is."

"Give it to me."

"George Washington and Alexander Hamilton were lovers. Secret, needless to say, but lovers. In the full carnal sense of the word."

"That's been rumored for years," I said. "Books have been written about it."

"Books based on conjecture and rumor," the man said. "But I can confirm it. I myself caught them once engaged in, well, you know. Imagine the reaction from the evangelicals and Trumpsters when you break the story! Hannity will soil his britches!"

"And your proof of this supposed relationship is a memory?"

"Oh, no, my dear Nicholas. What I have is more solid than that: A series of letters from one to the other that number more than a dozen. And all hidden up here in a part of this very steeple that I assure you no one but me could ever find. Doesn't your heart go out to them? Buggerers, their type were called back then. Universally scorned. Stoned or worse in some places when they were caught. No LGBTQ+ groups to advocate on their behalf. Lord. Sometimes I hate my own species. That's off the record. I wouldn't want misanthropy attached to my reputation."

"Thanks, I'll respect that," I said. "I have to go."

I turned to leave.

"Before you do are you sure you don't want to see them?" Ben said.

He poked around the rafters and found nothing.

"They were right here," he said. "I know for certain, for John handed them to me with the solemn promise I secret them away until the time was right to bring them to the light of day. Alas, I died before the time was right. So did everyone else in our circle."

"Who's John?" I said.

"The one named Hancock."

"How did Hancock get them?"

"From Washington, of course, who wanted the truth to be known some day and trusted only Hancock with their safekeeping. But Hancock was uncomfortable possessing them. So he gave them to me, entrusting me with their safekeeping."

"Except there are no letters," I said.

"There were," Ben said.

"But not now."

"No, not now."

"This only happens in a dream," I said.

"A dream?"

"What this is," I said. "A dream. My subconscious mind processing my waking reality, which is the life of a tired columnist transformed into the hottest reporter in America. Something that, I have belatedly realized, is a cruel joke. I'm starting to hate myself."

"Sounds suspiciously Freudian to me," the character said. "And if I may remind you of advice that I have already dispensed, don't put a word of this dream material in your book. As I said, the critics will kill you. They'll focus on your alleged dreams and completely ignore what I consider to be your valid and true evisceration of the media today."

"Maybe they'll also see me providing comic relief," I said.

"Without which your book would tend toward the droll."

"Exactly."

"Which genre do you envision this book belonging to?" the old man said.

"Satire," I said.

"Farce," he said.

"Wrong," I said. "According to Britannica, and I'm quoting, satire is 'a way of using humor to show that someone or something is foolish, weak, bad, etc.: humor that shows the weaknesses or bad qualities of a person, government, society, etc... an 'artistic form, chiefly literary and dramatic, in which human or individual vices, follies, abuses, or shortcomings are held up to censure by means of ridicule, derision, burlesque, irony, parody, caricature, or other methods, sometimes with an intent to inspire social reform.' As you, a man of letters, well know, it has a long history, predating even Chaucer and Swift."

"So you seek social reform," the man said. "Rather a grandiose ambition, wouldn't you say?"

"If I seek any reform, it's of newspapering," I said. "As for the genre you contend first my book, here's how Britannica defines farce: 'A comic dramatic piece that uses highly improbable situations, stereotyped characters, extravagant exaggeration, and violent horseplay.'"

"What kind of weird dude memorizes Britannica?" the man said.

"This kind."

"Well, there's no violent horseplay in the book. Not yet."

The Ben character stroked his chin.

"Perhaps both of us have it wrong," he said. "While there are satirical and farcical elements to this book, there also is fantasy: Me being here, as example number one. Remember that book you wrote in college, "What If He Came Back"?"

"Yes," I said. "No one bought it."

"Not even that university press editor, who wrote 'Decent imagination, mediocre writing, although your use of eighteenth-century English was a nice touch. You may have a career somewhere, but it won't be in books.' Do you know where that editor was headed? Toward the corner office at Penguin Random House, which she occupies today. I suggest you not submit this one to her."

He paused.

"Actually," he continued, "this book is so superior to that college nonsense so maybe go there first. Doubtless, she's forgotten your name. You were a nothing then."

We descended the stairs and walked to the back door.

"I have a confession," the Franklin character said. "There were no letters."

"No shit, Sherlock."

"I was just having a little fun at your expense. Which in your waking life SGM is doing. Turning you into a mockery. And you have responded by selling your soul. That gives your opus a tragic quality."

"I see that now," I said.

"Finally! Now it's time to do something about it—time to right wrongs. But I do have a tip for you. Maybe not the tip of the century, but a good tip, nonetheless."

"What is it?"

"This Chamberlain character is a fraud. What you heard is damning. His secretary wasn't kidding and she's got the goods. You know what to do with that. The man whose surname is like one of the seasons."

"I already have."

"Good man," the Franklin character said. "Before we go, may I ask you a question?"

"Of course."

"Has Jennifer ever said that I have appeared in one of Amber's dreams?"

"No. Why would *you* appear there?"

"Because I have some concerns. More accurately, a premonition, and not a good one. By way of background, you may or may not know that in my final days, when my mortal body was failing, John Carroll, the first archbishop of Baltimore and the founder of Georgetown College, now Georgetown University, provided comfort and relief. Did you know that his cousin, Charles Carroll, was the last surviving person to sign the Declaration of Independence when he died in 1832?"

"No."

"And that his brother Daniel Carroll II signed the Constitution?"

"No."

"And do you know what his last words were?"

"No."

" 'Of those things that give me most consolation at the present moment, one is that I have always been attached to the practice of devotion to the Blessed Virgin Mary; that I have established it among the people under my care and placed my diocese under her protection.' Now that's something your friend Jennifer might want to know, since she graduated from Georgetown."

"I'll be sure to ask her," I said.

"The point is, Archbishop Carroll's friendship heightened my respect for Catholics, of that era, at least. He is buried now in the Basilica of the National Shrine of the Assumption of the Blessed Virgin Mary in Baltimore. Which Pope Francis will be visiting on his American tour."

"How do you know that?"

"It's posted on the Vatican's Information Service site," the Ben character said. "Now, the premonition. Something terrible will happen when His Holiness visits Massachusetts. There will be injuries and perhaps loss of life. The details, sadly, elude me."

"I thought you could time-travel," I said.

"I can, but there are limits. Sort of like traveling on Southwest. You think you're booked somewhere and then you're canceled. Their pilots claim that's because they've not invested in modern software. Anyway, I'm not sure what you can do with this information about Francis in Massachusetts. Perhaps ask Jennifer if it rings a bell. And a final bit of wisdom. As I've said before, Jennifer's the one for you. I know you don't see it now but you will."

Cold weather and inaction on the miracle front had started eating away at the crowd before Jennifer's appearance—but the next morning, when my column was posted online and *The Trib* hit the streets, a new record number of people descended.

After reading my column, Elizabeth Turner called me at home. It was not yet 8 a.m.

"I must see you," she said.

I went right over.

Luke's Range Rover was not in the driveway and when Elizabeth answered my knock, she said: "Will you pray with me?"

"If you'd like."

"I would, Nick. Reach back into your childhood and connect to God with me."

We walked to the chapel and knelt at the altar. Elizabeth lit a candle. I lit one, too.

"Let's sit," Elizabeth said after a moment of silence.

We did, in the front pew.

"So, what's up?" I said.

"Your story today," Elizabeth said, "was your best yet."

"Thank you."

"But I wasn't surprised. As I've told you, I don't believe that things just happen. I believe God has a plan for everything."

Then explain Amber's end of the deal, I almost said.

"Your column had to appear today," Elizabeth went on, "because last night, without knowing what Jennifer had done—how could I, I didn't watch TV—I had another dream. In it, Mary revealed more of the Christmas event."

So now we have dueling prophets, I thought.

Elizabeth took her morning paper and thumbed to the passage halfway through my column in which Jennifer hinted at the magnitude of the event.

"Until last night," said Elizabeth, "I assumed—like everyone, I suppose—that Mary would perform her most majestic miracle yet, perhaps the healing of many, on Christmas Day. The thought even crossed my mind that Mary would bring back Kimberly. As I told you the other night, she would have been twenty-three on Christmas Day."

Uh-oh, I thought.

"But in my dream," said Elizabeth, "Mary cautioned me of embracing outrageous assumptions."

"What did she say?"

"'Out of the darkness shall come the light. The disciple shall show the way.' "

"Who is the disciple?"

"Mary didn't say and my dream ended after that. But of course it haunted me from the moment I awoke, and so I spoke to the cardinal just before calling you. The cardinal provided the answer. His Holiness is coming to Massachusetts right before Christmas."

I said nothing about my Franklin dream.

"On the news this morning, I did see that he was coming to America," I said, "but there was no mention of Massachusetts."

Taking what many observers thought could be the last overseas visit of his papacy, the pope had arrived last night in Los Angeles on the first leg of the American tour that would also bring him to El Paso, Miami, and Baltimore, ending in New York on December 22, when, after Mass at Saint Patrick's Cathedral, he would return to Rome. But the pope was closer to our cardinal than any other American bishop. Would he extend his U.S. visit by a day to come to Middleton? It seemed plausible.

"The pope's days on this earth are numbered, sadly, given his age," Elizabeth said. "He has unfinished business and nothing, not even a pandemic, can stand in his way."

"Will the cardinal talk to me about it?" I said.

"Not on the record, I'm sure," Elizabeth said. "Announcements of this sort must come directly from Rome."

"What about off the record?"

"Perhaps. Shall we see?"

We left the chapel for Elizabeth's study, where she showed me a printout of the cardinal's schedule. He was still in Los Angeles—he didn't leave for El Paso until this afternoon. Elizabeth picked up the phone, and the cardinal's secretary put her through immediately.

They chatted briefly, and then Elizabeth handed me the phone. I heard the voice of Jose Cardinal Cruz.

"I've been meaning to call you for weeks," the cardinal said. "Fantastic job with your coverage, Nick."

"Thanks," I said.

I was surprised—surely a cardinal would take offense at some aspect of the media circus I'd help create.

"No, thank *you*," the cardinal said. "In the last three months, attendance at Mass is up twenty-five percent throughout the archdiocese."

"Congratulations."

"The news from our Sunday collections is even better—across the board, we've seen a thirty-three percent increase in net income. You, Nick, deserve a lot of credit."

"Oh, I doubt that," I said.

"Don't. Your name keeps coming up in our pastoral explorations."

"Your what?"

"Pastoral explorations. Focus groups, in lay terms."

"You do focus groups?"

The cardinal laughed.

"How do you think we run the Church today—monks with quills stooped over parchment? This is twenty-first century America, where the faithful live in a market-driven environment. If we must fight fire with fire, then we will. Which is why I have blessed sales of certain items related to what is unfolding in Middleton. Not the Pastoral Pretzels or Fatherly Franks or Holy Hummus or Miracle Muffins, of course, but rosaries, crucifixes, bibles, and the like."

"But I thought you were—"

"Anti-materialist?" the cardinal said. "You bet I am. But I also am a realist. And the reality is that in such a consumerist culture as ours, the old methods don't work. That's why I also have been supportive of Elizabeth's chapel in that new mall. We are off the record, yes?"

"Yes."

"Between you and me, just last week I had a very fruitful Zoom call with your publisher. Once we settle a few little details, I think we'll be doing business."

"Business?"

"We call it spiritual convergence," the cardinal said. "Where media meets faith."

"I'm sorry, but I don't understand," I said. "It's been a while since I went to Mass."

"Three Hail Marys and one Our Father and you're forgiven," the cardinal said.

I said nothing.

"That was a joke," the cardinal said. "No need for forgiveness or repentance. Come back anytime without fear of consequence—we shall greet you with open arms. Now about convergence. We call it partnering. Synergy. A strategic alliance between your newspaper and the archdiocese in which both God and the bottom line are served."

"You mean the supplement," I said.

"Oh, no, Nick, much more than that. In return for sharing certain data from our latest diocesan census with Mr. Hill, we have agreed to advertise in *The Trib*. The campaign will be aimed at bringing even more people back to church by emphasizing all the good the archdiocese does for the homeless, immigrants, marginalized people, and more. We're not only about saving souls for eternity, Nick. While they're still hear on earth, we want folks to be housed, fed, educated and—I do not mean this as a pun—protected from ICE and kept warm in the winter."

The cardinal was right about that: On his watch, help to non-privileged groups had increased.

"The church does a lot of good," I said.

"Yes, with all of the aforementioned," Cruz said, "and also in trying to make amends to victims by ruthlessly identifying and bringing to justice those who abused. As you know, not every bishop can match my record."

"I do know," I said.

"Cardinal Law, for starters. I wish I'd had a moment alone with him before he departed for the fires of hell. I wanted our efforts to root out and jail the predators to be part of our media buy with *The Trib*, but your publisher refused. 'Bad news has no place in my paper,' he said. To which I responded: 'But it's actually good news, how we have been hunting these fucking bastards down and turning them over immediately to the authorities.' "

"You used the F word?" I said.

"Yes. Mr. Hill was shocked, I must say, but he did not relent. And I did not insist. Our record speaks for itself, whether or not Poop Man wants to acknowledge it."

"You know about that nickname?"

"Doesn't everyone? And you think I don't remember your column? Gave me a chuckle then. Never forgot it. Never ate an Olestra chip again after that."

"Thanks," I said.

"I suppose this has been a long digression and not at all why you wanted to speak with me," Cruz said. "Elizabeth tells me you want to know about His Holiness."

"I'd love to break the story about his visit if I can confirm it," I said.

"Are we still off the record?"

"Yes."

"You won't use the word 'cardinal' anywhere?"

I promised.

" 'Reliable source,' is okay," the cardinal said, "but not 'archdiocesan source' or anything like that. Because depending on whether or not he's just had another slugfest with those Conservative Resistance jokers who pose as cardinals, His Holiness would have my you-know-whats in a vise if that ever got back to him. So, yes, Francis is coming. He will bless the chapel inside the Minuteman Mall, then celebrate Mass, and following that, proceed to Middleton, where he hopes to meet privately with that dear woman and her daughter. Arrangements for that part are not yet concluded and that remains up in the air, so no mention of it. Barring some last-minute hitch, he arrives at Logan Airport from New York the morning of December 23, and proceeds by motorcade to the mall. You will be covering his visit, I assume?"

"No way I would miss it," I said.

"Then perhaps a brief meeting with him could be arranged. He thinks highly of journalists."

"I didn't know that."

"Oh, yes. Only last month, he bestowed the rank of knight and dame of the grand cross of the Pian Order to Philip Pullella, senior Vatican correspondent for Reuters, and Valentina Alazraki, Vatican correspondent for Televisa. Shall I read you part of what His Holiness said? It will do your soul good."

"Please."

"Francis said 'Journalism does not come about by choosing a profession, but by embarking on a mission, a little like a doctor, who studies and works so that the evil in the world may be healed. Your mission is to explain the world, to make it less obscure, to make those who live in it less afraid of it and look at others with greater awareness, and also with more confidence. It is not an easy mission. It is complicated to think, to meditate, to study more deeply, to stop and collect ideas and to study the contexts and precedents of a piece of news.

" 'The risk, as you well know, is to be overwhelmed by the news instead of being able to make sense of it. This is why I encourage you to preserve and cultivate that sense of mission that is at the origin of your choice. And I will do so with three verbs that I believe characterize good journalism: *listen, investigate,* and *report.*' Quite complimentary, wouldn't you say?"

"I would."

"And if you do get a moment with Francis, what might you ask?"

"Maybe 'are there really miracles?' " I said.

"Good one!" the cardinal said. "But of course, you already know the answer, don't you, Nick. Your Catholicism may have lapsed, but not, I believe, your sense of wonder."

I waited for the other shoe to drop: A crack about socks.

It didn't come.

I left Elizabeth's and went to *The Trib,* where I called Jennifer, who had recovered from yesterday. She said no one had officially informed her yet of the pope's visit, nor had the Vatican tried to reach her regarding a visit from Francis, but she wasn't surprised—one night before Elizabeth's dream, she said, the Virgin Mary had strongly suggested Francis would come to Massachusetts.

"In all the excitement, I forgot to tell you," Jennifer said. "What is most remarkable—and feel free to use this in your column—are the words Mary used: 'Out of the darkness shall come the light. The disciple shall show the way.' "

"Can I ask you something?" I said. "Has Amber ever mentioned Benjamin Franklin?"

"You mean the father of the free press?"

"Yes, him."

"Never," Jennifer said. "Why would she? What does Franklin have to do with Mary?"

"I've had dreams where Franklin time-traveled to today and he's been reading my stories," I said. "In my last one, he spoke of something bad soon to happen. He didn't know what exactly, but he thought Mary, through Amber, might have disclosed it."

"No," Jennifer said, "there's been nothing like that."

After speaking with Jennifer, I dashed off a story about "a reliable source" stating that the pope was coming to Massachusetts.

"This report, however, cannot be independently confirmed," I wrote in the second paragraph.

Then I texted Hill that it was ready. He'd been editing me lately.

"Another great one," the publisher said when he called me to his office. He had the column up on his screen.

"Thank you."

"I have just one criticism."

"You think I went too far."

"On the contrary—you didn't go far enough. Talk about good news— this is great news! The pope in town for the Christmas Event? What could be better?"

"What if my source is wrong?" I said. "We need a disclaimer."

"So the pope doesn't come in the end," said Hill, "what are people going to do—sue? It's an unnamed source, for heaven's sake. Arguably a journalist's mightiest weapon."

Hill tapped the delete key several times and started typing.

"Here," he said. "Let's try this."

Hill began to doctor my column.

I watched, increasingly uneasy as he deleted my disclaimer and rewrote entire paragraphs. When he was finished, I barely recognized the piece.

"A thousand times better," Hill said.

"It's not mine," I said.

"Sure it is. Your name and smiling face will be on it, same as always."

"But it's dishonest."

"And you're Nick Nolan, not Bob Woodward. Don't get weird on me, Nick—we've got too much riding on this. Now that we've settled that, let me show you the special section." It was being published tomorrow.

Hill called up page proofs of the Christmas Event supplement, which had grown from 96 to 128 pages. I watched as Hill scrolled through ads for cars, toys, furniture, home appliances, TVs, cigarettes, wine, and beer. Smith & Wesson had bought a two-page ad for its Equalizer handgun, with a photo of the handgun on one page and copy on the facing page that read "Level the playing field with our best-performing micro-compact to date. Next-gen EZ technology, low recoil impulse, and versatile magazine capacity all in a compact footprint, make the EQUALIZER™ an ultimate CCW," or concealed carry weapon.

"Take a look at the cover," Hill said.

A photo of Jennifer before the crowd yesterday appeared on his screen. It was spectacular, a shot of her arms uplifted, with rays of sunshine radiating down from the sky.

Fake, in other words.

"How'd you get it?" I said.

"One of those losers took it. He wanted a grand for the shot, but we talked him down to two hundred. Then Wright managed to Photoshop it nicely. Now what's the latest on the sacred oil? Have you gotten any?"

In truth, I hadn't asked.

"She won't part with it," I said. "She believes the contest's too commercial."

"Why don't you ask her if her GoFundMe account is too commercial. You really tried?"

"I really tried."

"Then we'll fudge it. And before you get on your high horse, let me show you this."

Hill went online and followed a link through *vatican.com* to a site for a small church in Eichstaedt, Bavaria.

" 'Genuine oil of St. Walburga,' " Hill read. " 'Flows from the stone slab on which rest the relics of St. Walburga.' And only fifty bucks a bottle. We'll have them FedEx it. And if they can't get it here in time, we'll use tap water. No one will ever know the difference."

CHAPTER TEN: CONFLICTS OF INTEREST

Leaving Hill's office, I went home and wrestled with the idea of sneaking into the system and undoctoring my column—and in the end I probably would have, if it hadn't already been sent to production. Midnight found me unable to sleep. When I finally did, nightmares roiled me.

What purported to be my column led the paper the next morning, and it brought the predictable response: a fresh onslaught of people trying to reach me, and yet another record crowd outside Jennifer's.

But I wasn't focused on Jennifer when I got to *The Trib.*

I was focused on our page-one centerpiece.

After what was described as "intense negotiations," Jennifer Lawrence late yesterday had agreed to play Jennifer in the movie, and while no one had informed me, Chamberlain had ordered all of his properties to feature it with a photo of Lawrence accepting her Academy Award for Best Actress and the photo—again—of me with Mickey Mouse.

I went to Lifestyle and beckoned the photo editor, my friend Cindy Leroux, aside.

"He told you to run that photo again, didn't he," I said.

"Yes," Cindy said.

"This time I'm confronting him," I said.

"After what he pulled down here yesterday, I hope you give him hell," Cindy said.

"What happened?"

"He unloaded on Marjorie Rudd."

"I thought he loved her," I said.

"He did—for about a week," said Cindy. "Turns out, she doesn't take shit. Behind the scenes, she's been a thorn in his side for months, slamming him for the budget and short staff. Things reached a head yesterday after Marjorie told Ham Whittier, owner of Capitol Hill restaurant, to go fuck himself."

"What did Whittier do?"

"Called demanding we run a correction on our review of Capitol Hill. We gave the place three stars—and Whittier ranted that it should have been five. When Marjorie said there'd been no error—and implied he was lucky for three stars, given how crappy the food *really* was, overcooked and cold and everything—he threatened to pull his advertising. That's when Marjorie hung up on him."

"So he called Hill."

"Right. Hill demanded we run not only a correction, but a whole new review—I don't know how we were going to explain *that* exactly. He also ordered Marjorie to call Whittier to apologize. 'No fucking way,' she said, and that's a direct quote. I guess she'd finally had it. Her anger must have caught Hill off guard because then he said he'd settle for five stars on the capsule summary we run in our weekly roundup. 'Over my dead body,' Marjorie said. It went downhill from there. She'll be lucky to keep her job. If she still wants it, which I doubt."

"I'm going to see Hill," I said.

"Since you're on the warpath," said Cindy, "why don't you ask him about this, too."

Cindy handed me her copy of this week's CoolBostonWeekly.

By now, I had grown accustomed to Courtney's hammerings—but her column, played on the cover this week, didn't mention me. Not a word about the screen and book deals or Trump.

Courtney had dropped two bombshells unrelated to me.

Citing a source inside the Office of U.S. Attorney, she claimed officials were secretly investigating "credible" allegations that Luke Turner had knowingly used inferior-grade iron on parts of the Minuteman Mall—and then bribed a state inspector to secure an occupancy permit.

I wondered how Winters would feel after reading this, given that Hill had killed his mall exposé. I was still waiting to learn what, if anything, he'd been able to find regarding the SEC.

Courtney's second bombshell was that Chamberlain had secretly put up ten million dollars of the seventy-five million dollars Turner had needed to finish the mall. Citing the same unnamed source, Courtney claimed the money had been channeled—legally, if furtively—through a SuperGoodMedia subsidiary, Tidewater Futures Inc., a company none of her sources had ever heard of.

"Of course," Courtney wrote, "this is hardly the first time a leading media company has invested in an enterprise it also covers. But this may be the first time such an unethical relationship is so nakedly based on greed. And if investigators bring charges, it may be the first time in years that a big-city newspaper becomes an accomplice in crime."

And that was not the only bad news about SGM that morning.

The Washington Post had published an investigation showing how deeply in debt the company was. Even with further gutting of newsrooms and closing more papers, *The Post* reported, Chamberlain could not get to a sustainable bottom line. With the exception of *The Trib*, the company was hemorrhaging.

I took the elevator upstairs and brushed past Hill's secretary into his office. I saw no one—but the bathroom door was closed, and Hill's dog was keeping watch outside. The publisher emerged momentarily. His face was pale and he walked to his desk slowly, as if in pain.

"Shouldn't you be in Middleton?" he said.

"I'm not going there today."

"You're not what?"

"I said I'm not going there today. Fire me if you want. I don't care. But I'm not going."

"You're burning out," Hill said. "I get that. Take the day off. Recharge. We'll use wire copy for tomorrow. And tomorrow, you'll be back there as good as new."

"Tomorrow, I will decide what I do, not you." I said. "Now about this."

I tossed The Scene on his desk.

"I look like an idiot," I said.

"And yesterday you were hung up on truth. Your point would be? Now if you'll excuse me, I'm late for a meeting."

"The picture's the least of it," I said. "Have you seen Courtney's column today?"

"Yes."

"Is it true Chamberlain invested ten million dollars in the Minuteman Mall?"

"Absolutely not."

"Then why would she run it?"

"Because her journalism is yellow?"

"She sounds credible on this to me."

"And she sounds desperate and reckless to me."

"What about the steelworker's allegations?" I said.

"What about them?"

"Will you run Terry Winter's story now?"

"Of course not," Hill said. "Luke Turner has been in business almost thirty years and except for Winter's story—an incredibly biased piece of journalism based entirely on hearsay—there's never been a whisper of wrongdoing. Turner is the best there is."

"Maybe he never got caught."

"And maybe Mike Huckabee will come to see the pope."

"We need to run Terry's story," I said. "We'll look like assholes if we don't. And since we're discussing investigations, what about the *Washington Post* exposé today?"

"Not my circus, not my monkey," Hill said.

"We're talking about the head of this company," I said.

"Maybe you should ask him yourself. I know nothing."

It was likely a lie, but I was not going to press the point, now.

Hill stood and put his arm around me. I recoiled at his touch.

"Look, Nick," he said, "don't think I don't appreciate your concerns. But it's not what we pay you for. You're the Mary News guy. You're the goose that lays the golden eggs. Let's not get sidetracked. Now I really am late for my meeting."

Embarrassed and angry, I left the paper. Mickey Mouse had reminded me of some important unfinished business.

And I was about to call my friend at Make-A-Wish when it occurred to me I didn't need his help. So I left my apartment, visited a travel agency, and stopped by a sports shop. I couldn't find what I wanted, but I bought the next best thing and had them gift-wrap it. Then I drove to Children's Hospital.

Jimmy was alone in his room when I arrived; his mother, he said, had gone home to shower and change.

"How are you?" I said.

The boy looked tired and still jaundiced, but he was off his IV.

"I'm okay," he said. "They finished with the new chemo. I go home in a couple of days."

I remembered Gina saying the doctors were trying an experimental protocol on the boy.

"That's great," I said.

"Yeah," said Jimmy, "just in time for Christmas. My father's even supposed to come over Christmas morning. But he always says that. Then he never does. It kind of sucks not having your father around, but you get used to it. So what's in the bag?"

"You can't open it until Christmas," I said.

"But Christmas isn't for five more days."

"I guess you'll have to be patient."

"Come on, Nick!"

"All right," I said, handing him the gift.

He ripped it open.

"Awesome!" he said. "A Tom Brady football!"

"I couldn't find one that was signed and I didn't want to fly to Tampa Bay," I joked, "but I figured you'd like it anyway."

"I do. Thanks, Nick. This is really cool."

"Want to toss a few around?" I said.

"You know we can't do that in here."

"How about in the lobby?"

"You can't do it there, either. The stupid guard will take it away."

"Not if we're careful," I said. "Let's go."

We took the elevator to the lobby. Jimmy stopped as we passed the wishing well.

"Do you have a penny?" I said.

"No one has pennies anymore," Jimmy said.

"But they do have quarters," I said.

I fished around the wishing well and pulled two out.

"Here you go," I said, handing him one.

Jimmy threw his quarter into the pool, then I threw mine.

"What did you wish for?" I said.

"You're not supposed to say. It won't come true."

"It's okay if you whisper it."

I leaned close to Jimmy and he told me.

"That's a great wish," I said.

"But it's our secret, right? You won't use it in one of your stories?"

"Absolutely not."

"What about you?" Jimmy said. "What did you wish for?"

"For you to have the best Christmas holiday ever," I said. "And to make sure you do, I'm sending you and your Mom to Disney World."

"No way!"

"Way."

I handed the envelope to Jimmy.

"You don't leave until after New Year's. Everything was booked until then."

"It's wicked awesome, Nick," Jimmy said. "Thanks."

But Jimmy's mood suddenly darkened.

"What's wrong?" I said.

"I didn't get anything for you," he said.

"I didn't expect anything."

"Yeah, but it would have been nice."

"Forget it, kid. Are you ready to send me deep?"

I handed Jimmy the football and trotted a few feet into the lobby. Jimmy connected with a bullet pass. Even sick, the boy had strength.

"Way to go," I said, returning him the ball. "Okay, deeper this time."

I ran past the reception desk and Jimmy lobbed a pass that I jumped to catch—and missed. The football bounced past a baby carriage and came to rest by the door, where a man in a uniform stood.

"Hey, pal," the guard said, "that's against hospital regulations."

"We're just having a little fun," I said.

"Somebody could get hurt. Hand it over."

By now, Jimmy had joined me. He looked nervous.

"That's the guy who took my ball before," he said.

"Hand the ball over, mister," the guard said.

"Sorry," I said. "The game is tied and there's only five seconds on the clock."

The guard seemed perplexed—but Jimmy got it.

"Here you go," I said, tossing him the ball. "Make it good."

I ran toward the wishing pool, turned, and Jimmy cocked his arm.

"Brady's looking deep!" I said. "He's being rushed but Nolan's in the end zone! Nolan's free! The clock's almost run out! The crowd's on its feet! Brady sees him! Brady fires! This is it, folks, a Hail Mary pass!"

Jimmy fired hard and high.

I leaped.

My fingers touched the ball and then I pulled it in.

Running, Jimmy and I escaped into the elevator.

It was almost suppertime when I finally left Children's Hospital. I decided to drop by Ernie's. I hadn't been in a while.

Destiny was at the bar when I arrived. She was sipping a beer and picking at a chicken salad sandwich, and her eyes were bloodshot, as if she'd been up all night.

"What's wrong?" I said.

"You weren't at the paper this afternoon."

"No, I wasn't."

"The shit hit the fan. I guess Courtney's column and the *Post* investigation were the last straws for a lot of people."

With Jones still in court, two dozen staffers had marched into Hill's office—but Hill was away at a meeting. Back in the newsroom, they'd circulated a resolution demanding Hill resign.

"That wasn't enough for Winters," Destiny said. "He quit, after telling me he's got an agreement to work with ProPublica. He's sure there is a lot more still to come out and they totally agreed. They've had their eye on SGM, too. And that was only the beginning. An hour later, Hill fired twenty-nine people. No buyout, no early retirement, nothing. Guards showed up with severance packages and told them they had ten minutes to get out or be arrested."

"Because of the protest?"

"No—that had been in the works for weeks. The consultants issued their final report recommending a total restructuring of the news department and Hill bought it. The city staff was cut by twenty-five percent, the suburban staff by half."

"But the paper is making more money than ever."

"Yes, but not SuperGoodMedia, as *The Washington Post* confirmed," Destiny said. "Have you seen the stock price lately? Twelve cents a share. Twelve *cents*."

My visit to Orlando came to mind.

"Hill didn't have the balls to face us after the layoffs," Destiny continued. "He sent an email. 'This assures *The Trib*'s brightest future ever,' he wrote. Merry fucking Christmas."

"Will the Guild fight it?"

"We're already drafting the suit," Destiny said. "By the time Hill exhausts the appeals, we'll all be dead."

"What about you?" I said.

"I'm taking Bud's place in Lynn—he got sent to the late-night copy desk. From now on, just call me Ms. Woman on the Street."

"I'm sorry."

"Why should you care?" said Destiny. "You're going to be in the movies. Don't think I bought that 'I-was-under-duress' crap you gave me and Terry over coffee."

That hurt.

"That came out harsher than I intended," Destiny said.

"Then what did you intend?"

"To say that you've changed. You're not the person I knew any more, Nick."

"You think screen and book deals have corrupted me."

"You were changing before that. Maybe it was the evening newscasts or People magazine or *60 Minutes*, but whatever it was, you crossed a line. And when you did, the story began to ruin you."

Destiny was right about that, though I'd have preferred a kinder description than "ruin."

But Destiny was wrong about something else.

"I didn't create this," I said. "I've gone over the top, way over sometimes—I admit that. But I didn't put that girl in a coma, or have her mother idolize the Virgin Mary, or make people flock to Middleton, or order monks to build an altar, or raise Tony Callahan's blood count. Nor is this some case of mass hypnosis."

"What is it, then, Nick?"

"I don't know," I said.

"Then why are you still writing about it?"

"Because isn't that what we do?"

"Don't we also right wrongs?" Destiny said.

"I know you think I've lost my conscience," I said, "but I haven't. I've listened to what you've said and I've thought about what Courtney's written. I've stood up to Hill—not as strongly as I should have, but at least it was something. And I can't tell you how many times I've almost confronted Jennifer."

"But you haven't."

"Not as forcefully as I should have. But you haven't been there in that crowd. You haven't seen the suffering—or the hope on this boy Jimmy Pulaski's face. You haven't felt the joy when Tony Callahan's doctor announced he was officially in remission."

"Nonetheless, you've gone overboard," Destiny said. "I'm telling you that as a friend—and someone who still believes newspapers should stand for something more than clicks. There's a time to charge in and a time to bow out—a time to say no to all the marketing and exploitation and hype. If we on the inside don't take a stand, who will? You need to right some wrongs and move on. Now can I buy you a beer?"

I tossed down a couple and went home, where I called Terry Winters, who said he'd been unable to get anything more about the SEC investigation of SuperGoodMedia than what *The Washington Post* had reported.

"Worked a number of good sources," Winters said, "and nothing. Of course, that doesn't mean there isn't more to the story. I'll keep digging."

"Will you be joining the staff of ProPublica?" I said.

"Yes," he said, "I start on January second."

I spent the remainder of the evening watching TV. WQZ led the eleven o'clock news with coverage of the first Mary lottery.

Apparently fearful of a charge of favoritism, the Sisters of the Sacred Heart had accepted an offer from worldwide lottery giant IGT to engineer the process, and starting at dawn, the faithful had formed lines at tables where nuns handed out what was estimated to be more than 3,000 tickets—only 100 of which revealed an image of Mary when the coating was scratched off. The lucky hundred then went to the semi-finalist's booth, where they deposited their tickets inside a Powerball-like machine. A blindfolded mother-superior type drew the day's ten finalists from the machine, then announced over a public address system that following the same procedure, another ten would be chosen tomorrow, and ten more the next day, and so on.

I was horrified. This could have been the set of a Fellini movie. And I'd help create it.

"Thank heavens she said this will be continuing," Officer Maloney told the camera, "or there would have been a riot out here. You can't do a one-and-done with Mary."

WQZ's coverage ended with an interview of a finalist and a sound bite from the cardinal, who'd joined the pope in El Paso, second stop on his American pilgrimage.

Mary News had just ended when my phone rang.

It was A.J.

"What is it?" I said.

"I need to talk," she said.

"About what?"

"About Middleton. I was there today. Of course, I wasn't a semi-finalist. Never did have good luck. So what I want to know is: Why only ten people a day? Ten a day isn't ridiculous—it's cruel. Why couldn't she let a steady stream through, morning to night? That way, everyone gets their shot. But no, she says it's Mary's wish, the hand of God, blah-blah-blah."

"Is there anything else before I hang up?" I said.

"Please don't," she said. "I called to ask a favor."

"Funny way you have of asking favors."

"I'm sorry, Nick. I know how badly I've treated you."

"What's the favor?"

"Take me to Amber."

"I can't."

"Sure you can. You go there every day."

"You don't understand," I said.

"Actually," A.J. said, "*you* don't understand. You don't understand what it's like getting up every morning too exhausted to make coffee, or always running a fever—and people think it's all in your head. You've never gone from doctor to doctor and still feel like crap every minute of your life."

"You're right," I said, "I don't understand what that's like."

"I'm scared, Nick. I don't have a job. I don't have any savings. I have nowhere else to turn. Please help me."

"I'd like to," I said, "but I can't."

There was silence on the other end.

"I can't because I'm just about done," I said.

"Done what?" A.J. said.

"Done with the story. I won't be writing much more Mary News."

"Before you stop, take me to Amber. Please. I'm begging."

"I can't."

"Just one minute with her. I'll never bother you or her again."

"If I took you," I said, "what could I say to all the others?"

"They wouldn't have to know," said A.J.

"They'd find out."

"You're my last hope, Nick."

"I'm sorry, A.J. Maybe when you read my next column, you'll understand."

I expected anger—and got what sounded like a sob, and then the dial tone.

A.J. was right.

I could never understand how painful her life had become.

But at least I could have empathy.

Midnight passed and I logged onto our website but found no denial of

SGM's investment in the mall. No word either about the restructuring or the resignation of Terry Winters. No surprise.

Mary News owned the site, again—not even the frenzy over Tony Callahan surpassed this. The main package was all-lottery: two stories and ten photos. A sidebar story involved the cardinal and the pope: according to Reuters, the cardinal's press secretary had announced that initial analysis of Jennifer's oil revealed it to be chemically identical to The Oil of St. Walburga, which the Church had recognized as sacred for centuries.

"While more steps remain before proclaiming the oil holy," the cardinal said in a media release, "this lends further credence to claims of Mary's presence. It is fitting, in this season of joy, for us to reflect on the hand of the Lord."

The cardinal had confirmed more big news: the pope would be visiting Massachusetts, as I had reported in my story that quoted a reliable source.

According to the updated schedule, the pope would arrive by jet from New York and proceed by motorcade to the Minuteman Mall, where he would celebrate Mass inside the chapel Elizabeth Turner had made her husband build.

"The Holy Father has consistently taught that materialism endangers the spirit," the cardinal said, "and so it is appropriate for Him to remind God's children what it means to love and cherish true values. For such a message, there can be no better forum than a mall."

CHAPTER ELEVEN: FULL DISCLOSURE

A light snow was falling when I awoke after another night of restless sleep. The day was bitterly cold. I dressed in a flannel shirt, jeans, and parka, and drove to Jennifer's.

It was December 21.

A Channel 14 assistant producer stopped me on my way past the remote studio.

"Where were you yesterday?" she said. "And what's with no story today?"

"I've been working on something big," I sadi. "Really, really big."

"More oil?" she said.

"Better that oil."

"A mass miracle?"

"Even better."

"Come on, Nick, tell me!"

"All I can say is see you tonight at six."

I pushed through the crowd to Jennifer's house. She seemed surprised to see me.

"I wasn't expecting you," she said.

"I was hoping I could see Amber."

"The carpenters are in there."

"Carpenters?"

"I've hired them to build a plexiglass wall and install an OSHA-rated air purification system. Now that we're about to have daily visitors, I need guaranteed protection; her health is so fragile, you know. I don't think she could survive the flu or another bout of pneumonia or, God forbid, COVID. She is fully vaccinated, but there are breakthrough cases. As you will see, the carpenters are wearing PPE."

"Amber is better today?"

"Yes, thank God."

"Then how about if the carpenters take a break," I said. "I'd like to visit. I won't be long."

"Is this for one of your columns?" Jennifer said.

"No," I said. "This is only for me."

"You won't be recording on your cell."

"No, and I don't have a notebook or pen."

"Five minutes, that's all," Jennifer said. "I need them to finish before today's lottery."

Jennifer excused the carpenters and we went through a new door into Amber's room, now sealed off from the rest of the house by the plexiglass wall. I noticed that Jennifer had placed a photo of her daughter before the accident next to the medicines on the bureau: it showed a pretty girl of about three in a red dress, smiling as she stood by a Christmas tree.

Jennifer had never displayed a photo before, nor shown me one, either.

"Do you mind if we're alone?" I said.

"No," Jennifer said, and left.

I sat in the room's only chair, which was at the head of Amber's bed; Jennifer kept her vigils here. Candles cast flickering light on the weeping Madonna.

I had never studied Amber's face before—could never bring myself to push past the G tube and IV pole and plastic tubing to seek the little girl beyond.

I did now.

I contemplated Amber's skin, the color of an ivory carnation, and her hair, freshly shampooed by Jennifer. Her lids were closed, but I imagined her eyes were blue. I imagined her voice was melodic, like a girl in a classic children's film.

Jimmy's question came into my head again.

"Are you?" I whispered. "Are you happy?"

She didn't answer, of course.

"It's not just my question," I said. "A little boy who is sick asked me to ask you. He also wanted to apologize for comparing you to a zombie. And mostly, he wants me to tell you he hopes you get better."

I reached out and wrapped my fingers around Amber's hand.

I felt a pulse, but nothing more.

And then, the two of us connected.

Energy passed between us, like a surge of electric current.

Amber opened her eyes—they were blue, just as I'd imagined—and she smiled, just like in the picture of her by the Christmas tree.

"I wasn't happy at first," the girl said. "I was in a long dark tunnel, but Mary rescued me. And then my mommy, who loves me very much, took care of me."

"But why didn't Mary make you better?" I said.

" 'Cause she needed my help."

"Couldn't you help if you were better?"

Amber laughed.

"You ask lots of questions, Mr. Nolan. But not every question has an easy answer, you know. Some don't get answered at all down here on earth. You must have faith."

"Faith's tough," I said.

"So is believing in what's important in this life," said Amber. "You don't anymore, Mr. Nolan, and that makes me sad. But I have hope. I see a light shining around you."

"What does it mean?"

"It means you will find that belief in the things that you've lost. It means you will find peace. I want peace, too. It's not that I haven't enjoyed helping Mary, but now I just want peace."

"It will come to you," I said. "And now I need your help. Please ask Mary to make Jimmy better."

"As I said, you must have faith," Amber said.

"I did once, when I was about your age," I said.

"What happened to it?"

"After my mother and sister died, I prayed for God to bring them back."

"But that's not how it works," Amber said.

"For years, my father and I visited my mom's grave and the grave of my sister, who I never met—she died during childbirth. When time passed and they didn't come back no matter how much I prayed, I got angry. And that's when I began to lose faith."

"I'm so sorry your mom and sister died," Amber said. "I understand now how you feel. Your mom and sister have eternal peace now. And you will soon come to a place of peace here on earth. And now, Mr. Nolan, I am very tired. I am glad you visited, but now you must go."

Amber's hand went cold and her eyes closed.

"Are you all right?" Jennifer said. She was standing behind me. I hadn't heard her enter.

"I'm fine," I said.

"You've been in here over half an hour. The carpenters are champing at the bit."

I looked at Amber—but of course she hadn't moved or spoken.

"I've come to a decision," I said. "I don't belong here anymore."

"You really don't believe, do you?" Jennifer said.

"It doesn't matter whether I do or not. I just know it's time for me to go."

On the other side of the plexiglass, I saw a carpenter standing impatiently with a drill. Jennifer signaled for him to wait, and then she smoothed her daughter's brow, ran her fingers through her hair, kissed her cheek, and smiled at me.

"I remember those horrible first few weeks, praying for her to come out of her coma," she said. "The doctors said there was little hope, but I refused to believe. When finally it was clear they were right, I was angry—angry at them, angry at me for being in that car, angry at God."

"Who wouldn't be?"

"I wanted Amber to pass. That sounds terrible, but it seemed merciful. I gave permission to disconnect the respirator—but, like Karen Ann Quinlan, she started breathing on her own. I'm ashamed to say that only made me angrier. But anger, I learned, slowly eats you up. You have to let go—and eventually, I did. I renewed my faith and I began to believe that God must have had a reason. And he did—although I didn't discover what it was until we came to Middleton. You know the rest."

"Should I say I'm sorry?" I said.

"For what?"

"For a lot of things."

"If you mean sleeping with me, don't," said Jennifer. "I have no regrets. But we're two very different people, going in two very different directions. My head knew that, but my heart didn't until now."

"I understand," I said.

"Do you?"

"Sure. I feel the same way myself."

"I have a mission now, Nick," Jennifer said. "I can't let anything get in the way."

"You have faith."

"My prayer for you is that someday you'll have faith of your own. Will you be here tomorrow?"

"I'm not sure," I said.

"Stay in touch if you're not?"

"Of course."

"Goodbye, Nick."

"Goodbye, Jennifer."

She walked me to the door, and we parted with a handshake.

I never expected to see her or Amber again.

I never did.

Amber, that is.

I was standing outside Jennifer's door wondering how I could avoid the assistant producer when an ambulance roared up. EMTs loaded someone into it and sped away. The commotion drew everyone's attention, so I was able to slip away unnoticed to my car.

I was getting in when Officer Maloney appeared.

"What was that about?" I said.

"Some crazy person slashed her wrists. Said she'd kill herself if Mrs. Abbott wouldn't let her in. But it was just a ploy for attention. No one serious about suicide slashes their wrists. They find a tall bridge."

"Not very empathic, Officer Maloney," I said. "I thought you were working on that."

"Sorry," the policeman said. "Tough for old dogs to learn new tricks. But I'm trying."

"Do you know who it was?" I said.

"As a matter of fact I do. It's what's-her-name—she writes for your paper. Or used to. I never see her column anymore. Not that I ever liked it to begin with. She was such a whiner."

"You mean Alice Johnson?" I said.

"Yeah, that's her," Maloney said.

"Where'd they take her?"

"Probably Mass. General," said Maloney. "They've got a unit for head cases there."

"People with mental health challenges, you mean."

"Yes, that's what I mean," Maloney said.

When I got home, I went online and ordered flowers sent to A.J. When the clerk asked what I wanted on the card, I gave Jennifer's unlisted cell number with instructions to call as soon as A.J. felt up to it.

Then I began to write my final column for *The Daily Tribune*.

I worked until nearly 3 a.m. but nothing I wrote satisfied; I had much to say but couldn't find how to say it.

I'd fallen into a fitful sleep when my cell rang. It was quarter past seven in the morning.

Hill was calling. I let it go to voice mail, then listened.

"Nick, it's Bruce," he'd said. "Are you okay? No story, no stand-up, no one's seen you in the newsroom, HR's got no report you're sick, WQZ says you made noise about something big but all we've got is nothing, what gives? If you need a vacation, how's two weeks in Cancun sound—but *not* 'til we get through the Christmas Event. Call me the second you get this so I don't send out the police. I need you back in action today."

I'll be back in action today, all right, I thought. *Just wait and see.*

I made coffee and logged onto *Trib.com*, where second-day coverage of the pope's impending visit to Massachusetts again filled the home page. It was all happy, cheery, holy stuff—all but a single paragraph at the end of the main story that described how the State Police, Secret Service, and Swiss Guards were working to keep Francis safe on his extra day in America.

"In light of recent threats," the story said, "security is expected to be extremely tight in Massachusetts, as it has been all during his tour."

And that was all: one ominous paragraph.

I figured *The New York Times* would have further elaboration, and I was right: citing unnamed sources, *The Times* claimed the existence of "credible" threats against the pope from some recently identified ISIS cell over some alleged papal slight. The pope himself seemed unworried. "His Holiness believes the Virgin Mary has protected him from threat before and will do so again," the paper quoted Philip Pullella, the senior Reuters Vatican correspondent. "The Third Secret of Fatima remains a very powerful force for him."

I went back to work.

By late afternoon, I had only one hole left to fill: Courtney's allegations, which I still could not independently confirm. The sources I'd once had in law enforcement were history and Terry Winters—the one friend who probably could have dug someone up for me—wasn't answering his phone.

That left only Courtney.

"It's me, Nick," I said when she answered her phone.

"You think I've forgotten the sound of your voice?" Courtney said.

"We're off the record?" I said.

"Yes."

"None of this winds up in your next column."

"No," Courtney said, "you have my word."

I thought she had agreed too easily, but I didn't care. I was all in now.

"I assume you didn't call to compliment me on my columns," she continued.

"Actually, I did. You've given me plenty to think about. This week especially."

"Thanks. From you it means a lot."

"I need your help," I said.

I was certain Courtney would laugh, but she didn't.

"For what?" she said.

"I'm writing my final column," I said, "and one last piece is missing."

"What's going on, Nick?"

"I'm done with Mary News because things have gotten out of control, as you have amply documented."

"You flatter me. But there must be more to it than that."

"There isn't. I only want to right some wrongs."

"But how could *I* help you?"

"I need to confirm the Turner investigation."

"You think I made it up?"

"I don't."

"Then run with it," said Courtney.

"I need more. I need your source."

"You know I can't give you that."

"I do. But you could call him or her. See if they'd agree to talk to me off the record."

My cell rang 15 minutes later. That seemed remarkably fast, but obviously Courtney was tight with her source.

He turned out to be U.S. Attorney Joseph T. Cicilline, a man who was rumored to be exploring a run for governor. I knew him or, rather, used to: he was the aggressive young prosecutor fresh out of Yale Law School who'd sent Brenda Davis's landlord to prison after my Forgotten Children series. I hadn't spoken to him in over a decade.

But Cicilline hadn't forgotten about me—he said he still read my stories "religiously."

I couldn't tell if he was ridiculing me, and I didn't want to know. He'd respected me, once upon a time.

"Times change, don't they," said Cicilline.

"Tell me about it."

"I liked the old *Trib* better," he said. "You guys may have been all over our ass, but at least you stood for something. This Hill dude is quite the trip. I hear he took his ax to the paper again."

"You heard right."

"I guess that's what happens when you lose local ownership. Someday, a hedge fund or a guy in Dubai will own every newspaper in the country. A sorry day that will be for democracy. How can I help you, Nick?"

We established the terms of our relationship: Cicilline would be "a high-ranking law-enforcement source," no more.

"So, yes, I can confirm everything Courtney had," Cicilline said. "She gets her facts straight."

I thanked Cicilline and was about to hang up when he told me he had more.

"Things have moved fast since I spoke to Courtney," he said. "We're no longer looking at spring to bring this case to a grand jury. We have new evidence that makes me confident we'll indict Turner shortly after the first of the year."

There was more still.

The new evidence, Cicilline said, had prompted him to subpoena Chamberlain and Hill.

They'd been served just hours before.

I finished my story, but another problem awaited: slotting it into the paper. Hill already suspected something funny was up; surely he'd left instructions for editors to be on the lookout for anything I wrote.

So I emailed my column to Bud Fuller, freshly demoted to the late-night copy desk. He called back saying he loved it—and he'd make sure it got in tomorrow's paper.

"Not Page One," he said. "It's already been put to bed. But tucked away somewhere inside metro/region—yeah, we can do that. And I'll make sure it's huge on the homepage."

"You'll get fired," I said. "Like me."

"I hope so," Bud said.

It was almost ten o'clock, the night of December 22. The snow that had been teasing Boston had grown into a Nor'easter, and the plows were already behind. But Ubers were still getting around, and I took one to Children's Hospital. Jimmy was supposed to be discharged tomorrow, and I wanted to wish him well. I wanted to tell him I'd visit him at his home on Christmas, if that was okay.

Gina Pulaski was at her son's bedside when I walked in. She was pleased to see me—but Jimmy didn't stir. He was hooked up to an IV again, and his eyes were closed. I couldn't tell if he was sleeping or something worse. But he still had his football tucked under an arm.

"He's been drifting in and out of consciousness," his mother said.

"What happened?" I said.

"Cytomegalovirus. CMV."

I knew about that from interviewing Tony Callahan, who'd undergone two bone-marrow transplants for his leukemia.

"An infection," I said.

"A raging one," said Gina. "With his immune system wiped out from this new treatment, he's susceptible to everything."

I remembered taking Jimmy to the lobby—a place crawling with germs. The thought that I might have contributed to his setback, however unwittingly, hit me hard.

"He'll be all right, won't he?" I said.

"I hope so," said Gina. "I don't know if you're still religious, Mr. Nolan—your columns give no clue—but if you are, please say a prayer."

Almost a foot of snow had fallen by the time I left Children's. It was midnight.

I showered when I got home and was about to log onto *Trib.com* to see where Bud had snuck my column in when my cell rang. I picked up and heard the voice of Hill.

He sounded insane, like Jack Nicholson in *The Shining*.

"Nice try, Nick," Hill said. "You almost pulled it off. Too bad I have friends on the late-night desk, too."

Hill said that after being tipped off, he'd driven through the storm to

The Trib so that he could personally fire Bud Fuller. "My only regret is you weren't there, too," he said. "It's much less satisfying shit-canning someone by phone. But you're fired."

Then he began to ramble—I believe he was drunk, the way he'd been at Luke William's party. He called the U.S. Attorney "the worst kind of political opportunist" and predicted that Turner would be cleared once he had his day in court. He defended our Mary News coverage, asserting that our circulation figures and market research prove "we're only giving our readers what they want, isn't that our job?" He defended his time as publisher, saying *The Tribune*, with its record profits, faced "its brightest future ever."

And by the end, he'd retracted my firing, saying he needed to sleep on it and wouldn't make a final decision until after he returned from Florida on a Christmas visit with Chamberlain.

"I thought we were tight, Nick," said Hill, "you and me, riding the rocket together. You should have told me something was bugging you. Is it money? We can take care of that. Or maybe it's something I don't see. You just gotta tell me, Nicky Boy. Tell your old Uncle Bruce."

By now, Hill was simpering. I couldn't bear listening to more, so I hung up.

My final column wouldn't run.

As it happened, that was a blessed development.

Daybreak on December 23 brought gusting winds, clearing skies, and almost two feet of accumulated wet snow; like any respectable Nor'easter, the storm had done its damage, then blown out to sea. I turned on the TV and found that Logan Airport would remain closed until at least noon. The pope wouldn't fly in—according to Channel 4's morning guy, Amtrak was still running and he would reach South Station on a special train at 10 a.m., and then proceed to Danvers and the Minuteman Mall.

Jimmy's condition had stabilized, the charge nurse said when I phoned Children's—he was still unconscious, but his fever was down. I asked to speak to Gina Pulaski, but she'd already left for Middleton. She'd always wanted to see the pope.

I dressed for winter and drove to the Minuteman Mall. I wanted to witness history, too.

Police had blocked side streets along the route the pope's motorcade would take, and a National Guard checkpoint had been established outside the mall parking lot, which was crawling with Humvees and police cruisers. Men with rifles peered down from the mall roof—police snipers, I assumed. Entrance to the mall was gained only by passing through X-ray stations and past bomb-sniffing dogs.

Seeing all this chilled me. The words of the Third Secret of Fatima, which *latimes.com* had reprinted in a sidebar, wouldn't leave my head: "The 'bishop clothed in white' makes his way with great effort toward the cross amid the corpses of those who were martyred. He too falls to the ground, apparently dead, under a burst of gunfire."

Inside the mall, the mood was a mix of anxiety, excitement, and reflection. COVID-masked teenagers with ear piercings mingled with masked older people clutching crucifixes and carrying Bibles. Reporters prowled for new angles, and souvenir vendors did a brisk business.

Mall management had suspended screens from the glass roof that covered the central atrium, which formed the spine of the mall. They were carrying WQZ's live broadcast and I watched as the pope was helped off the train at South Station. The motorcade—limos sandwiched between State Police cruisers and National Guard vehicles—left for Danvers. The highways had been plowed and the trip would take about an hour.

"Would you like to see the chapel?"

A woman wearing a mask had approached me.

It was Elizabeth Turner.

"Of course I'd like to see the chapel," I said.

She led me to the north side, where the chapel had been built on the first floor between an Imax theater and a food court. Recognizing Elizabeth Turner, one of the soldiers standing guard let us in. The chapel was smaller than I expected. An altar, baptismal font, confessional, and pews to accommodate about 100 people comprised the whole of it.

"The Third Secret of Fatima has everyone on edge," said Elizabeth. "They don't seem to understand that prophecy has already been fulfilled with the 1981 assassination attempt on Pope John Paul II. As you may remember, he survived, thank God."

"You can't be too careful," I said.

"Of course," said Elizabeth. "But Pope Francis will be safe here. My dreams last night were all blessed things."

Elizabeth genuflected, then knelt and bowed her head. I sat next to her. We were in the last pew. Except for the soldiers, we were alone.

"I've told you how my husband resented building this," Elizabeth said when she'd prayed. "But that will all be behind me soon. Our marriage ended yesterday when I told him to leave. The next time I see him will be in court."

Once again, Elizabeth had surprised me.

"You're divorcing him," I said.

"I will seek an annulment, of course. By court I meant the charges the government will soon bring. I have offered to testify."

Courtney's column, Elizabeth told me, had been the final straw in her marriage.

"For all his flaws, I never imagined he was a criminal," Elizabeth said. "And when I learned he was, I knew immediately the greater good could no longer be served. I told him I could not be a party to blood money."

"What did he say?"

"He denied everything," Elizabeth said, "and then he was on the phone to his lawyers. What I overheard didn't sound like the protest of an innocent man. It sounded like someone worried he will go to jail."

"The government has a strong case," I said.

"Very strong," said Elizabeth. "Agents raided his office last evening and then they raided our home—at my invitation. They would have sooner or later, but time was of the essence. I figured Luke might have already destroyed important evidence at the office, but I know where he keeps his backup drives."

So that was the new evidence Cicilline had mentioned to me.

"But no more of this now," said Elizabeth. "Let's not allow evil to spoil this glorious moment."

Elizabeth and I stood in the chapel doorway and surveyed the crowd, which numbered more than ten thousand. The pope's motorcade was just five minutes from the mall, according to the live cast. His schedule called for him to enter on the north side; bless the people watching from all five stories; celebrate Mass in the chapel for the select 100 who'd been invited, with the crowds watching from the TV screens; then leave.

I was struck anew by how crazy this was: a pope in a mall during a pandemic surge.

The motorcade pulled into the parking lot. The crowd fell silent, all eyes on the screens.

I looked up at the glass roof and noticed it was buried in snow.

And then we heard it: the sounds of glass shattering and steel twisting. The roof was collapsing.

A beam above the chapel buckled, sending glass and snow onto five stories of people. The lights dimmed and alarms sounded. A second and third beam buckled. A fourth. Screaming people stampeded.

I stood with Elizabeth, our gaze frozen on the roof. I was certain the whole thing would collapse but it didn't. Beams dangled and a broken screen swayed but nothing else fell.

Elizabeth clasped her hands in prayer.

I smelled gas emanating from the food court.

A restaurant erupted in a fireball.

"Mother of God," Elizabeth prayed. "Hear us in our hour of need."

A man on fire ran toward us. I wrestled him to the floor, then smothered him in snow. He fell unconscious.

Someone found a fire extinguisher and raced toward the restaurant, spraying foam as he went. I heard a terrible whooshing, like a steam turbine at full throttle.

More gas.

But suddenly, the whooshing stopped. A worker had succeeded in closing an emergency valve—nearly at the cost of his life. He stumbled out of the restaurant and I saw his singed hair and the horror on his face, and then his eyes rolled shut and he crumpled in shock. Elizabeth knelt by him, gently squeezing his hand as she prayed. He was a kid, all of seventeen.

Someone had found a second extinguisher and was beating back the flames when firefighters rushed toward us. I was focused on the people lying in wreckage and snow. I didn't know CPR but I figured I could free someone so I ran to a woman who was dazed and mumbling.

"Help me!" I shouted at the people around me.

I saw that a chunk of glass had nearly severed the woman's arm. I saw bone and gushing blood and I knew we had only seconds before she lost too much to survive.

"Give me your scarf!" I yelled to a teenage girl.

I tightened it around the woman's arm and the bleeding shrank to a trickle; tighter still, and it stopped. I shouted for an EMT and stood back as he went to work.

For the first time, I got a good look at the woman's face.

It was Gina Pulaski.

Over the next thirty minutes, Elizabeth, I, and many others helped the best we could—comforting the wounded, clearing off snow, working with the EMTs and firefighters. The pope had never entered the mall—but he blessed those on stretchers as they were brought out for transfer to ambulances and helicopters. Then he returned to his limo and the motorcade started back to Boston. He was returning directly to Rome.

According to later counts, thirty-six people had been hurt, though none with lasting injuries.

No one had died.

It could have been much worse.

That it wasn't, many soon began to declare, constituted a miracle.

CHAPTER TWELVE: EXTRAORDINARY THINGS

The next day was Christmas Eve—a Friday that year. *The Trib* led with the mall disaster, but I detected Hill's hand in the absence of even a sentence suggesting substandard materials might have contributed to the roof's collapse.

Calling Brigham and Women's Hospital, I learned that Gina Pulaski had been upgraded from critical to serious condition. When I called the charge nurse at Children's, she told me Jimmy also had been upgraded, to good condition.

"It's extraordinary," she said. "The docs don't know what to make of it, but he could be in remission. I'm beginning to believe in the power of prayer."

I would visit Jimmy and Gina soon, but I had a more pressing issue. I was determined to get my final story into print—with a few last-minute additions now.

I drove past the paper and saw that the management lot was empty. There no longer was an employees' lot but Hill had given me a card key to the managers' lot and I parked my Audi in his space. I left the key in the ignition. I didn't intend to drive it ever again.

It was almost noon, and just one person was in the newsroom: weekend editor Dave Roderick, a man who'd started at *The Trib* as a reporter and turned to editing after years languishing in a bureau. Roderick's forte was survival, and since SGM's takeover, he'd shamelessly ass-kissed Hill.

I went to my computer and called up tomorrow's news budget. My column wasn't listed, of course—so I made it the lead page-one story. "122521 XMASNICK," I wrote on the budget spreadsheet. "On Christmas Day, we reflect on the true meaning of the season. NOLAN/100 inches/file art."

Roderick was watching and when I left my computer, he called up the budget.

After reading what I'd added, he said: "I thought you were fired."

So Hill had informed him. I wasn't surprised.

"Actually," I said, "I was—for, like, a few minutes. Then Bruce and I talked things over. The upshot was that if I wrote a great story, he'd give me a second chance. So, I wrote it."

"Has he read it?"

"You bet," I said. "He loved it."

"How come I don't find it in the system?" he said.

I took a flash drive out of my briefcase.

"Because I'm still tweaking it," I said. "You'll have it by six."

"Deadline's five on Christmas Eve for local copy. No exceptions, not even for your pearly words."

I went back to my desk and got down to it.

It was closing in on five o'clock when I finished. I crossed the street for my fifth cup of coffee—and found Jones in his office when I returned. I remembered that the jury had been expected to return a verdict in the libel suit today.

"May I come in?" I said.

"Please," said Jones. "Sit down."

"Did we get a verdict?"

"Yes. We lost."

I was stunned.

"We should have won," I said.

"And if we'd had an ace defense, we would have. I could tell you ten things we could have done better if we'd been willing to spend the money. For starters, we could have hired Elizabeth Ritvo."

"Will we appeal?"

"That's up to Chamberlain and Hill now. I'm not optimistic. What about you, Nick? I hear you've gotten into some trouble of your own lately."

"And I'm still not done," I said.

I handed Jones my flash drive.

"Read this," I said.

Jones was silent until he'd reached the end.

"Extraordinary," he said.

"You don't think it's corny?"

"No. It's honest and real and it comes from the heart," Jones said. "It's the best thing you're ever written."

"I don't know about that," I said.

"Well, it beats socks."

We laughed.

"Now we just have to get it into the paper," Jones said.

With Hill in Orlando, we figured we had a shot.

Except Hill wasn't in Orlando—the storm had delayed his departure, and he walked into the newsroom as Jones and I were discussing how to illustrate my story. Evidently, Roderick had called the publisher.

"Well if it isn't the gruesome twosome," said Hill. "A little birdie told me I'd find you here."

"Good afternoon, Bruce," said Jones.

"Why don't you two come to my office where we can have a nice private chat," Hill said.

The publisher looked pale when we reached his office. He was clutching his stomach—and his dog lay at his feet, apparently sensing something was wrong.

"I've just gotten off a conference call with Chamberlain, our lawyers, and our insurer," Hill said. "If we agree not to appeal and we run a full-page apology, the other side will settle for smaller damages than we believe the judge in this case will award."

"So, that's what you're doing," Jones said.

"It's called cutting your losses."

"How do you sleep at night?" Jones said.

"Like a baby. I think of stock options and year-end bonuses and Paula Orton and I drift off to Dreamland happy as a clam. I sleep even better when I get to can an asshole. You're fired, Jones. You have an hour to clear out your desk. After that, I call the cops."

Jones said nothing. I suspected he had another sort of response in mind.

Hill turned to me.

"How *do* you sleep at night, knowing Terry Winters' story might have prevented yesterday?" I said.

"That story was built entirely on anonymous sources, which Winters refused to reveal to me," Hill said. "I smelled a rat. Even if we had run it, let me tell you what the response would have been: a round of denials, and the show would have gone on. The issue here is whether Turner acted wrongly. My money says he did not."

"I quit, effective immediately," I said.

"How melodramatic," said the publisher. "Do you deliver a passionate speech on your newfound principles now—or did you exhaust yourself in your insipid story?"

"I should have quit a long time ago," I said.

"When, Nick—when you became a star on the six o'clock news? When you accepted an Audi and a raise and a personal trainer and a line of credit at Brooks Brothers? Was it when you signed those book and screen contracts? Or was it when you banged Jennifer Abbott? At least I was no two-faced weasel. From day one, what you saw was what you got."

I was formulating a response when Hill doubled over in pain.

"Do you want me to call 9-1-1?" Jones said.

"I want you to get out of here, both of you," Hill said. "Clock's running. Fifty-six minutes and you'll be leaving in handcuffs."

"So where does that leave us?" I said as Jones and I walked downstairs.

"Praying he's having a heart attack."

"Do you think he really is?"

"I honestly don't care. Let's go. I need a beer."

"How about Ernie's?"

"Perfect," said Jones. "I haven't been there in far too long."

The place was deserted—except for Destiny Carter, who was drinking alone at a corner of the bar. Destiny was widowed and had no children, which made holidays tough for her. This holiday, of course, would be tougher still.

But she brightened on seeing us.

Over draft ales, we filled each other in on recent events. Destiny had more news: Along with the layoffs, Hill had ordered an end to all editorials, op-ed pieces, and letters to the editor. I'd missed that in my emails, but Destiny called it up on her phone.

"Done with wasting space on things that get no clicks," Hill had written.

"And the staff that got them in the paper," Destiny said.

"Nothing we can do about that now," Jones said. "But there is something we can do about Nick's story. We can get it published. Along with mine, which I have yet to write."

It was a quarter past nine.

"Time to go," Jones said. "We're coming up on deadline."

Two police cruisers and an ambulance were parked in front of *The Trib* when Jones and I returned with Destiny. Hill was on a stretcher, an oxygen mask over his face.

"I'm the executive editor," said Jones. "What's going on?"

"We think it's acute appendicitis," said one of the EMTs.

"Our Christmas bonus just arrived," Jones said.

"Excuse me?" the EMT said.

"Inside joke," Jones said. "You know how journalists are."

"Snarky?" the EMT said.

"Yes," Destiny said, "snarky."

We went into the newsroom. The handful of people needed to put a holiday paper to bed were busy. Deadline was only twenty minutes away.

Jones ordered Roderick to call up the front page. Here, Hill had not been remiss: an AP puff piece on the crowd building for tomorrow's Christmas Event was leading the paper.

"Kill it," Jones said. "And bring the second-day mall story out front, above the fold. Nick, we're leading with your story."

"But Hill left strict instructions," Roderick said.

"Hill's not calling the shots anymore," said Jones.

Roderick reached for his cell phone.

"Policy's clear on this," he said. "I need to call Chamberlain."

"You call him," said Jones, "and I will lock my hands around your ass-kissing little neck and squeeze until the life goes out of you. And if I somehow fail, I have two friends here who will be happy to finish the job."

Roderick's hands began to tremble and his lip quivered.

"There will be hell to pay for this," he said.

Then he bolted from the newsroom.

"Good riddance," said Jones.

Jones sat at a computer and began to work the mouse. Destiny and I watched, surprised that he knew his way around a page-design program.

"You think I've been living in a cave?" he said. "Let's get going, the presses roll in ten minutes and we post online ten minutes after that. Do you have a headline for your column, Nick?"

"Nothing worth mentioning," I said.

"How about: AFTER FURTHER REFLECTION, A TIME TO RIGHT WRONGS," Destiny offered.

"Perfect," Jones said.

He typed the headline and flowed my story in beneath it.

"Now, my story," he said. "Ideas?"

"How about 'TRIB CAVES TO MOB MURDERER,' " I said.

"Another winner," Jones said. "The subhead?"

" 'Publisher and chairman agree to cowardly terms in libel suit,' " Destiny said.

"We're on a roll," Jones said.

"But where's the story?" I said.

"I have to write it," Hill said.

"In eight minutes?" Destiny said.

"I've been stewing for hours," Jones said. "It won't even take that long."

In barely five minutes, he wrote:

BOSTON—Citing mounting legal costs, *Boston Daily Tribune* publisher Bruce M. Hill has decided not to appeal yesterday's guilty verdict in the biggest libel suit ever brought against the paper. Hill did so with the explicit approval of David W. Chamberlain, chairman and chief executive officer of SuperGoodMedia, the *Tribune's* Florida-based parent company.

"It's called cutting your losses," the publisher said.

Hill said *The Tribune* has agreed to pay an unspecified sum in damages and to run a full-page apology to former state Supreme Court Chief Justice Donald Sabella. Sabella sued the newspaper five years ago in the wake of a column regarding the brutal slaying of Robert Jones Jr., son of *Tribune*

Executive Editor Robert Jones. The column followed *The Tribune's* Pulitzer Prizing winning investigation that revealed Sabella was in the pocket of Columbian drug lord El Chapo, an investigation that led to the judge's impeachment.

The seven-member jury delivered its verdict yesterday after more than four days of deliberations. Observers said *The Tribune's* defense was hurt by second-rate lawyers, hired to save on expenses—and that the newspaper would have stood "an excellent chance" of winning with a better legal team.

"Once again, Chamberlain and Hill put profit before principle," said Jones, who testified at the trial. "This is a sad day for *The Tribune* in particular and newspapers in general."

Lawyers for Sabella could not be reached for comment late last night.

But Jones said he is considering the highly unusual move of independently hiring Elizabeth Ritvo, one of America's leading First Amendment attorneys, to head an appeal.

"More than my own reputation is at stake," said Jones. "Justice must be served."

It was ten minutes to ten. The presses would soon roll.

"OK," said Jones, "I'm hitting the button. Let's go, guys."

"Where?"

"To the pressroom. It's been a long time since I was there. I've forgotten the smell of ink."

"What about Hill's dog?" I said. "We can't leave him."

"I'll take him," Destiny said.

We found press foreman Michael Adams standing by the master controls. One of his staff was loading the redone page-one plates. Like me, Adams went back a long way with the executive editor.

"I'm sorry about the verdict," said Adams. "What a kick in the teeth, especially on Christmas Eve. If it means anything, I was with you one hundred percent. That son of a bitch got your kid, no question. Not that it don't take balls to stand up to him like you did. I admire you, Bob. It couldn't have been easy testifying."

"You'd do the same thing in my shoes," Jones said.

"Well, looks like we're ready to roll," Adams said. "You staying for the run?"

"The first few hundred," Jones said. "You, too, Destiny and Nick?"

"Us too," Destiny said.

"I read your story, Nick," Adams said. "Hell of a piece of work. Said a lot of things I've been thinking since the sale. 'Course, your ass is toast the second I hit this button."

"Actually, my ass already is toast," I said. "So is Bob's. We got fired."

"My only regret is Hill will be in surgery when this posts and hits the streets," Jones said. "What I wouldn't give to see the look on his face."

"Press time, folks," Adams said. "Maybe you'd like to start 'er up, Bob."

Adams passed us ear protectors and safety glasses, then showed Jones the start button on the control panel. Jones hit it and the presses began to turn.

"Sitting in an office all day, you forget the power this thing has," Jones said. "I remember my first job—Christ, it's a half century ago. We were just out of the hot-type era. Maybe I'm old-fashioned, but there's something about this that a monitor can't equal. This is real, not pixels on a screen."

Adams snatched a few copies of the paper off a belt and gave them a quick once-over. Satisfied, he let Jones rev the press up to full speed.

Adams handed us copies.

His story was the lead story.

Mine was the off lead.

They were the only stories on the front page.

The same would be true in a few minutes on our home page.

No ads, no click bait, only truths.

My cell woke me on Christmas morning. It was eleven o'clock on a raw and foggy day. I'd slept almost twelve hours.

"Hello?" I said.

It was Courtney.

"I just wanted to wish you Merry Christmas," she said.

"Merry Christmas," I said.

"You probably didn't expect me to call."

"I have few expectations now."

"For what it's worth, I loved your story. I don't know how you got it in the paper, but congratulations."

"You don't think I sounded like *Chicken Soup for the Soul?*"

"Can I be honest—in a couple of places, yes. But you told the truth. The truth can be devastating. Are you going out there today?"

"I'm not sure," I said.

"You have to," Courtney said. "You can't just slip quietly into the night."

She was right. It's one thing to speak truth, another to be held accountable.

"Strange mood here today," Officer Maloney said as he escorted me through the crowd outside Jennifer's, which numbered more than twenty thousand, according to his estimate.

"In what way?" I said.

"I can't tell if they're happy or sad. Or angry. I saw a lot of people reading your story. I heard grumbling."

"What did you think?" I said.

"Pretty heavy stuff," the cop said, "but you told it from the heart. It's the kind of stuff you don't see much of anymore in a newspaper."

"You didn't think the end was silly."

"Sentimental, maybe," the policeman said, "but not silly. Silly doesn't make you stop and think like that."

The shades were drawn on Jennifer's house and there was no sign of activity save for officers on horses behind the police tape. The authorities had never called out the mounted patrol before.

"Have you seen her today?" I asked Maloney.

"Only for a second, when I came on duty. She poked her head out and said she might come out later, but don't plan on it. Then she told me not to let anyone in—not even you. Sorry, Nick. I don't think she liked your story."

We moved toward the altar, where Mass was underway.

I was strangely calm as I ascended the altar when the Mass ended.

Seeing me approach, the priest guided me to the lectern.

"I know many of you have already seen this or read it online," I said, unfolding today's paper, "but I wanted to read it to you myself. A personal connection. Then I'll be happy to take questions."

I cleared my throat and began:

"Last September, a month after *The Daily Tribune* had been sold to an out-of-state chain that cares only about money, I got a call from a woman I once knew. Jennifer Abbott had become a mother in the intervening years, and her only child, Amber, severely injured in a car crash, lay in a rare kind of coma. My first story about them concerned their struggle for dignity, but my second introduced the possibility that the Virgin Mary, whom Catholics recognize as the mother of God, was speaking through Amber. Soon, I was writing about the possibility of miracles.

"From then on, the story mushroomed. Thousands of the faithful journeyed to Middleton, along with journalists from near and far. Rather than tread cautiously, the media only plowed ahead. As the exclusive source of first-hand accounts, *The Daily Tribune* uniquely benefitted, and it used every tool imaginable to exploit its monopoly: among them, an extensive social-media campaign, polls, and advertisements everywhere.

"Wrong, all of it.

"But as a result, circulation rose to previously unimaginable levels, our clicks went stratospheric, advertisers flocked to us, and a publisher who came to journalism from marketing potato chips began to capitalize on our monopoly.

"Led by me and my newspaper, we in the media transformed a story of mystery into Fellini. Sensationalism prevailed when reflection was needed. And we exploited a most vulnerable person: a little girl in a coma.

"Meanwhile, in areas where we should have been aggressive, we sacrificed principle to the bottom line. At *The Tribune*, this ridiculous concept of 'good news rules' prevailed, sacrificing integrity in order to enhance shareholder value. This is what happens when you lose local ownership to out-of-town vultures: the pursuit of profit reigns supreme as the corporate ghouls strangle newspapering and truth disappears.

"Although you didn't read it on these pages, SuperGoodMedia, the Florida-based parent company of *The Trib*, invested heavily in the Minuteman Mall, a major new advertiser. Once upon a time, this was called a conflict of interest. In SGM's view, this is called good business practice.

"Something else you didn't read was a story by Pulitzer Prize-winning reporter Terry Winters exposing the use of defective beams in the building of the mall. No one will ever know if that story could have prevented this week's disaster, but we do know this: Bruce Hill, our publisher, killed it—the very week that he accepted an invitation to join Turner's board.

"There is more. Even now, Hill refuses to let his reporters look into whether Turner bribed a state inspector for an occupancy permit. In fact, I have learned from a high-ranking law-enforcement source, prosecutors will soon seek to indict Turner. Hill and SuperGoodMedia Chairman and CEO David Chamberlain have been subpoenaed to testify.

"So *The Trib* was wrong. *I* was wrong, and I apologize from the bottom of my heart. And while I am sharing my sentiments, let me extend sympathy to my many colleagues who were just laid off by this soulless parent company that cares about money and nothing else—not people's livelihoods, not truth, not local journalism, so vital to our democracy. With this latest round of firings, *The Trib* is officially a ghost paper. My fervent hope is that a non-profit foundation or group of philanthropists will buy it, not only saving jobs but rebuilding the paper into the force for good it once was. I will do all I can to help make that happen.

"But I don't regret everything about my coverage this year because I've learned—or re-learned—some important lessons. This fall, I met a twelve-year-old boy named Jimmy Pulaski. Jimmy suffers from cancer, but except for the fact that he's lost some weight and all of his hair, you would not know it. Jimmy has a great sense of humor and a keen mind. He wants to play football when he grows up, but he probably should be a philosopher.

"When I first met him, Jimmy asked me a question. He wanted to know if miracles really happen. I dodged Jimmy that time, but I've since had the chance to ponder it at length. Were he to ask again, this is what I would say:

" 'While journalists believe they usually have the answers and typically they do, sometimes they don't. I don't know what made Tony Callahan and the others better—whether mysterious but natural forces science someday will explain, or the hand of God or blessings from The Creator, as Native Americans might say. I leave these matters to every person and their conscience. They cannot be resolved on the front page.

"So I couldn't tell Jimmy if miracles happen. But I would say without hesitation that extraordinary things do.

"One night recently, Jimmy was back in Children's Hospital, and together we visited the lobby wishing pool. Jimmy threw a coin in, and while I promised not to reveal what he wished for, I can tell you it was something exciting taking place in the future. And *that* is an extraordinary thing—that a child so sick still believes in tomorrow.

"Without intending, Jimmy reminded me that extraordinary things surround us, should we look. A newborn baby is an extraordinary thing. The look on a child's face by a Christmas tree or a menorah candle or on Kwanzaa or the Festival of Breaking the Fast is an extraordinary thing. A sunset is a beautiful thing. A barefoot walk on a summer beach is a beautiful thing. Holding the hand of someone you love is a beautiful thing. The rush to help injured strangers during a crisis is an extraordinary thing. Truth is an extraordinary thing.

"So, too, I am happy to report, is Jimmy's unexpected improvement in the last few days. 'Extraordinary' is the word one of his nurses used to describe his turnaround.

"In closing, let me note that I have torn up my book and screen contracts, and when the banks reopen tomorrow, I will return my advance to SuperGoodMedia. This is my last story for *The Daily Tribune*. I don't know where my future lies, only that it's not on these pages. Merry Christmas, everyone."

I closed the newspaper and gazed out over the crowd.

"Any questions?" I said.

The journalists jumped.

"Will somebody else be writing the book now that you've backed out?" a reporter from *Inside Edition* shouted from the crowd.

"You'll have to ask SuperGoodMedia," I said.

"You mean SuchGodawfulMuck, don't you, Nick?" cracked the TMZ correspondent.

"Yes, I do," I said.

"What's Jennifer's take on your story?" another reporter said. "Has she issued a statement? Has anything happened inside? Is she coming out?"

"I haven't talked to her today," I said.

"Do you see the irony I do in your name?" the *People* reporter said. "Nicholas, patron saint of Christmas."

"Also patron saint of merchants, brewers, sailors, and archers, so no," I said.

"Since you have no new Mary News maybe we should call you Scrooge," joked a TikTok influencer.

"Good one," I said.

"Will Bradley Cooper still play you in the movie?" a reporter said.

"Look," I said, "the reason I came here today was to explain why I'm getting off this story. I thought I was clear I didn't come to discuss movie deals except to say I've torn up my contract. Does anybody besides the press have any questions?"

An old man in a wheelchair shot his hand in the air.

"You, sir," I said.

"Who won the sacred oil contest?" the old man said. "It was supposed to be in the paper today."

"There's supposed to be ten winners," a woman added. "But I didn't see anything about it, either."

"I don't know," I said. "I wasn't involved in the contest. Sorry and I wish you well. Anybody else?"

"Will there be a lottery today?" a middle-aged woman asked.

"I have no idea," I said. "Perhaps one of the nuns can fill us in."

No sister did.

"So, what time's The Christmas Event?" a woman on crutches said. "What's it going to be?"

It was almost noon now.

Before I could answer her, the fog lifted, the clouds parted, and the sun shone. Elizabeth Turner and many others claimed they looked to the sky and saw the Virgin Mary, her arms opened in embrace, the infant Jesus cradled in her lap.

Not me.

I felt the heat of the sun, and then the fog and clouds moved back in.

The winter COVID surge, fueled by the Delta and omicron variants, was finally starting to ease when, on March 19, 2022, recently hired ProPublica Senior Reporter Terry Winters succeeded in completing the full story of the malfeasance inside SuperGoodMedia, with stunning new developments that *The Washington Post* had been unable to get.

Among them was how Chamberlain had accepted The Alkil Global Capital Fund's secret offer to buy SGM. Chamberlain was able to conclude the sale, given that he was the majority stockholder and was eager to bend the rules.

Commit fraud, that is, with Garth Vader his willing accomplice. That lunch of lobster tails and steak in Orlando, as it turned out, had been the invitation to the dance.

Winters and ProPublica would be nominated for a Pulitzer, and with good reason: The very day it was published, federal agents led Chamberlain out of his office in handcuffs. He made bail and then disappeared into obscurity and a cocoon of lawyers. I hope one day to see him led off to prison. I'm confident I will not be the only one cheering.

Also damning in Winters' story were two sordid substories.

The worst involved Vader.

With help from his FBI sources, Winters had been able to confirm that Vader for months had been under investigation for having sex with under-age girls he lured into his Palm Beach mansion. That he'd been a friend of the late Jeffery Epstein, as Winters reported, came as little surprise.

The surprise was federal agents arresting him on the day—at the exact hour, 12:01 a.m.—that Winters' story was posted. The timing, of course, was not coincidental. My educated guess is that during the final reporting, Winter's FBI sources apprised him of the pending arrests and asked him to hold the story until Vader was led out of his mansion in handcuffs. How else to explain how ProPublica had a photographer outside at midnight?

Chamberlain had a sick secret life, too, that *The Post* had not mentioned, likely because they had not found the evidence to support it.

But Terry had.

He proved that Chamberlain for years had been frequenting The Complete Treat, a massage parlor on the outskirts of Lakeland, Florida, about halfway between Orlando and Tampa Bay. His preference was for whips and chains, which his preferred prostitute, Madame Potpourri—who also was The Complete Treat's owner—used in his monthly visits.

Madame Potpourri had repeatedly taped Chamberlain using a hidden camera, then used the videos to blackmail him for a quarter of a million dollars. For that sum, she had given the files to him, swearing they were the only copies. She lied. Terry somehow had gained access to them. So had others. The source was never publicly disclosed, but I had a good hunch.

The day after Terry's story ran, FBI agents raided The Complete Treat and arrested Madame Potpourri—real name, Mary Potter—on seventeen charges of human trafficking. Chamberlain was charged with solicitation.

Terry, of course, did not publish any of the images, and his writing about the former chairman's sex life was straight down the middle, as it should have been.

But the *New York Post* and TMZ had no compunctions about publishing images from the "secret" tapes and both did, with bars across Chamberlain's privates—but none across his face.

As might be expected, given such a gift, the Post copy editors outdid themselves with their headline. It read: Mary's Miracle Masochist.

The cumulative coverage proved devastating for Super Good Media, which was placed in receivership until the criminal wrongdoings could be sorted out.

Like Chamberlain, Hill also went down with the ship, but he is unlikely to face charges as he was a loyal bootlicker and nothing more. Last I heard, he was running an IHOP franchise. I wonder if he has Olestra pancakes on the menu. I do know that he had to sell his Denton's Wharf condo, that Destiny gave Paula Orton his dog and Orton dumped him, and that the Down Town Club revoked his membership and banned him for life.

As for the rest of the SGM executives, I can report that CFO Peters, CMO Hawkins, CDO Winthrop, and SOS D'Ermo finally proved to have value. In plea bargains with federal prosecutors, all escaped prison sentences for being accessories to fraud in return for testifying against their former boss. They have no future in journalism, but I hear Disney World is auditioning for people to play characters. I think D'Ermo would be a lock for Goofy.

Like other SGM properties, during the receivership *The Trib* was reduced to publishing a print edition only three days a week. The online version was updated daily, but there was little of interest on the site. As spring wore on, I was told by friends—who were all working part-time, without benefits—that the newsroom most days was empty, with journalism, such as it was, conducted mostly by Zoom. It seems unlikely that there will be a physical location for *The Trib* for much longer, if the paper even survives, for the court-appointed receiver has put the building on the market, the proceeds from a sale to be used to pay off debt.

Not long after Terry's story was published, my phone rang. I don't answer numbers I don't recognize and so I let it go to voicemail.

It was Natalia Perez, calling from Florida.

"Give me a buzz when you have a moment," she said.

I called immediately.

She told me she was working at Publix now—she'd swallowed her pride and gone to her sister, who'd helped her get a high-paying position with great potential for advancement. I filled her in on me and *The Trib*. She knew, of course, about SGM imploding. She'd quit just days before the hammer came down.

Now, I got it.

"You were Terry Winters' source," I said.

"I was no such thing," she said.

"You had access to the files and images he needed and you shared them."

"Nick, you are barking up the wrong tree," Perez said. "If there was a source inside SGM, I have no clue who it might have been. But it wasn't me."

She paused and then said, with a chuckle: "I wish you could see the look on my face right now."

I pondered that for a moment.

"Well, it sure does seem like a coincidence," I said.

"Or perhaps another instance of how the Lord works in strange and mysterious ways," Perez said.

EPILOGUE: WHAT MATTERS

In September 2022, I sold "Enemy of the Paper: When the Hedge Fund Comes to Town. What Franklin Would Say" to a major publisher. Netflix bought the screen rights. I spent much of the rest of 2022 editing the book and working on the screenplay.

But writing, per se, is no longer my ambition.

Helping to save local journalism is.

With my advance money and contributions from generous donors who share my views, I incorporated The Franklin Project, a non-profit organization that will work to rebuild local journalism by supporting—financially and editorially—independent dailies and weeklies across America. We have formed a board, hired a staff, and opened an office in Washington, where I live now.

The Franklin Project will also help nurture the next generation of reporters: high-school and college students and other young people with passion for journalism. We will do this in partnership with ProPublica, Report for America, The Lenfest Institute, and the Institute for Nonprofit News, organizations devoted to real journalism with real impact on real lives.

Beyond this, we have two lofty ambitions.

One is buying papers that have been lost to the chains and finding local owners. Already, negotiations are underway with an individual I am not yet at liberty to name to buy and rebuild *The Boston Daily Tribune*. The second is re-establishing papers in news deserts, working with foundations and donors to provide capital and recruiting journalist-entrepreneurs who live in those communities or are willing to put down new roots.

Pie in the sky?

I don't think so. Pulitzer Prize winner Art Cullen, editor and co-owner with family members of Iowa's *The Storm Lake Times*, is among those who are showing the way. And he is sharing the secrets of his success—and offering internships at his paper—in service to the cause.

"The foundation of a functioning democracy is an informed electorate," Cullen said during a 2022 broadcast of "Story in the Public Square," the national public-television and SiriusXM show. "If you don't know what your tax rates are, how can you vote on 'em? If you don't know what that city council member stands for, how can you cast an intelligent vote, and have a functioning democracy? And without a newspaper or a legitimate credible news source that provides a common set of facts, the fabric of the community deteriorates, as those studies indicate, and as we all know.

"There is a direct relationship between the decline of newspaper readership that's been occurring my entire career, since say 1980, and it's been a steady decline, and there's also been a steady erosion of civic engagement. And it kind of culminated, and I'm not exaggerating, it culminated in that January 6th attack on the US capital, which had stage rehearsals both in Minnesota and Michigan, both places where these news deserts are spreading, and where civic ignorance is rampant. And because they're getting their information from some guy sitting in his underwear in Macedonia posting Facebook messages full of lies that are intended to destroy our democracy. And you know what, journalists are the final wall that protects liberty. And who do they go after first in Pakistan? The journalists. Who did Trump go after first? The journalists; called us enemies of the people."

You may be wondering about Jimmy and Gina Pulaski. Neither was sufficiently healthy to make that trip to Disney World—not that January. But both improved rapidly as spring 2022 approached and that May, they took the trip. Gina had recovered completely from her mall injuries, and Jimmy was declared in remission. He entered middle school that fall and made the football team as backup quarterback. I attended one of his games, and during his minutes on the field, he threw a touchdown pass.

I was on my feet along with the rest of the crowd.

You may also be wondering about A.J. In late December 2022, she sent me an email.

"With the one-year anniversary on my mind," she wrote, "I've been thinking about you and I hope you are doing well. Congratulations, too, on the Franklin Project—it's gotten a lot of good press in the right places, *The Trib* not being one of them, lol. Actually, not lol. I feel sorry for the few people that are left.

"More than thinking about you, I want to thank you. Words cannot express my gratitude for you giving me Jennifer's cell phone number. She never returned my calls, but in a final act of desperation, I texted her—and she returned it, with seven words: 'Let me and Amber pray on it.'

"Pray they must have, because my health has been steadily improving since January, to the point where my doctor now can find no sign of chronic fatigue syndrome. I feel really alive for the first time since I can remember! So thanks again, Nick. Just thanks.

"With all best wishes, A.J."

As for the Turners, Elizabeth pushed her lawyers to quickly finalize her divorce from Luke and, done with publicity, she moved from Boston to an undisclosed location. She continues to donate generously to many causes, religious and secular.

Luke Turner's case goes to trial soon, Meanwhile, the Minuteman Mall sits empty, its fate uncertain. Estimates of the cost to rebuild it with proper steel greatly exceed the cost of razing it, so it is likely that when the litigation surrounding it is settled, it will be torn down, the ground on which it stood a monument to deception and greed.

And perhaps you have wondered about Jones, Destiny, Bud, and Rose Redwing Brown, four of the best people I've been privileged to count as friends.

With his Social Security and his pension, which SGM had not been able to pillage since it was protected by law, Jones was able to buy a small condo on the Cape. We email now and again and he informs me that the sunrises and sunsets in Wellfleet are spectacular. He started writing poetry and says if it ever gets published, fine, and if not, fine, too. His surviving children and grandchildren bring him joy, he tells me, and he is grateful to have made it through the pandemic. One of these days we might meet at Ernie's for a draft or two.

Destiny brought her recording of the diversity meeting to the Massachusetts Commission Against Discrimination, which immediately began an investigation of Hill. Depending on its outcome, he may not be able to continue in his new career at IHOP. My advice to him? Practice saying "fries with that?"

Destiny had long admired Cory Booker, whom she had interviewed several times while on the staff of the *Newark Star-Ledger,* and apparently the feeling was mutual—when she applied for a position in his office, the senator hired her to fill a newly created position: Chief of Staff for Equity and Justice. We've already scheduled her to be a regular speaker to members of the Franklin Project.

Bud Fuller?

I tried to entice him to join the project, but the best I could do was get him to agree to be a regular speaker, like Destiny.

By Zoom, that will be.

Before moving back to his hometown, Deer Isle, Maine, Bud filed his age-discrimination lawsuit against SGM, which had hired a young person to fill the trend-setting job he'd applied for. He did not want damages, only cause SGM more hurt. Which the suit did, shining a light on ageism. That's one of the issues he will be addressing when speaking to Project members.

Journalism past, present and future will be among his topics, too. Back on Deer Isle, Bud accepted a position writing for the *Penobscot Bay Press*, which has its office on Main Street in Stonington. It pays "peanuts," as Bud phrased it, and the hours are long but it's good, solid local journalism and Bud is in his element. Ever a frugal man, he saved enough during his years at *The Tribune* to support himself, even without Social Security. In our last conversation, he told me he had started dating a woman, now widowed, from his high school class.

"I've fallen for her," he said during our last conversation.

In all the years I've known him, this was the first time I'd ever heard him talk like that.

"Wedding bells in your future?" I said.

Bud had never married.

"Yes," Bud replied. "No date yet but you'll be invited."

"I'll propose a toast," I said.

And Rose Redwing Brown?

With the support of Bill Gates, she folded her climate-change foundation into the Bloomberg Philanthropies larger efforts. There, she manages global recruitment from the grassroots to the corporate-donor level but her greatest contribution may be as a motivational speaker for the cause. Her latest TED Talk, "Mother Earth cries: We listen, then act," has been viewed more than twenty-five million times.

"Now who's the star?" I teased her recently.

"Too big, I guess, to teach that Franklin Project class you want me to," she retorted.

"No," I said, "not too big at all. The kids will love you."

In late June 2023, I returned to Boston to interview the latest round of applicants for The Franklin Project and visit old friends. On my way back to Washington, I stopped in Philadelphia for a meeting at The Lenfest Institute.

It was July 3, 2023.

After my meeting, I walked to Independence Hall, but a sign on the door indicated it was closed for the afternoon. With time to kill before the next Acela to Washington, I stopped by the Red Owl Tavern. I wanted to see it in real-life, not just a dream.

I was sitting at the bar when a man with an uncanny resemblance to old Ben sat next to me and ordered a Coke.

"Am I dreaming or are you Benjamin Franklin?" I said.

"No, you're not dreaming and no, I'm not Ben," the man said, "but I *do* play him every Fourth of July during the annual performance of the

Founders Thespians, of which I am a charter member."

"Sounds entertaining," I said.

"And informative," the man said. "You should come. Our play is a reenactment of the signing of the Declaration of Independence. Right over there, in Independence Hall. Tomorrow at noon. With luck, there are still tickets available. All proceeds benefit our little club."

"I'm afraid I won't be here," I said. "I'm just passing through."

"Well, pleased to meet you. And you are?"

"Nick Nolan," I said. "I'm a journalist."

"And I am Brian Flaherty, retired postmaster of Phoenixville, Pennsylvania. Also, a big history buff, in case you hadn't surmised."

Flaherty looked at his watch.

"Goodness, I'm late for rehearsal," he said. "Perhaps our paths will cross again another time. Have a good day, sir."

"And you as well."

I write this final passage on an autumn day in 2023 from my apartment in Georgetown. It's a modest place but it does just fine, and I certainly can afford it: In the first week of publication, "Enemy of the Paper: When the Hedge Fund Comes to Town. What Franklin Would Say" landed at number eight on *The New York Times* bestseller list. Matt Damon has just signed on to play me in the Netflix movie. My royalties will continue to accrue, allowing the Franklin Project to flourish.

I never expected to hear from Jennifer again, and as time passed, I thought of her less often, though whenever I did, I always felt empathy for her daughter and a sense that we should have spoken last words. Closure, you might call it.

But I did hear from her again, in an email she sent in early September 2023.

"Dear Nick," she wrote, "I hope this finds you safe and healthy. First, congratulations on the book! It should be required reading for every student, teacher, and politician, not to mention ordinary citizens like me.

"Second, I wanted to inform you that my precious Amber died three months ago. We had moved from Middleton a week after that Christmas into an apartment whose address I shared only with her doctors. Cardinal Cruz celebrated her funeral Mass, attended only by me, per my wishes. There was no obituary and she was cremated. At some appropriate date, I will give her one last ride on the Santa Monica Pier Ferris wheel, which she so loved, and then I will scatter her ashes in the Pacific.

"Between the tears since Amber's passing, I have pondered what to do with what's left of my life. I don't know what I can offer except conviction and dedication, but perhaps The Franklin Project could use a volunteer.

"Please don't answer or even reply to this email as an element of suspense is something I appreciate, as you know better than anyone! I will be at Washington Monument Plaza at 4 p.m. on October 5. If you come, there is more I have to say, but it must be said in person. And if you do not show up, I will understand and you will never hear from me again."

October 5 is my birthday. I would turn 50 on that day.

I debated whether to show up, but in the end, I did.

Jennifer was waiting on a bench.

"Happy birthday," she said.

"You remembered."

"Some dates you never forget."

"I'm so sorry about Amber," I said. "What happened?"

"Pneumonia followed by sepsis. Prayers and the staff of Boston Children's couldn't save her. She's with the angels now."

We hugged, wordlessly.

"I owe you an apology," Jennifer said. "Several, actually. First, for lying about the accident that put my baby in that coma. Second, for saying Father Silva died. He didn't, and he wasn't driving. I was. The shock of what I had done overwhelmed me and for years I lived with guilt and PTSD."

"Understandably," I said.

"A third lie pertained to miracles," Jennifer said.

"You don't believe there were any."

"Not exactly. I believed that Mary, real or imagined, wanted to help people, but whether Jimmy Pulaski and Greta Ricci and Tony Callahan and Henry Spinelli were restored to health by divine means or medicine or something else is for someone wiser than me to decide. Same goes for the weeping Madonna. I don't know where that liquid came from, I only know I did not rig it. Ditto the Mega Millions ticket. I heard that winning number, or imagined I did. It happened to be the day, month, and year I was born, plus the number of my landline when I was a kid."

"In other words, a number you might have played anyway."

"Yes."

"What about A.J. Johnson? I probably shouldn't have, but I gave her your cell phone number. And now she is healthy. Coincidence?"

"Maybe not," Jennifer said.

"So none of this was really lying," I said.

"Not in the strict sense of the word, perhaps. But putting aside A.J., I *did* portray all the others' outcomes as miraculous."

"I did my share of the portraying, too," I said.

"True," Jennifer said. "But you redeemed yourself, as it were, with your Christmas story."

"You read it."

"Repeatedly. Before and after Amber passed. It helped, Nick, not only in reaching a place of truth but in my grieving. So, thank you."

"I had imagined you'd be angry," I said.

"I was at first, but with time I found the wisdom of your words. And now for the end of my confession. Now for the last two lies. When I told of Mary speaking through Amber, the truth is I heard words but was never certain if they had been spoken or were only in my head. I chose to believe they were spoken. But my mental health was suffering."

"Continuing trauma," I said.

"Yes, and the pandemic compounded everything. The stress and fatigue we have all experienced may have caused me to hear things—auditory hallucinations, as my therapist suspects. Whatever, the last lie was about my prayer. The miracle I prayed for was not for others but for my daughter to be released from her coma."

"No one could fault you for that."

"No, and those prayers were answered. She was released, the day they pronounced her dead at Boston Children's Hospital."

We were silent for a while after that, two people on a bench enjoying a warm, sunny afternoon.

"You didn't say anything about me seeing a therapist," Jennifer said after a bit.

"It's helped?" I said.

"A lot. And early on in our sessions, she suggested I also see a psychiatrist, which I did. During one of my early visits, he made what in retrospect was not a surprising diagnosis."

"Your PTSD was intensifying," I said.

"Yes. I also have bipolar disorder. Bipolar II, a less severe form."

Memory brought me back to when we dated, and to many occasions at her house in Middleton. Hyper speed followed by darkness.

"Are you on medication?" I said.

"Yes," Jennifer said. "And happy to report that it works fine and I have no side effects."

"That's great news," I said.

"One more thing," Jennifer said. "Perhaps you are wondering about my faith today. I know from your last story about yours."

"Well, I am curious," I said.

"I have been thinking recently of a passage from Paul's Epistle to the Romans: 'For all have sinned and fall short of the glory of God.' "

"We are all sinners, aren't we," I said.

"Yes. But Romans also offers the chance for redemption," Jennifer said. "I focus on that. Does that mean I have faith? I can't say. I know I am not the Catholic I was before, but also that I'm not drawn to any other religion. Nor would I call myself an atheist. My spirituality these days comes in part from meditation, which I began on the advice of my therapist. It comes, too, from an appreciation for beautiful days. Just like Frank Beazley in your book."

"You read it, too."

"Yes."

"Would you call this a beautiful day?"

"I would," Jennifer said. "And not just the weather."

"I totally agree."

"Frank believed in helping others. You with The Franklin Project are doing that. And with what time's left to me, I hope to do the same."

"How?"

"By volunteering at soup kitchens and homeless shelters in the D.C. metro area."

"You live here now?" I said.

"I do, sharing an apartment with two old Georgetown classmates who also have dealt with mental-health challenges. We've become our own little support group."

"That's wonderful," I said.

"You know what else would be wonderful? If you could help me in writing a memoir. Not because I want more attention or a bestseller or anything ridiculous like that. I owe a lot of people explanations and a book would be a good way to offer them. If others find even a grain of wisdom in what I write, that would be a welcome bonus."

"I'd be happy to help," I said.

"One more thing," Jennifer said. "As I mentioned in my email, I'd love to volunteer for the Franklin Project. I think I might have something of value to share. About mental health, for starters."

"I'm pretty sure we can work something out," I said.

"Pretty sure?"

"One-hundred-percent sure," I said.

"There's still a lot left in my GoFundMe account," Jennifer said. "I believe the rules would allow me to contribute the balance to The Project, since it's non-profit."

"That sounds great," I said. "You know what else sounds great?"

"What?"

"If I went with you to Santa Monica at the appropriate time."

"I'm pretty sure you can," Jennifer said.

"Pretty sure?"

"One-hundred-percent sure."

The shadows were lengthening when we noticed an older man watching us from a distance. He had a book in his lap.

"He looks like Benjamin Franklin, minus the long hair and glasses," I said.

"He does, doesn't he."

"Get this: I've had dreams about Franklin. How weird is that?"

"Very. But tell me about weird dreams. Sometimes I think the last ten years of my life have been one long weird dream."

The man stood and walked toward us.

"I've never done anything like this before, so please pardon me," he said, "but are you Nick Nolan?"

"I am," I said.

He held out the hardcover book he was reading.

It was "Enemy of the Paper: When the Hedge Fund Comes to Town. What Franklin Would Say."

"It's brilliant," the man said. "Relevant. I hope it brings change. Could I please have your autograph?"

He handed me a pen.

"I'd be delighted," I said. "Make it out to whom?"

"Ted Sorenson," the man said. "Retired restaurant owner. But you don't need to write that. 'To Ted, best wishes, will do just fine."

I signed his book and handed it back.

"Has anyone ever told you that you look like the real Ben Franklin?" I asked.

"Frequently," Sorenson said. "And it can get annoying, believe me. But I'm not alone in this. Let me show you something."

He took a photograph from his wallet.

"Know who that is?" he said.

"Of course," Jennifer said. "Helen Mirren."

"Looks exactly like her, right? Actually, it's my wife, Diane Louise Sorenson. You can only imagine the number of times *she's* asked for her autograph. Which she gives, using her real name and making a crack about the only difference between her and Helen is that she's *not* a British Dame. Always gets a laugh."

The man chuckled.

"We do have our fun," he said. "Well, I have taken enough of your time. Thank you so much, Mr. Nolan. I will treasure this always. And I hope you write a sequel. Your project should give you the material. Now, I bid adieu to you and your rum mort."

"His what?" Jennifer said.

"You, his great lady friend," Sorenson said. "It's from a line in his book!"

"I remember now," Jennifer said.

"Now have a fine rest of your day, both of you," the man said as he walked away.

"I know a nice restaurant nearby; can I buy you a glass of wine?" I said.

"Merlot?" Jennifer said.

"What else?"

"Of course!"

"Let's go!"

Jennifer grinned.

"Do you realize what that exchange could be?" she said.

"No idea," I said.

"A possible ending for your next book, if you're writing one."

"The thought has crossed my mind. 'Fit to Print,' I'd title it. About The Project and how it could serve as a model for others who want to do their part in saving journalism."

"There's no question you have to write it," Jennifer said. "But you should seriously *not* include our exchange just now. Consider what Franklin would say if you did."

"Let me guess: Cheesy. Or the 18th-century equivalent."

"Exactly," Jennifer said. "Today, we'd call it a Hallmark ending."

"Ouch," I said. "But true. Let's try another. How about 'What isn't weird is wine. I know a nice restaurant nearby; can I buy us a bottle?' "

"Better, but still needs work," Jennifer said.

"Then let's work on it over wine."

"How would Franklin phrase that?"

"No idea," I said. "And if you'll forgive the pun, frankly, who cares?"

"Your readers will," Jennifer said.

"Good point. But let's forget books for now. We have more important business."

Jennifer took my hand and we walked away.

THE END

BEFORE THE CLICKS

There was James Gordon Bennett Sr., founder (in 1835), editor and publisher of the *New York Herald*, at one time the most profitable and widely circulated newspaper in America.

"The American reader consumes most avidly that which he detests most blatantly," Bennett is reputed to have said, according to Alfred McKlung Lee's 1937 book *The Daily Newspaper in America*.

There was New York's *Hawk and Buzzard*, a newspaper first published in 1826, which carried this motto on its front page: "Our gossip birds shall keep a bright look out and show the world what folly is about."

And there was *The New York Times*, about which Columbia Journalism Review in June 2020 wrote:

"In October 1896, a few weeks after Adolph S. Ochs had taken ownership of the 'quality' paper that had fallen on hard times, he rented the billboard space on a windowless brick wall of the Cumberland Hotel, later razed to make way for the Flatiron Building. It was New York City's first electric sign, with nearly 2,700 individual lights of white, red, green, and blue that could be arranged into block letters to spell out words.
NEW-YORK TIMES
ALL THE NEWS
THAT'S FIT TO PRINT
SUNDAY
MAGAZINE
SUPPLEMENT
HAVE YOU SEEN IT?

"For newspaper readers of the time, the meaning was clear: Ochs was taking direct aim at the two papers then dominating the New York market—Joseph Pulitzer's *New York World* and William Randolph Hearst's *New York Journal*—and their brightly colored and richly illustrated front pages, loud headlines, and heavy coverage of lurid crime, political scandals, and tear-jerking human-interest stories. The style was called 'yellow journalism.' Today it'd be called 'clickbait' or 'fake news.' "

AFTER THE CLICKS
Have the hedge funds and chains killed local journalism?
Not all of it.

And the epilogue of *Unfit to Print* is my argument that what's left can be maintained and enhanced, and that at least some of the news deserts and ghost papers can be brought back to life—and that new generations of journalists can be enlisted in the cause.

Many foundations, programs and benefactors already are engaged in the work. The Ground Truth Project, led by founder, CEO, and editor Charles M. Sennott, and its Report for America, are helping to lead the way. The Knight Foundation is working hard. Others who have joined the cause include American Journalism Project, The Lenfest Institute, the Institute for Nonprofit News and ProPublica.

Great inspiration can be found in Pulitzer Prize-winner Art Cullen and his family, who own, write, edit, and publish *The Storm Lake News*.

In Rhode Island, *Ocean State Stories*, *OceanStateStories.org*, which I co-founded and now direct, publishes long-form journalism about issues that often are neglected or under-reported—stories that explore healthcare, education, public policy, socioeconomic and racial disparities and injustices, domestic violence, food and housing insecurities, ageism, suicide prevention, mental health, veterans' affairs, and developmental and intellectual disabilities, among others. These stories are told with data, expert input, and most importantly, the personal experiences of Rhode Islanders.

LEARN MORE ABOUT THE DANGERS
OF LOCAL JOURNALISM'S DEMISE
The American Journalism Project has excellent background, a path forward and ways individuals, foundations, and programs can help: *https:// www.theajp.org/why-local-news/*

Penny Abernathy, retired Knight Chair in Journalism and Digital Media Economics at the Hussman School of Journalism and Media at the University of North Carolina at Chapel Hill, has studied news deserts exhaustively. Her work can be found at https://www.usnewsdeserts.com/

Abernathy also discussed news deserts and what democracy loses in an appearance on Story in the Public Square: https://www.youtube.com/watch?v=wviO5QPVnno

The Hussman School has carried on Abernathy's work since her retirement. Its latest report, "News Deserts and Ghost Newspapers: Will Local News Survive?", published in 2020, is available at *https://www.usnewsdeserts.com/wp-content/uploads/2020/06/2020_News_Deserts_and_Ghost_Newspapers.pdf*

The Poynter Institute has an informative report by Michael Bugeja, Distinguished Professor of Liberal Arts and Sciences at Iowa State University Greenlee School of Journalism and Communication:

https://www.poynter.org/educators-students/2022/how-we-got-from-there-to-here-and-what-comes-hereafter/

A NOTE ABOUT THE 18TH-CENTURY SLANG

Sprinkled throughout this book are many words and phrases from Benjamin Franklin's time. I went down the rabbit hole on this, spending hours researching them and finding many sources. None was as useful as "A Classical Dictionary of the Vulgar Tongue," published in London in 1785, and available on Google books at https://bit.ly/2VMFIxN

ACKNOWLEDGMENTS

Over the course of my career, I've had the honor of working with a succession of wonderful reporters, many of whom became friends. I've also had the honor of working for many fine editors. As the saying goes, I have been lucky and blessed. I'd like to think that I have paid back this privilege with my commitment to public-service journalism, notably my coverage of mental health and intellectual and developmental disabilities, which I began in 1983. More on that at *https://gwaynemiller.blogspot. com/2016/04/*

I extend gratitude to the many reporters who worked at *The Providence Journal* and moved on. They include A.G. Sulzberger, now publisher of *The New York Times*; Dan Barry, Sheryl Stolberg, Farnaz Fassihi, Helene Cooper, Michael Corkery and C.J. Chivers, staff writers at the *Times*; Mark Johnson, Kevin Sullivan and Paul Duggan, now at *The Washington Post*; Jonathan Karp, who was a staff writer briefly at the Projo right out of Brown University and is now the CEO and chairman of Simon & Schuster; Jennifer Levitz, with *The Wall Street Journal*, and her husband, Mark Arsenault, with *The Boston Globe*; and Mike Stanton, a professor at the University of Connecticut. More are listed in the section four paragraphs down.

My gratitude also to former Journal executive editors the late Chuck Hauser, the late Jim Wyman, Joel Rawson, Tom Heslin, Karen Bordeleau, Alan Rosenberg and David Ng. I had the honor of writing Jim Wyman's obituary, and Viola, his widow, placed the print version in his casket to be buried with him. Newsman that he was, Jim would have appreciated that.

Thanks to editors who held other positions at *The Journal, The Cape Cod Times* and the *North Adams Transcript* who supported me and helped me improve my journalism: Carol Young, Rod Doherty, the late Bill Breisky, Jim Concannon, the late Al Johnson, the late Larry Howard, Len Levin, Jim Rosenthal, Jim Sunshine, Pamela Reinsel Cotter, Dave Reid, the late Andy Burkhardt, Pam Thomas, Mark Silverman, Elliot Krieger, Tim Murphy, Dave Bloss, Phil Kukielski, Kathy Hill, John Granatino, the late

Don Smith, Sue Areson, Lisa Newby, Peter Donahue, Dave Weyermann, Kurt Mayer, Bill Corey, Mark Divver, Whitman Littlefield, John Kostrzewa, Mike McDermott, Eryn Dion and Michael Delaney.

The list of book editors who have been essential to my life as a writer is shorter but equally important: the late Alan Williams, who was one of Stephen King's early editors and who bought my first book, "Thunder Rise;" Jonathan Karp, who edited five of my books, including "The Work of Human Hands," my first non-fiction book and the first book Jon ever bought; Paul Golob; Lisa Kaufman; Phyllis D. Deutsch; Dawn and Stephen Porter; and David Dodd, Patricia Lee Macomber and David Wilson, of Crossroad Press.

Together with the former *Journal* reporters named above—and at the risk of leaving someone out (as I surely have, my apologies)—I express gratitude to the many fellow writers who have commiserated, critiqued, encouraged, and done all of the other things involved in a collegial writerly relationship, in no particular order: Peter Gosselin, Jay Bookman, Dean Starkman, Donna Hartman, the late Jack White, Randy Richard, Jack Perry, Tony Lioce, the late Carol McCabe, Ariel Sabar, M. Charles Bakst, Bobby McGarry, the late Bill Reynolds, Bob Wyss, Kevin McNamara, Irene Wielawski, Christopher Rowland, Elliot Jaspin, Alisha Pina, Andrea Panciera, Ira Chinoy, the late Pete Lord, Alex Kuffner, Ed Fitzpatrick, Wayne Worcester, Gina Macris, Tracy Breton, Kathy Gregg, Lynn Arditi, Amanda Milkovits, Patrick Anderson, Rich Salit, Brian Jones, Amy Russo, Bob Kerr, Gail Ciampa, Antonia Noori Farzan, Mark Patinkin, Tom Mulligan, Kate Bramson, Bruce DeSilva, Andrea Stape-Schussler, Jody McPhillips, Steve Eisenstadt, Berkley Hudson, Gerry Goldstein, Jan Brogan, Elizabeth Rau, David Polochanin, Chip Scanlan, Katie Landeck, Bruce Butterfield, Katie Mulvaney, Paul Davis, Tatiana Pina, Rob Levin, Lisa Vernon Sparks, Laura Meade Kirk, Brandie Jefferson, Randi Parent, Carol Kozma, Jackie Tempera, Linda Borg, Karen Lee Ziner, Froma Harrop, Wheeler Cowperthwaite, the late Greg Katz, Kein Andrade, Brian Amaral, Drake Witham, Jennifer Jordan, Jonathan Rockoff, Scott Mayerowitz, and Sumathi Reddy. Special thanks to my longtime dear friend and colleague, Tom Mooney, whose insights I value greatly.

At the Pell Center, home of *Ocean State Stories*, I am lucky to work with Jim Ludes, Teresa Haas, Erin Barry, Katie Langford, Kate Lentz, and to enjoy the support of Salve Regina University Chancellor Sister M. Therese Antone and president Kelli J. Armstrong. Thank you, all.

Gratitude, too, to my children, Rachel, Kate, and Cal, who when they were growing up woke many mornings to find their father banging away on a keyboard. And let's give a shoutout to my grandchildren: the creative spirits Isabella and Olivia Bernier and Vivienne Chu.

Lastly, a huge debt of gratitude to my wonderful wife, Yolanda Gabrielle. Thanks, Hon, for everything!

MEET THE AUTHOR

This is G. Wayne Miller's 21st book. He is also a journalist, a filmmaker, and director of Ocean State Stories, *OceanStateStories.org*, a new non-profit, non-partisan news publication based at Salve Regina University's Pell Center for International Relations and Public Policy that is devoted to the kind of in-depth coverage of important issues that is increasingly threatened as the hedge funds and chains continue to gut and close newspapers.

Miller is cofounder and director of the Story in the Public Square program, also based at the Pell Center. He co-hosts and co-produces the national Telly-winning public-television and SiriusXM Radio show "Story in the Public Square."

A full-time journalist since 1978, Miller has been honored for his work more than 50 times and was a member of the Providence Journal team that was a finalist for the 2004 Pulitzer Prize in Public Service. Three documentaries he wrote and co-produced have been broadcast on PBS, including "Coming Home," about veterans of the wars in Iraq and Afghanistan, nominated in 2012 for a New England Emmy and winner of a regional Edward R. Murrow Award.

Visit Miller at www.gwaynemiller.com

ALSO BY G. WAYNE MILLER

BOOKS

Non-fiction

The Work of Human Hands: Hardy Hendren and Surgical Wonder at Children's Hospital, 1993.

Coming of Age: The True Adventures of Two American Teens, 1995.

Toy Wars: The Epic Struggle Between G.I. Joe, Barbie and the Companies That Make Them, 1998.

King of Hearts: The True Story of the Maverick Who Pioneered Open Heart Surgery, 2000.

Men and Speed: A Wild Ride Through NASCAR's Breakout Season, 2002.

The Xeno Chronicles: Two Years on the Frontier of Medicine Inside Harvard's Transplant Research Lab, 2005.

An Uncommon Man: The Life and Times of Senator Claiborne Pell, 2011.

Top Brain, Bottom Brain: Harnessing the Power of the Four Cognitive Modes (with neuroscientist Stephen M. Kosslyn, PhD), 2013.

Car Crazy: The Battle for Supremacy Between Ford and Olds and the Dawn of the Automobile Age, 2015.

Kid Number One: A Story of Heart, Soul and Business, Featuring Alan Hassenfeld and Hasbro, 2019.

The Growing Season: Frank Beazley and the Meaning of a Life, 2020.

Fiction

Thunder Rise, Book One in the Thunder Rise Trilogy, 1989.
Since the Sky Blew Off: The Essential G. Wayne Miller Fiction, Vol. 1, 2012.
Asylum, Book Two in the Thunder Rise Trilogy, 2013.
Summer Place, Book Three in the Thunder Rise Trilogy, 2013.
Vapors: The Essential G. Wayne Miller Fiction, Vol. 2, 2013.
The Beach That Summer: The Essential G. Wayne Miller Fiction, Vol. 3, 2014.
Drowned: A Different Kind of Zombie Tale, Sequel to the Thunder Rise trilogy, 2015.
Blue Hill, 2020.
Traces of Mary, 2022.

Films

On the Lake: Life and Love in a Distant Place, 2009.
Behind the Hedgerow: Eileen Slocum and the Meaning of Newport Society, 2010.
The Providence Journal's Coming Home, 2011.

Screenplays

The Glamour Girls, with Jessi Sundell Cramer, 2008, WGA registration # 1288636
Summer Love, Harvardwood Books and Unlimited Publishing LLC, 2008, WGA registration: #1216146
Snyder, with Drake Witham and Drew Smith, 2008, WGA registration: #1217682
King of Hearts, 2009, with Drew Smith, WGA registration #1062014
Life Happened, 2023, WGA registration # 2222611

Curious about other Crossroad Press books?
Stop by our site:
https://www.crossroadpress.com
We offer quality writing
in digital, audio, and print formats.